Escape from Perdition

Malania E. Reynolds

●●● THREE SKILLET

Escape from Perdition

 THREE SKILLET

www.ThreeSkilletPublishing.com

v.3

This is a work of fiction based on actual historical places and events. The author has referenced certain historical figures for context and realism, but all characters are fictitious, and any resemblance to actual persons living or dead, except in a general historical context, is purely coincidental.

ISBN: 978-1-943189-11-3

"Indeed it was for my own peace
that I had great bitterness;
But You have lovingly
delivered my soul from the
pit of destruction.
For You have cast all my sins
Behind Your back."

Isaiah 38:17 KJV

1

Kaskaskia, Illinois

September, 1843

James Morgan stopped his plow horse at the end of a row of turned sod. His eyes darkened in anger as he gazed over the field he had worked in since early dawn, and he gave a loud, long curse of frustration. The row was crooked in one place. He took out a blue kerchief from a back pocket and wiped his damp brow as he caught his breath, the exertion of the day drawing ragged gasps from his chest. Leaving the plow in the soil and the horse standing in harness, he stumbled over clods of dirt and headed for the barn. Grabbing a knapsack in which he had hidden a change of linens, he removed his clothes and took a bath in the horse trough. He donned the fresh clothing and leaned down to wipe the sod from his boots, using a knife from a shelf in the barn.

He climbed the steps to the kitchen door, his eyes now gleaming in anticipation of the night's entertainment. He reached high on the top shelf for the old mended sugar bowl and stuffed the coins in his pockets. He ignored his daughter Charlotte silently stirring beans in a pot at the stove. He yelled to his hapless son Joseph to bring the horse to the barn and left the house without another word.

A tall, still slender woman, with her long blond hair twisted tightly in a knot at the back of her neck, saw him leave as he passed by the window near where she sat in her grandmother's rocking chair, reading her Bible. She rose and stumbled into the kitchen. She was dressed in a slovenly manner, her faded blue gingham dress wrinkled and dragging the floor as she went. She opened the door and peeped in to make sure he was gone.

"Has he left?" She shuffled over to the girl and peered into the pot of beans. "When are we going to eat?" There was a whine in her voice, and her eyes were dull and red rimmed.

"Yes, Mama, he's down at the corral saddling his horse. Do you want me to call him?"

The woman drew back as though in fear and left the question unanswered. She went back to her rocking chair and slowly rocked back and forth, her eyes gazing off into space, seeing something only she could see. Priscilla Morgan had long since given up trying to change the routine of her husband. She'd let herself become bitter and resentful of her life on the Illinois farm.

It had been an arranged marriage, planned and contrived by their separate fathers, each of whom hoped to benefit financially by the connection. James had known almost from the start that it was a mistake, because Priscilla had refused him access to her bed without coercion after the birth of her first child, a boy, who died in infancy. The fact that she'd given birth to two more children was purely luck or possibly God's will. She'd slept single and solitary in the front room since Joseph's birth. James took his pleasure in the town whenever he felt the urge for feminine companionship.

Charlotte went to the front room door, saw her mother sitting quietly and sighed. She returned to the stove and pulled the freshly baked bread from the oven. Later, when Joseph returned from stabling the horse, they sat and murmured to themselves about the foibles of their parents.

*****

The Golden Eagle Saloon was abuzz with excitement when James walked through the double doors. Two strangers had arrived the night before from the West, dressed like Mountain Men in leather, scraps of fur and old patched clothes. They stood in the center of the room, while the men listened, fascinated by their odd behavior and manner

8

of speaking.

The larger of the men, Elijah Perkins, bearded and with long black hair in a braid hanging to his waist, was extolling the virtues of the great mountains of the West. "Wild animals roam the meadows and sleep in the high grassy areas under the trees," he was saying. His midnight-dark eyes sparkled with excitement.

"I tell you, large spruce trees seem to touch the sky; and the shaking aspens turn gold in the autumn sun. Ponderosa pines as far as the eyes can see. Oh, it's a marvelous place, the Rocky Mountains of America." The Mountain Man proclaimed in his deep, bass voice, "There's high snow-covered passes and deep valleys carpeted with wildflowers in the spring. Mountain sheep cling to the rocks like they was in a painted picture hanging on yon wall."

James sauntered along the edge of the crowd and leaned his belly into the low wooden bar, then turned sideways, so he could see and hear the man speak more clearly. He'd never seen the room so full of customers this early in the day. He asked for a rye whiskey straight from the bottle. The room was dusky from the smoke of many cigars and pipes. Flies constantly buzzed around the spittle spots on the sawdust floor. The early afternoon sunlight filtered through the open windows and fell in pools among the patrons sitting around the bare tables of the barroom.

Taking one long swallow of the liquid, James turned in time to hear the fur trapper say, "Heh, you at the bar, would ya bring me a beer?"

Turning his eyes from left to right, James realized that the huge fur-clad man was speaking to him. He turned to the bartender and was given a large glass of cool, frothy beer. He put a silver coin on the bar for his own drink and enough to pay for the stranger's beer. Holding the stranger's glass in one hand, and his own drink in the other, he approached the Mountain Man with curiosity, and not a small touch of fear. Tall himself, James wasn't a match for the giant of a man who took the glass from him and said with a twinkle in his black eyes, "Thank'ee, son."

Someone called from the front of the room, "Mr. Perkins, are you acquainted with Dr. Marcus Whitman, the missionary doctor from the Oregon country?"

"No, can't say that I know the man, but I've heard of him. Was at the rendezvous one year at Bridger's place on the Green River, but I didn't get thar until the next day."

9

Perkins was about to elaborate, but there was a great roar of laughter from the crowd in the saloon. James thought at first that they were laughing at him, but as he glanced to his left, he saw the other stranger lift a short, squat man off the floor and toss him with little effort out of his way, as he marched with long strides to the bar. The unlucky man fell with a thump onto his backside on the floor. Picking himself up gingerly, he crept to the edge of the room, where he leaned against the wall, his face red with embarrassment.

"I'll get me own drink," said the Mountain Man. Dressed in a similar manner to Perkins, he was in no way like him in character. While Perkins was tall and broad shouldered, the other man was slight with narrow hips, and a glimpse of almost snow-white hair could be seen at the edge of a red knitted cap that enclosed his head. Otto Thibodeau moved with the grace of a mountain cat, stealthily quiet, his eyes darting from side to side as if searching for danger. He shoved his body into the place that had recently been vacated by James Morgan.

"Whiskey," the man demanded in a soft, gruff voice. There was a distinct accent in the word. French, thought James, or, maybe French-Canadian.

The bald-headed bartender reached under the counter for a bottle and brought a small clean glass to the counter. Opening the bottle and tipping a bit of liquid into the glass, he was interrupted by a commanding bark from the Frenchman.

"Give me a big glass, and leave the bottle." Thibodeau threw a coin on the bar and held out one thin, pale hand, pointing at the larger glasses on the shelf behind the bar. Surprised, the bartender obeyed the voice and turned to his next customer, but was arrested by the rebuke of the huge man in the middle of the room. He almost spilled the drink he was handing to the customer.

"Otto, now you behave yourself," Perkins bellowed to his friend. "You been so long out of society, you done forgot your manners." Then, taking a long sip from his own drink, thus emptying the glass, he started again to tell of wild dangerous cougars, monstrous black bears, and the mangy brown coats of the buffalo that roamed the plains and the mountains of the West. Hawks and golden eagles flew through the sky, and fierce winter winds froze a man's insides if he didn't have shelter.

"How come, if you like the mountains so much, you done come all the way here to Illinois?" called a female voice, scornfully, from the rear of the room. The crowd shuffled their feet and whispered amongst themselves.

"Well, it's like this, my good woman, I hain't seen me old ma in twenty years, don't know if the woman's still alive, so I come east to find out." And, for all his bluster and large size, the men standing near him, including James, could see a tear in the corner of the huge man's eye. "Came to sell my furs in St. Louis and just kept on traveling, me and old Otto thar."

James puffed out his cheeks and took a breath. He spoke from his spot at the front of the crowd as though the interruption hadn't taken place. "Dr. Whitman said that wagons could get over the mountains. He and his wife made the trip in '36 with Spalding. I heard from some men passing through town last month that more than a thousand pioneers started out from Independence in June. Did you run across those wagons when you were in St. Louis?" James concentrated on Perkins, knowing that his neighbors were now looking at him. His heart was racing and his breath shallow to think he had found someone who might have knowledge of what was his greatest desire: to go west.

"I heard that same thing. My brother read it in the St. Louis paper; wrote me a letter; how the wagons lined up for a mile waiting to cross on the ferries. Whitman wasn't with them though; he was at the Shawnee Mission. I'd make that trip if I knew for certain the wagons could get over the mountains." Burford Shaw was a slender man with a full beard and long nose. James had known him for a few years. He was surprised that the man was interested in going to Oregon.

His eyes went back to Perkins.

Perkins quickly gained control of his emotions and began to talk of the forts along the route to Oregon. "We missed the excitement at St. Louis, but we heard about it. Over a hundred wagons, I was told. Too many, I say. Bound to run into trouble along the way, unless they split up into smaller groups. But, it can be done if they take the Platte River, then over South Pass and the divide to the Green. Been there myself; met old Bridger. He gave me a map onct."

He dragged a torn, ragged piece of paper out of his pocket and placed it on top of one of the nearby tables. He pointed out the rivers, the forts and the landmarks along the route to the ocean. Every eye in the room was engaged in an effort to look at the map. Several burly men pushed and shoved others out of their way until those in the back finally gave up the idea and simply listened in fascination to the drone

11

of his voice.

Shaw and an older man named Cavenaugh expressed a desire to go to Oregon, and soon the majority of the crowd lost interest and left the building or started gambling and moving upstairs with the bar girls. They were joined by Sedgewick, a merchant in the town. The circle grew smaller as Perkins, Shaw, Sedgewick, Cavenaugh and James Morgan drank and talked, more seriously than earlier when the crowd hovered around them. Unnoticed at the bar, Otto kept pouring liquid from the bottle into the glass until he slumped in a heap on the floor, passed out and beyond the sound of his friend's bravado.

Long into the night, the discussion continued, and James was enthralled with the idea of going west. He could, in his mind, see the rivers and boulders and the trees described by Perkins. He could almost feel the rush of the wind in his hair, as he listened to the trapper speak of the trails he'd traveled. The boredom of the Morgan farm, the raising of animals and crops no longer had any appeal to his senses. He stumbled out of the bar, one of the last to go, into the dark night, mounted his horse, and headed home, his mind now befuddled with almost forgotten dreams. He had, at one time, before being held down by responsibility and family, longed to travel on the path of Meriwether Lewis and William Clark to the Pacific Ocean.

James arrived at the house, tied his horse to the porch rail, and stumbled into the large room where his wife lay peacefully sleeping on her cot. With a great sweep of his hand, he grabbed the covers off her, leaving her exposed to the cool, early morning air. She yelped like a beaten dog. He shouted, "Get up, woman! I'm going to Oregon country!"

He saw her eyes widen and heard her intake of breath at the violence with which she'd been awakened. She lay staring up at the mad man confronting her. She blinked in the half light of the room, tears forming in her eyes, for the lanterns had long since burned through the oil in their bowls, and only the faint glow of the still hot coals in the fireplace reflected light into the darkness.

"Are you drunk?" she asked unnecessarily, for it was quite clear that he was. His eyes blazed with fire, his clothes and coat were awry, and his hair stood up as if it had been raked many times with his massive fingers. "What's this talk of going to Oregon country? Where've you been, you crazy man?"

"I been down to the Golden Eagle, and I seen with my own eyes two men from the West. They was telling all about the mountains, and

12

the wild animals, and the white tailed deer, and the soil so tender and deep that you can plow without a mule. I've decided I'm going to see the ocean as soon as we can git ourselves packed up."

It was only in times of great excitement that his father's heavy Scottish brogue appeared in his speech, so carefully had he tried to erase it.

"You're out of your mind, you fool," she replied. "We can't just pack up and go 'cause you decide to go west. What about the farm, and our families, and the neighbors?"

"We'll take them with us, the whole darn bunch of them, that's what we'll do." He was beginning to visualize the long road ahead, with a string of covered wagons, all headed to the Oregon country. The dream in which he had seen himself as a very young man was now coming to fruition. He turned around when he heard a sound, and saw a body in white behind him in the doorway. It was his fifteen-year-old daughter, Charlotte, awakened by the sound of her parents arguing.

"Papa, are we going to Oregon?" Her eyes were round with wonder.

"How long you been standing there, girl?" her mother asked. "You should be in bed."

"I couldn't sleep with Papa gone so long," she said. "I heard the sound of his horse walking in the farmyard and knew he was home. Are we going to Oregon, Mama?"

"No, you silly child, it's just the liquor in your pa speaking. We ain't none of us going to leave this farm. Now, go back to bed, before you wake Joseph."

"But, I'm awake," said a small boy's voice from behind Charlotte, finally appearing from the darkness of the hallway. Joseph resembled his mother in many ways. He had light-colored hair and gray eyes, and even at the age of eleven he showed signs of the height he would achieve when he was fully grown. His eyes blinked at the two adults as he came from around his sister's skirts.

Priscilla turned on her husband angrily and started to yell and taunt James. He spun on his heels, and went into the bedroom they'd shared at the beginning of their marriage, before the relationship between them had soured, and slammed the door. He clumped over to the bed, lay across the mattress fully dressed and went to sleep while the rest of the house was wide awake.

13

2

Priscilla ordered the children to return to their beds. By this time, she was thoroughly agitated, and pulling a long wool coat over her nightgown, left the house and hauled herself into the saddle of the horse that James had left tied to the porch rail. The faint light of early dawn filtered through the mist of a heavy fog. Guiding the horse along the road toward the south, she arrived at her sister Eileen's farm. The house was dark and silent. She dropped from the back of the horse, stepped onto the porch, and pounded loudly on the front door.

"What the hell's going on out there? Stop that racket!" A deep male voice came from inside the house. Peter Kincade walked to the door and opened it wide. "What? Priscilla, is that you? What are you doing here in the middle of the night?"

"I want to see my sister." She shoved her way past the surprised man.

"Priscilla, why have you come here?" Eileen stood in the door of the room she shared with her husband, her hair hanging down to her waist, as she tied the strings of her night robe. "Are the children all right? Is James sick? Tell me, what's wrong?" she demanded. She led Priscilla over to a chair by the fire.

Peter left the women to their discussion and went into the kitchen, where he built up the fire in the cast iron cooking stove. Putting several small chunks of kindling into the firebox, he stirred the coals and added a few torn pieces of an old newspaper. As soon as the flames were built up, he went down the hallway to check on his two sleeping sons. The noise hadn't awakened them. He quietly closed the door.

In the living room, Priscilla loudly poured into her sister's ears all the tribulations that her hated husband caused her, including the most recent episode. She accused him of tumbling her out of bed and slapping her and yelling that he was going to Oregon. On and on she went, about his drinking, gambling and womanizing, until Eileen's patient ears were ringing with the accusations of cruelty and slander.

Eileen tried to calm her sister, and finally unable to stop the ranting which was quickly turning into hysteria, she slapped Priscilla on the face. Priscilla drew her head back in shock, and burst into loud racking sobs, her shoulders shaking with emotion. She began to calm down and looked around the room as though suddenly realizing where she was. "How did I get here?" Priscilla asked, dazed.

"Now, calm down and explain what you mean about going to Oregon," Eileen told her sister in a quiet voice. Priscilla started again on her tale of the early morning, but this time she made more sense, as she described how James had come in and uncovered her in her bed and told her that he was going to Oregon.

"Why does he want to go to Oregon? Has he mentioned the idea to you before?"

"No," Priscilla admitted. "Wait," she said and shook her head with remembrance. Timidly, she looked at the clear blue eyes of her sister, and at the same time felt a few remaining tears in her own eyes. "Yes, he did want to go to the Oregon country when we were first married. But, Father said he was being impractical and it was too dangerous to take a wife and children across the desert and mountains, so he stopped talking about it. I thought he'd forgotten." She sat drooping in the chair, and she covered her face with her hands.

"You never mentioned to me that James wanted to go west. Of course, I know we've never been extremely close, what with nine years difference in our ages, but surely I'd remember if my older sister had told me her husband had plans to do something so impulsive." Eileen looked at her sister as if trying to figure out who this unknown person was.

"No," Priscilla replied. "Father wouldn't hear of us going, so we

15

never made any real plans, and James put his maps and papers away in a drawer of the desk. I wonder if he ever pulls them out and looks at them." Her words were an acknowledgment that she and her husband never spoke of anything except the children and practical living matters.

Peter came into the room and looked closely at Priscilla to see if the drama was ended. "Breakfast is on the table if you're hungry." They went into the kitchen, where the children, Jesse and Neely, were picking at their food. The meal continued with small talk about common matters and gossip about the neighbors. It was an uneasy quiet. Eileen kept darting glances at her sister, but Priscilla remained calm.

After eating a good meal, Priscilla climbed on the horse and rode home, her mind going over the events of the morning. She worried that James really was serious about going to Oregon. At home, she left the horse tied for Joseph or Charlotte to put in the barn, and sat in the rocking chair as though she'd never left the house. The drowsy warmth from the heat of the fireplace took her into a daze, and she didn't know or care what happened in the house while she sat there staring into space until evening and everyone had gone to their beds. She rose and lay on her cot in the front room, oblivious to her surroundings.

3

James slept most of the day and finally aroused himself to leave the house for the afternoon chores, after eating a meal of corn pone, bacon, beans and onions prepared for him by Charlotte. His head was pounding from the liquor he'd consumed the night before, and he hadn't forgotten the events of the morning after the announcement of his intentions. But, all the outside tasks had been quietly accomplished. The horse had been stabled, the cow milked, hogs and chickens fed, and James was only half aware that his faithful children had done the work, while the adults in their life were indifferent to the work necessary to the running of a small farm.

When dark was almost upon the land, James went into the house, lit a lamp in the bedroom, closed the door, and took from his desk drawer the old faded maps and papers from so long ago, in which he'd dreamed and planned and prepared until his father-in-law, Nehemiah Prescott, had stopped the dreaming, the planning and the preparation in its infancy. James had been made to realize that he was selfish and cruel to think of taking a young fragile woman into the wilderness. Priscilla wasn't fragile; she was strong, and she would've enjoyed the trip. He knew that was true, but he'd let himself be swayed by the prejudice and weakness of his father-in-law.

But, it wasn't too late. Another wagon train would be leaving St.

Louis in the early spring, and James was determined to be on it. Old man Prescott was dead and buried on the hill above his farm. There was no one who had the power to stop him this time. James sat long into the night, dreaming, remembering and jotting down things that Perkins had reminded him of when he talked of the far off mountains and deserts of the West. He made lists of things to sell, things to buy, and what would have to be gathered together from the farm. The excitement ran through his veins like hot lava, and he didn't retire to his bed until dawn was breaking in the east.

Upon arising in the morning, James ate a breakfast of flapjacks covered in freshly churned butter and molasses, swallowed down with hot, unsweetened coffee. The sun was already in the sky when he arrived at the barn in time to help Joseph with milking the cow and mucking out the manure from the stalls. Joseph glanced at him with a questioning look in his gray eyes, but James didn't bother to explain his plans, for he hoped to keep them a secret until he could talk again with Elijah Perkins or Otto Thibodeau.

The days of the week passed slowly for the Morgan household, with each member of the family wary and struggling in his or her way to make sense of the turmoil that had erupted. Charlotte and Joseph continued with their regular tasks, and the family was fed and clothed as usual. Priscilla looked at her husband with resentment in her eyes whenever he came near her, but she didn't speak to him and pretended that he didn't exist when he was outside.

The truce couldn't last for long. On Saturday afternoon James arrived home from the sale of one of the farm horses and some chickens, changed his clothes, ate a few biscuits and a slice of beef, remounted his horse and rode toward town.

There was a crowd gathered in the Golden Eagle Saloon when he stepped through the doors. James didn't stop at the bar, but made his way to the table where Perkins sat, talking to his friend, Thibodeau. He asked if they had time to talk. Perkins answered in the affirmative and ordered drinks from a passing waiter.

James took his maps and papers from a leather satchel, and with the notes he'd made during the week, he and his new acquaintances spent the better part of two hours in a serious discussion of the trail to Oregon. Perkins said it could be done with careful planning. Thibodeau, with a nod of his snowy white head, and in heavily accented English and half-French, told him of things that Perkins couldn't know. Finally, the three men shook hands and said good-bye, with Perkins promising that if everything worked out at his home in Tennessee, he would meet with James in the spring in St. Louis.

The next day, to the chagrin of the people of the town, Elijah Perkins and Otto Thibodeau rode out as quietly and as mysteriously as they'd arrived two weeks earlier. The joy went out of the Golden Eagle Saloon as the men could no longer glean tales of adventures in the Rocky Mountains directly from the mouths of the Mountain Men.

About this time, things began to disappear from the Morgan farm: animals, implements and farm equipment. James quietly and quickly liquidated the assets of the farm, turning whatever he couldn't take with him into cash, either in gold or paper script. He didn't mention to Priscilla what he was doing, and she never came outside, for she wasn't concerned with the working of the farm. The children, of course, knew. James carefully explained his plans to be gone from Illinois before the weather turned bitterly cold.

On the Wednesday after James talked to the fur traders, he saddled his favorite horse, Lightning, and leading one of the farm horses, visited with his friend and neighbor, John Raymond. After explaining that he was going to Oregon, the men haggled over the price of the horse. Raymond agreed to buy several other items that James suggested, and the men shook hands with a promise from Raymond to visit the Morgan farm soon to gather together his purchases. James gave Lightning a small apple, pulled the saddle from his back, put it on the other horse, Blue Boy, mounted and rode away.

Three weeks after having made arrangements with the sheriff for the sale of the farm and the remaining assets belonging to the couple, James told Priscilla his final plans.

"You foul man," she screamed at him. "You never cared what I wanted, from the day I married you. What do you want to do with me, leave me to starve? You'd like that, wouldn't you, mister?" Her face was puffed and red by then, and she flew at him like a riled cougar, leaving scratches on his face.

"I—" He tried to get a word in to calm her down, and it only served to incense her more. She pounded on his chest with her fists, until both Charlotte and Joseph were required to pull her away from his person.

"Mama, no!" Charlotte grabbed her mother's arm, only to be knocked to the floor. Joseph was still a boy, but he was strong enough to protect his sister from a second strike of his mother's arm.

"Mama, please," the boy wailed, with tears running down his

face. "Papa said you're going with us!"

"Liars burn in hell," and she slapped her son. "Your pa ain't thinking of nobody 'cept himself. My father said he was kind, generous and peaceable. But, he's a drunkard, a gambler and a woman chaser." She turned to James and screamed, "How you going to feed two growing children when you reach the westward mountains? You don't know nothing." She raised her arm to slap him, only to have Joseph grab her arm.

"No, Mama!" He pulled his mother's arm to his chest, and held on as the tears ran down his face.

Throughout the whole pitiful tantrum, James kept his temper, but all respect for his wife was now wiped away with the vileness of her accusations. He didn't raise his voice, or his fists to her, but simply walked out of the house and stayed protected in the barn until she was gone, sorrowful that the children had stood up for him better than he had done.

*****

Charlotte and Joseph helped their mother pack her belongings. Often she changed her mind, all the while ranting and shouting about the injustice of it all, until Joseph left the house and joined his father in the barn. With wisdom far beyond her years, Charlotte carefully and patiently listened and obeyed her mother, then put back the items that her mother decided not to take. It took them several hours, and exhausted by her unexpected exertions, Priscilla fell into a deep sleep.

Awakened and told to dress and eat for the journey, Priscilla turned her bitterness and vengeance on her children. Calling out vile names, and hurling abuse about their innocent heads, the memory of that day would remain to haunt the children for years. Early in the dawn of a new day, Joseph drove the wagon in which Priscilla, along with her clothing, jewelry, and the other possessions she kept with her, traveled to her sister's home, knowing he would never see her again.

Charlotte, worry lines marking her plain face, watched in a state of awe and relief as the wagon left the farmyard and moved slowly over the ridge and out of sight. She loved her mother with a deep, passionate emotion, but she didn't want to live in fear of her ever again. After his return, her father put his arm around her weary shoulders, and she gave in to her relief.

20

The days quickly passed as the family awaited the sheriff's sale. They packed everything they could use on the trip to St. Louis. It wasn't much as far as value was concerned, mostly clothing and shoes; a few of his father's favorite salt water-splattered books brought on the boat; the miniature of Solomon Morgan and one of his parents and himself as a child; and the family Bible with the names of ancestors the children had never known. The gaily decorated trunk that Solomon James Morgan had brought with him from far away Scotland was stuffed full of dishes, flatware and linens for their comfort, as well as the familiar use of the items. It'd been suggested by Perkins and Thibodeau that James not take much with him in the initial portion of the trip, because everything could be bought in the city. James wisely took their advice, and although disappointed to leave their favorite articles behind, the children obeyed their father.

On a startlingly brilliant sunny day in the middle of October, James and his children watched near the barn while everything they owned was auctioned off before their neighbors and friends. Even Uncle Peter came and bought a few items to help keep some of the family traditions alive. Eileen had told him of some pieces that she was sure Priscilla would want once she settled into the household routine. He'd made arrangements with the auctioneer to come for the articles on the morrow. Most of the farm animals and crops had already been bought by their neighbors.

Peter leaned over to shake James' hand, and the joining of their hands caused the horse to shy away. Peter clasped the reins tightly, calling, "Whoa, boy!"

"Seems the animal senses a change coming." James chuckled. "Mighty smart animal."

"I wish we could come with you." Peter kept his eyes on the animal, running a hand down his neck to calm it. "Feel myself being driven to leave, sometimes, what with the poor soil and the drought. Another year of lost corn, and it might do us in." He shook his head and glanced at the men walking around the last of the farm equipment, trying to decide what they could use.

"Seems the sale is going well for you."

"It has to be. Everything's gotta go; need the money more than the equipment. Raymond's bought the other crops, will have his men do the harvesting. Wheat's already packed in barrels; I figure I can sell it for a better price in St. Louis. Garden crops not ready to pick." He sighed. "Gonna miss the milk cow and the chickens."

"It's not too late, James." Peter patted the horse twice, and turned back to the man. "Besides, the children need their mother. Even you know that. Anyway, with our troubles we can hardly afford another mouth to feed."

"Or ruin a household," James mumbled.

Peter looked hard at his brother-in-law, but didn't respond to the muttered comment. "That's a long trip. The young'uns have their playmates, and they could get back in school regular."

"Done's done, Peter. Don't try to change it."

"If that's the way it is." Peter sighed. "Godspeed, then." He gave Joseph a friendly pat on the top of his head, kissed Charlotte on the forehead, turned his horse and sadly rode away to the top of the ridge, where he stopped his horse and looked down on the farm that had held such promise of happiness in the early days when he'd first married Eileen Prescott. He waved and tipped his hat to James. He urged the horse to move faster as he turned toward his home.

Early the next morning, before the sun had reached the horizon, James Morgan, his daughter Charlotte and son Joseph rode out of the farmyard for the last time. Sustained in part by the food that Charlotte had prepared the night before for the trip to St. Louis, the family didn't look back, for there was nothing to see. The auction had taken everything, and the place already looked abandoned and ghostly in the dark shadows surrounding the buildings.

A small slice of moon and a million stars glowed in the sky, and Charlotte cast her eyes upward to keep the tears from flowing down her cheeks. She blinked several times, and finally wiped the remains with a finger. She'd lived in this valley her whole life; she knew no other place. The wagon creaked, and the farm horses pulled at their traces, as James, his mind on the journey ahead, carefully led them through the dark grassy ridge to the road which would lead them to their future. His chestnut stallion, Blue Boy, tied to the rear of the vehicle, lumbered along at a steady pace, following in the dust kicked up by the wheels of the wagon.

4

Several weeks later, the Morgan wagon stopped on the outskirts of St. Louis. They camped for the night beside a small gurgling stream and bedded down as soon as the meal was finished and the dishes washed. Early the next morning, untying his horse, James rode into town to look for a more sheltered place to stay.

St. Louis, Missouri, in the year 1843 was a bustling town, a major trading center for the east-west and the north-south traffic. Steamboats had first traveled the river in 1818, making trade easier to New Orleans and the larger Eastern markets. The town itself was built on limestone and dolomite cliffs high above the Mississippi River. James wasn't concerned with the history or geography of the town; he only wanted a temporary shelter for his family until he could join a party of pioneers to the Willamette Valley of Oregon, where land was free to settlers willing to brave the roughness of the wilderness.

After riding an hour, James found a rundown but respectable hotel in a quiet, commercial area of town where the proprietor Bertha Hightower told him he could park the wagon in the empty lot behind the hotel until needed. His five horses he could leave under the care of Moses Smith, proprietor of the livery stable on Missionary Street. He rented two rooms, one for himself and Joseph, and one for Charlotte. Accommodations included two meals a day, morning and evening. He paid for one month out of the funds he had gotten for the sale of his land.

James rode to the stream where he had left his children in the parked wagon. He tied Blue Boy behind the wagon and drove them to the hotel, where he dropped off the children and their luggage, then following the directions given him by the hotel proprietor, he drove to the livery to make arrangements to stable the horses. A tall, slight youth of uncertain age came out of the barn at his knock and told him he could put the farm horses in the corral at the back of the barn and put his chestnut in the barn for extra pay. James quickly decided to leave the wagon parked where it was beside the livery for the time being. The youth agreed to the arrangement, and James paid the stated price for the care and feeding of his horses for a couple of days.

Tired but encouraged, he walked the short distance to the hotel and said a pleasant good-night to his son and daughter before spending a profitable couple of hours in a local saloon. He kept a close watch around him as he left the saloon, and his hand tightly clasped on the pistol in his coat pocket, but even as drunk as he was, he found his way back safely, climbed the stairs and fell instantly asleep, still clothed.

*****

Charlotte awoke early in her room on the second floor of the Hightower Hotel in St. Louis. It had been good to sleep on clean sheets again after the rolling, jolting bed of the wagon. Through the filtered sunshine, she could see dust mites whirling and beating against each other. Her toes curled under the covers as she stretched out her limbs in the luxury of the bed.

"Ah," she said aloud, her voice echoing around the room. "This is wonderful." She stretched out again in the warm bed. "At least I don't have to cook this morning."

She'd only peeked into the large dining room the evening before, and she tried to recall how glamorous it had been, with its high, white ceiling and crystal chandelier hanging on a chain, as a dark-skinned man led them up the stairs. His hands were filled with their luggage, and it seemed he had something to say about everything they passed, from the cord by the stairs to ring for service, to the gas lamps that lighted the hallways. Her head was a-swim with the thought of it all. She did remember thinking how big everything was as he guided

24

them up the stairs to their rooms the night before. She couldn't imagine living in a place so grand.

The smell of coffee brewing and bread baking through the thin walls brought her back to the morning, and heaving herself out of the bed with a sigh, she made for the chamber pot enclosed under the small table near the window. Having finished her business, she shoved the pot back where it belonged. She took her brush and comb from her small portmanteau and began to brush her long, black hair. It fell almost to her waist and needed a good washing, but there was no hot water. She gazed at herself in the cheval mirror in the corner.

Shorter in stature than her mother, she had her father's dark hair and eyes. Her face was plain, her nose covered with freckles and her mouth too wide for her small pointed chin. Her father teased that the freckles were a gift from her grandfather who had come over from Scotland when he himself was a lad of eight. Grandfather Solomon James Morgan had flaming red hair, and freckles covered his arms and body. He'd died when Charlotte was two, so she couldn't begin to compare her own face with that of her paternal grandfather.

She asked her mother once about her Morgan grandfather. Her mother had taken her to the room she shared with her husband. There on the bedside table was a miniature of him painted by a traveling artist, when they'd lived far away in Maryland, but the red hair and freckles didn't show to good advantage. Her grandfather wore a black suit, and a snowy white cravat which covered his neck completely, even under his ears. His piercing blue eyes stared at her in a frightful manner, and Charlotte was glad that she hadn't known him. But, she liked the stories her father told of him. Priscilla said she could keep the painting if she wished. Charlotte had hidden the portrait in her stocking drawer so the eyes wouldn't stare at her in the night.

Turning from the mirror, Charlotte hurried to dress in the same clothing she'd worn the day before. She felt gritty from days of traveling. She pulled her brown leather coin bag from the pocket of her skirt and looked inside. Only a few coins in change remained inside. Well, she'd have to bring the hot water up herself, or ask Mrs. Hightower if she could bathe in the kitchen after breakfast.

Downstairs, Bertha was in the kitchen, cooking long slices of thick bacon in an iron fry pan, with steam rising around her person like a fog. A large pot of porridge was simmering on a back burner. The stove held prominence in the large room, with its black, ghostly burners and smoke stack. At least a dozen shelves were arranged

25

haphazardly on one wall holding stacks of plates, saucers, bowls and glasses, while another wall, near the back door, had rows of pegs holding long handled spoons, spatulas, and sharp, shiny knives. And, in the center, a table held wash basins and flour boards made of wood. The entire arrangement spoke of efficiency and endurance.

The smell of fresh coffee permeated the room, raising a deep grumble in the stomach of the young girl as she walked into the room and stopped at the entrance. Her long, dark hair still trailed down her back, for she had thought there was no need to braid it in her usual way if she'd soon be washing it. Charlotte took one long, wandering glance around the room then focused on the plump, gray-haired woman.

"Good morning, Mistress." Charlotte smiled politely, taking two steps forward, then stopped again, noticing the tall, slender black man, dressed in a dirty white cloth apron covering his gray striped overalls. Charlotte didn't know whether to acknowledge his presence.

He sat in the corner of the room, softly humming a merry tune under his breath. He was peeling a potato taken from the mound stacked high in a bowl on the table beside him. A large round metal container at his feet was already half full of dropped rinds. He looked up at the young girl in surprise, his eyes taking in her image at a glance. He didn't stop his work for a second, but continued carving a slow twirl of skin off the potato in his hand. His eyes lowered to his task.

"Good morning, Mrs. Hightower," Charlotte repeated cheerfully, deciding to ignore the man's presence. "I was told by my father that's your name. I'm Charlotte Morgan. We only arrived late last night and went straight upstairs to our rooms, my brother Joseph and I."

Bertha turned so quickly from the stove that she gave out a yelp of pain as her hand brushed the hot rim of the frying pan. Bertha Mae Browning Hightower was a bold, middle-aged woman gone to fat, with thick gray hair, which she couldn't seem to keep centered on top of her head. It somehow managed to slip to one side or the other as she moved about the room. She might have been better suited to leave it in a braid down her back, but she was a creature of habit. Her mother had told her as a child that a woman should keep her hair off her neck, and Bertha had never disobeyed her mother. The woman had a loud voice but a kind heart, and never turned aside a stranger, but somehow found a meal and a place for them to sleep, even if it turned out to be a blanket-covered mat on the floor in the storage

26

room back of the kitchen.

"Goodness, little girl, you scared me," Bertha shouted, turning back to the stove and her cooking. "Almost dropped the bacon on the flame, I did."

"Oh, I'm so sorry," Charlotte replied. "Can I help you? I'm a good cook."

"Well, that's a good turn I can't refuse. Bless you, Missy, grab that cloth and take the biscuits out of the oven. My helper, Gladys, slipped yesterday and broke her ankle on her way home. She seems to be feeling poorly this morning. She shouldn't have stayed out so late with that worthless man, Tom, she likes so well. Don't know what she sees in him. Keeps her up all hours of the night, so's she can't get to her chores in time for the guests, he does. Walking down a dark street at night never done anyone any good, that's what I say. And now I ain't got a helper for the kitchen 'cept Conk, here. This is Hezekiah Conklin, a free black man who lives in a lean to shed out by the woodpile. He's been with us since we bought the hotel. Does the heavy work that my husband can't do because of his health."

"I goes by Conk, mostly ma'am," he chuckled before getting back to his business. "Name my pappy gave me when I was borned in a place called Detroit. My pappy worked on the steamboats, but I doesn't like the water. Don't mind the brown and white spot. He be Nero, and he always be where I am."

Taking this fascinating information in her stride, for she hadn't had a chance to meet the occupants of the hotel, Charlotte moved around the dog lying on the floor, and walked to the table and picked up a cloth, then moved to the huge wood burning iron cook range. Opening the door to the oven with both hands covered by the cloth, she reached in and drew out a large flat pan filled with soft, brown mounds of bread.

"Um, this smells good." She took the pan to the table and leaned over it, taking a deep whiff. The aroma of freshly baked bread wafted throughout the room. Seeing a long handled fork hanging on a peg near the stove, Charlotte grasped it and turned to the pan of bacon as Bertha, her face moist with perspiration, brushed past her toward the dining room door with the steaming pot of porridge. Charlotte turned the slices of bacon so they were uniform in crispness.

Working as a team, the two women quietly and efficiently soon had the meal on the red-checked cloth-covered table in the large dining room. Plates and cups were set for ten people, with the

27

necessary flatware beside each plate. Opening a drawer of the sideboard, Bertha removed some red folded cloths matching the tablecloth that she had laboriously hemmed herself, and shutting the drawer with her massive hip, she handed Charlotte the stack of clean cloths and turned back into the kitchen to pick up the large blue-speckled coffee pot and bring it to the table. Charlotte had never used napkins at home, but she instinctively knew the purpose for such cloths, so she placed the fabric properly folded beside each plate as though that had been her chore for years at her home in Illinois.

Gazing around the dining room to make sure everything was in order, Bertha moved to the doorway into the hall, stretched up her hand, and taking a wood-handled metal hammer from a peg, she struck it against the bell shaped metal piece hanging on a leather strap. "Clang! Clang! Clang!" Three times she struck it, and the sound echoed up and down the hall and drifted up the staircase to the upper floor, warning the guests that food was on the table.

Charlotte heard the sound of several upstairs doors opening and shutting, and a mighty stamp of feet on the stairway; and the men and women shuffled noisily into the room, chattering among themselves. The last of the guests to enter were Joseph and James, who looked surprised at Charlotte standing in the kitchen doorway. He ignored her as he saw the plentiful repast on the table. He took a seat near the end of the table, and Joseph gave his sister a hug before pulling out a chair and dropping into it. The other people sat in what appeared to be their regular places and began to hurriedly fill their plates and bowls with the fragrant food.

Later, Charlotte looked at the faces of the people gathered around the long, rectangular dining table while she waited her turn at the pot of porridge. A couple of nicely dressed men, their hair slicked down and wet with pomade, sat across the table from a pair of sober widows. From their outdated mode of dress, they were down on their luck and living off the remains of their husbands' earnings.

One of the drummers, named Rachet Jones, sold housewares and sewing notions, and tried during the meal to sell a newly designed gadget to Bertha, but she had all the implements for her kitchen and sewing room she needed. She turned him down politely, turning and whispering to Charlotte that she didn't want to lose his patronage.

The other salesman sold vegetable and fruit seeds and tree saplings. Charlotte overheard him tell James, sitting beside him, that he had a catalog with colored pictures and many sample seed packets in the large carpetbag in his room. James acknowledged that he was a farmer, and they discussed the spring crops.

During the meal, the two old ladies told stories of their men, each trying to top the other one. Her husband had been a preacher, Sarah Warren whispered to Charlotte. She frowned at the other guests grabbing at the food as though they hadn't had a decent meal the night before. She lowered her head and clasped her hands to pray, but no one paid the least attention to her, helping themselves to the hot, fragrant biscuits. She talked about her grown daughter, who had married well and lived in the East.

Charlotte soon discovered that Margaret's husband, Thaddeus Brown, had been a store keeper who was killed in a robbery of his establishment one night about five years before. She was dressed in deep mourning, and kept a white lace handkerchief always at her nose, pretending to hold back sniffles, although no one was fooled into thinking that she cared for the missing man, since she flirted outrageously with the salesmen sitting across from her. She brought from her pocket a tiny jar of smelling salts, ever ready to bring it out when she had one of her "spells" as she talked of the tragedy.

Near the drummers were a husband and wife named Nassar who looked like they had recently quarreled; the woman's face was still red and marked by traces of dried tears. Charlotte peeked at her over her cup, and blushed when she saw the woman frown at her.

Lastly, a short stout man of uncertain ancestry with a heavy accent stood and poured coffee into his cup with an unsteady hand. Charlotte wondered if he had a hangover from a night of heavy drinking as her father often had, or if he had some debilitating disease.

There was a muttered sound in the doorway that led to the living quarters at the back of the house, and a man cursed as he struck his hand against the edge of the door while maneuvering himself through in a wooden chair sitting on wheels. Quickly Bertha moved to his side, but he brushed her away and rolled himself to the head of the table. Charlotte noticed for the first time that there had been no chair placed in that spot.

"Stop your fussing, woman," he said. "Damn door ain't wide enough, that's all. I should have had the carpenter cut a few more inches off the sides. Morning all! Looks to be a grand day outside after last night's rain."

Clayborne Hightower was a bald, portly man, and dressed in a suit and tie every day, even though he no longer left the building.

Charlotte soon found that he maintained an office behind the lobby, trying to keep up appearances. One whole side of the office from floor to ceiling was shelved with a thousand or more books, written in different languages, for Hightower had a degree from Harvard. Proficient in Latin and Greek, he spent many hours poring over the ancient world through his books, or practicing his violin. Once a real estate agent, he could no longer show clients properties for sale, but he was still keen on the assets and values of local holdings. He frequently sat by the fire in the parlor of the hotel during the day, smoking his pipe, and expanding on the growth of the city to any guests who happened to be whiling away the hours, especially in bad weather. An assistant called Jacobe Sinclair was often seen coming in or out of the office during the daylight hours.

5

Charlotte and Bertha were drying the last of the breakfast dishes. As the final cup was placed on the high shelf, Conk brought in an armload of kindling and sat down in his favorite chair near the corner. His dog Nero lay beside his chair and was soon fast asleep. He reached for the bucket standing beside the stove, and taking out a carrot, he began to scrape off the dirt and skin from the vegetable. A low humming sound issued from under his breath.

Paying no attention to her servant, Bertha picked and chose items from off the shelves and opened drawers in the pantry until she had the necessary ingredients for making bread and a raisin cake. Talking in her lazy drawl, she entertained Charlotte, dithering beside the table unable to decide what to do. Bertha told the girl a few stories of the crazy antics of some of the guests in the hotel, and all the time, her clever hands were busy.

Charlotte caught on to what Bertha was doing as she gazed at the different bowls and spoons and flour boards. While Bertha mixed flour, milk, and lard together to make the bread, Charlotte blended the ingredients for the cake. Bertha continued to talk in a sing-song manner, while in the corner, Conk hummed his lonesome tune. Finishing the carrots, he began to snap the ends of a passel of green beans. The dog, thinking his master was about to leave, stood up and lay his chin on Conk's lap, but when the man didn't move, the dog lay down, his head raised, but soon he relaxed and went back to sleep.

Eventually, Bertha had the dough kneaded the way she wanted it, and pinching it into three equal blobs, she dumped each of them into greased loaf pans, and covered them with a clean white cloth. In the meantime, Charlotte, working quietly and efficiently, soon had the cake batter poured into a long, deep cake pan, and grabbing a cloth, she positioned it in the center of the still hot oven. Without a word, as though a silent signal had passed between them, Conk put aside his beans, and rose to toss more kindling into the stove. The dog stood, gave a short bark, with his tail thumping back and forth. Conk patted his head, and scratched under his chin, and the dog was reassured. He stood on alert and waited for a signal, but apparently the man wasn't going outside, so the dog lay down.

Bertha, finished with one task, took her lovely porcelain tea pot, two cups with the pretty pink roses, and two matching saucers from the high shelf and proceeded to make tea. Telling Charlotte to sit at the table, she put a kettle of water on the burner to boil, and brought the tin of tea from the pantry, spooning out some of the fragrant leaves into the pretty pot. Setting a collection of sugar, creamer, and spoons on the table, she sat and waited for the water to boil.

Bertha was silent, more relaxed and gay. Her gray topknot had fallen and was perched precariously over one ear. She stretched her arms over her head and began to remove a few hairpins from the tangle of hair, then shoving the topknot back to the center of her head, she replaced the pins and sighed. Charlotte thought of her gritty skin and hair, as Conk in his corner calmly snapped beans. He arose from his seat, placed the bowl of fresh beans on the table, and disappeared out the back door with the discarded pieces of beans and carrots, Nero happily following.

Bertha finished making the tea, and the ladies sat in companionable silence for a few moments, sipping the sweet, soothing brew. Bertha loudly cleared her throat, reclaiming Charlotte's attention.

"I thank you kindly for your help this morning; don't quite know how I'd have managed without you. Do you think you could help me every day while you're here? No telling when that shiftless Gladys will be able to work again, what with her leg broke, and all." And she looked hopefully at the young girl.

"Yes, thank you, that would be nice, for I didn't know what I would do with my time before Papa decides to leave. I'm used to being busy with my hands, and I love to cook." This for Charlotte was a long speech, for she was normally very shy.

"Good, good, that's settled, then. I'll talk to your pa about your pay and make arrangements for the delivery of more supplies." Bertha was pleased, now that she had everything settled, for she truly hadn't known where she would find such a helpful hand in the kitchen in the middle of winter.

Sitting at the table sipping her hot tea with Bertha, Charlotte decided it was time to mention her most pressing burden. She wished she could ask for her own wages, for Papa would only gamble the money, but a person didn't speak of such things with a stranger, so she refrained.

"Ma'am," she started, "I'm wondering if there's a place where I can take an all-over bath. We've been on the road for weeks, and it's too cold to bathe in the creeks."

"Well, my soul, you poor child," Bertha said. "Here I am going on about things when I should have known what you needed most." She pointed her new friend toward a large room at the rear of the house where she would find what she needed.

Charlotte climbed the stairs to her room and unlocked the door. She went to her portmanteau and drew out clean undergarments and a fresh dress made of pale green wool. She took her comb and brush, as well as the small brush she used to clean her teeth, and locking the door behind her, went downstairs to find the magic room.

Her eyes widened in amazement as she saw one long rectangular shaped room that seemed to be filled with tubs of all sizes and shapes. Charlotte realized it wasn't only a wash closet for the guests, but a laundry room for the bed linens. She threw a couple of sticks of kindling in the grill and lit the fire under the stove. She brushed her hair while she waited for the water to heat. Her mind drifted back to the night before. She couldn't remember if her father mentioned the bath facilities.

Grabbing a thick cloth, Charlotte tipped the hot steaming water from the bucket into the large metal tub lined with cloths to protect her sensitive skin. Then lifting a bucket of cold water, she put in a small amount, trying to figure how much was needed to cool her bath. Putting the cold water bucket beside the tub, she placed a finger in the water. Just right! She tiptoed to the door to make sure she'd locked it, then removed her clothes, stepped into the tub and leaned back against the cloths. Ah, heaven, she thought, and taking a large bar of fragrant soap from the low table beside the tub, she bathed herself and washed her hair thoroughly.

Emerging from the laundry room, Charlotte looked to the right and then to the left, and crept up the stairs to her room, with her hair piled on top of her head, still damp from the washing she'd given it, and her soiled clothes wrapped in a large towel, for she had forgotten to ask Bertha what she was to do with them after her bath. Hoping not to offend anyone, she kept them with her. With the cloth bundle in one hand and her other holding the key, she opened her door and walked in. She placed the damp bundle near the door and closed and locked it. Oh, she felt so good. She had a job, with real pay! Surely her father would be pleased when he came home.

She withdrew her comb and the two brushes from her dress pocket, and lowered her hair. She would know better what to do next time, she thought, for her movements today had been awkward and shy. Charlotte had never lived in a place as grand as this one, and no one had explained what she was expected to do. Slowly brushing her hair to remove the tangles, she braided it and curled the braid into a knot at the back of her neck, making plans to explain everything to Joseph so he wouldn't be ignorant of the details as she'd been.

She saw a wide drawer under the table holding the ceramic pitcher and basin. She opened it and saw that it was empty, so she placed her undergarments and rolled stockings in it. She grabbed the smelly chamber pot that she had hastily used that morning, and carefully locking her door from the outside, slowly walked down the stairs. She knew where to empty the pot, so, she did and scrubbed it with the leftover cold water from the bucket, and returned upstairs. Her breath was coming in short gasps, for all this walking upstairs and downstairs, along with the fear of being seen by one of the widows, was wearying.

Her bed was unmade, for she had left the room thinking to return after the morning meal, but had stayed longer to help Bertha. She went over, and pulling the top covers aside, she smoothed the bottom sheet then neatly tucked the top blankets over it all. She fluffed the feather pillows until they were rounded and soft. She looked around for something else to do, and her eyes were drawn to her open bag. She spied some pegs on the wall next to the window, and hung her two slightly wrinkled dresses on the peg. One of the pegs already held her heavy coat, for she'd hung it last night. Her bag now empty, she slid it under the bed. She gave a great sigh, for the room was clean and tidy, and she was ready to tackle the next project, which she decided was to find what she was to do with her soiled clothing.

Embarrassed, Charlotte held the bundle of clothes away from her dress as she locked the door to her room again and went downstairs. She moved straight to the kitchen hoping to find Bertha there, but the room was empty. She placed the bundle near the stove, thinking they might dry more quickly, but she didn't dare open the package and spread the items out behind the stove. She would die of embarrassment if Conk saw her undergarments hanging there.

She looked around and saw the three loaves of bread, nicely rounded on top and ready to be kneaded a second time. The cake pan was also waiting for attention. With no further concern for the soiled clothing, Charlotte found the flour barrel and the board she had seen Bertha use earlier, and turned the first loaf of puffy dough out onto the floured board. She thumped and pulled and pushed the soft dough, while grabbing a handful of flour occasionally and scattering it on the dough until the blob was again a solid heap; and she threw it back into the pan, covered it with the cloth and started on the second one.

An hour later, the back door opened, and the dark-skinned man came in, went to the larder and grabbed an empty bucket, and then went out, without a single word or gesture that he'd noticed the woman working quietly at the range. The dog didn't come, and Charlotte wondered where it had gone. She blinked at the abruptness of his movements, and continued stirring the beans in the pot.

She finished kneading the bread and iced the cake, after finding what she needed in the storage bins. She'd found a thick juicy beef roast in the larder, and it was roasting nicely in the oven, adding to the delicious smells emitting from the kitchen. She took the large bowl of peeled potatoes, sliced them into small chunks, dumped them into the largest pan she could find and added water. Both the beans and the potatoes were noiselessly simmering on the stove. She put another small log into the stove and shut the door with a clang.

The kitchen door opened, but this time it was Bertha coming from the private quarters she shared with her husband. She stopped and stared, for a moment not recognizing the thin girl in the green dress and enormous apron, calmly stirring the contents of a pot on the stove. The fragrance of yeasty bread mingled with the sweet aroma of cake, and Bertha glanced at the table top. The cake was iced and the rounded tops of the bread could be seen peeping out of their pans.

"Goodness, girl, what you been doing all morning?" Bertha

asked.

Charlotte was flustered, and her face burned; she could feel each freckle on her nose and imagined they looked like tiny spots of dropped wax. She couldn't find a word to say in her shyness. She'd only been doing what she would have done had she still been back in Illinois on her parent's farm.

She stammered, "I'm sorry ma'am. I was trying to help you." She looked around as though she could undo what she had started. She picked up another oversized spoon and stirred the potatoes.

"Oh, don't look so stricken, love." Bertha grew red around her neck, now embarrassed herself, calling out, "I hadn't meant to rebuke you, girl; I was just so startled by what I saw that my words came before my discretion. A mighty fine helper you are, and I'm glad to get your services, for I stayed with my husband so long that I was afraid dinner would be late. But, here you have things in hand and me attacking you like that. Please forgive me."

The larger woman walked to the slender youth and gave her a hug. It had been so long since Charlotte had been comforted by a woman that she felt the bitter sting of tears and quickly drew away. Out of the corner of her eyes she saw the bundle of clothes near the stove and cried out that she didn't know what to do with her laundry. And, she felt her face warm again.

Bertha looked at the girl and shook her head. She gazed at the bundle and picked it up to note that it was slightly damp, but warm from the fire. In a friendly tone, she explained that the guest's soiled clothing was to be placed in separate barrels marked with their names in the laundry room, and the washing was done every Monday. She took the package to the laundry room herself, and spent some time hanging the clothes on the line to dry. When she returned, Charlotte had been joined by Conk, who was straining the cream off the bucket of fresh milk he'd brought from the barn behind the hotel. Charlotte began pulling plates from the high shelf to set the dining table as though she'd been working in the hotel her whole life. Bertha sighed, telling her, "If only Gladys had such an industrious character, then wouldn't life be wonderful?"

6

On their first full day in St. Louis, James set out from the hotel with his son walking quietly beside him. He saw the last puffs of dust trailing after the moving stagecoach pass from his sight, then turning left, moved slowly toward the livery stable. His stated object was to see to the safety of his animals and to move the wagon to the lot behind the hotel.

Joseph looked about him with curiosity as he strode beside his father. A stray dog got up from the dirt of the street, came slowly over to them and sniffed at their legs. Joseph reached out his hand tentatively toward the mongrel.

"Be careful, son, he may be dangerous." He looked around to see if the owner was nearby. The animal seemed friendly enough, and accepted the scratch on the head from the young boy.

"Who does he belong to, Papa?" the boy asked. "Do you think we can keep him?"

"Can't say, son," his father answered. "May be a stray someone has left on the roadside, and he wandered into town to find food. 'Spect that's what he wants, a good meal. Best leave him be; it won't do for us to take on a half-grown pup at this stage in our journey. It's enough to have to feed ourselves and your sister."

"Oh, all right, if you think that's best." Reluctantly, the boy tried to shoo the dog away, but the animal continued to follow them to the stable yard.

Standing as he had left it beside the livery barn, the Morgan wagon looked inconspicuous in the morning sunshine. Its sides were weathered and unpainted. The cloth covering spread over the full load of supplies seem dingy and gray. The wheels still bore the signs of the mud they had gathered after the last creek crossing outside of the city. James leaned over the side, trying to ascertain if anything had been disturbed during the night, but everything looked the same.

From inside the barn, a young lad about the same age as Joseph, but much heavier built, came out to greet them.

"Everything's all right, mister," the lad said. "I done took care to watch it myself. My name's Jasper Smith. 'Course that's not my real name; no one knows what my right name is, 'cause I'm an orphan. Mr. Smith found me as a baby out on the road one night, with my mam and pap dead in the bushes, and their wagon ransacked and everything stolen, and me screaming at the loss. He took me in and gave me a place to sleep. I work for Mr. Smith mostly, but sometimes I make a little extra by helping out with the chores of the townsfolk. Mr. Smith gave me a shiny dime if I'd watch this wagon through the night. This your boy, mister?"

"Yes," said James. "This is my son, Joseph. Our name is Morgan. You seem to be about the same age. How old are you? And, I thank you for watching after the wagon so well. It was a kind gesture for Mr. Smith to make. Who, by the way, is Mr. Smith?"

The young lad grinned as wide as his lips would allow, showing several crooked white teeth. He shifted his feet in the dust and said, "I'm ten, best anyone can make out. Leastwise that's what Mr. Smith thinks. Mr. Moses Smith is the owner of this livery stable, that's who he is. That dog you got don't belong to nobody. I done heard you talking about him when you walked up. He just hangs around, like you say, begging for food or a friendly scratch. I see he likes you, Joseph, well enough."

The dog sat on his haunches beside Joseph, and the boy reached down and gave him another pat on the head. He gave out a friendly bark, and James looked apprehensively at him, scared that he might bite the boy. The mutt's tail began to wag with vigor, so he supposed Joseph was safe for the moment.

Alerted by the barking dog, a short, stubby man wearing coveralls and an oversize faded blue shirt and scrubby-toed boots, came from the barn, a frown on his forehead and his jaw bulging with a new plug of tobacco.

"I thought I told you to keep that damn dog away from the barn." The livery man looked fiercely at his son, and his eyes moved to the dog sitting calmly beside Joseph, his tongue hanging out and his tail wagging back and forth, and his eyes sparkling with glee. Before James could say a word, Jasper burst out in the livery man's defense.

"Mister Morgan," the livery boy said. "This here's my father, Moses Smith." And he glared at James as if he would defend that title to the death.

James had no intention of questioning the boy's parentage or pedigree. He stepped forward with his hand outstretched. "Good morning, Smith. I'm sorry if the dog's barking has disturbed you from your work. I'm afraid he's taken a likin' to my son, Joseph, here." He looked fondly down at Joseph, who was still engaged in patting the dog's head in reassurance. Joseph looked back at him with a frown on his face. "We came in late last night from the East. There was another lad here then, and he said we could park the wagon until we find a better place for it. Those are my four sorrel horses standing in your corral, and the chestnut, too." He peered into the darkness as if the other boy might come out of the barn, somewhat worried now that he might have been mistaken in trusting the word of a stranger.

"Ah, I see," said Moses Smith. "That would be my oldest son, Abraham. He came home and told me that a new family had come to town. Happens all the time, people coming and going, what with all the excitement about wagon trains heading to Oregon. 'Spect you're one of them pioneers waiting for Captain Foster to gather all the people together to form a caravan?" His eyes focused on James, with curiosity in their depths.

"Yes, that's right," replied James. "My daughter Charlotte and the boy here. We came from Kaskaskia, Illinois. Not very far as the birds fly, but a long tortuous trek by wagon and horseback. Sold everything I owned and hope to start out for Oregon as soon as the grass is green enough in the spring. Who's this Captain Foster you mentioned? Is he the one I need to speak to about joining the train? Where might I find him, if I were looking for such a man?"

James glanced down again at Joseph as the boy moved forward toward Jasper Smith. He frowned with disapproval. The boys seemed to have grown bored with the adult conversation and walked off a little way by themselves. Whispering to themselves, they moved out

39

of range of the men's presence and began to toss what looked like a cloth bag back and forth playfully, separating more as the bag flew astray and fell on the ground.

Smith had also noticed the actions of the two boys and smiled. "Jasper doesn't have any boys of his own age nearby, and he's too young to be comfortable in his much older step-brother's presence. He's often abrupt with the boy. I keep him busy around the sables, but it's good to have someone of his own age around."

"What are they playing?" James watched the boys throwing the bag to each other.

"That's a bean bag." A big grin appeared on Smith's puffy, red-skinned face.

"What did you say?" asked James. "A bean bag?"

"Aye! My wife came up with the idea, sewed a piece of cloth together and put a couple of handfuls of beans inside and stitched it up. Makes a nice toy to play with, although I'm afraid my son Abraham has outgrown the game. He's seventeen now and thinks he's an adult. Probably is in most people's opinion, but I can't help seeing him as he was when a baby in my arms. Guess a man's got to let his young'uns grow up when they get as tall as my Abraham. A shame, though."

"Yes, I see what you mean." James stood for a moment watching the boys play. The dog was circling around them trying to catch the bag in his teeth, his tail wagging furiously from side to side. "Well, about this Captain Foster, where did you say I might find him?" James took his attention off the boys for the moment.

"Didn't say. Don't know him by sight, but I've heard tell he stays at one of those big hotels in the center of town on the main east-to-west road. 'Spect anyone in a saloon could give you the directions. Seems a fever's overcome the eastern half of the country. Everybody wants to head west. It's the talk of all the barrooms; heard it myself from a stranger when I happened down to the Red Rooster a few weeks back. A fancy dressed man with a pearl stud in his cravat; looked like a gambler man. Don't 'spect he'll last long out on the desert, but was bragging about the high mountains and the grassy plains. All the men were standing, slack-jawed and round-eyed, as though the western ocean was a thrill they must see 'afore they die. Me, I plan to stay right where I am; don't fancy no hot, dusty trail, nor no flooding rivers, neither."

James stared at the livery man, aghast that the man was so attuned with his own fascination with the idea of going to Oregon. He'd watched and listened in awe to Perkins and Thibodeau in Kaskaskia, exactly as this man was describing the men of the Red Rooster Saloon in St. Louis, Missouri. But, he hadn't thought of it as a fever, rather as an opportunity for advancement in the world. James decided it was time to change the subject before he was forced to defend his decision to go west. He looked quickly at the two boys, still tossing the bag between them.

"Guess I better check out my animals and see to their needs. That's what I came for. Is it all right to leave them here with you until I can find another place? How much do you charge by the month?" He moved toward the barn with Smith, all talk of going to Oregon forgotten as the two men discussed a mutually acceptable deal for the care of the Morgan horses and wagon.

Later, as James and Smith were coming out of the barn, Joseph and Jasper were sitting on the ground, with the dog stretched out beside them, asleep. They were talking as though they'd known each other for years.

Joseph jumped up from his seat and ran to this father's side. "Can I keep the dog, Papa?" Joseph's voice quivered with excitement. "I'll take good care of him myself. I will, I promise."

Jasper stayed back, then slowly made his way forward, as if unsure about the outcome of his new acquaintance's proposition and not wanting to call attention to himself if the plan they had decided on went astray.

"I can't say for sure, son, don't know if the hotel allows pets inside." He turned to Smith. "We're staying at the Hightower Hotel for now. Over that way." He pointed over his left shoulder.

"Sure they do," replied Smith, spitting on the ground. "That black helper of Hightower's keeps a dog of his own, name of Nero."

Joseph's eyes lit up like twin gray moons in his round face at this news. Jasper came to stand beside him and lend any support he could.

"Come along, then, and we'll ask Mrs. Hightower if you can keep the dog, but you mustn't get your hopes up too high in case she turns us down." James turned to go, but, Smith took hold of his arm and delayed him. James looked at him in surprise.

"Them boys seem to git along jest fine. I'll send your young'un home later, 'iffen you don't mind him staying a spell." He glanced at James and spat a long stream of tobacco.

"Fine, fine, that would make it fair to the boys, I'm sure." James agreed to the plan. In fact, it suited him not to have the boy trailing him everywhere he went.

There was silence between the boys as they looked deeply into each other's eyes, then a whoop of joy came bursting out of Jasper, and he hugged his father tightly, yelled at Joseph to "catch" and threw the bean bag high in the air. The dog raced to sniff the cloth when it fell in the dust.

7

James made his way down the side streets until he came to what looked like a retail establishment. On the outside in bold lettering were the words, "General Merchandise, B. Trice, Proprietor," and in various sized and spaced lettering, "Clothing, Dry Goods, Hardware, Mail." Eager now with this new knowledge of the name of the wagon train captain, he entered the mercantile store with a smile on his face. Using the natural charm with which he won many a poker game, James looked around at the contents of the store.

In the far corner, there was a square shaped cubicle with a caged window near the top. Across the top of the cage was a recently painted blue sign, MAIL. Shelves were spaced around the walls piled high with large and small boxes, marked with the name of their contents; on the floor were barrels and boxes. Several large wooden tables were covered with carpenter's equipment, hammers, saws, boxes of nails and cans of paint. On one shelf were lanterns of all sizes and shapes. Several rows of waist-high counters stood loaded with wares. On one row he could see horizontal racks stacked high with bolts of colored cloth, and behind it, hanging on pegs, were ready-made dresses and men's shirts. There were shoes of all sizes from which could be seen a small white tag informing the customers the cost. James knew it would take days to identify all the contents of the emporium. And, in the center of the vast room was a large pot-bellied wood burning stove, the heat from which radiated around the enclosure, and several empty chairs.

There was a woman standing behind a counter dressed in a high-necked blue muslin dress, talking to a heavyset woman with her head covered with a black felt hat. On the rim of the hat, James could see a bunch of purple wax grapes. The woman was dressed in gray, faded silk. James shifted his gaze to the left, hearing a male voice, and turned in time to see Benjamin Trice shaking the hands of a couple of women who had several packages in their hands. Looking more closely, he was sure they were the sisters with whom he had shared a breakfast meal at the hotel that same morning. Happy to find this opening to his quest for information, he stepped near the women from the hotel.

"Good day, ladies," he said, "If I'd known you were coming to the same place, I could have accompanied you on your way. I'm James Morgan, also a guest at Bertha Hightower's hotel. We ate at the same table this morning."

One of the sisters, Sarah Warren, sniffed the air, as though she found something tainted in the smell of the room. She started to turn aside and leave the store, her business with the proprietor finished, but her sister wasn't so quick to leave. She smiled and held her handkerchief to her nose, as though she too had caught a whiff of the pungent odor, but she stepped forward and welcomed James as though he were her long lost brother, come back from the wilderness of the West.

"Why, yes, Mr. Morgan, I remember you well. You're the father of that delightful miss who helped Mrs. Hightower with the kitchen chores this morning. Such a shame, poor Gladys breaking her leg like that, isn't it?" Margaret Brown, dressed from top to toe in solid black silk, as though she were going to a party instead of attending to her normal shopping chores, was always inclined to gossip when she could find a listener available. "What was your daughter's name again? I'm sure I should remember it, but I cannot."

"Charlotte," James replied, laughing inside at the tricks of the widow. He glanced at the other one, Sarah, and watched as she meandered over to the sewing notions as though she couldn't be bothered with the conversation between her sister and a man. Picking up a glass jar of buttons, she pretended not to listen to her sister's conversation, but James wasn't fooled by her antics. Although a dirt farmer by trade, he wasn't without experience in the company of the fairer sex.

Impatiently hoping to rid himself of the ladies and their prattle, James turned to meet the proprietor, a twinkle in his eyes, and quickly, but ever so politely brought the conversation to a close by reminding them that he would see them later at dinner. With a wave of her white handkerchief, Margaret wished him a pleasant day, and grabbing the arm of her sister, marched to the door. She paused a moment to look back, and a disappointed expression crossed her face when she saw that James had already started a conversation more to his liking with the man behind the counter. She gave a huff of disapproval, and slipped through the door of the shop, as if she were a China clipper in full sail.

Giving a sharp look toward the female behind the counter, who was now alone and waving a feather duster at invisible objects that offended her, James turned to the man. He held out his hand and spoke, eagerness in his voice.

"Good day, my name is James Morgan. Are you Mr. Benjamin Trice, the proprietor? I was told by a reliable source that you might know the whereabouts of a Captain Horatio Foster who's gathering together a list of pioneers for a wagon train heading west as soon as the weather turns warm enough for the grass to feed the animals. I should like to be on that list, if it's possible." He waited, his heart beating so loudly that he was sure Trice could hear it.

"Aye, that's me, Benjamin Clark Trice, owner and operator of this establishment. And, my wife Rebekah, as well." He motioned for the female behind the counter to come to his aid. She slowly moved to his side but didn't speak, leaving the men to their talk. She wielded her feather duster up and down the shelves behind her, but James knew she was listening to their conversation with interest.

"Captain Foster, you say you're looking for? Aye, and he's gone to Pennsylvania to hire a wheelwright or wagon maker for the trip west. Got shops in this town can make wagons, but none what can make a good wheel for rolling over rocks and hard ground. He told me himself, he did, that a master wheelwright is worth his weight in gold, once the train gets into the high mountains of the West. I expect him back in a week or two."

Disappointed, James continued the conversation for a few more minutes, purchased a few small items, a pretty blue ribbon for Charlotte's hair and a mouth organ for Joseph, just to keep on good

45

terms with the proprietor, and left the store.

Wandering aimlessly from place to place, James decided he'd have to take on some sort of occupation in order to keep paying the bills until the train was ready to leave. Seeing two men removing sawed logs from a wagon near the back of the hotel, he walked over to their side, and using his famous charm, began a conversation with them. He was certain he'd seen one of the men in the saloon the night before. Casually, so as not to alarm the men, he began to help unload the logs from the wagon to the stack in the enclosure. After a few minutes, he asked who was in charge of the log business.

The man from the saloon, whom James was later to discover was named Arthur Bingham, told him who to see about a job, and James, after a cheerful good-bye, left them to their work. He walked briskly to a side street about five miles from the hotel, where he found a saw mill and several men working. The sound of the buzzing saw was deafening as he got closer. The fresh smell of sawdust tickled his nose, and he sneezed in reaction. There was a wooden shack with a round metal smokestack to the rear of the area, and he saw a sign that said, "Office."

The manager of the saw mill was Major Sanford. He rose from his seat and gazed out the window as though it were something he did often to keep an eye on his employees. He was quick to point out that what he needed more than men were a good sturdy wagon and a team. He turned back into the room and gave James an inquisitive look over his wire-rimmed spectacles. "You say you've got a boy with you. I also need a loyal, sturdy helper to dust and clean. The sawing of the wood from the outside is a constant bother to the wife, and if the boy has a bit of schooling, he can help with the paper work involved and run errands. I'll train him myself. The boy can board with us so he'll be handy at all hours, for sometimes I work late into the night on a rush order for cut timber."

The Major added with a sigh of despair. "I have an older son who had the chance to work as apprentice for a prestigious lawyer in the main business area of town, but his mother's reluctant to have him leave home so young. If Robbie gets paid for the work he does for lawyer Thigpen, we wouldn't have that expense, so the few cents for the younger boy will save us money. If your family moves on in the spring, it'll be a temporary arrangement, after all. 'Course the dog will be a setback, but he can eat the scraps from the table. I'll have to discuss this with my wife, Wilhelmina, but I'm sure she'll agree in the end to take in the smaller boy."

The Major soberly shook hands with James and thanked him, promising to look out for his new, young employee, so no danger came to him. James was very pleased with himself. An hour after arriving, he had not only a job for himself, but a business agreement for the use of his wagon and horses. With a promise to arrive early in the morning with his wagon and team, James walked the distance back to the hotel, very satisfied with the day's affairs.

*****

When Joseph returned to the hotel, accompanied by Moses Smith and Jasper, Bertha said he could keep the dog, but it could sure use a washing. The Smiths left with a friendly wave, and Conk took the dog into the backyard, where he pulled the wooden tub with which he washed his own mastiff, Nero, from the peg. The mongrel and Nero sniffed and circled each other and growled, but Conk called his dog to heel, and put him in the kitchen.

"What ya gonna call your dog, Master Joseph?" Conk poured a bucket of warm water into the tub. Reaching for a bar of lye soap and a couple of cloths, he grabbed the dog and put him into the tub and held him tightly. "Here, young'un, take this here brush and rub the bubbles through his fur. I knew a feller once, had a dog he called Spotty. I thought it was a fine name. Looked a lot like this 'un."

While he was talking, Conk encouraged Joseph to scrub the dog's coat and pour clean water around his head and neck. The dog didn't like that, and scrambling over the side of the tub, escaped from the arms of the dark-skinned man. He shook the soap and water from his coat, sending drops of water in all directions, then rolled on the grass. Hezekiah Conklin laughed, his bass voice rumbling from deep inside his throat. Joseph ran to catch him. Together, the man and the boy finished washing and rubbing with the towels until the dog's hair was mostly dry. Conk went into the kitchen and gave the dog a small piece of meat as a reward for being so cooperative. He petted his own dog, Nero, and introduced him to Spotty, for Joseph decided that was a good name for the dog, and the two mongrels lay side by side near the kitchen range to warm themselves.

Joseph was sitting at the kitchen table eating a small sliver of the raisin cake that Charlotte had baked that morning when his father arrived back at the hotel. Told the arrangements for his new home and occupation, without a word of argument, he went upstairs to start packing his belongings. The dog, whose coat was now shaggy and clean, scampered up the stairs behind him, his tail wagging with joy.

*****

Turning to Bertha, who had followed the boy and dog with delight in her eyes, James said, "I'm pleased that you'll allow Joseph to keep the dog with him; he's already grown fond of the mutt. I came to tell you that the boy and me will be going to work tomorrow at the saw mill. The lad will board with Sanford and his wife on the week days, so he'll be available to run errands. He'll be here with me at the hotel on weekends, if you think that's alright."

Bertha replied, "That's a fine arrangement." She put up a hand to hold the knot of hair in position as it tried to slip to the side. She took out a couple of hairpins and poked them back into place. "I'm glad to have this time alone to speak with you."

Satisfied that her hair wasn't coming loose, she brought a cup to the table and filled it from the coffee pot. Scooting the cream and sugar near his cup so he could reach them, she pulled out a chair and prepared herself for the discussion in her mind.

"Sit yourself down, Mr. Morgan, there's something I been thinking on this morning. That gal of yours, she's a real good cook. My servant girl broke her leg, and I need someone like Charlotte to help around the place until Gladys gits her leg healed; sort of temporary, like, until you leave. The maid part would be making beds and sweeping the female guest's rooms, for they don't like for the black man to invade their privacy, but the cooking was what impressed me the most. She was efficient and followed orders without complaint, and we worked well together this morning. Could you see yourself clear to letting your girl help me?" Bertha puffed out her fat cheeks and nodded her head as if to help James decide the matter.

Thinking that with a little luck, the caravan would be leaving St. Louis in a few weeks, James agreed to the terms if Charlotte was willing to work. Secretly, James was determined to see that she did because it would give him extra money in which to gamble at the poker tables.

Bertha told James that she would make Charlotte's wages equal to the rent and food at the hotel, so they wouldn't owe her anything. The smile on her face said she knew what he was thinking, and James realized she'd surely seen men of his character before in her years as a hotel matron. He wasn't pleased with the arrangement, but decided free rent and food was better than paying for it.

He wondered if the woman would give the girl any money on the side, a stipend for her personal use, but that was a matter for later discussion. They shook hands, and Bertha called Clayborne in from the front room to witness the signing of the paper agreement.

8

St. Louis, Missouri
January, 1844

The wind howled outside the walls of the Hightower Hotel, and the kitchen door blew open. Conk quickly got up to close it, putting a chair under the doorknob to help secure it. He grabbed an old cloth and wiped up the flecks of snow that had blown in. Bertha, standing near the stove with an oversized spoon in her hand, murmured words of gratitude, and looked out the window. Snow still lay on the ground from the blizzard the week before, leaving some drifts as high as the roof of a house. The temperature was below freezing, the sun hidden behind heavy slotted gray clouds and Major Sanford had sent his employees home early.

"Damn snow, will it never end?" She reached up to push her topknot more securely onto her head.

"No, ma'am. Not as long as the sun don't shine," Conk proclaimed and sat in his chair to finish shelling beans. He threw the cloth on the floor beside him.

It was such an odd statement that Charlotte burst out laughing. "He's right, Bertha. Sunshine's the only thing that'll stop the snow. But, at least it's snug and warm in here. Do you want me to baste the ham again? Or, leave the oven closed until the bread's done?" She looked at Bertha with a sparkle of humor in her eyes.

"Oh, leave it for now, I guess, and wash these bowls and spoons. Conk, soon's you finish those beans, best go for more logs for the furnace. The guests will start complaining if they feel the cold. I just hope the wood lasts until spring." She sighed and missed the secret smile that passed between the man and the girl, and they went back to their chores. A clatter of dishes being washed blended with the low hum of Conk's voice as he finished the beans and rose to put on his heavy coat and scarf before bringing in more wood. He had trouble with the door. Charlotte closed it behind him and wiped the floor again with the dirty cloth.

*****

James grew restless and left the building shortly after the noon meal, taking a few of the dwindling coins from his paycheck in his pocket. He stumbled over a pile of clutter on the sidewalk and opened the doors of the Red Rooster Saloon, looking for more congenial companionship. Only a few men were there, drinking alone at different tables. James saw Arthur Bingham at the bar, but he didn't stay long, moving out into the street when his drink was finished. One of the saloon girls came downstairs and spoke to James for a while. But he was in a strange mood, so she drifted over to an empty table and began playing with a deck of cards. They knew each other very well, and occasionally she glanced at him; but he ignored her, and continued to brood and drink slowly from his bottle.

A couple of hours later the circuit judge wandered in and looked around. He decided there were enough men to start a poker game. The men gathered around a back table, and James won the first two rounds, then lost one, then won again. Slowly the day wore on into late afternoon. A couple of players left and new ones sat down in their place. James felt a knot in his stomach and realized he was hungry, so asked Jenkins to bring him a ham sandwich and two hard boiled eggs provided by the saloon. Hank Blessing, the bartender, kept his eyes on the men, swiped the counter several times, cleaned some glasses, and was kept busy pouring drinks as the room slowly filled with restless men hating the confined spaces of their homes. Several more girls came down the stairs and mingled with the men.

The manager told the dancers to start early as it would be a busy night. Duff, the piano player, struck a few chords and began to play while the dancers donned their gaily colored frocks. A short time later, he struck a lively note, and the dancers flew onto the makeshift stage and pranced around to the sound of the piano. Some of the patrons watched or sang along or flirted with their favorites, but the men at the poker game in the back paid them no heed.

James watched the dealer toss the cards on the table and glanced up at the scene around him. Everyone was drinking, laughing, winning and losing; and talking politics, the weather or whether there would be war with Mexico. He heard the swish of the inside doors as a stranger came in and shut the outside door behind him. He stood for a moment in front of the wide door of the saloon, the bright light making his eyes blink, and the music strumming in his ears with its tinny vibrations. James picked up his cards and tossed two on the table so the dealer would give him replacements. The betting started, and he forgot the stranger for a moment.

While the craggy-faced, slender man called Slim was making up his mind, James saw the stranger at the end of the bar, eating a sandwich and boiled eggs, and washing them down with a beer. James was distracted by the game, and the next time he saw the man with the black beard, he was sitting alone at a table, swirling his liquor around in the glass and accompanied by a bottle at his elbow.

A bar girl named Flavia, dressed in bright red and yellow with black stockings, stopped by and gave the stranger a gentle poke, leaned close to his face and asked for a drink. He declined her invitation and watched the dancers on the stage. James was amused at Flavia's tricks; he quickly returned his eyes to his cards when he saw the man look toward his table.

The wind whistled around the building, and a couple of men left the bar. James could feel the draft of cold air when the door opened and they went out. The dancers left the stage, to the disappointment of some of the spectators, who whistled and yelled for them to come back. He took a quick glance at the stranger sitting alone and returned to the game. He won the pot and drew the money to him. He lifted the bottle and tipped some more liquid into his glass. It burned his throat, but he was used to the stinging, burning sensation of the alcohol. He watched the dealer shuffle the cards, and the judge took out his timepiece and commented that it was getting late.

At the bar a couple of men were arguing over whether a girl's pearls were real or not. James listened to the men as they became more agitated and loud, sending curses flying so fast he was afraid it would become a brawl, but the bartender told the men to go outside. One man pinched the girl on the nose and left the bar, saying he'd see her later. No sooner had the man left than the girl went upstairs with the other guy. James laughed, because it was Maizie, his favorite. She gazed over her shoulder at him, and he waved and picked up his cards.

Slim threw down his cards and rose from his seat. "That lets me out; the stakes are getting too high for me." He picked up his winnings from the table and left the bar. Distracted by the disturbance, James saw the stranger toss back the last of his drink, rise and walk with a steady pace to the edge of the group and ask politely, "Mind if a stranger sits in, men?"

James looked up and said, "Sure, you can take Slim's place over there." Turning toward a man with long sleeves rolled to the elbows and brown corduroy trousers, with a dirty apron over his tight belly, he yelled, "Heh, Jenkins, throw some more wood in the stove, will you?" He lifted the half full bottle of whiskey near his elbow, tipped it and filled his glass on the table, then taking a long swallow, leaned his head back so that the bitter liquid could flow more smoothly down his throat.

Jenkins gave James an exasperated look, then slowly moved to the wood box and picked up a few pieces and threw them into the iron stove. He closed the door and went back to serving the customers.

The stranger sat down in the chair left empty by Slim, placed his hat beneath the seat, ordered a whiskey from Jenkins and watched as the dealer shuffled the cards.

"My name's Butler. I come from Virginia." There were five men playing poker, and they gave him their names, and the game started. It went on and on through the hours of the afternoon and evening. At some point, Jenkins lowered the hanging chandelier of candles and lit them one by one, but it didn't distract the players. He lit several lanterns hanging in sconces on the walls. The room was slowly filling as more men entered to drink or to come in out of the cold. Someone exclaimed that it had started snowing again. A groan encircled the room, but no one left to watch it.

Around the table, besides James Morgan and William Butler, there was Judge Moore, and a jolly man named Sylvester with fat cheeks and small beady eyes that seemed to disappear in his rounded face. He spoke with a German accent and laughed with a gravelly tone, as though the sound came from some deep well inside him. James could read him like a book. His eyes glistened with unshed tears when he had a good hand, and he cracked his knuckles before he shuffled or dealt the cards.

Across the table from James sat a traveling salesman named Priddy, who was sitting in on the game until his stagecoach left. He was dressed in a fine black wool suit, white shirt, with a big pearl stickpin in his wide tie. About five o'clock a man came in and told him that because of the high snow drifts the stage wouldn't be running that night. That didn't seem to bother Priddy. He told his informant to book him another night in the hotel.

The game dragged on past midnight with James winning some and losing some, but slowly losing more than he was winning. The new man, Butler, kept pace with the other players, winning more than he lost. The oppressive heat from the stove and the smell of urine and unwashed bodies were enough to make a man nauseous. He took a white cloth from his inside vest pocket and wiped his face.

Everyone in the barroom was drinking; the roulette wheel whirled, and men laughed. Over at the end of the bar, a man was half leaning, half lying, and the bartender told him to go home. James watched as he suddenly slid to the floor, and a heavyset man carried him to the back wall and left him to lie there. The music was playing loudly, and the dancers on stage hefted their petticoat skirts high in the air. Jenkins was kept busy manning the bar. Todd, the handyman and cook, brought fresh sandwiches and boiled eggs for the customers. He placed a jar of sour pickles beside the tray. Afterward he returned to washing glasses in the back room.

James became morose and bet higher stakes. He noticed he was down to his last few dollars, took a chance and made one large bet, which he lost to William Butler, as the other players had earlier called in their hands. James now owed William a significant amount of cash, over one hundred dollars. He realized he had no funds to pay, not even if he went back to his room at the hotel and raided his waist money belt.

He sat in shock, silently staring at the cards, while a sense of dread filled the air. The onlookers whispered among themselves, and soon the news spread around the room. The piano player stopped playing, and the dancing girls walked off stage, bewildered.

Judge Moore looked at James, and something passed across his face. Hank, the head bartender, looked down at the shelf behind the counter to make sure his shotgun was handy. Priddy, the fancy dressed salesman, backed away from the table. William, unaffected, and with a steady hand, poured himself another drink and downed it in a gulp.

James looked up at William, unsure how to proceed; if he walked away, he lost everything: his honor, his dreams of Oregon. As though the idea was dredged up from some lost nightmare, James said loudly enough for the nearby gawkers to hear, "I still got something you might want." His hand shook as he poured another drink, swallowed and felt the burning liquid slide down his throat. He coughed and his gut roiled as he searched the eyes of the younger man. "Game still in play?"

William eyed the cards in his hand, kings and aces. The bottle glistened in the dim light from the chandelier overhead; the liquid inside was a tempting amber, and cold, but he ignored it. "Game's still on. What might you have that I want?" He gave James a scornful sneer.

"I've got a girl." James heard his voice crack, and he forced it louder. He glanced at Sylvester and the judge, defiance keeping his shoulders straight and his head high. "A daughter, marrying age. You see she gets to Oregon safely, and she's yours, if you call us quits on the deal."

"Hell, man!" That was the judge. "You'd sell your own daughter to a stranger?"

"I said it, didn't I?" James slammed his cards on the table, two jacks, a four, a king, and a deuce. "You making a liar of me?"

William's face turned pale as he saw the losing hand. He slowly laid his cards on the table face up. The judge gasped in shock. William's eyes pinned him to the table. A movement across the room caused him to look, as the bartender, Hank, brought his shotgun up and laid it silently on the bar.

The whole room became deathly quiet as the men and women edged closer to the back table and saw the marks on the cards lying face up. Suddenly, a great babble of voices burst forth as whispers of what James had said passed from ear to ear around the room. "James Morgan bet his daughter and lost," a drummer from Chicago relayed to his neighbor. "His daughter?" came from a man in a checked suit and mustache. "Is he crazy?" A few men, not heeding the falling snow, left the barroom by the front door to pass the news to anyone nearby. Everyone was startled at the surprising turn of events. "It's a joke," one rather plump saloon girl with golden curls and dressed in purple said to her friend, Flavia, laughing loudly.

But James was deadly serious. He hardened his eyes, pressed his mouth tight, and sat rigid on his chair.

Sylvester, the fat troll, cackled with glee, his hand slapping his thigh. He growled in his German accent, "Guess we're done here." He leaned in closer, the lamplight gleaming in his beady eyes.

James shook his head, attempting to clear the fog from his brain. "Hold up, now," he cried angrily. "This ain't done yet. What do you say, Butler, my daughter worth a hundred dollars to you?"

"A real marriage? No strings attached? No going back on your word?" The silence in the room was broken by a cough in the background.

"A real marriage, only take her to Oregon, that's all I ask."

William looked at James and started to laugh. The sheen of drunken over-indulgence making his face shine, he muttered, "Damned ridiculous, but my beloved Martha's dead and buried in the peaceful hills of Virginia. I'm lonely and miss the companionship of a woman. Don't even care what the fool girl looks like." He glared cautiously at the other patrons of the saloon, and with a sudden jerk of his arm, he slammed his hand flat on the table, making the cards leap as if with joy, and yelled, "Done!"

For a split second, the two men stared into each other's eyes, searching for something they didn't understand. James, surprised that his offer was actually accepted, wiped some spittle from the corner of his mouth with a shirt sleeve. He solemnly stood up, took the few steps to circle the table and held out his hand. William firmly grasped it and the deal was set.

Suddenly, the room was alive with raucous laughter, and the bartender gave a great sigh of relief, removed his shotgun from the counter, picked up his dropped cloth and began to energetically wipe the bar. From somewhere there came a loud voice, "Do it now! Go get your daughter, Morgan!" James was stunned, and he shook from the bar patrons' reaction to his deal with the other gambler. His head felt like a giant hammer was pounding on his skull.

A couple of men who knew him well shoved Judge Moore forward, and the pressure began to build as the word spread. "There's going to be a wedding," came from a feminine voice. Someone said, "Here's the judge, ready and willing." "Damn, fool, bringing a decent girl into a barroom," proclaimed a tall, slender man dressed in a long black frock coat and red scarf. His head was covered with a beaver hat.

In the onslaught of noise, William took another drink, his hand now quivering with reaction. "My God," he murmured, "what have I done?" He looked up at the ceiling as if for an answer. The darkened wood and scuffed beams glistened from the glow of the candles in the crystal chandelier.

The women were hugging and calling out suggestions referencing the lewd behavior of a newly married couple, chiding William that he'd shaken hands on the deal. "A home and family, you naughty man," one bar girl teased, running her hand along his chin. His face went slack at her words. The patrons of the saloon continued to riot around him, with the piano player dashing off long, mournful ballads.

James knew what to do. He was a man of honor. Swaggering a little, he dodged the tables and fled through the line of men slapping him on the back and whispering encouragement in his ear, and walked out the barroom door. In the sudden darkness, he stumbled as he realized that the snow was almost ankle deep, and his feet sank into the soft white mush. He hadn't brought his coat, and the gale force winds tore across his unprotected body as he made his way to the hotel.

He burst through the door to the hotel, staggered upstairs and pounded on Charlotte's door. He yelled through the door, "Charlotte, get up and put your clothes on!"

When she opened the door, she was in her nightgown, still trying to get the sleeves of her wrapper on her arms. She shivered, the small movement telling of the chill in the room. "What's wrong, Papa? Is Joseph sick?" She blinked at the light from the flickering candles in the hallway sconces.

"No, he's all right. I need you to put your clothes on right now and come with me."

Bertha yelled from downstairs, "Is that you, James Morgan? What's all that yammering about?"

"I've come for my daughter. It's none of your business. Go back to sleep." James didn't want any interference from the hotel matron. The men were waiting at the saloon, and he had his honor to uphold. He muttered under his breath, "Damn woman! Always got her nose in another person's business."

Just before the door closed, James heard her huff a bit, and mutter something about him being a troublemaker, didn't know why she kept

57

him on. Her husband replied, "Come to bed, Bertha, if Morgan wants to take his daughter out in the middle of the night, that's his business."

Charlotte quickly dressed in her undergarments, cotton socks, lace up shoes and the same work dress she'd worn that day. She pulled on her heavy woolen coat, tied a colorful scarf around her head and opened the door to her father.

James impatiently grabbed her arm and practically dragged her down the stairs. "Outside, girl, we got places to go!"

In a flash they were out the front door and down the street headed toward the saloon.

Charlotte pleaded, "What happened? Where are we going?" She tried to twist her arm free, but he held it tight. A few minutes later she slipped on a patch of ice. "Stop, Papa. Where are you taking me?"

"Be quiet, Daughter, you'll find out soon enough." The snow was really heavy now, and with her father holding tightly to her arm, she pulled her scarf more firmly over her ears and nose with her other hand. The snow fell on her lips, and she licked it away. She slipped again.

"Come on, you clumsy girl," James said angrily, and yanked on her arm, almost causing them both to fall. He was shaking from the cold, and his teeth chattered, walking as he was without a coat or hat. He hurried her along. "Stop dawdling, girl; they're waiting for you." His heavy Scottish brogue sounded harsh in the silent night air. His toes felt frozen, and it was hard to keep his balance in the slush of newly fallen snow. James pushed the girl ahead of him, and she fell, landing face down in the snow. He grabbed her arm and pulled her up.

They came to the door of the saloon, and the sound of laughter and men's voices could be heard from within. Charlotte stopped, shivering. James opened the door and dragged her to where a group of men and saloon girls were standing, drinks in their hands.

Everyone turned when the door opened and stared at the girl walking beside James, but couldn't see her face because of the scarf. Her coat was splattered with flecks of white. One of the men grabbed the scarf and stepped back in admiration. "She's a looker, Butler. Can she cook?" He laughed uproariously.

"Of course she can cook." James was insulted at the slur on his daughter's skills. Hadn't she been cooking and baking since she was twelve? "Here she is, just like I promised." He angrily threw her toward William, who was standing in the center of the group of men.

She slipped as she came against his solid body. He caught her before she fell.

The drummer from Chicago asked the judge if he could marry people without a license. "Of course," he proclaimed loudly. "I have a lifetime federal appointment, and my duties include officiating at weddings." A couple of the saloon girls become interested in the conversation, and one asked if anyone wanted to make it a dual wedding, but she didn't get a response from the men.

One volunteered to let William use her ring for the ceremony. "She's purty, Mr. Butler. She'll make you a good, willing wife." And giggling like a school girl, she took a gold ring off her finger and handed it to the groom. "Here, but make sure I git it back before morning."

"So, she'll do?" James narrowed his eyes, wondering if the man would back out now. Surely, good God, not! If only the damned bar girls would shut up and let the judge do the deed.

William accepted the ring and looked closely at Charlotte. "She's young and pretty, I give you that. Guess she'll do for me." He turned to the judge. "Get it over with, Judge; ain't got time to waste. It'll be dawn before long."

James was satisfied. His head now throbbed, and he wanted this over and done with. He watched as the other man shook his head, blinking his eyes hard, before working one finger into an ear, and shaking his head again.

"Damn ringing!" William turned to call out to the bartender for yet another rye whiskey. "Want to get this done before the sun comes up."

"You don't have to worry about that, Mr. Butler." This came from one of the girls, Maizie, her blue eyes sparkling with fun, who handed him a glass, partially filled. "You can use my room for the night."

"Thank you, kindly, Maizie, I think I will." He swallowed the liquid and gave her a wink. She took the empty glass and moved to James' side, and he smacked her bottom at her boldness.

The bride stood very still, her brown eyes wide with alarm at the exchange between the bearded man and the saloon girl. A tick had developed in James' left eye. It was twitching, and he raised a finger to rub it hard. Maizie offered a dainty handkerchief, and he wiped his eyes. Through the blur of tears, James looked at the man standing near his daughter. He was tall, but not quite as tall as he was, with dark hair and gray eyes, and a full black beard. His coat looked to be of fine woolen cloth, with a white shirt and tie beneath the lapel. He glanced down at the floor, and he had black city-bought shoes, which seemed to be freshly polished.

At least the man wasn't bald, fat and toothless. He almost chuckled at that. Charlotte might have fainted dead away on her wedding day, to have been betrothed to a scoundrel like that. It wouldn't have mattered, but this way was simpler. He turned when he heard a sound to her left.

The judge cleared his throat, and his bulbous nose stood out like a red rooster's comb. "This is a bad business, Morgan." He looked at James closely. "Shouldn't it wait until morning?"

"Do it now, Judge. The snow's getting thicker outside." James pushed the girl from behind. Maizie giggled and clapped her hands. Sylvester leaned in and cackled.

Priddy interrupted him, "The man won her fair and square, Judge. We all know it." He looked around, and the men surrounding them agreed. A roar of angry comments erupted from the back at the delay. "Hurry up, Judge," came a shout from near the bar.

The judge turned to William. "Butler, you want this girl?"

William shrugged and nodded.

Judge Moore pulled his little black book out of an inner pocket and demanded his fee in advance. "One dollar," he said.

William drew a silver dollar from his pocket and handed it to the judge. He stepped beside Charlotte as the other men and saloon girls moved back to give them room.

The judge told William to take the girl's right hand, and he seized it. Charlotte's hand was small in the grip of the big man's calloused palm. William squeezed hard, and she let out a yelp in protest. He looked at her and grinned.

The judge started speaking, and her eyes widened as she realized what was happening, that she was being married to a stranger. She turned to look at her father, but he was grinning and poking the man next to him, very pleased with himself. The judge looked Charlotte in the eyes and asked her a question, and when she didn't respond, the man beside her said, "She does." Everyone seemed to be looking at her, and she nodded her head, her eyes glazed with incomprehension. The man beside her dropped her right hand, took her left and slipped a ring on her finger. She looked down at it with a blank look. It was gold and wide with some sort of design. By the time she looked up, a few more words had been exchanged, and suddenly there was dead silence in the room.

The judge looked expectantly at William. The gambler with the winning hand, the man who'd won more than just silver and gold, grabbed Charlotte and kissed her hard on the lips.

There was a spontaneous burst of applause, and everyone was yelling and laughing. The woman dressed in scarlet and blue, with the white feather in her hair, reached for Charlotte's hand, pulled the ring off and placed it back on her own finger. She sashayed over to the bar and yelled for a whiskey.

Charlotte was being hugged from all sides; tall men, skinny men, men who smelled like a brewery, stale tobacco and hair pomade. They smacked her straight on the mouth with slimy lips, and pinched her checks and her bottom. She yelped when one reached inside her coat, grabbed her breast in one hand and squeezed. She looked through the crowd, calling once for her father, but he was standing beside the saloon girl who had loaned her the ring. They were laughing, and the saloon girl pointed her way.

James looked his daughter's direction, took his glass and lifted it to the girl in a toast and gulped it down with one swallow. Now that the deed was done, it was as if a great, black storm cloud had dissipated, and he could finally breathe again.

*****

Charlotte was awash in confusion.

The crowd moved away, and a great hulk of a man grabbed her from behind, hefted her over his shoulder and headed for the stairs. Her last look at the mob of men and women on the saloon floor was from an upside down angle as she was carried up the stairs. She could see roulette wheels and tables in front of the bar. The last man she saw was her father, laughing with his arms around the prostitute. He gave her a long kiss, and Charlotte felt sick at the sight.

The man carrying her came to a door painted in a putrid green color, opened it and kicked it shut behind them. He threw his new wife—Charlotte now understood that and more—onto the bed and slammed down on top of her. She squeaked with surprise. He untied the scarf from her neck and shoulders where she had put it when she stood in the overheated room, and threw it onto the floor. His fingers began to unbutton her coat; he lifted her from the bed, taking her arms out of the holes, and twisted her body to remove the cloth. The coat followed the scarf onto the floor.

Charlotte was frightened, and her heart was beating fast. She wouldn't receive help from her father, she now realized. He'd been part of the plot to kidnap her and turn her over to the man who now held her captive. She was truly married, if that charade in the saloon meant anything at all. That had been what she agreed to when she nodded her head. This man was her husband. None of the men or women in the room downstairs would help her, she was quite certain of that.

For the first time in her life, Charlotte was in a situation over which she had no control. If she tried to fight her way out, the man would overpower her with his greater strength. If she tried to run away, the strangers in the room below would bring her back. Her best chance was to surrender to the man's desires and try for an escape in the morning. Where could she go? She couldn't leave her brother alone with her father.

Oh, God! Charlotte thought. Joseph! What would happen to Joseph? Her father must have been out of his mind, to put her in such a position as she now found herself.

She didn't even know this man's name.

*****

William could think of only one thing, the same thought that had consumed him coming up the stairs. He unbuttoned the dress, and he pulled it up and over the girl's head and slung it toward the foot of the bed. She was now covered only in some white cotton undergarments. He snatched one foot forward, unlaced her high top shoe and flung it onto the floor. Thunk! The sound was loud in the room. He could hear the voices down below, and someone had started to play the piano. The snowfall outside wouldn't stop the celebration, and it would probably continue until dawn.

He threw the other shoe on the floor and began to remove her white cotton stockings from her thighs. He couldn't resist. He leaned down and planted a kiss on the soft pink inner flesh of one thigh. It tasted sweet as honey, and he could see the dark shadow of hair through the thin cloth of her drawers. He smelled the nectar of woman, and he kissed that area through the cloth. Ummm. It was delicious, but he must touch her skin.

William clutched the girl by the elbows and pulled her to his

62

chest. Her soft rounded breasts felt so good. With skilled fingers of long practice he removed the rest of her garments, and she lay before him naked and vulnerable. Her dark brown eyes gazed at him in something resembling shock. He could even imagine an innocent fear lingered there. She was an untrained virgin. But, he wasn't going to be stopped. He'd bought her, and he would have her before the night was further advanced.

Leaving the girl on the bed where he could watch her every move, William stood beside the bed and removed his own clothes. First, off came his jacket, then his tie, his vest, sweater and white cotton shirt. He sat on the bed beside the girl while he unlaced his shoes and dropped them on the floor, and he rolled his stockings down over his ankles. Standing, he watched the eyes of the girl dilate and become curious as he removed his trousers in one easy pull over his slender hips and dropped them down around his ankles. He stood very still as he watched the surprise in Charlotte's eyes. But, she didn't flinch from the sight of his manhood.

He stood a moment longer, and when the girl's eyes drifted up to his face, he grinned, and surprisingly, she smiled back. It was a timid, weak smile, but a smile nonetheless. Encouraged, he jumped down onto the bed and covered her with his body, landing kisses on her cheeks, her eyes, her chin, then as softly as the brush of a butterfly wing, on her mouth. She didn't resist. Her lips moved with his in curiosity. He pressed harder, grinding his lips onto hers. He touched his tongue to her lips and teased. She shivered, and it sent a thrill through his already overcharged body.

Smoothly, he slid his hand down her waist and over her hip, and with the pressure of one large masculine hand he spread her legs wide to receive him. Without a signal or thought for her innocence, he plunged deep inside her and threw a hand over her mouth in case she began to scream.

Charlotte jerked her head sideways, and when he removed his hand, she gasped for air, crying out, "You're hurting me." Tears filled her eyes, and she tried to pull away.

"You're mine, sweet Charlotte," William whispered, aroused even more by her agitation, and the rising and falling of her bare breasts. "Mine forever; do not try to escape. Your father sold you to me."

She fought for her freedom. She raised her fingernails to his face and clawed with all her strength. She tried to lift her legs and kick, but he was too heavy. She struck at his back and sides with her fists, but he subdued her with his long arms.

William caressed her face once she finally relaxed in his arms.

"Oh, God! What do you mean, my father sold me? You paid money for my person?" she asked her captor. "White people can't do that, can they? Buy or sell another white person?"

"Oh, yes, my pretty wife," William replied. "They can and they do. Your father lost you in a card game. He had no more money, and I agreed to take you in proper payment as chattel for his debt."

"A card game? My father gambled and lost all his money? How can that happen? He had plenty this morning when he left the hotel dining room. I gave it to him, ten dollars in government script that I saved from my wages."

William rolled off the girl and lay on his side looking at her in surprise. One thick strand of hair fell onto his forehead, and he brushed it away, impatiently. His eyes darkened with concern.

"Your father took your wages to gamble in the saloon? Damnation, does he have no honor at all?"

Charlotte turned her head aside.

"What, girl?" William saw the look on her face, and he wished to comfort her.

"My father." She looked at him, her eyes red with tears. "My mother called it an addiction, a disease that couldn't be cured. He often is unable to stop himself from gambling away money that isn't his. She was right. Now he's gambled away me." She spat the words with scorn, and her eyes closed as tears began to run down her face.

William paused in dismay, and he moved from the bed and reached for his clothes. He couldn't attempt to figure out the puzzle of James Morgan; he was too drunk. He felt a sickness like he'd never felt before come over him. He looked sadly at the girl, who was now his legal wife, whom he'd just cruelly treated and felt guilt for his own part in the scheme. But, what had been done couldn't be undone. He must take responsibility and not condemn her father for his own part in the shame of this night's business. He must make restitution for his own actions.

Quickly, William dressed and told Charlotte to dress, too. He would take her to her home and leave her until the morning when he was sober and thinking clearly again. He watched with a feeling of shame as she dressed and sat on the bed to lace her shoes. He knelt at her feet and finished the lacing for her. The smell of sex lingered in the air and blended with the heavy perfume of the saloon girl who worked her magic over her customers each night. The thought crossed his mind that the situations weren't all that different, for he'd taken a sweet innocent girl's most prized possession in the bed of a prostitute, and with his money, too.

Turning his head, he saw Charlotte before the looking glass, arms raised, tucking the loose strands of hair into the knot at the back of her neck.

"Come, I'll take you out the back way, so no one will see us. I'll take you home if you tell me where you live. Is it far?" he asked.

"No, not far. Just on the other side of Trice's Mercantile Store." Leaving her hair, Charlotte looked down at her coat to make sure it was buttoned correctly, then turned and crossed to the door. William was ahead of her, and he unlocked and opened the door for her to pass in front of him. He noticed her colorful scarf on the floor and went back for it.

They walked the length of the hallway and down the back stairs. The icy wind blew against their exposed skin and surrounded them as they left the door to the saloon. The snow was coming down in soft white crystals. He could barely see, and he wasn't familiar with the town.

But Charlotte seemed to know her way. She guided him down the alley beside the saloon and around to the front, then moved off to the left. Walking as briskly as they could in the slush of newly laid snow, they came to the entrance of the hotel. It was never locked because people came and went at all hours. William opened the front door and Charlotte stepped inside, with her husband following. She shook herself like a wet dog and brushed the flakes of snow off her shoulders, then turned to the stairs. The heat of the building seemed oppressive after the cold of the outdoors.

William took her arm, thinking to assist her up the stairs, but she brushed his hand aside and moved ahead of him. He followed more slowly, feeling his way through the situation that had developed through his own selfishness and pride. Arriving at her door, she turned and whispered for him to come inside. He complied with her request and found himself in a bare room with nothing but a bed, one hardback chair, a cheval mirror and a small table on which was a ceramic pitcher inside a wash basin. There was a multicolored rag rug on the floor which added a bit of softness to the place. It was stark but it was clean. He shut the door behind them.

Without a single word, Charlotte began to remove her outer garments and sat on the chair to remove her shoes. William was bewildered. Did she expect him to stay the night? Should he go and leave her alone? While he puzzled over the matter, Charlotte rose and crawled into the bed. None of the ladies of the night at the saloon could've offered so blatant an invitation. He was just sober enough to understand. He undressed as fast as he could, followed her onto the bed, and no longer troubled by her innocence, although the girl was awkward and stiff, William spent the most pleasing of nights.

*****

Charlotte awoke in the darkness of her bedroom, aware that a male was gently snoring in her ear, and a heavy arm was wrapped around her waist. She lay still, going over in her mind the events of the night before, after her father rushed her out of the hotel and into the snowfall. She remembered that terrible scene in the saloon with the drunken men kissing and pinching her, the humiliation of being carried upside down while the piano player pounded on his instrument, and her father cuddling the prostitute. It was all there in the early morning air, whispering, condemning her. She couldn't see the face of the man lying close beside her, but she could smell the liquor on his breath.

Oh, God! She moaned silently; she was married to this man. She couldn't remember the words of the ceremony, but she knew what they meant. Hadn't her mother blamed her father enough times for the facts of marriage to be made clear even to the ears of a young child? And, her body was sore in places she'd never known could be hurting. She'd been bought like a horse at the auction sale in Illinois, before they'd come to this place in St. Louis. She belonged to this man until death.

What about her brother? What about Joseph? She couldn't leave, for what would happen to him? She must stay and protect her brother from her father's wayward gambling and womanizing. If that Maizie woman was any indication, then her father was lost to all decency and honor. Charlotte stared at the dark ceiling that she couldn't see and made a vow to herself and to the tall, dark man lying beside her. She would remain with him, if he wanted her, no matter what degradation or humiliation he might put her through, for she was bound to him by law and her own pride and honor. She'd be his wife and bear his

66

children for her brother's sake. Having made her peace with herself, Charlotte rolled as quietly and gently as she could manage from underneath the heavy arm of her husband, and rose to start the new life in which she was now trapped.

9

Downstairs in the kitchen, a curious Bertha wanted to know what had happened in the middle of the night to bring James Morgan to the hotel in such a state of drunkenness. It was a miracle that the whole house hadn't awakened to the noise, as he snatched his daughter from her room and ran out the door into the snow.

The cold crept into the building in spite of the warmth of the heating system. Snow glistened in the early morning sunlight, and she knew it wouldn't take long to melt. Conk brought in more logs and kindling and threw them into the box behind the stove. Flecks of snow covered his cap and coat, and he shrugged them onto the floor, ignoring the frown of his employer.

Bertha put the coffee on to perk and started making biscuits.

Charlotte entered the room with a determined look on her face. She greeted Bertha and the dark-skinned man cheerfully, and told them of the events of the night. She didn't include what happened in the prostitute's room, or afterwards in the room upstairs. She shyly said that her husband was asleep in her bed. She looked down, embarrassed.

"Well, bless me; and you just a child, yourself." Bertha wanted more information, but didn't want to embarrass the girl more than necessary, so she gently asked a few questions. She noticed that Conk was listening and sent him to fetch the milk and bring in the eggs. 'Twasn't the man's business what had happened to the girl. The door opened, and Clayborne rolled into the room, seeking the warmth of the stove. Bertha rushed to him and gave him a peck on his bald head. She burst out with this new information about her friend, and he looked at Charlotte with a boldness he hadn't displayed before.

"Who is this man you've married, Charlotte; some old gray-haired man with dirty fingernails and no teeth?" He turned the chair so he could look her fully in the face, and she cringed.

"No." The girl quietly described her husband as tall, dark-haired and with a full beard.

"It's not as bad as I thought, then. I'll have my assistant, Jacobe, inquire more about the man to see if he's respectable, but since the deed's already done, and my friend Judge Moore performed the ceremony, nothing can be changed. You'll have to live with the man; no way to annul the marriage if he's asleep in your bed." He sighed and moved his chair away from the stove. There was a sparkle in his eyes as he looked at the women. "The whole assembly will know when they come down for breakfast. You'd best be prepared for their questions, young lady. What's his name again?"

"Yes, sir. His name's William Butler. He's up there now." She blushed and turned to stir the porridge with an oversized spoon, her face pink with embarrassment. Bertha snickered and smiled at her husband.

"Charlotte, honey, go set the table while I finish cooking the sausage." Bertha took a fork as the girl left to obey her, and she started lifting the sausages from the skillet to a platter.

As soon as she was out of the room, Bertha whispered to her husband, "What's to be done, Clay? She's such a child. Can't you get the judge to forget what happened in the barroom?"

"No, it's obvious that she's a real woman now. It's too late to stop the march of time. What if she has a baby within the year? She'd be in trouble for sure if the man leaves her stranded with us. I'll have Jacobe look into his background, but there's nothing I can do."

*****

With a frown on his face, Clayborne took his cup of coffee and rolled into the dining room, his mind perplexed by this affair. Somehow, he wasn't surprised when Moore appeared at the door of the dining room, having been let into the house by Conk. They put their heads together, and although the judge was aware of his own selfishness in the matter, he didn't see what else he could've done. He described the events of the night from his side of the bargain. He took out the coin and showed it to his friend.

Clayborne looked at the coin and frowned. "I blame it all on James Morgan. I usually don't interfere in my wife's running of the hotel, but that man's been nothing but trouble since he came, drinking, coming in at all hours, and now this fateful marriage. I'll wait and see how the young man appears when he comes down. If he's an honorable man, Judge, he'll treat Charlotte with respect and goodwill, no matter the circumstances of the wedding ceremony and the night of degradation in a brothel. But, we can't interfere in the man's business, since the father gave his consent to the marriage."

"I was drunk, myself, Clay. The men of the night were whistling and yelling for the marriage, and you know how it is when a man's in his cups. It was a debt of honor. A man's gambling debts are sacrosanct. If Morgan hadn't paid the bet, he would've been run out of town on a rail or tarred and feathered. And, once he'd shaken hands on the deal, Butler couldn't refuse the offer of the girl as chattel for the debt. It was a bad business, for sure. I was caught up in the middle of it. But, I'll make it right, soon as I see the man this morning. It'll be all legal and proper, quick as I file it with the county clerk. If he's honorable, Butler will keep the vows he made even if he was drunk." The two men agreed on that fact and turned to other matters of importance.

10

William Butler awoke that morning to the harsh sound of a clanging bell, and at first he thought it was inside his head, for it was pounding like a blacksmith's hammer against an anvil. There was a sour taste in his mouth, and his tongue felt as thick as a slab of calf liver. He opened one eye, looked around the room, and suddenly realized he wasn't where he was supposed to be. The wallpaper was covered with green grape vines, not the bawdy, lewd colors of a prostitute's room. Sitting up abruptly, his eyes widened in horror as he realized he was naked.

"My God, where am I?" he asked out loud. He heard the clang of the bell again, summoning the patrons of the Hightower Hotel to breakfast. Slowly, as if in a bad dream, the events of the night began to unfold before his mind. He couldn't precisely remember all the details, but he was pretty sure he'd gotten married and spent a most pleasing hour with a dark-haired girl. But, where was the girl now?

Hearing the scrambling of many footsteps in the hallway and down the stairs, he decided he'd better get up. Then, holding the side of his head with one hand, where the pain seemed to be the worst, William edged out of the bed and over to the table upon which sat the ceramic wash basin and pitcher. He opened the door underneath the table and found a metal chamber pot, which he put to good use, feeling much better once he'd relieved himself. He searched on the floor around the bed for his money belt and found it intact.

He poured some of the clean water from the pitcher into the basin. It was cold to the touch, but he didn't care. It was just what he needed to wash away the last of the dregs from his night of heavy drinking. Splashing water liberally onto his face and arms, he reached for a used flannel towel on the peg beside the table. He didn't even mind the usage; at least it was partially dry. Finding his clothes, wrinkled and smelling of stale tobacco and whiskey, he was ashamed to appear in them, but had no choice, for he didn't know where he was.

He pulled on his wool coat, which he found under the bed, raked his hands through his hair hoping to get it into some sort of arrangement, then taking a deep breath, stealthily opened the door to the room. The aroma of freshly brewed coffee permeated the hallway, mingled with the smell of baked bread. Keeping as quiet as possible, considering his bulk, he moved down the stairs and headed toward the smell of coffee. He saw people sitting at a long table and entered the room with considerable trepidation.

There were at least a dozen people at the table, and they all looked up when William entered the room. The silence was broken by a large matronly type who immediately rose from the table and went to the sideboard to bring a large dark blue coffee pot to the table.

"Come in, come in," Bertha said. "No need to feel shy; we ain't going to bite." She laughed so loudly the knot of hair on the top of her head began to slide to the side. "There's a chair next to my husband. Sit yourself down and dig in before the food's all gone."

He glanced around the room and saw at least two people that he recognized. One was the man he'd spent the greater part of the evening gambling with the night before, James Morgan. Sitting next to him, red of face, and with her eyes firmly placed on the spoon she held nervously in her hand, poised over a bowl of still steaming porridge, was William's new wife, her freckles standing out like brown dew drops on a white rose. There was no denying it, what he'd hoped was a dream was a reality that he must face in the harsh light of the sun.

Sighting the chair the woman had pointed out, William made his way to the other side of the table, rounding the end where a man in a wheeled chair sat, calmly eating. He sat down and picked up the red napkin beside his plate. The man in the wheeled chair mumbled something under his breath, then looked up at William, held out his hand and said, "Name's Clayborne Hightower. This is my wife's hotel. Glad to meet you."

Surprised, William shook his hand, and with a glance around to see the others, found a dozen pairs of eyes on his face. He gave them all a nod of his head, found the pewter plate of hot buttered biscuits in front of him and took one for himself. The woman on his right handed him a bowl half filled with squashy yellow eggs. He took the spoon, dipped into the eggs and came out with a generous portion which he piled on his plate. The woman, leaning very close, so that he could smell her rancid perfume, handed him a jar of marmalade, and he took some of that, too. The woman was dressed in deep mourning, and William tried to puzzle out if she was flirting with him. He soon dismissed it as his imagination and took a bite of the delicious biscuit, covered in marmalade.

The conversation at the table became general in nature, and William was able to eat without feeling embarrassed. Occasionally, the woman in black would lean over and ask if he needed some more eggs or another biscuit. He thanked her politely, although he would have liked some more eggs, but he didn't want to be considered greedy on his first day at the breakfast table. He took a deep swallow from the water glass at his plate, and looked up into the solid brown eyes of his father-in-law. There seemed to be a hint of guilt in those eyes, a feeling that William had become familiar with over the last few minutes. It dawned on his weary mind that everyone at the table knew exactly what had happened in the Red Rooster Saloon last night and the aftermath that had taken place in the prostitute's bed.

Fearing retribution of some sort, William continued to eat, watching with a wary sense of impending doom, until some of the patrons of the hotel left to go about their business. Setting aside his cutlery, and dropping his napkin onto his empty plate, Clayborne pushed his chair a few inches away from the table and began to talk.

"Where you from, Mr. Butler?" Clayborne asked the question in a calm, soft voice. Everyone at the table became still and looked his way. William refused to squirm in his seat. He wasn't a child; he was a grown man and had married the girl, legal and with her father's permission, by God. In fact, the father had sold her to him. Money had changed hands in a rather provocative way. There was no denying the fact, for there had been near a hundred witnesses in the saloon.

"I'm from Virginia," William said, his voice strong and unrepentant. "Wythe County, in the southern part of the state. Left there over a year ago. I'm a mule skinner or oxen driver by trade. Been working in the magnesium mines and driving the iron ore wagons before I lit out for St. Louis hoping to find a position in the coal mining business."

"Well, well, a miner. That's a change, for most of the pilgrims that travel through here on their way west are farmers or horse traders." Clayborne looked straight at James Morgan while he was speaking.

William caught the cut of the man's eyes, but whether his piercing expression was given in condemnation or criticism, he couldn't tell. William refused to look at Morgan to see his reaction to his host's opinion of him. He continued to keep his eyes centered on the man in the wheeled chair as Clayborne continued.

"I heard that over a hundred wagons were on the train that left last June; Sinclair came back from Independence full of the news. He said emigrants had been congregating for up to three months; they came from all over Missouri, Illinois, Kentucky, back East, all wanting that free land they're advertising in the papers. The politicians were making speeches on the village green; talk was rampant in the saloons."

William heard a sound and noticed it was James clearing his throat. His face had turned red. There was a squeak of chairs as Charlotte and Bertha rose simultaneously, as though they had a secret signal between them. Charlotte gathered plates and flatware from her side of the table, while Bertha stacked the ones on the other side. The other ladies began an exit from the room as though they imagined that if they stayed longer, they'd be asked to help with the kitchen chores. They were followed by James, who left without a word to his daughter or her new husband.

William watched them go but wasn't disturbed, for with his headache now gone, and his mind clear, he was prepared to answer truthfully any questions, while he wondered to himself why Hightower felt it necessary to interrogate him if the girl's father hadn't concerned himself with his background or pedigree. There was left in the room only one other man beside William and Hightower. He looked at him closely and discovered that he was the judge who'd officiated at the marriage ceremony. Slightly worried, William took the initiative and began to pose questions of his own.

"Do you have knowledge of the mining industry around here, where a man might find a position? I only arrived yesterday and haven't had a chance to look around." He was startled at the look on the judge's face.

"You only got to town yesterday? Then you're not looking to join Captain Foster's wagon train in the spring?"

William looked from one man to the other, and suddenly he remembered what Morgan had said when he offered his daughter in marriage. It bore the stipulation that he take her to Oregon. He moaned under his breath. "No, I came to work in the mines, but tell me about this Foster and his wagon train. Is Morgan going with them? I heard him in the saloon talking of Oregon, but thought it was just talk; didn't realize he was serious."

"Oh, he's serious, alright. That's all he talks about, when he talks at all. Keeps quiet most of the time; works at the saw mill, delivers wood and kindling to the businesses in town." Clayborne sat back and glanced at the judge.

"Foster went on a trip to Pennsylvania, to find wagons and oxen for the emigrants bound for the western country." The judge pulled out his timepiece from an inner pocket. It was pinned to his vest by a long golden chain. He looked sharply at it and returned it to his pocket. He frowned.

"I heard he's already back from his trip," Clayborne responded. "My assistant saw him yesterday at the courthouse when he filed some papers for me. I'm sure that's good news for the travelers. Brought back about a dozen wagons with him, Sinclair heard. Good strong Pennsylvania Conestoga wagons, built to last, and has a wider wheel base than the ordinary farmer's wagon. You'd be wise to get one if you can afford it." He gave William a sharp look. "I suppose you'll be going with Morgan when he leaves?" It was a mild question, but William could tell he was being tested.

"Brought several families, too, from what I've heard." The judge picked up his part in the conversation. "The captain plans to build a proper town in Oregon, with blacksmiths, coopers, wheelwrights, bakers and cobblers. All kinds of trades are welcome to go west for a better future. I'd go myself if I were twenty years younger. But, you bright young men, that's the place for you. Good soil for farms, too, but town life is the thing. Need to build a new St. Louis right near the ocean. I hear tell there are trees as big as a house and so tall a person can't see the top, standing underneath."

William was sure the judge was exaggerating, but he wouldn't contradict him. He'd heard many stories on his travels from Virginia, for it seemed everyone was talking of Oregon these days. He'd picked up a few newspapers along the way, too, the editorial columns full of Dr. Whitman, the missionary, and the advantageous liberty of Oregon's forests and mountain grandeur. And, enough free land for all, it appeared.

"Which do you think would be better suited for these Conestoga wagons, mules or oxen? I've driven both, and my personal choice is the oxen, strong and reliable. Mules tend to kick and raise a ruckus early in the morning. I've spent many a cold dreary morning chasing after a mule that didn't want to get into the harness." William felt compelled to go along with the men until he had more information from his wife on her family's plans.

"I've never seen a team of oxen at work." Clayborne placed his empty cup on the table and rolled a bit away from it, seeming to settle in for a long conversation. "I've heard they have more stamina in the mountains, steady plodding, but they get there finally. What do you know about mountain travel?"

"Wythe County is high country; mostly covered in trees, large oaks and walnut and pine, but not nearly as high as the Rockies, I've heard. That's where they get their name, large boulders, mighty trees, dangerous cliffs, landslides and enough rocks to make a man wild with fear. The Rockies are so high the trees only go so far up, and the snow covers the passes half the year. It'd be dangerous to try to cross the mountains in snow, on horseback or by wagon. And, there's no shelter to speak of from the cold wind and rain." William had talked to several men who'd been over the high passes of the Rockies, but never in a wagon. He'd been told horses can't easily breathe in the thin mountain air.

Back and forth the conversation went between the three men, until the judge pulled out his timepiece again from the inner pocket. "I have to make a trip to the courthouse this morning, so I'll be saying good-bye for now. I wish you luck, Mr. Butler. I'll probably not see you again before you leave since I have a big murder case to be heard in the next few weeks." And, with those ominous words, the judge walked out of the dining room. The click of the front door could be heard as it shut when he left the building.

William turned away after the judge left the room and cast his eyes back to the man sitting quietly at the head of the table. He took a deep breath, prepared for the questions he knew would be coming now that they were alone. But, surprisingly, the lame man continued the conversation about the West and the man leading the wagon train. Captain Foster, it seemed, had been raised in one of the Indian villages spotted throughout the West and had visited many times with Clayborne in his hotel. Finally, after another half-hour of conversation, the real estate agent rolled his chair away from the table, and using the excuse of tiredness, went toward the back apartments in which he lived and worked.

William, now alone with time on his hands, decided he should talk with his wife. He rose from the table and walked toward what he assumed to be the kitchen. Standing together at the wash basins were the two women, Bertha and Charlotte Morgan, now Butler. The stout woman had her hands deep in a pan of hot soapy water, washing dishes, while Charlotte was drying a plate with a white linen towel. William cleared his throat to gain their attention, and the women turned toward him.

A big smile spread across the older woman's face, and she said, "I'd better see if Clay needs anything before his nap," and she was gone in a flash of green cloth.

Charlotte finished wiping the plate and put it carefully on the stack of others matching its pattern. She smiled shyly at William, crossed the room and continued to the dining room where she sat down on a chair. William had no choice but to follow and noticed that she sat in the same chair in which she'd eaten her breakfast. She folded her hands politely in her lap and waited for him to speak.

He cleared his throat, needing time to get his thoughts in line. He sat down in the chair next to Charlotte. Quickly, before he lost his courage, he began to speak.

"Miss Morgan, uh, that is, Charlotte, my dear," William started, his heart beating fast and large butterflies fluttering in his belly. He felt a little sick, but took a deep breath and continued. "Uh, we need to settle where we're to sleep tonight. I think you'll want to remain here where you're needed and have friends. I have no objection to that, if it's your desire. Or, I could find a small room at another hotel, if you would prefer it. Please tell me your preference, and I'll abide by your wishes." William stared at the wallpaper on the opposite wall, feeling exposed and vulnerable.

Charlotte replied, squeezing her hands tightly, clearly nervous. She caught a button on her dress between her finger and thumb, and began to fondle it. "I think it would be proper if we remained here where I'm known. Besides, there's my work. I'm cook and maid for

77

Mrs. Hightower. My room and board are my pay for the work that I do. But, you're my husband, and my place is with you, so if you feel uncomfortable around my father, I'll go with you to your home."

William felt relief wash over him. "You're willing to accept me into your bed and acknowledge me as your husband before the other tenants?" He turned in her direction, his gray eyes willing her to say yes.

"Yes, I'm willing," she answered, her voice steady.

"Then so be it," William answered, letting his breath silently leave his throat. "You're now my wife in word as well as deed. I promise that I'll always treat you with respect, and honor my vows of fidelity and take care of you to the best of my ability, so help me God. I'm a miner, not a farmer. I came to St. Louis looking for work in the mines, but I understand from Hightower and the judge that your father is headed to Oregon when the weather permits. Is that your desire, also?" He held his breath for her answer.

"Yes, my father's been waiting to speak with the leader about joining a wagon train west. We left Illinois in October for that very reason. We've been living here in the hotel since then." She looked strained, and William wondered why, but he didn't ask her.

"Do you want to go to Oregon?" His voice was low and gentle.

"Yes, that's my wish. But, what do you want to do?" She twisted the button in her hand. William watched, and gently took her hands in his. She looked up, her eyes troubled.

"Then we'll go to Oregon. Don't worry. It'll be a long and a dangerous journey in which there's the possibility that one of us might not survive, but I'll protect you if I can."

He took another deep breath and paused, one hand drawing up tightly into a fist, for it was painful for him to speak of Martha and his infant son. "You must know that I've been married before. My first wife died just over a year ago of cholera, and my infant son with her. I have many happy memories of the time that we had together and cherish the memory of my son. His name was Samuel. If this knowledge causes you pain and you wish to change your mind, tell me now, for I won't turn away from my past life, nor reject the happiness I've known."

"There's no need for you to turn aside from your past. I have sorrow in my heart, too, for we left my mother behind in Illinois because she refused to come with her family. You've seen with your own eyes how cruel my father can sometimes be to his kin. He and my younger brother are my burden to bear alone."

"You've no need to feel alone, my dear Charlotte. I'll take care of your brother, and your father, too, if necessary. I'm a man of my word. You can trust me with your sorrow as well as your future joy. How old is your brother, and where is he now?" William felt that he was sinking into a bottomless pit with his brave words, but he thought of himself as a man of integrity, in spite of the shameful way he'd behaved last night. He promised himself that he wouldn't drink to excess again.

"His name's Joseph, and he works as a cleaner and clerk at the saw mill where my father works. He lives with the manager of the mill, a Major Sanford and his wife. But you'll meet him tonight, for he comes to the hotel for Saturday dinner. He'll be pleased to see you, I'm sure. He has a shaggy dog he calls Spotty."

"Very well, I must go now and let you get on with your chores. I'll arrange a meeting with Captain Foster to discuss the purchase of a wagon and a team of oxen."

William barely had the words out of his mouth before Charlotte exclaimed, "Oh, that's the same man my father wishes to meet. Do you say that he's back from his trip to Pennsylvania? Papa will be so happy!"

"Yes, he's back. I've spoken with Mr. Hightower about him. I believe they're friends." He was puzzled why Hightower hadn't passed on this information to Morgan at the table this morning.

"Will you please tell Captain Foster when you see him that my father also wishes a meeting with him?" She looked with anxious eyes at William.

"Yes, of course, I'll tell him. But, I must go now. I'll see you tonight at the table," and with a quick kiss on her forehead, William was gone.

His mind now in great turmoil, William strolled around the commercial area. The snow had turned to slush with the coming of the sun, and someone had shoveled the sidewalks along the thoroughfare. He asked at several places along the street for information on the mining industry and got different answers. Walking by a huge edifice with a sign on the front wall that said, in various shaped lettering, "General Merchandise, B. Trice, Proprietor, Clothing, Dry Goods, Hardware, Mail," he stopped for a moment, gazed in the window at some items on display on a table, and there in the bottom corner of the glass was a poster: "Oregon, Free Land, See Cpt. H. Foster, Room

100, Hotel Durango, Market Street, St. Louis." William could hardly believe his eyes. Free land in Oregon country! That's what James Morgan was talking about in the saloon last night when he said he must take his new wife to Oregon.

He tried to see into the store, but the light was dim, so he went to the door and walked in. A tinkling sound was heard, and he looked up to see a small brass bell which had sounded when the edge of the door came in contact with it. Looking into the gloom he saw several men sitting in chairs around a pot-bellied stove, with smoke curling around their heads from their cigars and smoking pipes. He walked toward them and held out his gloved hands to the warmth. After a few seconds of silence, he greeted them and began to pull off his gloves. He asked if they knew anything about the poster in the window.

"Ain't no need to go there, Mister. Captain Foster, he's gone," a stout, red-faced man said with a shake of his wooly head. William turned in his direction, and stepped back from the heat of the stove.

"That right?" William was disappointed. "Do you know when he'll be back?"

"Nay." The man took a long draw on his pipe and blew a puff of smoke into the air. It seemed to circle his head and disappear with the haze of other smoke in the room. He was dressed in a brown town suit with a green tartan scarf around his neck. "Heard tell he went to Pennsylvania, but couldn't say for sure, 'cause I don't know."

William looked more closely at the men. They all seemed to be city men from the way they were dressed, with pressed pants and white shirts and ties. A couple had suspenders tight across the shoulders and chests. He decided not to tell them that Foster was back, hoping to gain more information.

"I've been told a man can get free land in Oregon, just by clearing off the timber and building a house." He waited a second, then continued. "Sure would be nice for a farmer to have land with good soil and plenty of water that he don't have to pay his money for. Could build a nice town for the women and children, too, with schools, and churches and businesses like this one." And he looked around in admiration at the neatly stacked goods and farm equipment.

"Sure would, but I'm not a farmer, I'm a banker," said a large man with a mustache and ears that stood out from his head like sign posts. "A man can't just pack up and go across the country until someone builds a town. I'd say maybe five years from now might be a good idea for a person of stature to go west."

80

Another man took the cigar out of his mouth and waved it in the air to stress his point. His bulbous nose twitched as he spoke. "Well, Townsend, there might be something in what you say, but there won't be no town until a great number of farmers clear the land and kill off the vermin that might invade the town, once it's built."

Townsend again took up the subject. "But, how are the farmers going to get supplies into the area? It's too far inland to come by boat, and too far to freight from Santa Fe."

Emptying his pipe by knocking it on the edge of the stove, the first man felt of the bowl to see if it was cool enough, then placed it in his vest pocket, and spoke again. "A clever fellow, now, could start a freight line from Fort Hall or even down from Fort Vancouver, if he had the gumption and the money." He looked sharply at the banker and rose to throw another piece of kindling in the stove and closed the door.

William listened to the conversation as it continued around the stove, each man having his say, whether good or bad, about building a town in Oregon, but that didn't help him find a way to get there. He glanced toward the back and noticed a woman standing behind a counter, making notes in a large, thin book, probably the daily tally ledger. She looked up and saw him, then dropped her head back to the notes she was making. He could tell that she was listening carefully to the conversation. Trice, the proprietor, seemed to be nowhere around. William waited a few more minutes, and in a quiet break in the conversation, he wished them all a good day, and left the building. He went to the livery stable, saddled his horse, put all his possessions on the horse's back, and rode through the muddy streets to the Durango Hotel.

11

William arrived at the Hightower's hotel less than an hour before the evening sound of the bell for dinner. He'd stabled his horse again at Smith's livery and brought his personal possessions with him. He quickly went up the stairs and left them in their bedroom, for Bertha had given him a separate key before he'd left the hotel that morning. He retraced his steps and went into the kitchen to give Charlotte a wave so she'd know that he'd come.

Charlotte's face was damp from the steam of the fire coming off the stove, her freckles clearly visible in the mist. Tiny ringlets of dark hair had come loose from her braid. She acknowledged William's presence with a nod and continued stirring the pot on the stove. Bertha, in a similar condition, gave a shout of gladness to see him and almost dropped the pan of cornbread she was carrying to the table. Ducking quickly out of their sight, William went into the parlor and was immediately confronted by a row of women.

The two sisters, Sarah Warren and Margaret Brown, were accompanied by two new guests at the hotel, a Miss Neva Divine and a Mrs. Prudence Filbert, niece and aunt. Josiah Filbert was upstairs in his room taking care of some business. He was a lawyer, and the family was traveling to Kentucky, Mrs. Filbert told the guests. William felt a little awkward in a room with no man but himself, but he was up to the challenge, for he felt impregnable after his success in purchasing a newly painted Conestoga wagon. He'd also made a bid on six strong healthy oxen.

Margaret rose from her seat by the piano and sat beside William. "Oh, Mr. Butler, how pleasant to have your company tonight." With her handkerchief fluttering around her face, she gave a condescending look toward the other women, as though she'd captured a prize at the fair. "I'm sure that darling Charlotte will be so pleased that you returned safely. It's entertainment night, you see."

Sarah's nose twitched at her sister's coquettish words, and she muttered in a peevish manner that she'd hoped to have the pleasure of Mr. Butler's attention later that night. William had noticed all four women's eyes on him when he walked in the parlor door, and he was certain they'd been discussing the odd circumstances of his marriage the previous evening.

With the insinuation he was available for the evening, he wasn't convinced they fully realized he was now committed to his new bride. He was soon enlightened as Margaret, with short-tempered outbursts from Sarah, informed him that it was a Saturday, and Mr. Hightower always played his violin, accompanied by Mrs. Hightower on the piano.

William agreed that it would be a treat to hear the sounds of music wafting through the halls of the hotel, and was about to expand on his theme, when the man in question came through the door, his wheels whispering on the wooden planks of the floorboards. William took the pause in conversation to look at the young lady in the corner perched skillfully on the edge of her seat. He wondered casually how she was able to keep from tipping over; she was so close to the edge. He glanced in the direction of the aunt and received a frown for his trouble. Carefully shifting his eyes back to Clayborne, he rose to greet him with a handshake.

Clay greeted the women graciously, and rolling his chair near the piano, he placed his violin case on the top. That brought a squeal of pleasure from Margaret, and she moved her seat nearer to his chair. He asked how the ladies had spent their day, to which there was a chorus of acclamation. With the charm and goodwill necessary for a host of a public inn, he kept the women from forming a barrier around William. He had a captivating manner that was nonthreatening, secure in his own masculinity, despite his disability.

Ignoring the conversations swirling around him, William was

thinking about training his oxen, for the farmer who had offered them had promised him free access to his pasture and entrance to the road heading west. He jumped, startled out of his thoughts as the great bell in the hallway rang out, "Clang! Clang! Clang!"

Everyone made a quick exit for the door of the dining room except Clay, who with unspoken word gestured for all to lead the way. He followed, moving his chair into the dining room and taking his place at the head of the table.

Josiah Filbert, having heard the dinner bell, came downstairs and entered the dining room. He was a portly gentleman dressed in the modern manner of a dandy, with a black suit, white shirt, black tie and silver vest. He glanced around the room, found his wife and sat beside her. Clayborne introduced him to those whom he hadn't met, and continued talking as though he hadn't been interrupted by the change of rooms. It was a friendly crowd around the table that night, and the conversation at the head of the table flowed smoothly.

James entered the room from the hall and took his usual place near the bottom of the table, away from Clayborne. A few steps behind him, with a sheepish grin on his face, marched Joseph, his clothes freshly dusted and his face glowing from an appointment with soap and water.

There were two traveling salesmen in attendance at the table, one a short, stout man from Baltimore, with an aroma of pomade from his slicked down blond hair. The other one, average height and slender, was from Clinton County, Missouri, and had several exciting tales to tell of the Dragoons at Fort Leavenworth across the river. He soon had the attention of the young lady seated next to him, Neva Devine, and no matter how many times her aunt frowned, Miss Devine wouldn't be distracted from the stories of the Dragoons. She waved her fan and batted her eyes in agreement to his statements that the Army was a good life for the men of America.

Charlotte carried the platters of food into the room and placed them on the tablecloth. A plate of cornbread was placed at one end of the table and a large platter of biscuits at the other end. Steam rose from a pot of beef stew as soon as the lid was lifted. William felt like he should rise and help her, but none of the other men offered to help, so he remained in his seat. He wasn't accustomed to the rules of the house, and had only eaten once, and that at breakfast, a generally more casual meal. Even so, he felt a thrill when Charlotte touched the sleeve of his jacket as she leaned in to place a large bowl of cabbage soup nearby.

A huge coffee pot was tipped one-handed by Bertha to fill cups, and a large pitcher of water was placed on the table for those who didn't indulge. A canning jar filled with sweet buttermilk was placed in front of Clayborne, for that was his favorite drink when served beef stew. Next, a bowl of turnips and a platter of hot, crisp fried fruit pies were carried to the table.

The other men hadn't waited for Bertha and Charlotte, but William felt compelled to wait for his wife, so he sat politely until she sat and placed her napkin on her lap. She was seated between her brother and her husband. She leaned toward Joseph and put her hand over his. He lowered his head in embarrassment at the sentimental gesture, but he grinned, and his crooked teeth gleamed white in the sunburned face. Slanting her body in the other direction toward her husband, she whispered in his ear, "My brother, Joseph Morgan."

William tipped his head forward around the head of his wife, and holding out his hand solemnly, shook the boy's hand. During the whole scene of affection, James sat stoically eating his food, not taking any part in the conversation around the table.

The meal progressed with the sound of cutlery against crockery as well as the occasional ting of glassware being carelessly knocked together. The candles flickered with the movement of air, and it seemed a congenial time for some, if not for all, as the final courses made it to the table, ending in a deliciously presented crème brulee for a final treat.

In a mutually silent agreement, plates were pushed back, napkins returned to the table, and the party at the table broke up. The ladies moved into the parlor, while the men sat talking politics and the weather, which appeared to be warmer than usual, with the snow swiftly melting with the return of sunshine. Conk passed around a tray of port for the men, leaving the bottle at Clayborne's elbow.

James watched as Joseph turned the pages of a picture book that Clayborne loaned him. He looked up at the men occasionally, but didn't speak. James sipped slowly on the remains of his port, and smiled at something Joseph showed him in the book.

Those who chose to smoke removed their cheroots from hidden places on their person. William looked toward the other men and watched as Filbert took out a long-stemmed pipe and a small tin of tobacco. He elevated the process of filling the pipe and lighting the tobacco to an amazing degree, as though he were a performer on stage.

When the discussion seemed to stall, William decided to quiz Clayborne with what was most important on his mind, knowing that the man was familiar with most people of the neighborhood.

"Hightower, I've bought a Conestoga from Captain Foster, and put in a bid for a team of oxen with a farmer named Webley who lives near the river. He said that I might board the stock there until we leave for the western country. Perhaps you know the fellow. Can you assure me that he's an honest man and will abide by his promise? I dare not purchase the animals only to find that when they are trained for the journey, he's fleeced me out of my investment."

There was a clatter as James overturned his glass, spilling a few drops of liquid on the table. He righted the glass and wiped the spill with his shirt sleeve. He gave William an odd look, whispered something in Joseph's ear and left the room without a gesture of farewell to his daughter who'd just entered to pick up their empty glasses. William gave James an angry glance as he passed from the room, and he looked to the head of the table in time to see a frown cross Clayborne's brow. Joseph followed Charlotte from the room, his book forgotten.

"Why, yes, Butler. I do know Webley and have always considered him to be a man of honor. He has a large, well-managed farm, and his animals are of good stock. I'll have my assistant speak to him to let him know of our acquaintance. I've also had a profitable day. Sinclair, my assistant, has informed me that he's sold two tracts of land near the river which have been difficult to obtain. What with all the traffic from the wagon train in the last year, the farmers have had enough of wagons and animals tramping through their property without permission." He laughed and put out his cigarillo in a dish near the piano.

Filbert cleared his throat and proceeded to drown out the other voices with his recent case in which a merchant sued a customer who had backed into a barrel of pickles, which had poured onto the counter top and caused damage to the display of sewing notions.

The salesman who had talked of Dragoons at Fort Leavenworth seemed uninterested and started a lively conversation with speculation on the chance of war with Mexico, explaining that a troop had been dispatched to accompany a Mexican caravan on the road to Santa Fe. Clayborne cautioned against unwarranted alarm and left the room to go into the parlor. With his exit, the men talked of other matters.

Much later, when the kitchen duty was finished, Bertha, quietly and with a grace not commonly seen in a woman of her bulk, entered the parlor and lowered herself onto the piano bench and began to touch the keys in a warm-up practice session. From the black leather case on the piano top, Clayborne lifted his beloved instrument and fondly caressed its smooth tan and brown surface as though it were the face of a child. The room grew silent as the ladies and gentlemen prepared themselves for a night of gaiety and pleasure. The violin gave out a squawk of displeasure as a wrong string was played, and Bertha rolled her nimble fingers up and down the scale. Looking fondly at each other, Clayborne nodded, and they began to play the soft smooth sound of an Irish ballad. Next, they played a lively folk tune, and the audience began to clap and sing along as the couple chose familiar songs. The faces of the two sisters were a picture of absolute joy and wonder. Even Mrs. Prudence Filbert began to clap and sing as she took in the beautiful sound of the well-known tunes, and her husband tapped his foot.

Finally, Clayborne, tired from the extra exertion, laid his violin back in the case and bowed as best he could from the confines of his chair. Bertha, her hair tipped over one ear, stood and curtsied to the audience. She followed her husband's chair from the room.

12

Charlotte awoke to the sound of stumbling feet in the hallway and heard the flinty sound of the opening of a door. She knew with an instinct from old memories that it was her father, creeping in, hoping not to awaken the boy in his bed, fast asleep. She glanced at the window and knew that dawn was approaching, left the bed, went to the wash stand, poured water into the basin and doused her face and arms with the cold liquid. She turned when fully dressed, and glanced at the sleeping man in her bed. Only his dark hair could be seen above the covers.

She opened the door and went downstairs.

*****

The soft click of the door awakened the sleeping man, and he groaned and rolled over. His eyes were gritty, and in the dim light from the shaded window, he gazed at the green leaves on the wallpaper and noticed some water spots and a small torn place near the ceiling. A fly buzzed around the room. He watched until it flew from his sight.

"Damn," he said out loud. He knew the sound of the closing door had been his wife leaving to start her work in the kitchen; he could smell coffee brewing. He lifted a hand and felt of his soft beard. He scratched a spot on his chest. He threw the covers back and, stark naked, went to the chamber pot. The warm bed was so enticing he lay back down, covered himself and thought of the day before and the meeting with Judge Moore and Clayborne Hightower. But, he couldn't concentrate; into his mind came a vision of the soft blonde curls of his Martha, and the laughter of Samuel as he crawled across the floor. He rubbed his eyes as a tear fell from his lashes. "Damn," he repeated. Trapped in a marriage with a girl of sixteen. He reached for the pillow and smelled the sweet fragrance of her body. He angrily tossed it onto the floor at his foolish pride and willfulness; he was trapped into marriage by a game of cards.

His thoughts drifted to the past, as they often did when he was troubled. He rolled to his stomach and buried his head in the pillow to stop the memories, but they continued. The fly buzzed his ear, and he flopped onto his back. He let his memories flow as he stared at the ceiling.

One day coming home to the empty house on Vine St, he'd been confronted by the feeling that he was a failure. It was the silence; that was what struck him as he walked in the door; the eternal, blinding silence where once there had been singing and laughter. His wife Martha and infant son Samuel, dead of a fever, the boy gone in a few days. Martha, lingering for more than a week, growing so weak that she could hardly press his hand when he held it. And, one long, dark night, she gave up the effort. She smiled and closed her eyes for the last time.

William felt the pain in his gut even now because she wouldn't return to him.

The kindly doctor said there was nothing William could have done. The whole county had lost loved ones; gone in a flash from the epidemic of cholera that raced through the area like the sweep of a giant hand, bringing sickness and death to many lives. But the quiet, calm assurance from the doctor didn't ease the guilt that had racked William's body, lying night after night in the bed they had shared with such joy and promise for the future. His daily life became torture. Gone, all gone. His dreams, his hopes, his plans for the boy. Long nights were spent in self-recrimination, filled with vivid dreams in which ghosts haunted him and he awoke in a panic, wet with perspiration. Many nights, William left the lamp burning, afraid of the dark shadows.

The pain and sorrow of the double deaths continued for over a month, then one day William quit his job as a mule team driver for the Virginia Iron Ore Mining Company, went home, packed a bag with his clothes and a few personal items, and crossed the street to his mother-in-law's house. They sat for a long time. She tried to talk him out of leaving, but he told his mother-in-law and Martha's family good-bye and rode his horse out of their sight and out of their lives.

He stopped his horse many times on the road during the last year, taking a job as laborer anywhere he could, until he had saved a considerable amount of money in gold and silver coins, and paper government script, which he carried in a money belt around his waist. A solitary man traveling by horseback, he stayed off the main roads, and went into the towns and villages only when he needed supplies.

Arriving at the boundary mark that announced the town of St. Louis, he'd walked his horse down the dirt road into a small commercial community until he saw a sign over a large, unpainted barn, "LIVERY, Moses Smith, Proprietor." The snow had stopped, and he gazed at the weathered building with relief.

With a huge sigh William Butler spoke to the fly now landed on his quilt. "I should have kept on riding. I should have never taken part in that card game. Damn. I'm trapped, just like you." He swatted at the fly, and it flew away. The sound of the bell aroused him from his thoughts. "Clang. Clang. Clang." He laughed and rose from the bed. He quickly washed, dressed and went down the stairs to eat his breakfast.

13

After that joy-filled Saturday night of music, the days seemed to march ever closer to springtime. Some days were mild, and the sunshine felt warm on a person's face; but on other days the cold north wind chilled the exposed skin. There were no more blizzards, but a cold, frozen rain fell several times, leaving ice-covered streets and sidewalks in their wake.

Everyone seemed busy these days. James continued in a self-imposed silence to eat his meals at the hotel, but he didn't linger during the day. He worked hard at the saw mill, delivering logs with his own team and wagon to his neighbors and the factory and wagon yard. On the days he didn't work, he spent those final weeks equally in gathering supplies to take with him on the long journey, and in gambling in the White Horse Saloon. He found the company more amiable and the gamblers more free with their money there. He would occasionally return to the Red Rooster but found that the men hadn't forgotten his brief indiscretion. He pretended it didn't affect him, but he couldn't slough off the guilt so easily.

He was pleased to find that his daughter—Charlotte Butler, she was now called—seemed happy with her situation. He was uneasy in the couple's company, and the distance between him and his children grew larger as the time for departure came. He became impatient with

Joseph's childish antics and his friend Jasper Smith and the dog, so spent less time than he could have with his son.

William spent many hours training his six oxen to work as a team. He yoked the recalcitrant male with a docile female, and they worked well together. The Conestoga was parked beside the barn at Moses Smith's livery stable. He'd visited many times during those weeks of preparation with Smith and his sons, Jasper and Abraham, and had learned some useful facts about animals. Smith gave him some tins of salve and ointments guaranteed personally by him to work on carbuncles and open wounds.

William had also had several occasions to become better acquainted with Joseph, his young brother-in-law, for he came as often as he could with his dog to play with Jasper. He noticed that the boy had bought a length of rope and spent time trying to throw a loop over the head of a pony. The boys would squeal with laughter, whether the loop fell wide of its mark or over the pony's head to be shaken off as though it were a snowflake. Joseph had grown taller and his arms become stronger working in the saw mill. There was an air of independence about him now that he received a stipend that he could spend as he desired.

When he wasn't training his oxen team, William was gathering supplies for the trip. He visited Trice's store many times, and sat with the town's men around the hot stove, listening to their tales of former glory days or current complaints about business or families. He bought certain articles from Trice, but had found a larger, better supplied store on Walcott Street and made purchases there, too. Great mounds of crates and barrels began to fill the Butler Conestoga, and other items hung on hooks on the sides and underneath. He placed the more sorely needed selections near the back for Charlotte's convenience. He packed extra dried and cured meat for the dog, and hay and oats for the pony. He distributed his coins and paper money in secret places so that it wouldn't all be in one place in case there was a thief among the pilgrims.

Bertha knew that the time for the departure of her friend was coming fast. Gladys' leg had long since healed, leaving her with a slight limp, but she was well enough to assume her duties. The girl was slow in her movements, but cheerful and willing to help anyone. She had broken her betrothal to Tom Giddings at the advice of her mother, with whom she lived, which pleased Bertha.

Bertha had a long discussion with her husband because she

wanted to reward Charlotte with a gift in honor of her faithful service under their roof. She finally decided on a length of calico cloth in a pretty pale pink with a design of darker pink flowers and green leaves. She bought matching thread and oyster shell buttons, and a pattern she thought would suit Charlotte's shorter stature. Bertha wrapped them all in brown paper and tied it with a pink silk ribbon with which she could decorate her dark hair. Clayborne agreed that it would be both practical and give Charlotte something to do with her hands while on the trip. While in Trice's Mercantile, Bertha noticed a short pen knife with a leather scabbard and wrapped it for Joseph, for she had grown fond of the lad while he'd been under her roof.

At long last, the wind blew warm and strong from the south, and the icicles melted off roofs and tree limbs. Heavy coats were discarded for lighter sweaters and shirts. Several of the pioneer men rode far along the western trail they would soon follow to check the grass and streams for flooding. The hustle and bustle of St. Louis City seemed to increase, and wagons lined up along the riverbanks ready for the push off. The wheelwrights, gunsmiths, blacksmiths, and farriers were kept busy night and day. Last minute decisions were made in households from Missouri to Ohio, for time was running out if a person was bent on traveling west this year. Captain Horatio Foster was seen everywhere; warnings were spread, and encouragements multiplied. The men grew impatient, and quarrels had to be broken up. Hastily written letters to loved ones back East were mailed at the local postal stations.

*****

During those gray winter months spent in St. Louis, Charlotte wrote three letters to her uncle Peter Kincade in hope of receiving news from her mother. And at last, on the second day before the end of February, she received her reply. Benjamin Trice at the mercantile store sent the tattered, ink-spattered missive to the hotel by the hand of a small boy hanging around the door with time on his hands.

Charlotte tore open the letter with eager hands, but her eyes began to tear up, and her heart sank like a stone. She was sitting at her leisure in the kitchen with Bertha and Gladys, the ladies taking a short break while they waited for a cake to bake in the oven. It was several hours before time to prepare the evening meal, and the ladies had been drinking hot tea from Bertha's finest cups. Unable to see the words on the page, she handed the letter to Bertha. Her matronly friend quickly grasped the tone of the message and rose to gather Charlotte into her bountiful arms, sheltering her head in the soft comfort of her breasts.

"I'm so sorry, my dear," Bertha exclaimed. "'Twas not the news you were expecting, I'm sure." She looked at Gladys and shook her head. "Her poor mama is dead," she whispered, and held the girl even tighter, until Charlotte pulled back in protest.

Charlotte drew her lace-hemmed handkerchief from her apron pocket—a suggestion from Margaret, who was never seen without her own cloth—and blew her nose, coughing at the fragrance of the handkerchief. She reached for the letter, still tightly clasped in Bertha's fat hand. She read it again and sighed.

"Poor Mama, nothing ever seemed right for her after the death of the baby." Charlotte's eyes were moist but clear as she explained to her friends the lost infant buried in the shade of a tree in the church yard in Kaskaskia. Her voice quiet and deep in her sorrow, Charlotte told them of those last weeks and her mother's refusal to come on the trip with them.

Then she was silent as she took a sip of her cooled tea, and she dabbed at her eyes as she read the horrific news she had received from her aunt Eileen. One stormy night a few days after Christmas, Priscilla had risen from her bed and left the house. They didn't realize she was gone until she was called for breakfast in the early light of day. Peter and the neighbors searched for three days before they found her scratched and mangled body at the bottom of a ravine in the woods, not far distant from the Morgan farm. Peter surmised that she must have had a dream and wandered from the house, distraught and crazy in her mind, circling, walking, pausing for breath and running to find her home and family.

Eileen concluded in the letter that the neighbors had been very kind, and the wake had lasted for hours. The new owners of the Morgan farm had built two rooms on the house, for they had a large family, and the season had produced a nice crop of rye, still in the ground when Charlotte had left Illinois. Finally, Eileen was with child again, so Peter's hopes of joining the family in Oregon would have to be postponed until another year. She sent her love to Charlotte and Joseph, but didn't mention their father in her epistle.

Bertha sent Conk with a written message to the saw mill for James to come home; there was an emergency, but it was a couple of

94

hours before he finished delivering his lumber and arrived at the hotel. In the meantime, the women began preparations for the evening meal as though it were a normal day, for there was nothing they could do until James returned.

*****

William rode to the saw mill and brought Joseph home with him, slowly walking his pony. He and Charlotte tried as simply as they could to explain the tragic details of his mother's death. Joseph went completely still and didn't shed one tear. He rose from his chair and went into the bedroom he shared with his father and locked the door. No amount of pounding on the door or calling out his name received a response.

The meal had been eaten and dishes cleaned before James arrived. Told that his wife was dead, he took some money from his waist pouch and headed for the White Horse Saloon; where he proceeded to drink until he fell on the sawdust floor, uncaring of the smell of urine and spilled liquor. Several of his friends brought him home across the saddle of a horse, and being very vocal, he spent an hour with William talking about the tragedy of his arranged marriage, the loss of their first child and Priscilla's mental illness.

"I could have loved her once; if only she'd let me. She was tall and gawky, but she had lovely eyes. Her hair was like silk." He cleared his throat as though the lump had come up to choke him. "But something changed in her when the baby died. It was a boy, so tiny, no bigger than my fist." He opened and closed his hand in remembrance. Then, he pounded it into the sofa, as though to drive the demons away.

William watched as he rocked unsteadily, as if his grief was a tangible being, a heavy burden carried alone through all the years.

His words grew bitter. "She must have carried a hard place in her heart. Some women do."

William nodded in commiseration.

"I was happy then, and I thought she would be, too, if we could have gone to Oregon like I dreamed." He sniffed with a sour laugh. "But, the old man, he said I was selfish and cruel to take a young woman across the prairies and mountains."

"You wanted to go to Oregon even then?" William took on a new level of understanding at the revelation.

95

"When the children were small, people thought I was a jovial sort of soul, bouncing the tots in the air, and teasing them no end. Joseph squealed with laughter." He wiped his eyes.

"It must have been a good time." William nodded his head in agreement.

James looked up at this son-in-law as though seeing him for the first time. "My father was a great man, strong and independent-minded. Charlotte takes after him. I read to them from his books. It was a grand thing, telling them the old stories of the green highlands of Scotland where I was born and the ocean waves and the big ship on which I crossed to America in 1800." His words began to slow, and when his breathing turned to slumber at last, William put him to bed on the sofa in the parlor.

*****

The next morning, Joseph, red-rimmed eyes, and uncombed hair, rode back to the saw mill, and without any breakfast, started to work as though it were any ordinary day in February. Fortunately, the weather was mild and the wind calm. His mother had been lost to the boy on that solitary ride home from his Uncle Peter's house in Illinois last September.

No one ever heard Joseph Morgan mention his mother again.

14

In the first week of March, the remaining wagons that hadn't already crossed, prepared to camp on the banks of the Mississippi River. The rafts were lined up one by one, and each wagon driver took his turn pulling his animals up in a steady line to board one of the long, flat boats. Among the throng of pioneers were a sober James Morgan and his son Joseph, sitting in the old weathered wagon from home, and Charlotte Butler perched majestically on the seat of the Conestoga, with her husband William walking behind his team of six oxen with his saddle horse tied securely to the rear flap of the wagon. He held, curled in his left hand, a long, wicked black whip.

The family left the hotel the day after receiving the letter from Eileen. It was a sad but amiable departure. Bertha presented her wrapped gifts, and Charlotte cried. Joseph whooped with joy over his new knife and scabbard. Clayborne contributed a box of books and old magazines, for he knew well that nights would be dark and lonely on the prairie. Even the sisters contributed to the merriment by presenting Charlotte with a wide-brimmed sunbonnet. She hugged them both. Sarah gave Joseph and William matching woolen scarfs, forgetting perhaps that the winter was over. Margaret was more pragmatic; she gave all three males white cotton socks purchased from Mr. Trice's store. Charlotte and William had presented small gifts of their own to her friends, including a metal box for Conk's tobacco to keep it from getting wet on rainy days while bringing in the wood. He grinned from ear to ear and told her she was a kind lassie. The last sight Charlotte saw, looking back, as William sent his whip flying over the backs of the oxen, and they stepped proudly in a westerly direction, was the snow white handkerchief of Mrs. Margaret Brown waving in the air on the steps of the Hightower Hotel.

James collected his pay and Joseph from Major Sanford at the mill office and drove by the livery so his son could say farewell to his friend Jasper and his father. Jasper solemnly handed Joseph the bean bag, and they promised to write each other. The boy shook hands with Moses Smith like a man twice his age would have done and walked away with tears streaming down his cheeks. He was silent on the road to the camp beside the river. The dog stood behind the seat wagging his tail in excitement.

It was a short drive to the edge of the river where the other wagons were camped. They spent the night separately: James and his son in one group, and Charlotte and her husband in another, for James still refused to speak to the couple.

Supper was cooked over an open fire for the first time since they had arrived in St. Louis.

*****

At almost the last moment, that final night on the eastern shore of the mighty River of the East, James grew restless, and felt deeply that he'd made a mistake to choose a life in the West. Guilt sat heavily on his shoulders, like the thick muslin quilt that his mother had once made in Scotland. Guilt over the death of his wife. Guilt over the hasty marriage of his daughter. Even guilt over the shortened childhood of Joseph.

James put the boy to bed in the wagon, covered him with blankets and started walking to find some type of solace in his grief and solitude. He strolled along the line of parked wagons until he saw a campfire with several men sitting or standing. As he came near the fire, he heard the men talking about Captain Foster. He stopped at the edge of the group and listened. They were discussing a few single men who'd missed the deadline for the trip, and the good captain wouldn't let them join the train unless they had the required supplies. He remembered the long list of things that he'd bought to satisfy the requirements of the journey. He'd checked them off one by one: enough to feed a family of four, farm equipment, a chamber pot, lanterns, candles, blankets and an India rubber mat to sleep on the ground when the weather was fine.

As those around the fire continued to discuss the hopeless situation of the excluded men, an idea began to form in his head, but he needed more information. Several men noticed the stranger in their midst and raised their heads, but didn't speak. He crept up to hear their conversation and began to ask questions.

"Who are these single men? Why don't they wait for another train? Rumors are flying that a man named Johansson has begun to form a caravan to Oregon."

The answers came in a whirl of male voices; each had his own opinion of the matter. Gradually James realized that one of the single men who had arrived too late to join the train was sitting in their midst. He complained the loudest. The conversation took a different direction as one of the men decided it was late and they needed to get some sleep, because the rafts would be loading before dawn, and each wanted to be the first across the river. The group was breaking up, and James stepped close to the man who had no supplies.

"My name's James Morgan. I came from Illinois. I might have a solution for you, if you're interested."

The man's attention was struck, because he angrily pitched the long thin tree branch he held into the flames, causing sparks to fly into the night sky like fireflies. He looked closely at James.

"It occurs to me, if we can get Captain Foster to agree, that you can come along with my son and me, if you're willing to drive the wagon most days." James waited for the answer with his heart racing.

No answer came forth, however, so he tried again.

"I have plenty of food for one more person, 'cause my son doesn't eat much, and I packed away enough for a grown man. He's eleven, but tall for his age, smart and a hard worker. He won't bother you none. Been working in the saw mill all winter, mostly sweeping floors, running errands, and filing paper work for the manager. If we're careful with the cooking and don't waste any, we might have an abundance for three, the boy being only a child."

"You say I got to drive the wagon?" The man stood and gazed at the flames that consumed the middle of the stick. One of the ends fell from the pile. He reached and pitched it back in. He turned to look suspiciously at James. "What you going to be doing while I do your work?"

"Well, for one thing, I'm an expert with a rifle and pistol, and I have both with me. Plenty of shells for them, in addition." Now that he had his fish on the hook, James used his natural charm. He smiled at the man engagingly. "I could help with the hunting party or scout ahead for game or wild Indians, if I didn't have the responsibility of the boy always on my mind. Another thing, I don't give away anything for free; every man has a job to do, so your food and comfort would be the pay you receive for driving the wagon."

"I don't got to pay you, then." The man sounded hopeful.

"What's your name and where you from?" James asked and smiled winningly to set the hook.

"My name's George Remmington, and I come from around these parts. A few miles north of St. Louis as a crow flies. I just got booted out of my inheritance by my older brother. Pa always said we'd receive equal shares of the farm, but he died a few months back, and now Melburn says it's all his since he's the oldest. Got a passel of kids and he claims there isn't enough land to feed us all. Hired a smart lawyer, and the lawyer says he's entitled to the lot. I rode my horse out of there and came to the city looking for work, but I heard about this wagon train heading west, and thought I may as well try that. I've got no reason for staying in Missouri, now."

"Have any experience driving a farm wagon?" James began to press for more information.

"Sure have. Any boy growing up on a farm knows how to drive a wagon come harvest time. Can handle mules real well, and plow, too." The man bragged, puffing out his chest and pulling up his pants with his hands.

"Well, that sounds fine." James decided to let the idea settle for the night and approach him again in the morning. "Got any friends in this bunch you been talking to that can vouch for your honestly or character? Where've you been staying since you come to St. Louis?"

"Look, you," Remmington said angrily, his eyes glowing in the reflection from the fire. "I don't know any of these people, and I bet you don't know them either, else you would've come right up to the fire and sat with us. And how do I know you're trustworthy? I might do all that driving and taking care of your son, and then you leave me starving out in the desert."

James laughed, and Remmington backed away from the fire as though to leave. James stooped and tossed loose dirt onto the fire, and the man paused to watch him. James casually shrugged his shoulders. "If you're interested, come and see me in the morning. Name's Morgan, and that wagon about three back is mine and my boy, Joseph's. If you don't find me, go back one more wagon. That'll be my daughter and her husband, William Butler, in that monster of a wagon from the East, called a Conestoga, they tell me. They'll know where to find the boy."

George spun on his heels and headed toward a nearby tree where he'd left his horse. He swung aboard and galloped away.

Feeling that he had succeeded in finding the right man for the job, James watched until the coals were turned to ashes, and walked to his own wagon, not looking back.

*****

Taking a long drink from his secret stash of whiskey in the wagon, James felt good as he removed his clothes and prepared to climb into bed next to his son. Dropping his head on a rolled bundle of cloth, his vision swam for a moment, and blinking his eyes, he saw the face of Priscilla, ranting and yelling at him; telling him he was wicked and God would see that he was thrown into the fiery furnace of hell. His good mood disappeared, and he was left immersed in the dregs of a life gone sour. He pulled the bottle from its hiding place and emptied it before dawn, all the while with his son Joseph sleeping soundly beside him.

*****

"Papa!" called the treble voice of a young man. The dog Spotty was growling low in his throat.

James awoke from his alcoholic haze. He opened his eyes and saw that Joseph wasn't in his blankets beside him. In a panic, he sat up, his mind still fuzzy, and his arms like lead weights were tied to them.

"Papa," the voice came again from the tail of the wagon, and James looked in that direction, craning his neck. A sort of halo caused by the early morning dawn seemed to settle around the boy.

"Papa," Joseph repeated a third time, his plaintive voice calling for attention. "There's a man here looking for you."

The conversation of the night before at the campfire came back to him, and James jerked awake. He looked down at himself to see if he was fit to welcome company. He was dressed only in his undergarments.

"Wait a minute, son. I'll be right out." He saw Joseph disappear from the opening. He could hear him explain to the visitor that his papa was getting dressed. Grabbing his trousers and shirt, he quickly donned both and pulled on his boots without socks, then ran shaking fingers through his hair to get it into some semblance of order. Putting a hand to his face, he felt the beginnings of a scraggly beard. He clambered over the end of the wagon, and almost fell in an ignominious heap at the stranger's feet. Fighting dizziness and the painful throbbing in his head, James stood up and shook himself awake.

Standing a few feet from the boy was the man with whom he'd discussed driving his wagon. The dog sat with his tongue hanging out, breathing heavily. What was his name? He tried to think. Ah, George. George Remmington, that's it. James glanced at his son but couldn't read his expression. He stepped forward and shook hands.

"Good morning, Remmington, I'm a little under the weather, as you can see." His most charming smile was on display again. The smooth lines of his face and jawbone belied his age, for even after fifty years of hard living, James was a handsome man.

George stepped forward and shook the hand offered to him, his surprise reflected in his eyes as he noticed no resemblance of the boy to the father.

"This is the boy I'll be with?" He pointed toward Joseph, who was shuffling his feet as though he wanted to get away from the men. "If, mind you, we come to a deal."

"Yes, this is Joseph," James acknowledged; his sluggish mind trying to think why that was important. The realization rolled over him that perhaps the man didn't want to travel with a drunken sot. James bristled. The man could go to hell for all he cared, that was if he didn't need him to drive the wagon, so James could engage in more interesting endeavors, those of a more entertaining nature.

The man turned to Joseph, looking him over from the top of his brown hair to the brown scuffed boots on his feet. "How old are you, boy?"

"Eleven, sir," Joseph looked up at the stranger with soulful, intelligent eyes.

"Your father said you've been working at the saw mill this winter, that right?"

"Yes, sir," Joseph answered in a steady, strong voice, with a touch of pride in his stance.

"What you been doing at this saw mill?" George gazed over at James, then back at Joseph.

"Mostly sweeping floors, emptying trash, fetching and carrying for the manager, but sometimes he let me file his papers or write down figures he gave me from his big ledger book." He looked off in the distance and grinned at something only he could see.

James was getting impatient. He shifted his feet again, wishing he had a drink, and his stomach was growling for want of food. He looked toward the other wagons and saw men beginning to hitch up their teams, and the women cleaning up from breakfast.

Damn, he thought. He hadn't eaten yet, and it was near time to pull out. This was turning out to be a hell of a day, and it was barely started.

"Morgan, I admire the spunk of your boy, so I'll take your offer to drive the wagon to Oregon. This is it?" He walked around the wagon looking at the wheels and the axles, and he shook the side rails to see if they were sturdy. Then he thrust himself underneath and banged on the floorboards.

He yelled from underneath, while Joseph knelt to see what he was doing. "How old is the wagon? You had it caulked with tar so's the water don't come in through the cracks?" George moved to a different place and hammered it again.

"Yes, sir, he did." Joseph answered for his father. "I saw him at Mr. Smith's Livery. I was watching with my friend Jasper while he and Mr. Smith fixed the wagon. Why are you knocking on the bottom, sir? You going to drive this wagon to Oregon?" Joseph grabbed the dog's collar as he tried to go under the wagon. He pulled him up, and the dog ran toward the Butler wagon. Getting no response from his master, he ran back to stand near Joseph with his tongue hanging out.

As George pushed away from the wagon and stood, so did Joseph. He demanded to see the horses. James led the way, and they made a parade, with George following him and Joseph shuffling along behind, his hands in his pockets against the chill of the morning. The dog followed the boy.

Both looked as hungry as James felt.

After a half-hour spent looking at the horses, checking their teeth, their withers, and running his hand up and down each of their legs,

George seemed satisfied and asked about his duties. By this time, Joseph had run over to Charlotte's wagon and eaten two biscuits and some ham and gravy, talking with his mouth full. Charlotte couldn't give the boy an answer about why their father wanted to hire someone to drive the wagon, so William walked over to find some answers.

He found the men standing next to James' horse Blue Boy, which he used only for riding, never having hitched him to a team. James introduced William to the stranger as his son-in-law, as though there had been neither friction nor the ongoing silence between them since January. William invited them to their campsite where Charlotte had breakfast ready.

Charlotte looked at her father and greeted him cordially. She acknowledged the stranger and invited him to eat with them. She served hot biscuits with ham and gravy, with molasses, and the last of her butter, washed down with strong black coffee. Since they left the hotel they'd no access to fresh milk, and the eggs wouldn't last many more days.

The wagons encircling the Morgan family were all busy with preparations to board the rafts to cross the Mississippi River. Cutting their meal short, the men separated to their respective animals and began to hitch the teams, while Charlotte cleaned the dishes and put things away neatly in the Conestoga. James rode ahead for information on when it would be their turn to board the rafts.

As he rode out of sight of his family, he wondered if he'd lost control of the situation that he himself had instigated. For it was clear even to his alcohol befuddled brain that his new employee recognized the leadership qualities of his son-in-law over his own. He saw the captain ahead with the officials involved with the crossing of the river, and decided that wouldn't be such a bad thing after all. Let William make the hard decisions.

*****

That night, the family gathered over the campfire on the western bank of the river. It had been an easy and exciting crossing. The raft drivers were experienced and careful of the dangerous undercurrents of the river. A string of lights could be seen as though they were fireflies along the bank. Charlotte counted thirty-seven wagons and about one hundred men, with maybe half that number of women and children. She cooked fried potatoes with onions and pieces of ham, and roasted corn for their dinner.

As soon as he had the team of horses unhitched, George withdrew to a solitary tree he'd chosen to bed down under and seemed to be reading a book, his belongings laid out in an orderly fashion.

Joseph was put to bed in the Morgan wagon, with the dog off on an exploring trip of his own. William went to his oxen to make sure they hadn't received any bruises or cuts on their first major experience with river crossings.

"They've performed well," he told Charlotte when he joined her at the campfire, while she put the dishes away. "Only a small amount of temperament, and I'm well pleased with them. Webley gave them a good start, and the weeks of training have proved a bonus." He laughed, "Even the stubborn one, Lucifer, pulled well with the female I call Jezebel. They took the lead as though instinctively they know it will be a long slow haul across the forests and plains. He's older, but he seems to be a leader. I hesitated to buy him, but now I'm glad I did." He walked over to sit beside James near the fire.

Music and frivolity could be heard at some of the campsites, and Charlotte hummed along with the gay tunes; but most of the pioneers were serious, hard-working people. They bedded down early for the dawn start of the trip. She hadn't met any of the campers, but William and James told her about a few of the ones they'd worked with on the crossing. Her natural curiosity arose, and she hoped the ladies proved to be companionable, for a lone woman with three men and a boy would prove to be tedious without the rapport of other females. She already missed the friendly company of Bertha and Gladys.

She was puzzled by her father's new attitude. He seemed to be letting William and George do most of the talking, where always before he'd dominated the conversations. She glanced at the males in her life. James and William were sitting by the tempered coals, apparently discussing the next day's plans. She was glad that the men had called a truce between themselves, but she'd never forgive her father for that walk through the snow and the humiliation she'd been forced to bear. Finished with her chores, she sat in her coat beside the wagon writing in her journal. She shivered in the cold, damp air. She planned to leave a record of their trek across the plains and mountains for Joseph to read to his grandchildren.

She jotted down her impressions of the river crossing and the night's activities along the bank, paused a moment, and closed her book. She put her pencil away in her pocket, rose from her seat and started toward them. She watched silently as William shook his father-in-law's hand and turned to help her into the wagon bed. High in the confines of the wagon, she glanced at her father one last time, and sighed as William tied the straps and they prepared for bed.

*****

Left alone at the campfire, James felt an intuition that the two men might have become friends if not for that foolish poker game. But, broken cups couldn't be mended, so they would each have to live with the mutual consequence of that night. Restless, for he had no one with whom to talk, he picked up his coffee cup and tossed the last dregs into the night. He'd grown accustomed to the loneliness of the past weeks, but tonight the string of fairy lights from the campfires and the gay tunes of the musicians gave him a sense of loss as if grieving for a loved one. Instantly, into his mind came the image of Priscilla Prescott as she'd come to him a tall, slender young bride.

He carried that picture with him as he went to see about his team of horses. He patted his horse Blue Boy, caressed his neck and gave him a piece of the apple he'd taken from the barrel in his wagon before they crossed the river. He had to be stingy with the apples and carrots now, for the humans would get first priority with the food; especially as he'd agreed to share with George. But, he didn't regret that decision, for George had done a fine job today guiding the horses on and off the raft.

Having said good night to his horse, James went to his own wagon, crawled inside, and pulling off his jacket, trousers and shirt, stretched out under the covers. His last thoughts were again of that night so long ago when he first met Priscilla. He sighed. There was no reason to pine for lost causes, he thought, and turned over, hitting his toe against a box at the back of the wagon, and went to sleep.

15

On the second day after the crossing of the river, Charlotte glanced down from her high perch on the wagon seat. She wasn't used to having nothing to do with her hands all day, so she called to William to stop the oxen. He looked over his shoulder with a quizzical look on his face, and she realized he could see her making hand gestures at him, and perhaps see her lips move, but he couldn't hear her words.

He yelled, "Whoa," and the oxen slowly staggered to a stop. "What's wrong? Are you in pain?" He walked to the lead ox and stood at the animal's shoulder so the beasts couldn't graze from the sweet grass at their feet.

"No, I'm fine, but I'd like to walk for a while, if I may." Charlotte was still shy around her husband and could see that he was annoyed at having to stop.

With a frown, William stretched out toward the wagon as far as he could while holding the yoke in one hand and his slack whip in the other. "You want to walk? Why would you want to walk while the grass is still moist from the early dew? I can't hold the animals much longer. The wagon behind us will get too close, and I'll have to move out of line."

"Please, William, can I just get down? Then I'll explain to you why I can't ride in the wagon seat any longer." She stubbornly insisted that she needed to walk.

"All right, come on down." William waited patiently, calming the lead ox with a hand on his neck, while Charlotte grabbed her thick skirts and, rather skillfully for a slender woman, edged her way over the side of the wagon. As soon as she was steady on her feet, William moved to the side and called for the oxen to "Giddyup." He cracked his whip over the rumps of the nigh oxen, and they began to move.

Charlotte, slightly embarrassed, walked as closely as she could to William. Besides being bored, there was another reason for disembarking the wagon. She explained her predicament. They were going through a forested area, on the road west of the river crossing. The road had been traveled for several years but was narrow enough that no more than two wagons abreast could transverse at one time. The wagons were going in single file, in case they met a traveler coming from the opposite direction. William told her to go to the side of the road and hide behind some bushes. He started the oxen moving, telling his wife he'd keep a sharp eye out for wild animals or transients that might bother her. He was well past the spot where she'd gone into the forest when she came out and started to dance around with her arms wide, swinging and skipping along to the tune of some inner music. She saw William laugh, and she didn't care. She could be foolish if she wanted.

She was having a marvelous time. She felt free, free for the first time in years. No hot, stuffy kitchens, no more washing other people's clothes, no more dirty dishes. She swung around in a circle, her arms akimbo; her feet skipping to a rhythm she made up in her head as she moved along. Her skirts flew modestly around her. The heavy sweater she had donned that morning seemed too warm and cumbersome, but she couldn't stop to take it off.

Spotty, running alongside the wagon driven by George, barked exuberantly at her antics, and Charlotte thought it a wonderful accompaniment to her marvelous day. The dog moved to join her, running in circles, barking and wagging his tail excitedly.

Sitting beside George, Joseph leaned out and waved to her. He leaned to his left and grasped George's arm, pointing to Charlotte. George looked where Joseph was pointing, and he nodded in agreement with something the boy said.

George stopped the team of horses by yanking hard on the reins and simultaneously using the brake by his left side. In a flash of corduroy trousers and flying feet, Joseph was over the side and skipping toward his sister and his dog.

Yet another wagon stopped, and down climbed two boys, about the size of Joseph in stature, but looking a year older in age. They were twins and seemed ready for an adventure after the confines of the wagon bed all morning. The four young people marched along as though they were soldiers on patrol, the dog following faithfully close by. Stopping occasionally to look at a special tree trunk, or a pretty flower, they fell farther and farther behind their respective wagons.

For over an hour the marchers let a greater distance grow between them and the wagons. They reached an especially rough patch of tangled vines and downed trees, and the wagons slowed considerably from their previous speed. With a gesture and shout from Charlotte, the boys followed her through a break between wagons so they could be on smoother ground on the left side of the train. There they had more freedom to scuffle with each other, and laugh at each other's antics. Charlotte kept a close eye on the wagons to make sure the boys didn't get near the hoofs of mules or oxen. Abruptly, the vehicles drew to a halt. One of the twins exclaimed, "They stopped," which when one thought about it was silly, and so his brother pushed him to the side, laughing. The other boy stumbled but caught his balance before he fell.

Charlotte said, "We'd better run and catch the wagons while we can. I'll see you tomorrow."

The four vagabonds and the dog hurried to the side of their tenders. The wagon train was completely still now. Joseph obeyed Charlotte and ran past William with a shout. George was talking with the driver from the wagon ahead of him.

*****

"Ahh, another delay," George growled to the man at his side. They'd both climbed down to stretch their legs from the uncomfortable position on the wagon seats, keeping a close eye on their respective teams. He watched as Captain Foster rode his horse toward the back of the train. "I wonder what's the problem?"

"A day like that, huh?" The man took a stick of tobacco from his pocket, and bit off a piece and chewed it a moment. He offered his plug to George, but he shook his head. He held out his hand. "Name's Harper. Ain't had a good day, myself, since we crossed the river.

Damn mules. I should've brought oxen." He chewed and spat on the ground. "You with that Butler outfit in the Conestoga? Heard tell he married his woman in a saloon. Her father lost her in a card game."

"That right? I hadn't heard. You talking about my boss, James Morgan?"

"Yeh, that's him. My friend Silas was there and was an eyeball witness. Morgan lost a pile of money and couldn't pay his debt. A matter of honor, ya know? So, he sold his daughter for the turn of a card. Bad luck, I call it. Silas said they was married right there in front of everybody. Old Judge Moore's an honest man. Spoke the words, same's they was in church. Butler took her upstairs to Maizie's room. No one saw them after that, Silas said." He spat again and laughed so hard George was angry. "I'd give a dollar to a seen it. What's that Morgan like?"

Captain Foster and three men rode by, and George thought it was a good time to withdraw from the conversation. "Here comes my ward. We'd best be getting back to our animals, or they'll start off without us."

Joseph rushed up to him, out of breath from running. Spotty sat on his haunches, his tongue hanging out, trying to regain his breath after so much activity. He looked up at Joseph with mournful eyes, as if to ask why they'd stopped their adventure.

George helped Joseph and the dog into the wagon. After hearing Harper's words, he felt uncomfortable with the boy, but shrugged off the feeling. Wasn't none of his business what his boss did, as long as he was left alone to drive the wagon in peace.

*****

"Ah, you've returned." William smiled, calling to his wife. Charlotte halted beside William and the oxen team, her eyes anxious. He reassured her by asking if she had fun.

"Oh, to stretch my legs! Thank you, Husband." She climbed back to the wagon seat, her expression tired but her actions exuberant.

William wasn't as complacent as he appeared, for he'd begun to truly worry over Charlotte's absence. He often forgot that she was so young, almost twenty years younger than him, and had led such a sheltered life. She worked hard every day, cooking and helping around the wagon. He couldn't begrudge her a little time with her brother, but he felt concern in the light of their situation in the wild.

A short time later, the wagons began to move again, and in the afternoon came to a wide meadow where they could spread out and travel more swiftly, three or four abreast. The rumors began that the Johannsson party was at the riverbanks ready to begin boarding the rafts to the western side. This caused a stir among several of the drivers, for if the second wagon train overcame them, their animals would eat all the grass. At camp that night, clusters of men congregated to discuss this new development, and Captain Foster decided that they'd rise an hour earlier each morning and travel one hour later at night until they could gain more of an advantage over the other party.

The next morning after breakfast was eaten and everything neatly tucked away in the wagon, neither Charlotte nor Joseph climbed aboard their wagons, but walked together, hand in hand, beside William and his team of oxen. An hour later, they were joined by the twins and their older sister, Francine Landers, whom they called Fannie. The twins were called Arthur and Amos, and it was difficult to tell them apart, they looked so much alike. Soon the boys and the dog separated and began to roughhouse again. Charlotte walked at a sedate pace with Fannie, and they became close friends, finding they had a great deal to talk about, secret things that only young girls would know.

16

The days stretched long and monotonous before them. On most days, James rode his saddle horse up and down the train, leaving room behind the wagon for George's horse and the pony, Petey. Naturally gregarious, he couldn't sit for long hours on the top of a wagon seat. It suited him to ride so that he could feel the breeze in his hair under his large brimmed hat. That had been a good purchase. He'd found it in a little shop off Market Street and found it to his liking right away.

At night around the campfire, while Charlotte prepared their evening meal, James and William talked of the odds of getting to Oregon before October, for no one wanted to get caught in the Sierras in a snowfall. Perkins and Thibodeau had warned him about the danger in the mountains. Sometimes, George joined in the conversation, but he was found most nights with a book in his lap, reading. James was curious about that book. Must be a good one, to keep a man occupied for hours on end. He himself would sometimes take out one of his favorites from the box that he'd packed so carefully in Illinois.

William told anecdotes of the balky mules and stubborn oxen he'd known in Virginia. That was when he shone the brightest, and Joseph would sit goggle-eyed listening to him. He told them he'd started as a boy digging the ore from the gloomy walls deep in the coal mines, a candle on his hat to light his path. His face became somber when he spoke, and his hands twisted into fists, then he laughed and told of how he'd been saved from that fate by a kind mule skinner who'd taught him that a life aboveground was better.

One dark, calm night when the stars were bright and the moon gone behind a small cloud, a cool breeze whispered through the camp. It was a magic night, one that seemed to bring secrets into the open. A lonesome violin played in the distance, and a man sang an Irish ballad. Charlotte separated the dirt and rocks from a quart of beans, carefully looking for weevils or bugs, washed them thoroughly and put them in the Dutch oven among the coals to cook during the night. James brought some extra fuel for the fire, and William tended to his oxen. When he finished, he told of his childhood in Virginia. His life had been hard: his father and he had worked in the mines, and his mother had taught the children in a one room school house in the hollow. He told of the great heaps of slag and the dirt that never seemed to be removed from their clothing and fingernails. A reddish haze hung low over the mountains from the constant smoke and grime of the village. Even the water in the fast-moving creek seemed pinkish-brown from the colored sky. His mother had died when he was seventeen; and his father when he was eight and twenty, his lungs filled with the dust of many years in the mines.

George sat near the fire, and listened as William talked. He tossed a small stick into the fire. He startled everyone by speaking out.

"My mother died of the poison."

"Poison?" James remembered Priscilla and wondered if the man's mother had gotten on someone's bad side.

As gently as she could, Charlotte asked, "What happened?"

"My father found her one day in the kitchen vomiting; but she couldn't tell him what was wrong. She was so weak and pale; she pointed to a box on the shelf; but he wasn't sure if that was what caused her sickness. He threw it away; and several other boxes and tins, too. We had an old goat called Charlie. Pa fed him samples of things in the kitchen, but they didn't make him sick. She lingered on for two more days, her face convulsed; her body racked with dry heaves, for we couldn't get any water to stay down, then she died."

He sat, silent, and the others didn't know what to say. The fire crackled, and a stick popped free, and he seemed to rouse himself from his memories.

"My parents had a wonderful life; they laughed and sang together.

113

We had a tree swing, and Ma would swing us high in the branches, and Pa taught us boys to fish, hunt and swim. One time, old Charlie got caught in the mud, and just called and called for help. Pa waded out to see why he wouldn't come out of the mud. He slipped on a rock, and Ma laughed until I thought she'd die from it." George looked around at his audience. "My ma was from Maryland, and she came to Missouri to visit her aunt." He scratched his head. "Pa married her, and she never went back to her home and parents."

"It's time we were getting some sleep; the captain'll be wanting to head out early in the morning." James picked up the sleepy Joseph and carried him to the Morgan wagon. "Don't forget your beans, Daughter. They'll make good eating tomorrow, if you've any left."

*****

Charlotte had brought a box of paper and pencils, and bottles of India ink, and water colors, for she intended that Joseph continue his schooling. She spent a little time each night with the boy poring over his efforts while sitting at the small table she used to cook supper. Sometimes, they would sit on a log by the fire, and she would have Joseph repeat the number scales, or spell words out loud, so she could test him. She wrote in her journal while Joseph silently read from the books that Clayborne had given them. Altogether, they'd brought three heavily caulked boxes of books, but William had suggested they'd have to be thrown away in the high mountains, for weight would be more important when they reached that stage in their travel.

James and William made arrangements to combine their supplies, for it wasn't right that Charlotte cooked from William's wagon when James, Joseph and George ate with them every night.

They shifted two boxes of hardtack, a bag of potatoes and one of onions from James' wagon. Charlotte requested the butter churn, along with a barrel of salt pork in brine, one of flour, and tins of salt, sugar and molasses also be moved from the Morgan wagon to the Conestoga. As they rearranged the items, William decided his kit for casting bullets, his powder and lead would be more conveniently located if moved to the back of the Conestoga for easier access.

Those first weeks crossing Missouri to Independence City were uneventful, for the food and game were plentiful, and the animals remained healthy and strong. There was plenty of firewood from dead limbs fallen from trees and brush along the way. Charlotte dreaded the

114

time when the forests were behind them and she would have to gather manure chips from the animals for firewood. She couldn't imagine a land void of all trees. She closed her eyes, but the picture wouldn't come to her, for she'd always lived in the forested land near her home.

The caravan pulled into Independence City on a late afternoon. Captain Foster called for two days respite from traveling, so the animals could rest and be looked over. The women lined the embankment of the river to wash clothes and bedding. George reluctantly handed over his soiled clothes to Charlotte, embarrassed at the thought of a woman seeing his undergarments. She assured him that a man's garments all looked the same, and she wouldn't notice the difference between his and her husband's, or her father's.

*****

While James rode into Independence to take advantage of the gambling halls and saloons, George took advantage of his absence to take Joseph fishing. He found a sturdy limb from a tree on the riverbank and used his draw knife to remove the outside bark. Happy to follow his directions, Joseph proudly pulled out his own knife and did the same with a smaller branch. George didn't think that the limb would be strong enough to hold a wiggling fish, but he didn't discourage the boy, and soon they had hooks from George's stash in his saddle bags on the end of a string. George had been fishing all his life, having been taught by his grandfather, and loved the taste of fresh fish cooked over an open fire.

"Mister George, where you from?" the boy asked after several silent moments of sitting with the pole in his tight grasp. Spotty trotted back from sniffling in the underbrush for some small creature.

"Why, I was raised on a farm, just like you, north of St. Louis." Surprised by the question, George realized that he hadn't told anyone but James that first night about his home. He still harbored resentment after the treatment of his older brother and didn't like to be reminded of his lost inheritance.

"Did you have brothers and sisters? Did you have hogs and chickens and cows?" the boy continued and gazed at the man with admiration, much as a younger brother might look at a much-loved older sibling.

"Yes, one older brother," and with the skill of an accomplished fisherman, George began to weave tales of escapades with his brother and the neighbor boys with instructions on lifting the pole from the water, putting a new worm on the hook and dunking it back into the water. The afternoon sun began to lower in the sky, and George knew that he should get the boy back to his family. He gathered together his fishing gear and the poles, for he decided if they were still there on the morrow, he would return with or without the boy.

George took the several fish they'd won out of the icy water of the river from where he'd lowered them on a heavy twine, so they'd stay fresh. He proceeded with no small amount of pride to show Joseph how to cut and scale the squirmy, slimy critters and put them in the pail he'd brought for that purpose. Together, they walked back to camp, with Joseph chattering like a bird about whatever came into his mind on the way.

Nearing the wagon of his sister, Joseph ran ahead of George and shouted, "We caught some fish, Sister! And, George brought them to you for cooking." His clothes were dirty, his hands still wet from helping clean the fish, and his gray eyes were twinkling like two bright stars in the early morning sky. The dog, barking and wagging his tail, leaped into the air to catch an insect that flew by.

Looking up from the potatoes she was stirring in the pan, Charlotte smiled at him. George slowly followed behind the boy, his hands full of fishing gear in one and the small pail dangling from the other. Her eyes widened, and he was certain she'd wondered what he was up to when he asked for the pail. He held up the fish, with a grin on his face as big as the boy's.

"Fish, you say? My, my. That will be a treat for supper tonight, won't it? Did you catch them yourself?" She looked at George for confirmation.

"I got two!" the boy exclaimed proudly. Glancing at George, he admitted they were very small and had to be thrown back in because they weren't fully grown yet. He shuffled his feet in the dust and looked chagrined.

"Two fish? Well that's good news, and you were wise to throw them back in the water, for someone someday will thank you when they're grown." Charlotte, her eyes gleaming with hidden laughter, hugged the boy and told him he needed to clean up for he smelled like the fish. The boy trotted off to his father's wagon, his dog running after him.

"Thank you, George, that was a wonderful sight, to see my

116

brother so happy." She took the pail he held out to her and looked inside.

"There's six or seven, but you can't tell because they're piled on top of each other. I made sure your brother at least had the pleasure of catching some of his own."

She smiled at him, but he muttered something about cleaning up himself and moved toward the Morgan wagon.

*****

James returned from Independence, drunk and well paid, for he won one hundred dollars in a poker game. No one condemned him for his behavior, and he gave the money to Charlotte to save for him. He also remembered to bring a bag of candy for Joseph, which he took with a smile of surprise, and looked inside to examine the contents. There was licorice, and cherry gum balls, and a peppermint stick. Joseph formally thanked his father with a manly handshake, kept the licorice and gave the bag to Charlotte with a solemn face. William, a witness to both events, guessed that it was a ritual that they'd started much earlier when Joseph was younger, which was confirmed by Charlotte.

On a warm sunny day, with puffy white clouds floating through the deep azure sky, a troop of mounted Dragoons, their banners flapping in the wind and the light glistening off their ornaments, met the first of the wagons. They stopped and inquired of the wagon master. When Captain Foster appeared, the officers stepped down from their horses, and the leaders of the wagon train squatted in a circle and talked. The enlisted men dropped from their mules and passed the time with smoking or cleaning their muskets or just lying back enjoying the sunshine.

Charlotte didn't see the Dragoons, but Joseph did. He was riding behind his father on Blue Boy when the soldiers appeared, and James hastily brought the lad and his dog to the wagons, then returned, for he wanted to hear what the men had to say. Later, he explained that they were two days out of Fort Leavenworth, and the Dragoons had come to accompany them to the fort. Joseph couldn't stop talking, and Charlotte remarked to him that she was pleased that he saw the men. When he ran out of truthful facts, he began to make up a few until George quietly told him he didn't think that his sister was as thrilled with the weapons of war as he was, so Joseph subsided, but his eyes

117

sparkled with excitement, and it took a long time for him to fall asleep that night.

James saw it differently. He now had a new bevy of compadres he could charm out of their funds, and they would have a lot. What did a soldier have to spend it on, anyway, besides having fun?

And gambling? What was better fun than that?

17

If Joseph had been excited when he saw a glimpse of the United States Dragoons on horseback and dressed in their finest uniforms, it was nothing to compare with what his sister felt when the wagons crossed the Missouri River and camped on the plush green lawns outside the gate of the fort. Charlotte's heart was thumping, and her eyes blinked to keep the excited tears from flowing down her cheeks. The sun was high overhead and dust was thick in the air from the movement of wagons and animals. Oh, she had never seen anything like it in her life! She wanted to clap her hands and dance and sing for joy. But, William said that wasn't the proper way for a married woman to behave, so she did it in her mind, where no one could see her.

The word was passed from Captain Foster that as soon as camp was made and the livestock settled, the people were free to visit the fort or to shop for supplies at the civilian sutler's store. Shelter was available for about ten people, but the rest would have to remain with their wagons and animals, for their protection as well as the orderly business of the fort. James somehow managed to be among the lucky ten settlers. George and William enjoyed Charlotte's venison stew with corn bread and turnips that night.

Even stolid and sensible George was impressed with the sight of the army fort. There were a few civilian houses clustered near the high walls of the stockade. The United States flag waved proudly on a tall tree pole. The troop of Dragoons led by Lieutenant Graham who had escorted the wagon train to the stockade stood at attention on their horses and mules before the gate, and Charlotte was able to see what had charmed Joseph so much. The men sat high in the saddle, their identification banner fluttering above their heads. A military band was playing somewhere, and the civilians were gawking at the pioneers from the East, and the Easterners were staring at the army.

The wagons formed a circle. The drivers and herders unhitched the teams and led the animals inside the protective loop. Preparations were made either for supper or visiting the inside of the fort. The Dragoons retired to their barracks, and all around was human activity. The noise could be heard of baying mules or the snorting of oxen. Dust tickled Charlotte's nostrils, and the smell of wood smoke permeated the air.

William expertly moved his team behind the Morgan wagon driven by George and joined the circle of wagons. Charlotte saw her father ride by on his horse with Joseph on the back, hanging on tight to Papa's waist. It was a thrilling sight to see Papa again like his old self, before the gloom of dark shadows and melancholia had threatened their home. She prayed quietly to herself that he wouldn't find a poker game tonight. Or, a bottle of whiskey, she added as an afterthought.

About two hours later, Charlotte was gathering her family's clothing articles together, for she'd heard from Fannie's mother that a person could hire one of the soldier's wives to wash and iron the garments for a small fee, and she was going to ask William if he would pay for the service. Before she could blink, the man that she was thinking of jumped onto the wagon and found her inside. Joseph was standing on the ground with his dog beside a front wheel. She was yanked around the waist and brought close to her husband's chest. He kissed the side of her neck and then laughed when she squealed.

"Come, Sweet Charlotte, we're going inside the fort," William said, and he kept a tight grip on her waist. "George has agreed to remain and watch the wagons if I'll stay with them this afternoon so he can have a turn. He said he needs to buy some boot polish and tooth powder."

"Oh, William, Fannie's mother says that if we take the laundry to one of the soldier's wives, we can get it done for a small price. It would be such a treat not the have to do the washing, just this one time," Charlotte pleaded. "I've got them all collected except George's things."

"Let George take care of his own laundry. Where's your bundle? I'll toss it down to Joseph, and we'll be off to the celebration." William seemed more excited than usual. Charlotte had never seen him in such a playful mood.

"What celebration?" Charlotte wrinkled her brow with consternation. "Fannie didn't say anything about a celebration."

"Why, the celebration of our arriving safely at Fort Leavenworth, of course," and he kissed her this time full on the lips. Charlotte was so surprised she had nothing to say, just handed him the bundle of clothing. He tossed it down to Joseph after giving him a warning to catch it. He helped Charlotte from the wagon and followed her. Joseph sulked because William had asked George to keep the dog tied up so he wouldn't follow.

Joseph's gray eyes were big and bright as he took in the sights, sounds and smells of an army barracks for the first time. He walked sedately beside his sister, because she was trying to act like a proper wife. And, not doing too good a job at it, she supposed, for her head was shifting from right to left and back again as she watched the antics of the mules with Dragoons on their backs. They paraded up and down the field, and the soldiers jumped off and lay on their bellies and pretended to shoot at some objects far off. The mules would stand perfectly still where they were left, not even swatting a fly, until the soldier jumped back on and raced to the other end of the field, then repeated the maneuver.

They were slowly making their way to a long, low building with a sign out front, "Sutler, A. Timothy; Proprietor," although Charlotte had no idea why. William guided his charges up the double steps and into the store. It was dim inside and smelled of fresh paint. It was small compared to Trice's large mercantile store in St. Louis. He encouraged Joseph and Charlotte to look around. Joseph went toward a display of knives and guns locked in a glass case. Charlotte spied some store bought clothing and proceeded to look for a new pair of trousers for Joseph.

William went to talk to the man behind the counter. They seemed to have a lot to discuss, because Charlotte looked at them twice and they were still talking. She made a note of the price of trousers of

Joseph's size, and her attention was caught by a tiny white christening dress, with lace ruffles and a white ribbon at the neck. Oh, she thought, that is so lovely. She put out her hand to touch it but brought it back, for she didn't want to soil such a pretty garment. Beside the dress was a pair of the tiniest brown leather shoes she'd ever seen. She gave a sigh of delight and heard a sound behind her. William had a small package in his hand and a bag with a twisted green ribbon tied gaily at the top. She told him the price of the trousers and asked if he had enough to pay for them, for she was certain that her father didn't. He gave her an odd look, took the trousers to the clerk, and told her to wait outside, he wouldn't be much longer.

Joseph was already on the porch waiting, because the soldiers appeared more interesting to him than the contents of a store. Charlotte came up beside him and slid a short glance his way before turning to watch the Dragoons on the parade ground.

"Did you enjoy your rides with Papa? Is that more fun than riding your own pony?"

"Yes, it was ever so much fun." Joseph turned from watching the soldiers and looked up at Charlotte with a sigh of frustration. "We went to the river and back. Papa won't let me ride Petey on the road because he says I might get lost or a wild animal might attack us." He paused a moment, then with a frown on his brow, he asked, "Sister, do you think Papa's bad spells are gone?"

Charlotte looked at her brother in surprise. She didn't quite know how to answer him. She blurted out, "No, I don't think they'll ever go away, but I pray every day for it. He has to drink and gamble and that's bad, but I don't think Papa's bad. He can't help himself, Mama said. It's in his Scottish blood."

"Did Grandfather Morgan drink and gamble? He was from Scotland." Joseph looked puzzled.

"I don't know, because I was just a baby when he died, but I know Grandfather Prescott did, because I heard Mama and Aunt Eileen talking about it one day. Aunt Eileen said he was a real skinflint, wouldn't give anyone money for frivolities, she called them. I looked up the word in the book and it means silly. Mama didn't let us have silly things either, because they needed the money to whitewash the walls of the barn, she said. I think it was because Papa gambled and drank, and Mama hated him."

Charlotte turned to find William at her side. She smiled at him, but he pretended he hadn't heard the conversation between his wife and her brother. Even if he had, she was certain it only answered a lot of questions he hadn't asked about the family. He told them he was through shopping, and they should go back to the wagon. In addition to the small package and the bag of candy he purchased, there was now a larger package wrapped in brown paper. Charlotte assumed it was Joseph's trousers, so she started walking in the direction he indicated, but she mused about the talk with Joseph, wondering what else the boy would have to say about their father the next time they talked.

Later that night as the family was finishing the meal, William rose and gathered the dishes waiting to be washed. He often did that to help Charlotte have more time for teaching Joseph and the children who stopped by the wagon. George was hanging around at that time, too, and Charlotte suspected William worried that George was pining after her, but she knew that it was Fannie that he wanted. One day she had seen George with Fannie in his arms and wondered if she should tell the girl's parents, but had decided it wasn't her business. This afternoon, she'd seen them walking together near the fort's outside walls. It was a dark corner, and she suspected that they had become intimate. She told William he should talk to George. He would do that soon, he'd promised, but right now he had some more pressing business.

There were only three children at the wagon that night for their lesson, Fannie and her twin brothers. She couldn't be counted as a child, since she was eighteen, but it was clear that she hadn't much schooling. Charlotte supposed the other children were tired after a day at the fort, looking at the sights. After presenting him with the new trousers and telling him to try them on, she sent Joseph to the other wagon where the faithful George was waiting. She collected the papers and pencils the children had used and tidied the table she used for the lessons, so William could put it in the wagon later.

She climbed into the wagon and began to undress for the night. She put on the nice cotton gown she had bought with some of the wages she received working at the hotel. She didn't wear it often, because the pioneers were always on the move, but tonight they would stay at the fort. She was almost asleep when she heard William return. He didn't come to the wagon right away, and she was beginning to doze off again when he pulled back the sheet used for a door and came inside.

"Charlotte, my dear; are you awake?" William sounded nervous, and his deep voice penetrated the darkness of the wagon.

"Yes," she answered in a sleepy voice. "I am."

"Then come with me, please," William said in his most persuasive voice.

"But, I have my gown on," she complained.

"Well, leave it on and put your coat over it. Please, I want to show you something."

Wide awake now, Charlotte felt around in the dark for the coat she kept on the box near the back of the wagon, in case she needed to get away from the wagon in a hurry. William had planned for all emergencies. This didn't sound like an emergency. The wagon creaked, and she knew he'd moved away. She put her coat over her gown and buttoned it, then slipped her shoes on, without stockings. She started to climb over the side of the wagon, but William's strong arms caught her and lowered her to the ground. Her long black hair was untied to stream down her back because William liked to see it down when they weren't traveling. She turned to him. "Where are we going?"

He pulled her to the side of the wagon away from the other campers. He had one hand behind his back as though he didn't want her to see it.

"What?" She was awake enough now to giggle at the silliness of it all.

"Charlotte, my dear, I think you have something to tell me," William murmured softly in her ear. He seemed so tall and formidable in the darkness.

"What? I don't have anything to say." Charlotte started shivering, whether from the cold night air or the excitement of the strange moment, she wasn't sure. William had never frightened her before, except on their wedding night.

"Yes, I think you do." His voice was more insistent.

"Do you mean about my parents? Did you hear me talking to Joseph?" That was the only thing she could think of that he didn't know about her, for she'd told him about her mother's death and her father's dark moods.

"No, that's not what I want to hear. Your parents' or grand-parents' drinking and gambling have nothing to do with us." William dropped his head and planted a sweet butterfly kiss on her lips. Then, as though he couldn't stop, he kissed her until she could hardly breathe, his arms warm and welcome around her body. Her heart was racing, and she hardly felt the cool gust of wind that blew through the camp. She had noticed cloud cover earlier slowly filling in where the stars had been. Charlotte wasn't concerned with stars or clouds. She wanted more of his kisses, and she strained to get closer to his warm body. He drew away from her, and his arms dropped to his sides. She felt bereft, and wondered what had happened.

"Why were you looking at the baby shoes and gown today?" he asked softly, his gray eyes dancing with merriment.

"Oh, you know!" She was so glad he knew because she hated to keep the secret that for the last few weeks her nipples had stung and her breasts were swollen, and she hated to cook bacon because it made her nauseous.

"Yes, my sweet Charlotte, how could I not know when you are so generous in your affection, and never reject me from your arms when I come to you in the night? You are with child, aren't you?" She nodded for she was suddenly shy in his presence. He brought the package up for her to unwrap. She pulled on the small piece of cloth, and barely visible in the dim light from the lantern, was a shiny wide gold wedding ring. She gasped with surprise, then threw her arms around his neck and kissed him until he had to take her arms and pull them from his neck.

William grinned. "I hadn't expected such an exuberant thank you, but I'm satisfied that you're pleased." He took the ring from her fist where she hid it so it wouldn't fall to the ground, and with great ceremony, he placed it on her ring finger, and lifted the finger to his lips and kissed the ring. "My sweet Charlotte, I love you. You are my own dear wife."

Charlotte couldn't believe her ears. He loved Martha in her cold, dead grave in Virginia. He had told her so many times. Was this because she was having his child? She had to know or go insane.

"William, what about Martha? You said you would love only her until you die. How can you say you love me now? Please, don't say it if you don't mean the words. That would be cruel." Charlotte implored him to tell her the truth.

William looked deeply into Charlotte's brown eyes and repeated, "I love you. You are my heart, my life, my love."

Charlotte chose to hear sincerity in his voice, even if his words sounded flat. They must be sincere, or he wouldn't say them, and she hugged him again.

*****

He kissed her as fervently as his need for a woman, any woman demanded. But, love? He scorned the emotion. He loved only Martha, who had wasted away in their wedding bed and now lay beneath the stars of Virginia, his home.

William kissed Charlotte one more time. He helped her into the wagon and gave her the package with the lovely christening gown and tiny shoes that she'd admired in the store. There was a length of soft cotton cloth to be used for baby clothes, and a large size dress for her to wear with her expanded waistline. Afterwards, he took her in his arms and filled her with his seed, although his child was already living deep within her womb. She fell asleep in his arms, content, but William stayed awake through the night pretending that she was Martha, as he did every night that he held his bought wife in his arms.

18

The next day dawned dreary and gray. There was a slight mist in the air, but by noon, the sun shone with a brilliance that hurt the eyes. They were ten days ahead of the Johannsson party, according to the scouts. The hunting party set out to look for game, and James came back with news of a herd of bison.

Three days later, the train was surrounded by the heavy lumbering beasts, as they moved slowly across the flat plains, grazing from the tall summer grasslands. It took two days for the train to wind its way through the herd of bovines. Their shaggy coats and black eyes were a delight for the children, and the ladies gazed at them in wonder. The result was a welcome relief to the pioneers, for there was plenty of meat for all. Captain Foster ordered the men to distribute the meat among the settlers. A few of the hunters, including James, kept the hides and better parts for themselves.

A few weeks past Fort Leavenworth, a massive windstorm came from the northwest. Before the emigrants had time to stop and gather their possessions, the wind blew canvas tops off a few wagons, with tin cups, papers, clothing and buckets flying everywhere. The women tried to retrieve what they could. A couple of the mules broke their harnesses and ran away, frightened. Women's skirts rose about their waists, and men lost their hats. Suddenly, the sky darkened, and

Captain Foster called for the wagons to circle, leaving the teams still hitched. Great billowing clouds rolled across the heavens; streaks of lightening appeared on the horizon, and loud claps of thunder sounded in the distance. Before twilight, the major brunt of the storm hit, and sheets of rain and hail fell for almost an hour. As quickly as it had come, the storm was gone. The next day, the adults added up the losses, waited a day for drying out, and the train moved forward again. There were no lives lost, but much damage to their possessions.

The days grew longer, the weather warmer and the wagons rolled on and on, through the forest and plains until there were no forests, only plains. The number of children who walked with Charlotte grew, but she never again danced freely in the grass. Sometimes only the twins and Fannie came, while on many days other children joined in her trek. From the beginning, she'd made sure that Joseph kept up with his schooling, and now she was attended at night after dinner by a cluster of children: small children barely able to walk, accompanied by their parents, and larger children eager to hear Charlotte tell stories she'd read in her grandfather's books. Occasionally, Charlotte would make up the stories herself.

There were tales of stormy seas and pirate ships, of wild animals and imaginary ones, of faraway lands; and stories of Oregon and California, and of brave Texans at the Alamo. Charlotte encouraged the parents of the children to tell of their experiences, and soon, several families on the train clustered around the Butler campfire on a Saturday night for the warmth, laughter and good times. A wiry old man with a long white beard brought his violin, another held his mouth organ in his hands, and a third slender young man made a homemade drum. He pounded along with the melody. The emigrants returned to their wagons cheered and whispering among themselves.

George kept to himself, reading from a book by the campfire if the light was high enough to see the words, or ensconced with his lantern if not. He slept in a bedroll a pace away from the Morgan wagon. He took Joseph fishing whenever there was a stopover and showed him how to cut and clean the silvery fish, or showed him some animal tracks. He taught him how to trap rabbits, and their bonding grew as the days flew by.

*****

One day Charlotte was walking along with her friend Fannie and the twins, when another woman of about thirty years joined them in their daily walk. They greeted each other with politeness, and while the young boys raced ahead, the woman cleared her throat and asked in a heavily accented voice if Charlotte would allow her two children to join the party. Charlotte looked at her sharply; and saw sadness in her eyes. She looked haggard and drawn and very thin. She asked her name.

"Matilda Johnson, and my husband's name is Bartholomew, but everyone calls him Bart. We got four young'uns, but only two are big enough to run and play like your boys."

Charlotte introduced Fannie and explained that the twins were Fannie's brothers, and Joseph was her own brother.

"They won't be too much trouble. I'll tell them to behave and obey you. It's so hard to keep them busy while I take care of the baby; he's only five months old. I told Bart it was too soon to come out west, but he said that if we waited another year, there might be another baby, and that would make five, so we might as well go now."

Charlotte watched as Matilda drew up the tail of her apron and started to pleat the cloth, a clear sign of nervousness or stress. She felt compassion for her and said that she'd be glad for the children to join them on their excursions. It turned out they were a boy named Nathaniel and a girl called Molly.

The next day, and every sunny day after that, Charlotte gathered her brood together. The boys ran and played, while Fannie, Molly and she walked more sedately along. Charlotte pointed out flowers, or birds, or something to amuse them. Often the younger ones returned to their wagons with grasses or flowers, a feather or a pretty rock. As she walked along, Charlotte told stories of cloud formations that became red roosters or magic horses in the sky. Maybe, she told them, they were dragons or witches or trolls or flying fish.

Joseph laughed at that one.

*****

William watched his wife in amazement. She seemed to be blooming with health in front of his eyes. He concluded it was the freedom from the chores and responsibilities far beyond her years that had released her natural talents. He noticed also that she never went beyond the boundaries he set on that first day when she had danced and raised her arms wide in joy. She was like a much older matron who could entertain the children, but not join them in their fun.

Along the whole train, the women and children walked, while the men rode their horses or drove their wagons. William cautioned them about the chance meeting with snakes or scorpions or other poisonous insects. He also encouraged Charlotte to carry a pistol in her apron pocket and a long tree limb in one hand as a precaution.

19

The wagon train had been gone about a month from Fort Leavenworth when Charlotte was awakened by the sound of barking, growling, whining, whimpering, and what sounded like a yelp of pain, and then silence. She nudged William lying beside her, "William. William."

"Yes, dear, I hear it. Stay here." He was reaching for his trousers. He grabbed his rifle and jacket and descended from the wagon. He called to her, "George, James and Joseph are already out searching, my dear."

Charlotte peered out. George held a lighted lantern high over his head. One of the men from the wagon ahead of George also had a lantern. He said, "Over here, I think there's something over here." George and James moved in that direction while William stayed close by Joseph. Charlotte could just make out the worried face of the youngster in the dim light of the moon.

"I think it's Spotty." She heard Joseph whisper in a little boy's treble voice, his lips quivering.

William placed his arm around the boy's shivering shoulders. He took off his jacket and draped it around the boy. "Why do you think it's Spotty?" he asked Joseph.

" 'Cause he didn't come back with us when Papa took me into the bushes."

At the sound of her brother's words, Charlotte's heart caught in her throat. Shivering in the night air, she reached for her coat. Her brother needed her nearby, if his fears were correct. She could keep his thoughts occupied, if indeed it had been Spotty they'd heard. William had no experience with frightened children.

Pulling back the flap, she saw men coming and lanterns weaving to and fro. When they got near enough to see the boy with William's arm around him, one kindly neighbor returned to his own wagon, presumably to reassure his family, while James and George walked to Joseph.

She could tell that George wanted to say something, but he shrugged his shoulders, and leaving the lantern behind, walked toward the skittish animals. Her father knelt before his son. William released his hold on Joseph but didn't retrieve his jacket and turned aside to his own wagon.

James said, "Joseph, it was Spotty, and he's gone."

Charlotte gasped, putting her hand to her mouth. Her father glanced at her through the opened flap, and he nodded at her, motioning with his hand for her to join them, before turning back to his son.

"Gone, where's he gone to?" Joseph asked, his eyes shining from unshed tears. "Why don't you go get him?"

"Son, he's dead," James replied in a sad tone and tried to take the boy in his arms, but Joseph jerked backward as if he couldn't bear to have his father touch him. William quietly leaned into the wagon, and told Charlotte to come outside, that she was needed. He waited while she buttoned her shoes.

She climbed down from the wagon with William's help. She saw Joseph standing in William's jacket, so large it almost dragged the ground, with James standing beside him with a puzzled look on his face. "What's happened?" Charlotte asked, concerned for the boy. Joseph stood stiffly and stared, defiance in his face.

William whispered, "The dog's dead, and I believe from the sounds we heard earlier that he's tangled with some kind of animal, probably a raccoon or other small night creature." Charlotte went over to where her brother and father were standing. William remained where he was beside the tail of the wagon. There was nothing he could do.

Charlotte, very carefully, so as not to frighten the boy further, stooped down to his height and said calmly, "Honey, William says that Spotty was very brave and tried to protect you, but he wasn't strong enough, and he's dead now."

Suddenly, like a small whirlwind gone astray, Joseph jumped and threw himself against her, flung his arms around her neck, and began to cry loudly. Charlotte almost fell to the ground from the impact, for she was overbalanced by his weight pressing hard against her, but she was able to catch herself by shifting her feet, before they both fell on the damp ground.

Charlotte looked up at her father over the head of the boy. She imagined she saw tears glistening in his eyes, but he brushed across his face with the sleeve of his shirt, shrugged his shoulders and walked away. Charlotte gave a little sigh of despair.

"Shush, Honey, you can't stay here. You need to get in the wagon out of the cold air," Charlotte told Joseph, hoping to reassure him and protect him from becoming ill.

He reared back from her arms, his tears now dry. "But, Sister, he was Jasper's dog. He told me to take care of him, and I didn't," and he began to cry again.

"No, Joseph, he was your dog. Don't you remember, you brought him home from Mr. Smith's livery stable?" She lifted the hem of her large nightshirt from under her coat and dried his eyes.

"Mr. Smith wouldn't let Jasper have a dog 'cause he might bite the horses or scare them away with his barking, so Jasper asked me to take care of him, but I didn't and he's died."

Charlotte felt the bitter sting of tears in her own eyes, and blinked to keep them from falling. She looked at William standing near the wagon, hoping he could tell her what to say. All of a sudden, it came to her what was wrong. Joseph wasn't mourning the dog; he was mourning the loss of his friend Jasper.

"Sweetheart, I'm sorry that you had to leave Jasper behind, but he belongs with his father and brother. You remember that he said he was an orphan, because his parents died on the trail to St. Louis, and Mr. Smith took him into his home and fed him and gave him some clothes? You wouldn't want him to leave a kind, helpful man like that, would you? I know you miss him, and you'll miss his dog, too. But sometimes we have to say good-bye to someone we love so that we can grow strong and kind, like Mr. Smith. I think you should write a letter and tell Mr. Smith how much you enjoyed taking care of Jasper's dog for him, don't you?"

Joseph separated himself totally from Charlotte and stood looking at her. She rose from her stooped position and wiggled her toes and stretched her legs, for she was beginning to get a cramp from sitting so long.

"A letter?" Joseph asked, looking at her sharply. "I've never written a letter before. Papa and Mama got letters, and Aunt Eileen wrote you a letter telling that Mama died, but I don't know that I can write a letter, too."

"Yes, Sweetheart, I think you should write a nice long letter and tell Mr. Smith and Jasper how brave and faithful Spotty was and how he tried his best to save you from harm, but was killed himself. I'll help you tomorrow, but I think you should try to go to sleep now." As she was talking, Charlotte was slowly moving Joseph toward the wagon in which he slept with his father. George was standing there to receive him, a reflective gleam in his eyes, and James was hovering in the shadows nearby. Charlotte left her brother in their care and returned to her own home on wheels.

Neither William nor Charlotte got much sleep that night, for she lay in his warm arms and told him about Joseph and his grief for the loss of his friend, Jasper. William comforted her and held her tightly until she had no more words. Charlotte went to sleep, only to wake a short time later to the sound of running feet and stubborn mules trying to make a break for freedom. She sighed and woke William, for another day was starting on the road to Oregon.

That evening Charlotte released the other children early from their lessons and spent the time laboriously helping Joseph explain to Jasper and his father how brave and loyal the dog had been and how he had died. They would have to wait to mail the letter until they reached a place that accepted letters for the East. But it seemed to comfort Joseph after he had written the facts on paper.

20

William noticed that George left the campsite earlier than usual one night and decided to follow him. George walked briskly until he came within sight of the Landers' wagon and slowed down. A shadow appeared to the left, and George walked toward it. In the dim twilight reflected off the lantern light, William saw two shadows merge and become one.

"Damn." The fool was meeting with Fannie Landers again, after he'd been warned to stay clear of the girl. William withdrew into the shadows of the wagon a few feet away and waited, worried and alert. It wasn't long before he saw the shadows separate, and he waited until George was near him and began to hum under his breath as though he'd been for a stroll so as not to frighten the man. William yanked the younger man aside when he came even with him and said, "Keep walking, I need to talk to you. What the hell are you thinking, man, to meet Fannie where someone from the Landers wagon can find you?"

"I'm sorry, Mr. Butler. I came because the girl said she wanted to tell me something. I won't do it again, I promise." George quickened his steps, his eyes glancing furtively William's direction.

"Damn, that makes it even worse, using the girl as an excuse." William kept pace with him, refusing to drop the matter. "You're a grown man. You should know not to give in to such talk from a girl that age. She's bored or fancies she's in love with you. You should tell her that her advances aren't welcome and keep the hell away from her unless there are other people around." He was growing angry as they approached his own Conestoga. He could see Charlotte was finishing the dishes, and even through his anger at George, he was pleased to see she'd taken his advice to relieve the pressure of the day's headache by releasing the tight knot she kept at her neck. Now her black hair trailed behind her back.

William was startled when George gripped his arm and pulled him to the side, away from sight of the wagon. He seemed to be even more agitated than he'd been when William had rebuked him.

"Mr. Butler, you mustn't think badly of me, for that's what she said, that she wanted to talk. Nothing else. She wants to marry me." He chuckled at that proclamation, but it had a sour sound. "She said Charlotte is two years younger than she is, so there's no reason why a girl of eighteen couldn't get married. I told her I didn't want to settle down yet, and I ain't got no material possessions or future plans, so I can't support her, but she won't let me be. I don't know what to do. She wants to kiss all the time and hugs me tight so I can feel her breasts under her shirt."

William could barely see the young man in the semi-darkness, and he knew what would happen if this wasn't stopped immediately. He thought of a good idea that might work, but it might as easily backfire, and the poor fellow would be in trouble.

"Look, I think you'd best go to the girl's father and tell him just what you've told me; that you like the girl well enough, but that you don't have any property or money, and you can't marry her. If he's any kind of father at all, he'll want to protect her from young men like you. He'll keep an eye on the girl from now on, I'm sure." William stopped speaking, took off his hat and scratched a spot on his head that had been giving him trouble lately.

"Do you really think so?" George sounded hopeful.

"Now, I'm not saying that would work. He might decide to make you marry her, thinking you've already done things you shouldn't, but at least it would be out in the open air, not sneaking behind his back, like you done tonight. That's dishonest and leads the girl to thinking that you want to marry her. You think on it for a while, and decide what's best for you and the girl. I'm going to check on my animals, especially my saddle horse Jimmy; he don't seem to be eating right, lately."

When the men had satisfied themselves that the horse was well, just off his feed for some reason, they separated to their individual sleeping places. William crawled into the wagon and could tell by the stillness that Charlotte had already gone to sleep, so he quietly removed his clothes and, lifting the covers gently, lay beside her. He turned over and went to sleep, tired from the day's driving of oxen.

*****

From the sounds of men's voices raised in anger, and a woman's screams, there seemed to be an argument going on at the campsite behind them. William looked up from where he was checking an oxen's yoke for tiny cracks in the wood. He looked to Charlotte, but she was leading her children in their letters. There were only three tonight, the two Johnson children and one other whom he didn't know by name, a little girl of about ten years. Charlotte looked up and into William's eyes with worry. He decided he'd better check out what the ruckus was about, for he wouldn't sleep if there was real trouble in the camp.

Coming close to the Landers' wagon, William could see there was trouble brewing. Mr. Landers was standing rigid, with his rifle in his hand, yelling at the hapless George, while his wife was hysterical, wringing her hands and red-faced. The twins were standing back as if they'd run if they had the chance, and there in the middle of it all was Miss Fannie Landers, shouting and pointing her finger at George.

"He did it, Pa. He kissed me." Fannie was accusing, and her mother stood beside her as if to protect her from this evil man. "Ever since Fort Leavenworth, he's been after me, grabbing my breasts and things. I told him it wasn't proper for him to see me alone, but he wouldn't stop. He was here just a few nights ago." Thinking she'd made her point, Fannie stepped back, and William could tell she had a gleam of mischief in her eyes.

Oh, God, thought William, she's accusing him of things he didn't do, so he'll be forced to marry her. The sly fox; he hadn't expected that.

George stood with his back straight and his eyes on Fannie. A crowd was forming around them, the men silent; the women whispering among themselves. George glanced his way with a helpless look, but William couldn't help him. He began to defend himself.

137

"Mr. Landers, sir, that's not so, what Miss Fannie said. Yes, I kissed her, and I fondled her bare breasts, too. She wanted it; she said I was handsome and just the kind of man she wanted to marry. But, it ain't true that I grabbed her; nor accosted her person in any way except what I already told you before." George looked the man straight in the eyes, and he kept his hands relaxed by his sides.

John Landers lowered his rifle, and a sigh of relief went through the onlookers. He looked closely at his wife and daughter, and frowned. He held up his hand, and everyone looked at him. Fannie dropped her arms and stood very still. She cast a quick look at George and shoved her mother aside. Surprised, Mrs. Landers moved back into the shadows away from the lantern's light, and her husband's eyes followed her actions. He turned back to the crowd and spoke with a touch of humor in his voice.

"I don't see any harm in a young man's kisses as long as he knows where to draw the line. Remmington came to me tonight with his intentions clear. He admitted his guilt, just as he done now before witnesses, and I believe his words." He chuckled and continued, "Sometimes young girls get fancy ideas in their heads, and my daughter's no different, but I don't see no real damage done, so all you gawkers, go on about your business. I'll settle this matter in my own way. Good night!" He walked toward his wife, hanging back in the darkness.

No one knew what was said between husband and wife in the Landers' household that night, but after a short conversation with Captain Foster, the Landers wagon was withdrawn from the line of vehicles and placed farther back in the train, where Fannie wouldn't see George every day. The twins no longer came to take their schooling from Charlotte and play with Joseph.

William didn't question George over the matter of his non-marriage, thinking if he wanted to talk he'd come to him. But James wasn't one to let such a thing go easily, and he harassed George about it and watched him carefully. He began to find fault with the way he handled the horses, and criticized his driving habits. He completely forgot that showing Joseph a good time on the trip and caring for his physical needs was why he'd hired him in the first place, to allow himself more freedom to roam alone. The plan had worked out well, but James remarked on more than one occasion that George was encroaching on his own rights as a father.

William mentioned his observations to his wife, but she said she had other things on her mind. She mourned the loss of her friendship with Fannie greatly, and she couldn't help but blame George.

When William told her of the deception Fannie had participated in against George, Charlotte remarked on several instances when Fannie apparently had used her friendship with Charlotte to see George, and discussed them with her husband. They decided there was nothing more to be done.

George spoke to William one evening while looking over one of the oxen. He was relieved that the episode with Fannie had been settled satisfactorily, but he didn't understand this new attitude of his employer. He had answered his questions with honesty, withholding only some of the grittier details to save the young girl's modesty. William suggested he withdraw a small distance whenever he could from the family group, but he was also glad to see the man eat and talk with his usual openness and amiability when called upon to do so.

Late one evening George shared that he felt he owed William a great debt, for the man had given good advice. He took his leave for the night, pulling out his Bible, and searched for Scripture in the dim light from his oil lamp, undoubtedly to ease his loneliness and guilt over the matter.

21

One day James rode up behind the Butler wagon and pointed to a large dirt formation in the distance that looked something like a house chimney. Charlotte gazed at the object with wonder, for it stood like a solitary sentinel on the prairie. She looked at William, driving the team of oxen, and shouted to him, "Look, William," and she pointed.

William had seen James ride up, with the swirl of dust he created rising into the air, and he tried not to become alarmed. He'd noted several strange sights the last few days. The landscape had changed from the flat plains and tall grass in which they'd been traveling the last weeks. The color of the soil was fluctuating, with more pinks and grays in some locations, and in others, browns and tans. He'd noticed several of the farmers walking in the tall grass, then stooping and digging up a few hands-full of soil, sniffing and tasting the dirt. Some took a sturdy stick and poked it deep into the soil, and beamed with pride as though they'd discovered the Promised Land of the Bible. He'd puzzled over the meaning of their actions.

"What is it, James?" William shouted at the man on horseback, who still gazed into the distance as though in a trance. He cracked his whip over the rumps of the oxen, and they picked up their pace.

"Called 'Chimney Rock' by the old Mountain Men; it means we're close to the bluff." James turned and looked at his daughter, as though he was trying to convey some important message, but Charlotte continued to look in the distance at the unusual formation.

"Bluffs, you say? What bluffs?" He was curious about the dirt formations, although he'd only gotten a glimpse of the chimney rock, being on the ground on the other side of the oxen.

"Just one bluff, rises out of the flat ground like a great mountain, all by itself. Perkins said a body can climb the bluff if he wants. When you get to the giant bluff then you're close to Fort John. A few weeks, maybe a month; depends on the weather and the speed with which the animals plod along." James gave a rather distrustful look at the oxen.

"That sounds good. What were those farmers doing the other day; digging in the soil and sniffing it, poking holes in the ground?"

"What! Where was this?" James turned his attention from the formation and rode closer to William. He lowered his voice as he drew closer. "Who were the men? Farmers, you say?"

"Well, they looked like farmers to me, by the way they dressed, might have been engineers thinking to build a road through the prairie. It was a few days back, before the grass seemed to taper off and the ground grew more rocks and gullies, said something about the soil being good to plow. Don't know why a body would want to farm here; there are no trees to shade a person in the hot sun. Looks like it doesn't get much rain, either."

James was no longer listening. He dug his heels in the flanks of his horse and rode out of sight toward the front of the train.

William looked at his wife with a question in his eyes; maybe she could fathom what the man was about. Charlotte shrugged her shoulders, still entranced by the rock formation. He realized that his wife's attention had withdrawn from him, so he turned to the animals, plodding along in their slow gait.

*****

From Chimney Rock, they traveled near what looked like two giant rock formations, one large and one small, which towered above the plains like ancient stone cathedrals made of clay. They were about five miles from the river, and the train didn't stop, although several of the men complained about it that night. Captain Foster explained they had no time to spare. He hoped to be in Fort John within the month.

The landscape changed almost daily, from long flat surfaces where a person could see for miles, to white or tan ditches and gullies where the dust was so thick, Charlotte had to cover her mouth and nose with a woolen scarf to breathe. They observed craggy earth fractures from an unknown source; tall spires of sandstone and wind-blown ancient volcanic ash in pale brown and gray brown; as well as scraggly shrubs and small trees that dotted the area. One early afternoon the bluff was seen on the horizon. It seemed to rise from the floor of the earth like a great monster in the open space. This magnificent geological formation forced the emigrants temporarily off the valley floor for there was no place wide enough through which wagons could pass.

Captain Foster called a halt for two days, since the scouts reported the Johannsson party had fallen further behind, at least two weeks, and there no longer seemed a danger of the second train catching them before they reached Fort John. Several of the men, including James, walked through the thick grass and rocks up the bluff and raved that they could see to the fort, but William was unimpressed with that conclusion. James brought back several small odd-shaped stones made of sand crystals and hard limestone with impressions of insect and beetle tracks. Captain Foster called them fossils.

William and Charlotte stayed near their wagon, because he'd noticed Lucifer limping a bit and wanted to see to his hoofs. In the end, he had to remove the stubborn ox from his yoke with Jezebel and replace him with one of the other animals called Brownie. Two weeks short of Fort John, Lucifer was killed and a great feast was enjoyed by the train, but William couldn't bring himself to eat of the flesh, for the animal had served him well in the march toward Oregon. Jezebel didn't seem to care which of the oxen was yoked to her. She stepped out lively when the trek was continued, just as the woman for whom she was named would have done. The spare ox named Atlas was tied securely behind the wagon.

Past the bluff the travel grew easier, and the flat surface of the sand caused the wagon tracks to become ever deeper. The train spread out three or four abreast and picked up speed. The men had their goal almost in sight, if you listened to the emigrants who had climbed the bluff.

*****

One night by the campfire, Charlotte dismissed the children early for the night, but some of the settlers still lingered to enjoy the camaraderie of the shared company for a while yet. While he fashioned bullets from William's molten lead and long-handled tongs, James looked around at them, seeing many he recognized, and a few that were unfamiliar. He bragged to the listeners, hoping to improve his standing among them.

"You do know Fort John's not the first name for this place." He worked the press, as if his statement were nonchalance and far from premeditated.

"Ah, there's the fool that knows nothing." A grizzled, shrunken man who had ambled up in hopes of some hooch spat on the ground, wiping his chin with his sleeve. "Never heard such a thing."

"I heard it from Perkins, that Fort John was formed by William Sublette as a private trading post. Named it Fort William, after himself." James looked up, his eyes glistening, and he let out half a laugh. "I believe it was only recently purchased by the American Fur Company and renamed Fort John. Old Man Bridger comes there often on scouting trips for the Army."

"Man's right," called another voice, the speaker unseen in the darkness. "It sits at the confluence of the North Platte River and the Laramie, a tributary of the Platte. Been used by the Indians since ancient times as a rendezvous. Old Bridger and the fur trappers camped while trading with the tribesmen."

The old coot, determined to get a last word in to show his intimate knowledge of the subject, called out, "Shallow streams. Yes, you betcha, it was the shallow streams, made for safer and easier crossing the rivers." He nodded his head like that said it all.

A young man, dressed in a blue jersey shirt and corduroy pants, spoke up. "I heard it was settled by a man named Jacques La Ramee in the 1820's, so Sublette didn't settle first. Some of the man's bones were found near the mouth of the river and that's where it got its name, Laramie."

"That might be so, but it's called Fort John now. I'll be glad to get there; I'm aiming to trade for some fresh flour and cornmeal if there's any to be found. My woman says she needs more salt, too," spoke up a heavyset man with a long white beard, named Harper. "If those things can be had at the store, I don't care who settled there first."

"There's a store, alright. People come from all over these parts. Indians camp outside the fort to trade with the trappers. Bound to be freight trains coming through from Santa Fe or Fort Hall." James had used the last of the molten lead, and lined several bullets on the tray to

143

cool.

William was impressed with the talk and began to think it might be a good place to live. He heard the fascination in his father-in-law's voice, and knew that the older man was enjoying the spirit of the adventure into the wild country. He watched Charlotte as she wrote in her journal, and George sat quietly listening to his employer speak. Joseph sat on a stone, wide-eyed and still. A coal fell in the slowly burning fire, shooting sparks into the air, and startled him. A cool breeze had arisen from the south and he rose to prepare for the night.

"Best let the rest go until next time, James, it's getting late."

The lingerers wandered back to their wagons, mumbling amongst themselves whether the story was true. "The man's a fool," declared Harper to his neighbor. "He don't know any more about the fort than we do. Likes to brag." After a time, the voices drifted away in the night.

James gave him an angry glare from his dark eyes, and put the cooled bits of lead into his leather pouch. William noticed that he didn't realize that he'd used William's lead and tools. Instead of making an issue of it, he calmly picked up the tools and remaining chunk of lead and put them away in his kit. George watched the tableau with smoldering eyes, but didn't speak.

Charlotte closed her book, rose and dropped it into her pocket. She dipped some water from the barrel at the side of the wagon and gathered soap and a cloth and helped Joseph wash his face and hands. James strolled away to his horses, as though untroubled by the actions of the emigrants.

William watched him go, a frown on his face.

144

22

A great shout was heard from the head of the train when the high clay walls of the fort were seen in the distance. William called to James to see if he could tell more of what was going on.

James mounted his horse and rode forward to see the sight, returning after some time. His eyes were red, and he could hardly speak. Eventually, with a gruff clearing of his throat, he told of the view he remembered from the top of the bluff, and how he had dreamed of crossing those mountains to the west. The fort was actual proof that the tall tales of Perkins the Mountain Man were true.

William was looking forward to seeing the fort for an entirely different reason. From what he'd heard of the vicinity of the fort, north and west, the grazing for cattle or horses was good, and trees could be found in the high plains of the eastern slopes of the mountains. The Laramie River was narrow and shallow, and was constantly fed by the snow melts and smaller streams coming down out of the higher grades. He'd never been enthusiastic about the Oregon country. He planned to talk to the people at the fort; see if it was plausible to start a freight line or trading post further north or west of the fort, maybe raise a herd of oxen.

George got up from his uncomfortable seat near the fire and followed William toward the roped line surrounding the animals. He caught up to William and cleared his throat. William stopped his pacing toward the animals.

"Yes, George, did you want to speak to me?" William assumed that George had finally decided to talk about the problem with Fannie Landers, but his eyes opened wide with shock when George began to speak.

"Mr. Butler, I have a respect for your opinion, and I don't want to cause trouble in your family, but I need some advice, if you would be so kind." George scuffed his feet in the dirt, and lowered his head. He cleared his throat again, and rubbed his chin with one hand.

"Go on. What trouble has stirred itself up?"

"It's like this, sir, for a long time now, I been thinking that I have to leave this wagon train and Morgan's employment. I've stood his taunting and criticism as long as I can. I been thinking if I can find a cheap mule at Fort John, I'll gather my belongings and hightail out of this area. Maybe, even head to California. I know I owe Morgan for the chance to work my way west, but I can't go no further with him or there's gonna be a fight or a killing."

William had no idea that the situation had grown so serious. He'd noticed an estrangement between the men, but assumed it was formed out of James' desire to remain independent. "George, I can't make a decision for you. You have to follow your own destiny, but let me tell you something that might help make up your mind. I've been talking with a group of farmers about the soil content and the water sources of this area, and I've been thinking of leaving the train myself at Fort John, and trying for a place of my own here. I wasn't as set on this trek to Oregon as Morgan and his daughter, but I started out for her sake."

"Here?" George looked around, as if surprised, but his voice had calmed. "Thought this was just an Indian trading post, and not much else."

William took a deep breath and continued walking toward his animals. "I had a good man tell me once that a man full grown has to make his own path through life, and I heeded that advice. Now I pass it on to you. I'm stopping here. I haven't talked to Charlotte yet, and if she wants to go with her father, I'll have to respect her decision, but I'm hoping she'll stay with me and have my child here."

He stopped at the animal corral and went over to his saddle horse Jimmy, which he seldom rode because he had to drive the oxen team. The horse traveled tied to the back of the Conestoga wagon. William rubbed the horse's neck and opened its mouth to look at its teeth, but his mind wasn't on the horse. He stooped and lifted one leg to see if a clod of dirt or stone had gotten in the space between shoe and hoof.

"Mr. Butler, if you stay here and don't go to Oregon like you planned, can I stay and work for you? You said you ain't a farmer, but I am. Been working on a farm all my life. I know about crops and irrigation, and planting and harvesting. I can help you build a house for your missus and a barn, too. I'll work hard for my food and shelter. You don't have to pay me nothing except for the essentials like clothes and boots."

"That so?" William looked into the breeze, and he tried to keep from smiling. He'd thank his father-in-law, if the man wasn't so low in his treatment of others.

George continued in a rush of words. "I know about animals, too, but you seen that for yourself these last months. I'm good at fishing and hunting, and I can cook when I have the food supplies." George stopped talking, and he cleared his throat, fiddling anxiously.

William's mind swirled with possibilities. If he had a partner like George to run the farming part, he could use his large wagon and haul supplies from the fort to the outlying areas. Or, he could go to Santa Fe or to some other stronghold and haul freight or logs down from the mountains. He could hardly wait to gain more knowledge of the foothills and land.

The two men made a complete contrast: one taller than the average man, with broad shoulders, slender hips and long legs, his hair black as the dark mines in which he had worked, his gray eyes piercing and a black beard that covered his lower jaw and chin. The other man was younger; with light brown hair and greenish-brown eyes, tall, but shorter than William, and slender almost to the point of emaciation. George was strong of body and of character, William could see that. He'd been faithful to the boy and taught him things that William didn't know.

He hadn't finalized his plans to stay at Fort John, however, so in a clear, concise manner, William tried as best he could explain that his own plans were still unformed, only an idea that had come to him since they left the bluff behind. The two men shook hands and went to their separate places of rest, a new understanding and secret between them.

*****

147

The secret didn't last long, for the next day a great argument started between James and George. The fight started simply enough. James rode his horse close to the wagon driven by George, his plan being to take Joseph to get his pony, Petey, and the two of them would ride closer to the fort, so that James could point out the Indian villages and the blockhouses. But, when he reached for Joseph, the boy balked at the idea of going with his father.

"No, Papa, I want to stay with Mister George." His treble voice quaked with his protest of independence.

"Now, come on, Son, it ain't often that a lad gets to see a sight like I seen yesterday." James remembered the excitement with which Joseph had welcomed the Dragoons at Fort Leavenworth.

"No, I won't go." He clung to George's arm as though he were his anchor in the storm. His eyes shone with defiance.

"Let go of that man's arm, Joseph Morgan, and come with me, now!" His Scottish brogue came out in his anger. Again he reached for Joseph to pull him off the wagon seat, but his horse sensed something wrong and shifted to the side; and James had to yank hard on the reins to keep him under control. He trotted back to the wagon.

"Mr. Morgan, the boy don't want to go with you, can't you see that?" George pulled at the reins, for the wagon had begun to slow and shift to the left, and he had to hold the reins hard to keep them steady. Joseph clung to the seat with both hands, being shifted from side to side with the motion of the wagon.

Without warning, James rode around to the other side of the wagon seat and butted his horse into the lead horse on the side of the driver. George was forced to bring the team to a halt, hoping that William driving behind him would see in time to stop his team from running into the back of the extra horses tied to the wagon. George had little time to react, because as soon as the team stopped, James rode back and grabbed forcefully at George's leg, taking him off balance. He fell in the dirt, face down, winded and hurt.

James dismounted from his horse and walked to the fallen man, grabbed him by the arm and shoved him back down again. By this time, George had regained his breath, and while he favored his arm, he rose to defend himself. The two antagonists stared into each other's eyes for one second, and the fight was on. Fists flew, and dust stirred up around them as they poked and swung and jabbed at each other. With an arm around George's throat, James swung a hard left into his

148

back, and George yelped with pain, then broke free and slammed a right fist into James' face. James could hear the sound of a voice yelling, "A fight!" and the shouts and taunts of men's voices with a few screams from the women who'd come to watch. He could make out a collection of faces, but didn't have time to identify them as George swung again at him. He was able to shift a bit, and the blow went wild. George threw another punch at James' face, and he felt a pain in his nose. Blood was in one eye, and it felt swollen. He gasped for breath and swung at George, but missed. George landed another blow to James' belly, and he bent over with pain. James hit George in the chin, making his head jerk back with a grunt.

James could hear the continued shouts of various men, and somewhere in his foggy brain came the sound of his daughter's voice yelling, "Stop, Papa, you'll kill him." But he was too full of hatred and jealousy to pause his attack now. He lifted his arm and tossed another punch.

The two men continued for some time to pummel and claw at each other. Finally, Captain Foster arrived, dismounted from his horse and yelled at some of the other men to stop the fight. Foster pulled on James' arms until he had to let go of George's neck.

The two men, now subdued by the strong arms of other men, looked at each with hatred. Hearts racing, breaths coming in gasps, they shouted at the same time, "I quit!" and "You're dismissed!" The men holding them loosened their holds. James and George stepped back and each walked away to find relief for their wounds and the solace of their neighbors.

James found himself in a circle of his gambling buddies. They tried to help him stand until he told them he was all right. He walked to his horse, which was still standing near the wagon. He jumped into the saddle and rode away without a backward glance.

*****

In the meantime, George gathered himself together, went to the water barrel, took a mouthful of the warm liquid from a gourd dipper, and spat on the ground, then went to see to the animals. He backed the team a bit, startling the two horses tied to the rear of the wagon. They had to move quickly to keep from being crushed by the wheels. He had the team pull forward and to the right and out of the line of other wagons.

"Mr. Butler, I'm taking the wagon to the fort. I'll leave them with the hostler, if I can." He yelled at the tall man standing with his wife and the boy. He couldn't look at Joseph, for his eyes were full of bitter, unshed tears, and his face was bleeding from the blows he'd received.

"Go on, George, I'll see you at the fort." William waved him off.

He drove directly toward the high walls encircling the buildings ahead of him. Inside the enclosure, he skillfully dodged a couple of loaded wagons setting out in the opposite direction, bent on some remote post on the frontier. He stopped the wagon, applied the brake and jumped down from the seat. He could see a few white men milling around, curious to see the stranger with the wagon. There were a couple of women standing near a tree, wearing the skirts and bonnets of emigrants bound for the west. He noticed the feathered hats and buffalo robes of many Indians striding singly or in groups here and there, or reclining on the ground near the walls of the buildings. He wasn't caring of how he looked, or what people thought of him.

George released his saddle horse from the rear of the wagon, left the reins dragging on the ground, found his saddle in the wagon and put it on the horse. He dug in the wagon for his personal possessions, grabbed a cloth bag and filled it with some staple foods; he figured he was owed a couple of days food, then he marched over to the nearest man, and told him to see that the wagon was given to a Mr. James Morgan when he arrived at the fort.

Spying a water trough, George led the horse to it, removed his hat, laid it on the ground, cast his head into the icy water and came up dripping. He shook his head, than put his hat back on, his hair still wet. A large red handkerchief was lifted from his back pocket, and he used it to dry his face. He turned to a man standing near the trough and asked if there was someplace he could stay the night. Surprised by the question, the man replied that he guessed a stranger could sleep in the hay of the horse corral, and told George where it was located.

George, now sober, wet, tired and angry over the sudden turn of events, took the direction the man pointed out and walked into a large open area. He scooped a pile of clean hay from a wagon to make a nest, tied his horse securely to a nearby post, removed his hat, dropped his saddle bags, then fell heavily onto the blanket-covered bed of fresh-smelling hay. Finally, his body aching from the blows it had suffered, George was able to drift into a deep, restful sleep. Near

150

sunset, he was disturbed by the arrival of maybe fifty or sixty horses and mules, under the care of several mounted guards. He jumped up, gathered his belongings and made his way outside the gate to the bank of the river, and sat against a tree watching the activity of the Indian encampment on the other side of the river.

23

Fort John
Wyoming Territory
June, 1844

James rode straight to the fort, and after asking around, found an older man in his late fifties to drive the wagon. The man, a retired army officer, he told him, was familiar with the trail to Oregon. James was afraid that George, in vengeance, would leave it standing out on the prairie unprotected. Everything he owned, except what was on his back, was in that wagon. He paid the soldier a five dollar retainer fee, promising to pay him more in Oregon, but for now he'd have to settle for his food. It wasn't a satisfactory bargain to the former officer, James admitted, but living at the fort trapping beaver pelts and taking handouts from his friends was surely no good life. The man agreed and jumped at the chance to go west.

The man's name was Lieutenant Jackson Taylor and he persuaded a friend to take him to the wagon train to pick up the Morgan wagon. When they got to the caravan, which was moving toward the stockade, he was told that the previous employee had taken the wagon. His friend drove him back to the fort, and Jackson gave him a small token for his trouble. He found that the wagon was in good condition, but the horses looked worn out.

James, of course, had found a bar and was proceeding to take out his frustration and guilt with a bottle of cheap gin. His horse remained tied up at the hitching rail outside, still saddled. When Jack found James, he was already half drunk, his face looking puffy and his nose broken. He had bruises on his hands and his trousers were torn. Jack told him that he'd found the wagon and it was fine, but James needed to buy mules to take them over the high mountain passes. James, his mind only taking in half what the new employee said, pulled out a worn money belt and told him to see to the mules, and continued to drink.

*****

William watched both of the men leave, his father-in-law on his saddle horse, and George, his new partner, high on the seat of another man's wagon. He supposed he'd leave the wagon at the trading post, saddle his horse and strike out for the next place he could find. William hated to see him go, for it'd been a practical plan, to stay at the fort and find a place here. He turned to see Joseph, traces of tears in his eyes, standing near Charlotte. They both looked despondent, but he would have to wait to talk with them. Right now he needed to get his team going, for with the fight finished, the train was moving forward. Standing beside Brownie, his whip in his hand, he waited for Charlotte and Joseph to board the wagon. He realized that Joseph hadn't only lost his best friend of the moment, but his home as well. With a call of "Giddyup," and a crack of the long, black whip, the Butler wagon headed toward Fort John.

The caravan pulled to a halt outside the imposing gates of Fort John the same night. The captain said they would stay two days, and leave early on the third day. That gave them time for buying supplies, repairing of the wagons, healing the animals that needed it, or washing clothes. They wouldn't linger longer, for the season was getting late and he wanted to get to Oregon before October.

Charlotte collected her supplies for the meal, but before she could start cooking, William told Joseph to go find his friends, the Johnson children, and stay with them until he came for him. He knew the boy would be safe with Matilda Johnson. Spreading a wool blanket on the ground near the fire he'd started, he asked Charlotte to sit beside him.

Charlotte placed her hands in her lap and composed her face. "William, I'm fully prepared for your condemnation of my father for his treatment of the younger man after his faithful care of his wagon and horses during the trip from St. Louis."

"Sweetheart," William began, taking her hand. He wasn't planning to talk of James except in a general sense. "My dear, I don't wish to upset you further than already today, but I have for some time been thinking of making a change." He looked at the fire, as though it would give him the right words to tell her his decision, because the behavior of his father-in-law had hardened his resolve to remain at Fort John.

Charlotte tightened the grip on the handkerchief in her hand. "My father fighting with a hired man was shameful. Is that what you wish to say?"

"Darling, there is that, but this is a far greater decision we must make. I've spoken with several of the farmers traveling with us about soil conditions and water, trees and grass. I plan to go into the fort tomorrow to ask the people about finding land here on the river for us to live. I cannot in good conscience travel to Oregon with your father any longer. He has proved to be a man of dishonor. I first noticed it when I played poker with him, long ago, and today he's proved it again." He paused for a moment to gather his thoughts before the final plunge.

"And me? My father expects me to travel with him."

"You'll have to choose, my dear, which of us that you'll accept for your protection. I've promised to honor my vows of fidelity and respect, but I can't keep the promise to take you to Oregon, which was part of the bargain I made with your father in the saloon the night of our marriage. I know he has dreams of a farm in the Willamette Valley, but it was never my dream. I'd like to start a freight line or build a trading post, for which I'm better suited. I'll make sure you have shelter and food, but you would be left alone for long periods of time, as much as six months, maybe. I'll ask tomorrow if there's a man available and trustworthy enough to help you with the work, but it'll be hard for you to live in such a way, alone with the child. I'm giving you your freedom, Charlotte, if that's your desire. I won't hold you to your marriage vows if you want to go to Oregon with your father and brother. You are free to go."

And, with the words that filled his soul with anguish, William also gave up his dreams of a child like Samuel, for if she left with her father, she would take the unborn child with her. William knew with a certainty that he would never marry again. He would remain alone forever. Marriage was too painful.

Charlotte spoke, her voice strained. "To leave for as much as six months? To hire a stranger to help with the work? To abandon me with a baby coming? You cannot be so cruel, if you truly love me."

William felt despair grip his heart. He could not travel on, and he could not lose his chance to have a family. He watched Charlotte's face, as she considered his words, what she must do.

"Charlotte? What are your thoughts?"

"It isn't me I must think of, but Joseph. My father isn't evil, but he's weak of character. The time will come when he'll get into a drunken fight or gamble away his funds as he did on the night of our marriage. I can't leave my brother to such a fate."

"You must tell me quickly, my darling wife. I can bear the suspense no longer." William took her hand, and it was moist and warm.

"I must sacrifice in order that my brother might live." She took a deep breath and squeezed her husband's hand in hers. "William, my husband, I'll remain with you and be your loving wife forever on one condition."

He looked down at the entwined hands and awaited her decision, his heart in his throat and his veins running as cold as the tomb. "Yes, my Charlotte, what is the condition?" He looked into her eyes with acceptance and regret, for he was certain he couldn't fulfill her terms.

"I'll remain with you as your wife, if you'll also take my brother, Joseph, and raise him as your own son, or as a younger brother. I'm convinced that if he goes with my father, he'll not live long. My father will abandon him or sell him as a slave as he did with me. My father cannot be trusted any longer. Will you take my brother as your own child?" She watched his face closely for his answer.

He and Joseph weren't close, not like the boy and George, but he liked the child, so he answered in the affirmative.

"My dear, I give you my solemn vow that I'll take your brother as my son and provide for him to the best of my ability. It'll be a hard life for you both, for I know not what the future holds. I'll have to speak tomorrow to the authorities about it. But, I will not go to Oregon. My mind is set and will not be changed. It may be that we'll

155

have to go to Santa Fe, although I worry about this talk of war with Mexico. Or, somewhere else where I can build a life for us, but not in Oregon." She nodded her agreement. He squeezed the hand he still held in his own, leaned over and kissed her to seal the vow. "I'll go fetch Joseph and tell him of our decision."

He collected his new charge, thanked Matilda Johnson for her care of him and started back to the Conestoga, but stopped halfway where they could be alone. He stooped and balanced himself on one leg, the other curled under him. Joseph looked at him with a puzzled expression.

"Joseph, there's something you must know, and Charlotte has agreed that I shall tell you. For now it's a secret, but will be known in a few days. We aren't going to Oregon." He stopped to let that fact soak into the boy's mind. "Your father has proven to be false and must travel his own road alone. Your sister wants you to live with her, and I've agreed. Tomorrow I'll go into the fort and search for land here on the Laramie River for a small farm on which we'll live. Until the matter of the land is settled, we'll continue to live in the wagon."

Joseph looked at William with his big eyes. "Where will Papa go?" His voice quivered with confusion.

"Your father will probably go on to Oregon. We'll remain here, or move to some other place if there's no chance for land."

"What about Mister George? Will he go away with Papa? They had a big fight, and it was because I wouldn't ride with Papa. He dragged Mister George off the wagon, and I was scared and jumped down, but I couldn't make them stop fighting. And Mister George is hurt."

William had suspected something similar had happened, because he'd seen James go to the wagon, and then George was on the ground. He'd had to stop his oxen team quickly to keep them from injuring the horses trailing the wagon. He could hear the guilt in the boy's voice, and he had compassion for him. He'd lost his mother, his friend Jasper, his dog Spotty; and now he would lose his father.

"I've already asked George to work for me, and he's agreed, but I can't say where he is now. He left to take your father's wagon to the stockade. Perhaps he's still there. Would you like to go with me to meet him?"

"Oh, yes, please, I would like that ever so much." Then he pulled William by the sleeve of his shirt, and whispered as though someone might hear, even though there was no one there but the two of them.

"Mister William, do you have enough money to buy my sister some clothes, 'cause she's getting fat, and her dresses are too tight. I saw her one day, and she was tying a sheet around her because she didn't have time to make a dress out of the cloth that Miss Bertha gave her. Could you get her a dress when we're in the fort tomorrow?"

"Why, yes, we'll look for several dresses, but we may have to settle on cloth, because they might not have store-bought clothes here. This place isn't as large as Mr. Trice's store." William found the boy's response amusing, and he rose to his great height and put his finger on his lips. "Shh, it'll be our secret. Don't tell your sister."

Joseph skipped ahead of his brother-in-law, and nearly tumbling over his feet, he grabbed Charlotte and gave her a hug. Surprised, Charlotte yelped, almost dropping the frying pan she was holding in her hand. She reprimanded him, "Joseph Morgan, you scared me. Don't jump on a person like that without warning."

Joseph smiled. "Mister William says I can stay with you, and he's taking me to the fort tomorrow to find Mister George."

Charlotte exchanged glances with William, and laid the frying pan on the grill that covered the open flame. She began to place the bacon slices she'd already prepared into the pan.

"Joseph, I've said that George may not be at the fort; so don't get excited. Wash your hands, for you're a grubby little boy after playing with the Johnson children." Charlotte watched as he obeyed her. "I think as a special treat you won't have your lessons tonight, so you can talk to Mister William about your visit tomorrow at the fort. Would that please you?"

Joseph gave a shout of joy, and after his hands were washed and dried, he sat on the grass before the fire and volunteered to help her if she needed it, but Charlotte said she was almost finished. William watched the exchange between brother and sister and thought of the life they must have led when they were in Illinois. She hadn't told him any details, but he'd learned some things from Bertha and Clayborne Hightower before they left St. Louis. This new responsibility loomed heavy on his mind that night as he lay beside his wife.

*****

The next day, the sun was hot and dust clouds marched along with a person's footsteps. It'd been days since it had rained, and the oppressive heat seemed to cover the earth like a blanket.

William's first sight of the fort at close hand was from the saddle of his horse, and he paused a moment to take it in, with Joseph gazing upward beside him. The walls were about fifteen feet high, built of sun-dried bricks. Common blockhouses stood at the two front corners, and men stood looking suspiciously down at them. Off to one side, near a scraggly tree, a broken, one-wheeled wagon drooped to the dusty ground. A dog was tied to the good wheel, so it wasn't abandoned. It gave rise to the possibility that a blacksmith might be in residence. The ground near the entrance gate was rutted with wheel imprints, and hardly distinguishable in the soil, the prints of many horses, leading to the corral.

The main entrance gate contained a high square window, through which a person could hold a conversation without opening the gates, decreasing the danger of intruders entering without permission. The bottom edge showed the rough-hewn assemblage of sturdy log construction, but the window was of finished wood, with iron bars running through it. There were heavy brackets built of iron on the interior surface of each gate, and to the side was a sturdy plank that could swing down to secure the doors when they were closed. But, since the caravan's arrival the night before, the gates were open wide.

William and Joseph rode through without restrictions.

The interior was composed of a large square area divided by small apartments containing the homes and businesses of the few residents, the storerooms, offices, and a large animal corral. The ground was rough dirt, with occasional tufts of coarse grass where wood met soil. On the far side of the square was a pile of unfinished lumber, and several men were toting a board into a shop that was a black cavern. Sounds of milling came from inside. A walkway of crude planks rimmed the homes and business fronts along the perimeter.

A tall pole extended from the ground, with a carefully assembled series of stones around the bottom, and the company insignia painted on a linen banner attached to the top occasionally stirred, indicating a breeze in the open air. The air within the fort itself was still, with the aroma of humanity pervading the place. The office and apartment of the manager was reached by way of a stairs, a long rude balcony, and entrance through a thick wooden door. There were other rooms along the top tier surrounding the fort, and from where William sat, it looked as if there was a sod roof to provide protection from the brutal sun of summer, and the cold snows of winter.

William and Joseph dismounted and tied the horses to a wooden railing. A group of men was standing nearby, and one of them spat, the spot on the ground a great lump, with the dirt around growing brown with the juice of the used tobacco. Another one held a cigarillo, and the sweetish odor in the smoke floated their direction, making Joseph cough. William overheard the elder one lamenting the lack of rain. He tipped his hat and led Joseph along the boardwalk to a long, low building with a slanted roof.

Their first stop would be the store to see if there were any ready-made clothes that Charlotte might wear during her pregnancy. The door was wood planks, held together by cross members. The only light came from two oil lanterns and one small window comprised of a wooden shutter that lifted to attach it to the ceiling. The low ceiling was of log beams holding the rough planking above. Someone could be heard walking overhead, with glimpses of light glimmering through the boards, and from time to time, a fine-grained dust would filter through a crack. There were two plain calico dresses displayed on a hook on the wall. The proprietor remarked that he had taken them in on trade just the week before, but they were freshly laundered, and there were no vermin in the seams. William was confident Charlotte would find them more comfortable than what she now wore.

William bought Joseph a couple of cherry balls, but the boy protested that he was too old for candy, and William replied that no man was too old for candy, and bought a licorice for himself. Joseph looked up at the tall man in awe, as William took a bite of the licorice and smiled in pleasure at the taste. William paid with a few coins as a woman came in from a side door and wrapped his purchases in heavy paper and twine. Joseph thrust himself from the store as William collected his goods. Coming out, William heard Joseph give a shout of joy, and he thought he'd hurt himself.

Joseph was running as fast as he could go toward a man with brown hair and greenish-brown eyes. It was George.

Will Joseph ever feel affection toward me like he does George? William asked himself. He didn't think so, but, he mustn't get jealous or he would end up like James Morgan, with only hatred and malice in his heart. He greeted the younger man with a handshake, and they started walking toward a sign on a two-story building marked "Office." George held back, confiding, "I'm hiding from Fannie Landers and her mother. They came into the fort about an hour ago. I got some of the information that you wanted. I'll meet you at your wagon," and he was gone, to Joseph's immense disappointment.

William and Joseph walked up the half log stairs and to the office. He glanced over the scene across the fort, now able to see the sod roof clearly. From this vantage point he could better view the sentries. One was standing, looking out over the landscape beyond the fort wall, and two others were involved in a game of some sort. One of them glanced at him, frowned, and went back to his game. He and Joseph went in the door. There were several people inside the room and a stack of animal hides on the floor, from which came a bad odor. Joseph wrinkled his nose and sneezed. William smiled in sympathy, but went toward a man who looked to be in authority. He held out his hand and introduced himself.

"Aye, your partner done been in this morning. Wait a moment, please." The man turned to continue his business with an Indian whose hair hung in two braids past his shoulders.

William moved out of the way, as several people talked to the man, and Joseph glanced about with wonder in his eyes. In a few minutes, the man came back and said they should take their conversation outside onto the balcony.

"Ah, Mr. Butler, I understand you be lookin' to buy land upriver-way, thar on the Laramie. That be right?" He looked at William with a query in his eyes, but seemed distracted and transferred his attention to some Indians standing below. He frowned and spoke to them in their language, and they disbursed. He glanced at the boy and turned his attention back to William.

"Yes, that's correct." William's eyes followed the Indians as they moved away, and he placed a friendly hand on Joseph's shoulder. "I've heard from several farmers who were on the train that the soil is good and there's a plentiful water supply from both rivers. I'm not looking for a large place, maybe a hundred acres or less. Land enough for a house, barn and corrals for my animals, and possibly a large garden spot. I must confess, Mr. Pedigrew, that I may be competition for you. I'm not a farmer. I'm a wagon driver. That is, I hope to build a freight line or even a trading store for goods coming from the east or maybe Santa Fe. I'm worried for there's talk back east of a war with Mexico. Perhaps you have more recent news on that rumor?"

"Nah, don't have no reliable information on no war with Mexico, but I'an heard rumors of raids by the Texicans further south a ways. Occasionally, there'n be troops comin' through, but they t'ain't said nothing 'bout hostilities. Been some trouble with a few Indian raidin' parties, but they'rn mostly quiet around these parts. In answer to the question ya came to hear, there be such a site a ways up the Laramie. A settler came in, built a house and barn, but could'na make a go of it. Left it abandoned and weeds took over his garden and wheat fields. Don't know the whole story, but seems his wife got sick, and he just up and left when she died."

William winced, and Pedigrew looked at him. "Doesn't seem right to make a woman's death the reason for taking over a farm." It was more, though. He remembered his own beloved wife. He'd done the same, just up and left to be gone from the sorrow. It'd followed him, however. This farm? It might be the very thing, both for his family, and for his peace of mind.

"There be a few scattered farms, but most of the bid'ness around here be from trappin' and huntin'. Wild animals what be in abundance along the rivers and lower reaches out towards yonder mountains. Not far from here, maybe three, four days ride, be a great open space, then the trail leads northwesterly direct to the mountains." He shook his head. "Cummings ran a few head of cattle and horses, but I cain't say what happened to 'em. Man named Robertson gots a place on the river; he might help you with information."

William said, "It sounds like the place I'm looking for, and it'll be a stroke of luck if the buildings are still standing. Do you think we could move right in? My wife's in the family way, and will sure be glad to get off that rocking wagon seat."

All the time they'd been talking, Joseph had watched the speakers as though he understood every word, and he probably did understand better than William, having been raised on a farm. Joseph grabbed William's shirt sleeve with a look of fear in his eyes. William looked up, and coming toward them was James, and he looked very drunk, staggering from side to side. Quickly, William told Pedigrew that he'd come back, because they weren't leaving with the wagon train. He and Joseph turned in the opposite direction from the one in which James was coming. Holding his packages tight in his arms, they made their way to the horses, and left the fort.

Neither said a word on the way back to the wagon, but William could almost read Joseph's mind, and now he understood better why Charlotte wanted to keep the boy with her. The boy was actually frightened of his father. William didn't know of any specific reason for it.

The next day, James rode out to the Conestoga on Blue Boy, his

161

coat wrinkled, his eyes bloodshot and his hands shaking. From the alcohol or nervousness, William couldn't say, but he stood with his rifle hidden nearby while James apologized and tried to make amends for his behavior. He accepted the blame for his part of the fight, and said he'd been under a lot of pressure lately.

"I brought a length of gingham cloth and some thread. With the baby coming, you'll need more clothes. Some flannel cloth for nappies and baby clothes, too." He offered Charlotte the package with a sheepish grin. She took the brown wrapping paper with a tight smile on her face and backed away.

"Here, Son, I found you a new hat." He reached to place it on Joseph's head, but the boy took off running and stood at the back of the Conestoga. James handed the hat with a feather stuck in the outside band to Charlotte, and she held it at her side, with the package in her other hand.

Stiffly, with a voice of deep regret, Charlotte began to speak.

"Papa, we're not going to Oregon. We're staying here with William. He's going to make a home for us along the river if he can find a place."

She had barely gotten out the words, when James exploded with anger. He cursed and called them ungrateful children and started forward as though to strike Charlotte, but William blocked his way. Standing toe to toe, the men stared into each other's eyes, and James backed down. He bowed his head and tears rimmed his eyes.

James hugged his daughter and wished her happiness. He shook hands formally with his son, and held out his hand to William with his eyes downcast. His son-in-law received the token of acceptance of his own authority over James' offspring. There were a few more words spoken in which he asked William if they were remaining at Fort John, and William acknowledged that they were. James said he'd write to let them know when he'd safely reached Oregon.

The last the Morgan children saw of their father, he was riding away down the dusty road to Fort John. James didn't look back. As soon as he left, George came out of the wagon, and Joseph ran into his arms. William turned aside and placed his rifle back in its leather scabbard. Charlotte, her eyes glistening, watched her father go.

"My darling, regrets?" William called to her.

"My grandfather's books and Bible are still in my father's wagon. I feel my family's history is riding away with my father. I wonder if Joseph remembered his mouth organ and his clothes in the wagon."

"We'll be safe, and your brother will have clothes. Let's not worry about that now." William kissed her cheek and saddled and mounted his horse, and striking out, he rode to Fort John. He went to see Pedigrew, and the men talked for hours about furs, horses, cattle and land. He was surprised to learn that the hired man, Lieutenant Taylor, had left a pile of crates and barrels from the Morgan wagon for him. He told Pedigrew he'd pick them up on his way to the homestead on the river.

When William returned to camp that evening shortly before supper, he carried with him the legal papers to 160 acres of land north of Fort John on the Laramie River, bought sight unseen. Also, he had the deed to any animals, tame or wild, that might be on the land, and water rights to both banks of the river for three miles.

Tied to his saddle horn, and trotting beside him, was a sorrel yearling with white markings on two legs, and a saddle big enough for a tall man. He called to Joseph to come see his new mount.

Joseph looked at the horse with wonder in his eyes, formally thanked William and shook hands. William asked George if he'd help him become accustomed to the larger horse, and said he had something to discuss with Charlotte.

While Charlotte put the finishing touches on the meal, William explained that Pedigrew didn't know in what condition they'd find the house and barn. It had been abandoned for years, but it would be her home for as long as she wanted to live there. It should have been a night of celebration, but there was a somber mood at the Butler wagon that evening, as Charlotte went to say good-bye to her many friends and the children whom she'd grown to love.

Matilda gave Charlotte a clean, used baby dress, and kissed her on the cheek. Charlotte exclaimed that she didn't want to take her baby's clothes, but Matilda said it was already outgrown and laughed. She wouldn't need it for at least another year. Charlotte laughed with her, and Matilda promised to write as soon as she found a place where mail could be sent.

Early the next morning the sky was streaked with red, and the clouds lined with gold and silver, as the wagon train moved out bound for Oregon. The Butler family watched them go and turned aside to make preparations for their own departure for their new home in Wyoming Territory.

24

About midway through the afternoon of the waning days of June, the call of birds and the chatter of ground squirrels were briefly interrupted as William's large, lumbering Conestoga topped a ridge and moved onto the floor of a wide valley carved by ancient glaciers. He was on the way to his new home, and occasionally, through the willows, oaks and brush along the banks of the river, he could see the reflection of the sun on a band of water flowing down from the high mountains in the distance. On the left lay a massive limestone rock formation.

Following Pedigrew's instructions, he turned his oxen team in a north, northwesterly direction away from the river and continued for about two miles, until he came to a broad meadow. In the midst of the meadow was a low, dark brown structure covered in greenery and surrounded by trees.

With a suddenness that startled the oxen so that they jerked with surprise, George and Joseph, on horseback, gave a whoop of joy and dashed off at a gallop toward the building. William flicked the lead ox with the tip of his whip and hollered, "Haw," and the animal pulled his mate to the left to realign the team.

Walking beside the wagon, dressed in a man's dark blue shirt with a pale pink broad-brimmed sunbonnet on her head, Charlotte looked up when the riders went flying by her, the hoofs kicking up dust in the green and lush grass through which she was strolling. Her hands clasped a bouquet of wild flowers. Across the meadow were yellow, pink and white flowers, with a touch of bright red here and there. Charlotte couldn't resist picking a few as she rambled along on this perfect summer day with high puffy white clouds in the sky.

She looked across at her husband, caught his answering gaze, and laughed, for peeping out of the sod on top of the house were bunches of the same type flowers that she carried in her hands. She pointed to the wild flowers and started running toward the house, uncaring if he later gave her a lecture on proper decorum for a lady.

Driving his team more slowly, William pulled up near the wide porch of the dwelling. The two riders had left their horses tied to the front porch railing. They came walking around the side of the house. The younger of the two ran to his sister as though he hadn't seen her only moments before. He grabbed her around the waist and hugged her tight.

George gave William a solemn look and shook his head. "Lots of work to be done, Mr. Butler. The barn roof needs repairing, the fence is down in one spot, the garden full of weeds and briers, but it can be fixed. It'll take us time. Looks like a large plowed area up the slope, might be a wheat patch, but it's covered in weeds, can't tell from this distance, and corn in the crib out by the barn. Shelters for the animals, but we didn't go in the barn; likely some hay and feed in there."

William hooked a lead rope to the yoke of Brownie and Jezebel and threw a weight on the ground so they wouldn't stray. He walked to the back of the wagon, released his saddle horse from the tail of the wagon and brought him around to tie next to the other horses. He went back and released the reins of a pony and handed the reins to Joseph, for the pony was his.

He looked at the house. There was an old ladder back chair lying near the door of the cabin, possibly blown there by the wind. There were two windows in the front of the house, boarded up tight. William noticed grass growing between the floorboards of the porch.

"Do you think the corral will hold the horses until we can get it mended? Did you notice how far to the river? Any recent signs of flooding?" William was concerned about the river after talking with Pedigrew on the last day at Fort John.

"Nay, didn't see no sign of a river, but there's a trail down that way, must lead somewhere." He pointed toward a line of bushes and trees in an easterly direction. "Easy enough to put up a barrier against the flooding if we can find enough rocks; won't know until it rains about the flooding. Corral will hold the horses if we repair the downed logs."

Charlotte had moved up the double steps to the front porch of the house and was standing patiently while the men were talking. She tried the door handle but it was locked. Joseph tied his pony to the porch column and joined his sister on the porch.

William turned his attention to his wife and walked up the steps. Taking a long narrow key from his pocket, he inserted it into the keyhole and turned. There was a small resistance, and the door opened wide. All four of the pioneers walked through the door, Charlotte and the boy, then William and George.

There was a large rectangular room, and at one end stood a massive rock fireplace, which centered the cooking area. High above the open fire area was a mantle made of one solid half log, the rounded side down. On each end of the mantle sat hammered tin lanterns with an enclosure for a candle. In the center of the mantle stood a wind-up clock covered with a thin coat of dust. Enclosed in the rocks near the opening was a flat metal surface which looked like the door of an oven. And spindles hung from the side of the blackened opening. Several pegs with long handled forks, spoons and three frying pans of different sizes hung on the left wall of the fireplace. In the same corner space were long shelves containing dishes, glasses and various-sized bowls. In front of the shelves about two feet from the wall was a cabinet made from old wooden boxes with the printing still visible, "apples," and inside the boxes were shelves for flatware and knives, and stacked pots, pans; and on the floor, two wooden buckets.

Standing in front of the fireplace was a large, handmade table surrounded by a long bench and three ladder backed chairs matching the one on the porch, room enough for six or seven people to be seated comfortably. In the middle of the table was a glass lamp, with chimney and bulb-shaped tank for oil; it appeared to be half full. Charlotte walked toward the kitchen area, and looking around found a tall glass canning jar, into which she placed the now wilting flowers she had picked in the meadow.

In the other corner next to the fireplace, draped from a string of rope, was a dark gray blanket. William walked to the blanket and opened it, thinking it might be an outside door, but proved to be a dug out sod root cellar. Dust flew from the blanket in a fog. The earthen floor sloped down into a room lined with shelves of canned goods, tobacco, salt, and cones of sugar. Spider webs were visible in the corner and between the shelves. A small table held a container of coal oil, two boxes of empty glass canning jars and a wooden bucket. Hanging from the ceiling were heavy cords with hooks on the end containing hams, long thin sausages, two slabs of salt cured bacon, and several canvas bags of onions, garlic and peppers. On the floor were barrels of flour, cornmeal, apples, turnips and cabbages. The smell coming from the cellar was so strong that William backed up and almost crashed into the table.

"Whee, this has to be cleaned out, and quick!" William dropped the blanket and continued his exploring. The exact center of the room was empty, and the wooden floor was bare. The other end of the room had been made into a living area, with a rocking chair, with a leg tied with thin cord, making it wobbly when William set it to rocking back and forth. Beside it sat a large stuffed horsehair sofa. He thumped the back and a cloud of dust emerged and caused him to sneeze. Near the sofa was a table with a glass lamp that matched the one on the kitchen table. Under the lamp was a lace cloth, and in front was a Bible. "The man left in a hurry, if he left his Bible behind," William told Charlotte, who'd come up behind him.

George and Joseph hadn't waited for the others to explore what was behind the blue blanket on the right side of the room behind the living area; and now they came back into the area to announce that there were two bedrooms, the smaller one an attached lean to shed with a sloping roof where a grown man couldn't stand with ease. With George holding the blanket up for them, William and Charlotte moved into the large bedroom. It was a twin to the room Charlotte had slept in at the Hightower Hotel containing one large handmade bed that centered the room with a tall enclosed wardrobe for clothes, and a ceramic pitcher and bowl set on top of a cloth covering a table near the door. On a shelf above the table was space for a lantern and various toiletries. The floor was covered with a twisted rag rug. The bed was covered with a homespun quilt, made of many colorful scraps of gingham or calico cloth.

Charlotte went to the quilt and ran her fingers lovingly over it. "Oh, look, William, isn't it lovely? And, very old. I wonder if the woman who made it was the same one who died here." She turned to her husband, but William appeared not to be listening; he'd gone into

167

the other room where he had to stoop so low his head almost touched his knees.

"This will do for Joseph, I guess. Only has a small bed and a couple of pegs for his clothes. Pedigrew said they didn't have any children, but guess they were prepared for the future." He backed out of the room and was glad to be able to straighten up again. "The quilt is pretty, dear, but I'm not sure it can stand a washing, it's so old." William ran his fingers along the pattern and remembered the quilts that covered the beds at his home in Virginia. He gently lifted the quilt and found dusty sheets and a feather mattress, with matching goose down pillows. He thought to himself that the couple must have been well off when they traveled west to bring such luxuries with them. He was sure the mattress and pillows would have to be burned, because he didn't know what disease or fever had caused the woman's death. He remembered too well the cholera that had killed his beautiful Martha, and they'd burned her bed linens and clothes. Better to be safe, he thought, but didn't say anything for now. No need to worry the others.

"Oh, I'll be very careful, but it seems to belong here. Maybe I can follow the pattern and make a new one like it." With William out of the smaller bedroom, Charlotte stood in the doorway looking in, but she didn't enter. Returning to the kitchen, she remarked, "I can barely wait to get started cooking in here, but I suppose everything will have to be scrubbed with lye soap, so we'll stay in the wagon for another few nights." With a sigh, she went back out to the wagon to start their supper.

William stood in the middle of the front room, pondering the fact that there was only one door. He didn't like that idea. What if there was a fire, or an Indian attack? "I wonder if this old clock works," he muttered under his breath. Working at the face, he got the curved glass door to release. Putting a slight pressure on the hands, he was pleased they moved freely. Underneath was a key, and he inserted it in the hole and wound it a few turns. It started a melodic ticking, and he replaced the key where he found it. He decided it would need oil before any more winding was done, or the dust might damage the workings.

William went out to mention the lack of a second door to George. George and Joseph had already left the confines of the house, and William found them circling the outside perimeter more carefully than the first time. Near the cabin an outhouse was lying on its side a few feet away from the hole over which it had once stood, either blown over by the wind or pushed over by some large animal.

George and the boy walked toward it, but Joseph called out that he wasn't interested in an old structure lying on the ground. He headed toward the barn.

"Don't go far, Joseph," George called out with a hand to his mouth. "We don't know what's here until we look around more."

Joseph acknowledged he'd heard him with a wave, and stopping a few feet away, he uncoiled his length of rope and began to wrangle a tree stump.

"I don't quite trust the boy in this new situation," he remarked to William. "He's curious, and he'll stray if given a chance, so I feel compelled to keep one eye on him." He glanced that way repeatedly as he examined the outhouse to see if it could be brought upright again.

"So, is the old privy still functional?" William laughed. He thought the boy would be fine. He would be living here, and he'd have to learn the surroundings one way or another.

"If we use one of the oxen and a rope, we might be able to lift the wooden frame. I think a new hole should be dug first. Over there, maybe." He pointed to an area about six feet to the left, and about five yards from the side of the house.

"You'd know best about that, George, but I've been looking in the root cellar, and all the food seems to be rotten, by the smell. Do you think we can fill that hole with the stuff from the cellar and cover it with soil before we start to dig the new one?" He looked at the half filled hole over which the toilet had once stood. "But, that's not what I came to talk to you about."

Joseph let out a whoop, having encircled the stump with the rope, and William glanced at the boy.

"What is it?" George turned from the deposed throne room, and he laughed at Joseph. "The boy has the ability to have fun with no more than a stump. All our lives should be so easy. Now, what do you wish to talk about?"

"I looked the house over good, and it only has one door. I don't like that idea; a person could be trapped in there if the place caught on fire. As soon as we get this little chore done, we should see about making a hole in the side of the house, but the question is where, the small lean to bedroom? What do you think?" William looked at the cabin as he spoke and noticed a window in the area of the large bedroom that he hadn't noticed when he was on the inside, probably because it was boarded up. There were two large wooden tubs hanging on the wall of the house, he supposed for the washing of clothes or bathing. He started walking toward the house, with George following him.

Joseph coiled his rope and followed, avoiding the smelly hole in the ground. The men went to the boarded window, poked and prodded, opened the window, and George went inside, while William continued to pound on the wall from outside, stooping to the ground and moving upward while George banged on the inside. Joseph stayed close by as George had instructed.

Charlotte, standing near the wagon, looked at William stooping near the foundation of the house. She waved at Joseph, who called back, "Sister, look at Mister George and Mister William. What are they doing?" Joseph pointed at the men.

William yelled at George, inside the house, to pound on the wall to locate his position. They would be hungry soon, and he looked toward Charlotte. "Wife? How's the next meal coming along?"

She waved, calling that she had work to do. To Joseph, she said, "I don't know what they're doing. You're helping me, if you don't mind. Take this pail of lard, will you, please?" She handed him the tin, and she brought out the ingredients for supper with Joseph babbling like a trout stream.

Nothing was done about the new door that day because the sun was low on the horizon, filtered through the trees and bushes, causing dark shadows around the buildings. William examined the corrals and sheds. It was a split rail fence, and he saw that with a few heaves and tugs, the enclosure could be repaired. With Joseph's help he lifted the logs into place and made sure they were tight. He circled the corral, found a few more fallen logs, and was soon finished with the chore.

He marched his oxen into the corral and unyoked them. But, as a precaution, he tied their lead rope to the pole shed. Taking the small feed trough from the side of the wagon, he gave them some hay and grain. He separated Star and helped George to lift the outhouse to an upright position, and leaving George to start the digging; he put the ox back with the others and tied him securely.

He hadn't been to the barn yet, so opened the wide double doors and went inside. There were four open stalls and a small room that held harnesses, a plow and other farm equipment, shovels, rakes, hoes, a scythe. In the dim light, he couldn't tell if they were rusted, but that would wait until the morrow. Swiftly scanning the area, he saw a wagon and wheelbarrow made of wood, a few stacked crates, an extra harness and a couple of barrels. He didn't take the time to look inside. In one corner stood a sharpening stone for honing tools, with a three-legged stool for sitting while a person turned the wheel.

He was pleased to see the sharpening stone but more interested in looking around the room to measure its size. He thought it would make an adequate shelter for George, if he wouldn't be offended by living in the barn. He would need a bed and maybe a small table on which to put his things. He ran through his mind the objects still packed in the Conestoga wagon, and thought of the small table that Charlotte used to assemble ingredients to mix her bread. That table should be all right for George, since the house had the large table near the fireplace. He could have one of the ladder back chairs in the kitchen area. They wouldn't need so many chairs with the bench for Joseph.

He pondered those things and walked toward the far end of the barn, which was very dark. He couldn't see into the gloom, so went back to the entrance and pulled down the lantern hanging on a metal hook. He shook it and heard the sound of liquid in the tank. He dusted off the glass with his shirt sleeve, opened the glass and felt for the wick with his thumb. He took his flint from his pocket and lit the lantern. It smoked but gave off a weak light. Strolling to the back of the barn, William could see what looked like a large stack of logs. Upon closer examination, he saw stacked almost to the ceiling, long round logs, short tree branches, and cut timber. His heart jumped with glee. He turned and left the barn, taking the lantern with him, and leaving the doors securely fastened behind him.

The afternoon drifted into twilight, and he could see Charlotte by the light of a lantern, cooking over an open fire she must have started herself because the men hadn't been there to help. Joseph was standing on one foot, his hands waving around, as though he were in the middle of a long yarn. He stopped talking when he saw William, and once again the man was struck by the heavy responsibility that Charlotte had placed on him. He waved at the boy and continued to where George was standing to his ankles in a hole of his own making. A pile of dirt was slowly increasing in size as George pitched another shovel full. When he saw William approaching, George climbed out of the hole.

"George, have you been in the barn, yet?" He felt the anticipation building, and led up to his surprise with a slow grin forming on his face.

"No, sir, didn't have a chance before; thought the outhouse might be more important to your missus."

"I'm mighty pleased that you've taken on that job, for it's not something I find I'd enjoy. She'll be able to protect her modesty now. But, I think you'll be happy to see what I just found in the barn, nevertheless." William turned and looked at the barn, now becoming a hulking, shadowy shape in the long summer dusk. "Earlier you said that it might contain some hay or animal feed, but there's none. There's a nice room, though, full of farm equipment that you'll need, and a sharpening stone and stool."

George's eyes brightened at this information. Although there were a few tools in the wagon, and they'd brought a plow with them, a sharpening stone was a treasure indeed.

"The whole end of the barn is filled with cut logs and timber." William waited for a reaction from the man.

George blinked at William, and without a word, started walking at a fast pace toward the barn. William had a hard time keeping up, even with his long stride. He grinned when Charlotte looked up from the fire and stared after them. Joseph had been watching her, and when he saw her reaction, he looked at the men and took off at a run toward them. They arrived within minutes of each other, and George, with the help of William, opened the barn doors. Lifting the lantern high so George could see, William followed his employee inside. Walking steadily down the aisle of the barn, with George in the lead, the three men stopped and gazed with awe at the pile of wood. George would have moved closer and examined the mound, but William touched his sleeve. "Best wait until tomorrow. There might be snakes or rodents hidden in the wood, and it wouldn't do to get bit at this point in your life."

George nodded and turned back to the open barn door. Blowing out the lantern and placing it on its hook, the group walked to the place where Charlotte was putting the finishing touches to their dinner. They explained about the timber, and for the next hour, the group discussed the day's events. William, Charlotte and Joseph slept in the Conestoga, but George took his gear out of the wagon, and sitting near the dying embers of the fire, he took his Bible from its leather pouch.

Far into the night, William stirred and looked towards the fire. He could see George, tired, sweaty and dirty from the digging, and when the fire finally burned away, the man lay down with a smile on his face.

William dropped the canvas and rested on his pillow, glad he'd invited Joseph's protector to join them on this new adventure.

25

At breakfast, William reminded George of his find the day before in his newly acquired barn, for he wanted the man to look over the store of worked logs. It was a boon he'd not expected, and it would make life on the farm much easier, as the fall season would be on them soon.

After examining more closely the timber in the barn, and finding no snakes, George finished digging the hole for the outhouse. He helped William dump the spoiled meat and vegetables from the root cellar into the previous hole, and covered it with the soil that had been dug from the new site. William brought Atlas, and the men moved the wooden toilet over the hole. George finished by staking it securely to the ground and putting dirt around it. He took a couple of the cut boards from the barn and made a new bench seat, and the family had an outhouse fit for royalty.

While George finished the outhouse, William took a shovel and dug more deeply into the root cellar. Joseph brought out the soil with buckets and dumped it in a pile in the yard. William wasn't sure that the spoiled meat and vegetables hadn't contaminated the walls, floor and ceiling of the root cellar, so he dug a half foot deeper on all sides and top. The pile of dirt became higher and higher, and William was thinking of what it could be used for when George suggested leaving it alone for now until he had the garden patch plowed. He could use the fresh dirt for the garden. William left the farming decisions to George, for he wasn't a farmer.

At lunch, Charlotte announced that in order to stay out of the way of the menfolk and their digging, she'd stripped the beds in the two bedrooms, and she asked for William's help to take the mattresses outside to lie in the hot sunshine. She washed the linens in scalding water with lye soap. William wasn't sure about using the bedding, but Charlotte insisted that it had been nearly five years; surely any lingering fever would be gone. He let her have her way, but he wasn't satisfied with the idea. He'd seen first-hand the results of cholera and didn't want to lose the new baby.

After seeing to the animals, cleaning out the farm wagon that had been standing in the barn and checking the wheels and axles, William noticed the water barrels were very low, since they'd used a considerable amount of the liquid in washing down the house. Hitching Brownie and Jezebel to the farm wagon, he hauled the two barrels down the trail George had pointed out. George and Joseph followed on their horses, and Charlotte sat primly on the seat. Not knowing what they would encounter, William kept his rifle by his side and the whip coiled around his shoulders. George had his weapon in the scabbard on his saddle horse.

Just as George had thought, the trail led to the bank of the Laramie River. The trail had at one time been clear of the tangle of briers and weeds, but now was grown wild in places. The men stopped, and while William used the scythe, George raked and shoved the weeds out of their way. They both wore heavy gloves, and William told Joseph not to get down from his horse in case there was a poisonous weed or snake in the brush.

When they reached the water's edge, they found the Laramie narrow and shallow, with a swift-flowing current. In other places they'd come upon, it widened to several hundred feet, and was about four feet deep, with a sluggish, sleepy flow. The sound of the flowing water was a welcome melody to counter the building heat of the day.

They formed a bucket brigade. George lifted the bucket down into the river; handed it full of water to William, who gave it to Charlotte, and she lifted it up to Joseph in the wagon beside the barrels. Using two buckets, it took a long time to fill the barrels. Once finished, they decided a break in the day was in order, and Charlotte pulled out the blanket she'd brought for the purpose, lay it on the soft sand of the riverbank and read a book, while the men took out George's fishing gear and proceeded to win their supper. William hadn't been fishing since a boy, so it was a special treat to sit relaxed in the sunshine. He watched the closeness between George and the boy, and thought back to the days when his grandfather was still alive. He commenced dreaming of the soft green mountains and tall trees of Virginia, and was startled awake when a fish grabbed his line. He pulled the fish from the water and added it to the catch of his friends, pleased with his attempt at fishing.

It was hard to tell which of the adults was more proud on the day of the fishing trip to the banks of the river. William, using minnows, had caught one nice sized channel catfish, and George caught several brown trout. Joseph caught one small trout and a catfish. The boy's sad, bewildered look had begun to disappear, and he laughed and talked more than he had since William had known him. William looked at Charlotte and thought she seemed more content, too. It was only at night when he lay beside her that she was withdrawn and quiet. He tried not to think of the suffering she must be going through after the dishonor of her father, and to have given up her dream of Oregon. For the sake of his child she carried beneath her heart, William resolved to be more kind and gentle toward his wife.

That evening, after a supper of boiled potatoes with onions, beans and fresh fish, Charlotte brought out an iced cake, slightly burned on the bottom, for she wasn't used to the oven in the fireplace. She'd hidden it in the bedroom until they ate, so that Joseph wouldn't find it. Joseph's eyes grew large as he saw the cake, and clapped his hands when Charlotte announced, "Happy Birthday, Joseph!"

William was stunned, for no one had mentioned that it was Joseph's birthday. George gave him a Jew's harp he'd purchased the day he'd hung around the office of the fur traders at Fort John, promising to show him how to use it tomorrow. Charlotte presented him with a new blue shirt she'd sewed on the trail by the campfire while listening to the children read or write their numbers. William had watched her make the shirt but hadn't given any significance to the matter. Trying his best not to choke on the lump of jealousy in his throat, he asked as cheerfully as he could, "How old are you, Joseph?"

The boy, his mouth full of cake, answered, "Twelve, Mister William." He didn't even look at him, but took a swallow from a cup of water to wash down the cake. George gazed at William with surprise.

"Why, that's a great old age, and I'm proud that you caught more fish than me. George has taught you well. Now if you ever get that rope of yours around a real steer, you can feed yourself. Your sister will have to show you how to bake a cake. This one's fine, isn't it?" And William took another bite of his cake, but his heart was saddened that his wife hadn't included him in the surprise.

When the house had been thoroughly washed down with lye soap and vinegar to Charlotte's satisfaction, they let it dry out for another day until the strong odor subsided. They moved some of the items from the wagon into the root cellar and kitchen area. George had gone over the garden plot, kicking up dirt, and tugging on some of the bigger weeds to expose their roots. Finally, working the ground with a rake and building a small fire to burn the accumulation of debris, he decided that they might plant some seeds, hoping they could be harvested before bad weather set in. He noticed the cord bound around the rocking chair, replaced the leg with a new one and hammered it to the glider. The chair could now be rocked without wobbling. Charlotte, wearing one of the enlarged dresses William had bought in Fort John, often sat on the porch as the sun was going down, until the stinging flies drove her into the wagon.

William was sitting in the yard of the barn, working at the sharpening stone which he'd brought out, for he needed more light than provided in the barn, and he enjoyed the heat of the day. Sitting on the stool, his legs working the pedal, William was honing the plow. He looked up and saw Joseph coming toward him, but continued his work.

"What you doing, Mister William?" Joseph scuffed the toe of one boot in the dust, looking curious. William knew he'd been practicing his Jew's harp, for his lips were red and slightly swollen. William had heard the sound but ignored it.

"I'm sharpening the plow so George can get started on the garden plot yonder. Didn't your father have a sharpening stone when you lived in Illinois?" William slowed the pedal and turned the plow to the other side for a more even edge.

"Don't know. I was only little then." The boy wrinkled his brow in thought.

William ran his finger cautiously along the blade to see if it was sharp enough. "Come here, Joseph, take your thumb and very slowly run it over the blade. Careful now, it's very sharp." Joseph moved forward, reached out his thumb and ran it over the blade edge.

Startled, he yelped and drew back. William chuckled and said, "Sharp?"

"You teased me. I never thought you could tease like George."

William rose from the stool, and laid the plow carefully on the ground. "Come around here, Joseph, and sit down." The boy sat, although his legs didn't quite reach the turning pedal. "Scoot forward." And William helped him move the stool closer so his legs could reach the pedal. "Now push with your right leg and then with your left." It took several tries before Joseph was able to get the stone moving. "Now, take your hand and feel the stone while it's moving. See how rough it is? That's what sharpens the blade, the friction of the rough stone against the metal of the blade. Do you have your knife with you?" Nodding, the boy jumped off the stool and took the scabbard out of his pocket, holding his most prized possession, and handed it to William.

"Sit back down." And the boy sat. William handed him the knife and told him to hold the sharp side close to the grinding stone. Joseph carefully held the small knife in his hands while he pedaled hard with his feet. The stone began to move, and the knife vibrated in Joseph's hands as the stone rubbed against it. William only let him work a minute, for he didn't want the knife so sharp that it would hurt the lad. "Stop!"

Joseph stopped and looked at his knife, running the ball of his thumb slowly over the blade. "It's sharper, now."

"How old are you, Joseph?" The boy looked at him, puzzled.

"Twelve, Mister William. Don't you remember yesterday was my birthday?"

"Then, don't you think that you're old enough to call me William without the mister?"

William walked away from the sharpening stone and toward the water trough. Picking up the half-filled water barrel that had been placed there after being taken from the wagon, he planted his legs apart to give himself balance, then picked it up in his strong arms. Holding it close to the rim of the trough, he poured the water into the wooden vessel. His arm muscles protruded below the sleeves he had rolled above the elbows to keep them away from the stone. He put the empty barrel back on the ground.

"Papa said a boy shouldn't call a grown man by his first name without mister in front of it." Joseph took a defensive position in front of the tall man.

William cursed under his breath, not for the first time, at the way James Morgan had treated his children. But, he guessed he was right this time, for even though he himself had called grown men by their surname, men he'd worked with side by side in the mine shafts, it wasn't polite for a young person to call a much older one by his given name.

He pondered the difference in the boy's life and his. He'd done a man's job long before he was the age of Joseph.

"That's fine, Joseph, for a lad of eleven years, but I think you're old enough at twelve to call me William, since I'm your brother." William looked toward the house, where Charlotte was organizing her new kitchen. She'd asked him to accept Joseph as his son, but his son was dead in Virginia. He quickly turned away from the painful thought.

"You're not my brother!" Joseph said scornfully, and his chin stood out in challenge.

"Yes, I'm your brother since I married your sister. That makes us kin." He waited patiently while Joseph worked it out in his mind.

"You're my brother because you married my sister? Nobody told you to marry my sister! We was getting along fine without you. She worked for Miss Bertha, and I worked at the saw mill."

William winced; alarmed at the way the conversation had turned against him. Stooping, he picked up the barrel and carried it to the farm wagon, lifted it, and placed it inside ready to be taken to the river. Without turning to look at the boy, he said, "It's time I got back to my chores." He walked to the corral to see about his animals.

*****

Charlotte was sitting in a chair with the pink material that Bertha had given her. She made a few tiny stitches, while she thought of the lovely christening gown and the baby shoes that William had bought, and she began to dream of the little one inside her. Growing drowsy, she was startled awake by the slam of the door.

Joseph ran into the house, quickly found Charlotte sitting near the fireplace sewing and went to her, a belligerent look on his face. She gazed at her brother. She was so proud of him. He'd worked hard the last few days, helping the men, but she wanted him to have some free time to play while he was still a child.

"Is Mister William my brother?" Joseph angrily spread his legs, and planted his hands on his hips as though ready to defend his honor.

"Why, yes, Joseph, I thought you knew that when I married William, that made him your brother, since I'm your sister. Didn't Papa tell you that?"

"No, Papa never said, and you didn't tell me. He said I can call him William now without the mister in front, since I'm twelve and I'm his brother." Joseph relaxed his stance, but he didn't let go of the subject. "I don't want him for my brother. I want George to be my brother. How come you didn't marry George?"

Charlotte was surprised at this information and tried not to laugh. She didn't want Joseph to know that she would much prefer the strong, sensible man she had married rather than the immature George. Even with the marriage happening the way it did, Charlotte had come to love William and was happy she was carrying his child. But, he doesn't love you, some little imp of mischief tried to say in her head. She swatted the imp away and realized that Joseph had backed up, thinking she meant to strike him.

She gestured for him to come closer and took his hand. "Sweetheart, I didn't know George until the day we left St. Louis, and I was already married to William by then. I should think it's a great honor to call William by his name. And I don't think George will mind if you call him by his name, now that you're a grown up twelve, instead of eleven. But, you should ask him if it's all right with him. He's just the hired man, so he might not like for you to call him that."

Charlotte knew she'd made a mistake as soon as she uttered the words, for Joseph took on a defensive look and stiffened.

"He's not a hired man; he's my friend. We had hired men in Illinois, but I wasn't allowed to play with them." He snorted, and without another word to his sister, Joseph grabbed his rope from where he'd tossed it in his rush to confront his sister, and raced out the door.

*****

Joseph uncoiled his rope and let it fly over his favorite tree stump. He walked over to where he saw his friend. George picked up the hammer and nail can he'd been using to repair a board on the barn wall and put them inside the shelter.

Joseph kicked up some dust, unsure what to say. George was his friend, but Joseph wasn't allowed to be friends with hired men.

"Hello, Joseph; how's your roping arm doing? Caught any cows yet?" George often teased Joseph about roping the pony or his prowess as a fisherman.

Joseph looked at George. He'd forgotten the rope in his hands. He grinned. "Ain't no cows here to catch." He stopped talking, for now he didn't know what to call his friend. Then he blurted it out as though he needed to get it all in one big gulp. "Mister William said I'm to call him by his first name, 'cause I'm his brother now he's married my sister and I'm twelve. Sister said I could call you George if you don't care, so can I, Mister George, can I?"

"I'd be honored if you called me George. I been thinking about it a while, but decided it wouldn't be right you calling me George, when you call your own brother Mister William, now would it? Twelve is a fine age, and you're not a boy anymore, but you're not a full grown man either. Why, any day now, your voice is going to come out in a squeak something awful, and you'll be embarrassed, but it's just your throat getting used to speaking like this." And George lowered his own voice an octave, to show Joseph how he would sound as an adult. He had a smile on his face.

Here was something else that Joseph had never considered, that he might someday sound like his new brother and his friend George, but he was pleased at the thought. He tried an experimental lower range and surprised himself how low his voice could go

George went to the plow that William had left lying in the dust beside the sharpening stone. He ran the ball of his thumb over the edge, then gazed toward the garden spot. Leaving the plow by the barn, he walked to where William was grooming Star, one of his oxen.

Joseph followed him, experimenting with his voice, wondering if the sharp edge had felt as rough on George's finger as it had on his.

"Guess it's time we get to that garden plot. I figure if we plow now, we might get a few crops before winter sets in, but you're the farmer, what do you think?" William glanced at Joseph, and he nodded at him, before looking back to George.

"I was thinking the same thing, Mr. Butler. I found some wheat seeds in a can in the barn, but it'd be better if we get some potatoes and turnips before we start on the wheat. I don't know whether they'll grow in the fall season, but I suppose it's worth a try."

"You'd know better than me, but I heard that some Germans back in Virginia plant their wheat in the fall and let it set during the winter, and come the spring, it's nice and green."

"I've heard that, too. But I don't know about the higher elevation. I suppose we could try it since these seeds seemed to be an added bonus like. If it don't work, we still have the seed you brought from St. Louis. Which team do you want me to use today?"

"Take Atlas and Juno, they haven't been used for the plow. See how they work together."

"Can I go?" Joseph didn't know much about plowing, but he wanted to spend the day with George.

"Not today, boy." George reached for the lead rope of the two oxen standing near the water trough and attached the plow to the yoke with a chain. Telling Joseph good-bye, he headed toward the garden plot.

William watched him go, and turned to Joseph. "How about you and me going into the house for a spell? Reckon Charlotte could find us some of that left over cornbread from last night?" And, looking into the distance where George was now tramping in the high weeds behind the oxen, he sighed. "Sure wish we had a cow and some chickens."

Joseph thought of George leaving, and William offering him a spell of his time. He grinned, the idea of food appealing to him.

After their short meal of cornbread and coffee, strong for William, very weak for Joseph, William told Charlotte that Joseph would be with him, so she wouldn't worry, and he picked up his rifle and left, with Joseph at his side. Together they hitched Brownie and Jezebel to the smaller farm wagon, and went to the river to fill the water barrel they had emptied for the animals.

Joseph couldn't wipe the smile off his face. He wasn't disappointed at all.

26

Coming back on the river trail, William was surprised to see an old man he didn't recognize walking his horse slowly from the opposite direction. The man rode up, and William stopped his animals. He glanced over at the rifle in the wagon at Joseph's feet, ready for trouble.

"Ahloo, my friend, I'm your neighbor." He pointed toward the northwest. "Got back yesterday from the fort, and Pedigrew said some people had moved onto the old Cummings place. Always thought it a shame the way Ralph Cummings rode off and left the place to run down. Name's Julius Caesar Robertson, but most folks call me Jules. You can, too, if you've a mind to."

William looked closely at the man on horseback; he seemed friendly enough, but he was cautious from experience. They were too far separated to shake hands with the stranger on horseback, and William walking beside the nigh ox. Joseph sat silently on the seat of the wagon.

"I'm William Butler, and this is my brother-in-law, Joseph Morgan. I was on my way up to the house. Why don't you come along, and I'll introduce you to my wife?" And he started the oxen on the trail to the house.

Stopping the animals near the front porch, William went around the wagon and helped Joseph down. He fastened the lead rope to the porch column and patted Brownie on the shoulder to keep him calm. They dropped their heads as far as allowed by the heavy yoke and started to graze. Casually taking his rifle from the wagon, he turned to the stranger, who had followed him. "Come inside and meet my wife," and held open the door.

"Charlotte, we have neighbors," William called out from the door.

She turned from the fireplace where she was stirring a pot of soup. Leaving her soup, she walked toward the men. Joseph stood near William, his gaze never leaving the stranger. Charlotte moved closer to the man, smiling shyly.

"Dear, this is Mr. Julius Caesar Robertson, come for a visit." He removed his hat and placed it on the peg by the front door. He took Joseph's hat and placed it beside his own.

"Pleased to meet you, sir. Won't you come in, and I'll put on a pot of coffee."

"No, no, water will do, thank you kindly, ma'am. Coffee in the middle of a hot day makes a man sleepy."

The old man was dressed in dirty tan buckskin with the remnants of what looked like a red plaid shirt hanging out under the top part. There were perspiration stains under the arms and down the center of his back. He had on Indian moccasins rather than store bought boots like most men wore. His face was deeply brown and wrinkled, like a puckered, overly ripe apple. There was the smell of stale tobacco and something else that William couldn't define.

"Pardon me, then." She took the gourd dipper and put some cool water into a coffee cup and took it to Robertson, then turned away to start peeling potatoes for supper. Joseph joined her, taking out his knife and helping. She gently reminded him not to cut so deeply. He gave her a sheepish grin and continued what he was doing.

William guided his guest to the other end of the room and offered him the rocking chair while he sat on the end of the sofa. "How long you been on the Laramie, Mr. Robertson?" He was glad to know that they had a neighbor, but didn't completely trust the man, not like Pedigrew whom he had liked at first meeting.

"About eight years, give or take a few months." Robertson took the question literally. "Come out from St. Louy with some fur trappers in '36, tried it 'bout a year, and decided I liked farming better; built me a cabin north of here, and went back East for the missus and chil'uns."

Near the fireplace, Joseph and Charlotte exchanged a glance. She shook her head and cut away another curl of potato skin.

"Then you must have known Ralph Cummings, the previous owner of this place." William hoped to find more information on the type of fever that had killed the woman.

"Nay, cain't say I knew him; kept to hisself. My wife came over a few times to visit with the woman, but she didn't feel welcome. Poor woman was sickly, didn't have no young'uns."

William decided to change the subject. "My friend George who works here said that he wanted to try planting some wheat seed this fall. You think that might be a good idea? He's out in the garden patch plowing now. You might have seen him when you rode into the yard. He thought we might get in a small crop of vegetables before the cold weather hits." He looked inquiringly at Robertson.

"That's wise thinking, Butler. Only June; should be able to get some carrots and squash; 'taters might grow, but cabbage and onions, best left to the early spring, February mebbe. Wouldn't hurt to try corn, beans, peas, or okra, though, might come up before winter. I've done a little 'sperimentin' myself; some things just don't take to the cold nights." He cleared his throat and looked at the floor. "Reason I came over to see you though, Pedigrew said you come out from St. Louy on the wagon train last week. He said you don't have no cow or chickens or pigs. And, I got a letter for you came with a party from Fort Leavenworth the day after you left, Pedigrew said. And, a parcel."

He took a wrinkled, water-speckled paper from his pocket, and from inside his buckskin vest came a brown, wrapped parcel about the size of a small book. Joseph ran over from the kitchen area to give them to Charlotte. She held the letter to her breast, then put it in her apron pocket for later when Robertson had gone. The parcel she opened with a kitchen knife. Inside the wrapper was a selection of various seed packets, and she saved them for George.

Robertson looked around the room, taking in the woman and boy at the table. He sat back in the chair, crushing his hat, as though embarrassed. "Thought you might like to buy some of them critters. I got plenty. Or, if you've a mind to trade, my wife sure has had a hankering for some sweet fruit pies. Cain't hardly get dried fruit around these parts, unless a wagon train comes out from the east. Tried planting some peach trees from the seed, but didn't do well; died the first winter. Sometimes a trader comes up from Santa Fe, with some oranges or lemons from Californy, but that's a long way off." He gazed expectantly at William.

"Why, that wouldn't be a hardship; we've a little dried apples and a few fresh ones left. There's another train behind us, should be here in another week. A fellow by the name of Johannsson's leading the train. It's been dogging our tracks all the way from Missouri." William turned to call out to Charlotte. "We've got a few apples we can let Mrs. Robertson have, don't we, dear?" William was quite aware that if they gave some of their precious fruit away, they would run out, too, but he figured it would be worth a few pies for the goodwill alone. If Robertson had a cow, chickens and pigs, then that was to their good luck, although he would offer to pay for those.

Charlotte called out in the affirmative, and William turned back to Robertson. "As for the animals, I'll pay a fair price, for I was just telling my boy there, that I sure would like to have fresh milk, butter and eggs again. We ran out before we reached Fort Leavenworth."

By the time the visit was over, Charlotte had handed over some of her dried apples, enough for one pie, and four shiny red apples from the barrel in the root cellar, but she refused to give out any more, no matter what William said. Robertson thanked Charlotte and promised to bring the wife and children with him next time he came. He gave William directions to his place, and left on his horse.

Joseph watched him go and started throwing a loop around the rotting stump. After a while he tired of the game, and sat down near the stump. He took out his knife from its scabbard and began to carve his initials, J M. The M came out all right, but the J was crooked, for it was hard to form a half circle with a knife. William remarked positively on it and stepped back into the house.

Charlotte was displeased. "Honey, I wish you weren't so generous with the dried fruit; I like sweet pies, too." She sighed.

William grinned sheepishly, "I'm sorry, dear. I figure it's a fair trade, some fruit for the chance for fresh milk and eggs." He poured some water into a cup and sat at the table. He took several sips and absentmindedly reached under the cover of a basket for a biscuit. "Robertson reminded me how much the people of the territory need a good freight service. If I can see Pedigrew next week when the new trains from St. Louis come in, I'll ask him about the best routes and weather patterns. He's bound to have that information from the trappers that bring him furs. Maybe I can also meet one of the trappers." He became silent as he gazed off into space.

William was distracted from his dreams when he heard Charlotte call out, "William, I have a letter from Bertha." She held it in the air, so he could see it. She started reading, sometimes stumbling over Bertha's tiny squall.

"I've heard from Sarah Warren, and she seems happy with her traveling salesman from Baltimore," Charlotte recited. "They've gone to New Orleans on a steamer out of St. Louis. Poor Margaret is grieving something awful for her sister. Clayborne had a bad spell with his lungs, and coughed for a week. The doctor says he needs to go to a dryer climate, but how can we do that and leave our major source of income behind? Do you recall that drummer named Hammond, the one who sold seeds? He's come by, and Clayborne bought a number of seed packets to send to you. They should be on the government train, for I've sent them by the hand of the army to be taken to Fort John, if you are still there. And, finally, Gladys and I send our love and affection. We surely miss your smiling face of a morning. Best wishes: Bertha Hightower."

They went over the letter several times before Charlotte reluctantly finished the preparations for the evening meal, and William went outside to talk to George.

*****

Shortly after dawn, while William was preparing for his visit to the Robertson farm, George went into the barn, lit the lantern and brought out a piece or two at a time of what he thought he would need of the cut lumber and stacked it neatly near the shed in which the proud Conestoga stood. With his hammer and nails, he proceeded to build chicken coops and a fenced area for the pigs.

The rain had cooled the air, and Charlotte insisted that Joseph wear a sweater, although he protested loudly that one wasn't needed. William chained a yoke of oxen to the smaller farm wagon, and with his brother-in-law sitting on the seat in his hated sweater, they started northwesterly in the direction that Jules indicated that his farm lay. He took some of the money he had secreted before they left St. Louis to pay for the animals.

Several hours later, William and Joseph returned from the visit at the Robertson farm with news and a wagon full of noisy animals: oinking pigs, clucking chickens, and strutting behind was a jersey cow, udders drooping with milk. Joseph found that the Robertson

187

children were older than he was. He expressed his disappointment that they wouldn't become playmates. The Robertson family promised William that if needed, they'd come to help with the planting in the spring or the harvest come fall, if he would likewise help when it was needed at their place.

George hadn't finished the chicken coops, so the fowl were left to cluck and peck at the ground in search of seeds or berries. There was a magnificently colored Rhode Island Red rooster, with his reddish brown beak, yellow feet, and startling red comb, with a harem of five hens. William gave Charlotte a sorrowful look when she first saw them, thinking she would feel he was mocking her, but they decided it was coincidence that Robertson had the same birds for which the saloon had been named. Two small pigs, one male and one female, promised the start of a long line of hams and sausage meals. Robertson swore they would breed well.

William was pleased to tell Charlotte that although it was small and primitive, the Robertson home was clean and the beds neatly made. There was a wood-burning kitchen stove similar to the one in the Hightower's kitchen but smaller and compact. There were only two burners, an oven, and no hot water well. Robertson had had it shipped by special freight from Santa Fe. Charlotte greeted this news with gladness, remarking that if one could be brought over the mountains and plains, than maybe someday when William had his freight business started, another could find a home in her kitchen.

She wore her new pink dress and the pink ribbon from Bertha in her hair. She had wanted to surprise William and Joseph, so had put on a large pot of beef stew and mixed a batch of dough for bread, then worked to finish her pink dress to wear at dinner. William was pleased to hear of it, telling her he was genuinely surprised, and the dress was beautiful.

For William, the moment was much more. He looked at Charlotte in surprise, for he hadn't anticipated a celebration on his return. The pink of the dress was reflected in her cheeks, and for the first time, he saw the real beauty in his wife's face. It awoke a desire in his heart for her that he hadn't known was possible, and the memories of his Martha began to fade into the past.

Charlotte mentioned that the green meadow reminded her of a painting that had hung in her Grandfather Prescott's home. She said they should call the place Green Meadow Farm. She laughed and said it was only temporary until she thought of something better.

George found a flat, square board in the pile of lumber in the barn. He smoothed and rounded the ends of the board and took some black paint and painted Green Meadow Farm on the board. With William's approval, he hammered it on the fence near the entrance to the place, and the name stuck. Whenever anyone at Fort John or those few settlers on the high plains and in the mountains spoke of the Butler place, it was always Butler's Green Meadow Farm. The name of Cummings was no longer mentioned.

27

George waited one Saturday until William came out of the barn from cleaning the stables and tossing fresh grass to the cow and horses. He'd spent all day yesterday using the scythe to cut the tall grass in the area behind the barn. The smell of fresh cut hay lingered in the air for days.

"Hello, George, you get the peas and squash planted?" William rubbed his shoulder, stretching his arm out and swinging it around in a circle a couple of times. "It sure is different, this farming business, from walking slowly behind a yoke of oxen. Got a sore shoulder from using this thing."

"I learned that as a boy. I got everything planted, what few seeds we had; maybe Hammond will send more." George looked down at his feet, then raised his eyes and looked at William. "Ah, Mr. Butler, I been thinking since I done finished with the plowing and planting, if you don't mind, I'd like to spend some time in Fort John. Met a couple of fellows there last time and would like to see them again, if they're still around. I'll bring back any supplies you need."

William stopped swinging his arm and looked up at the plowed and planted wheat field; he nodded as if pleased at what he saw. "You go ahead, spend the night if you want. There's nothing around here that won't wait a day or two longer. Don't forget your rifle."

George felt a wave of relief, gave his boss a big grin, shook his hand, and went to saddle his horse. In a moment, he'd gathered what he needed and flew up the trail at a gallop.

Upon arriving at the fort, he noticed a wagon train had arrived. All around were strangers passing by as they shopped for goods or tried to unload things they had packed, but now couldn't see the need of. He loitered near the office of the fur company manager, wondering if the trappers might be in the bar, when he saw Pedigrew come out the door and hook his finger at him. He looked around, for he couldn't think why the man wanted to speak to him. Pedigrew wagged his finger again, so George mounted the steps to the office and followed him inside. Over by the stack of furs was a man dressed like an experienced Mountain Man. He was fingering the furs and mumbling under his breath. Near the counter was an Indian wrapped in a smelly blanket and smoking a pipe.

Pedigrew drew George aside near the door so he couldn't be heard by the other men. "Remmington, how things going upriver?" Before he could answer the question, Pedigrew continued, "Been meanin' to drop by, but t'ain't had time, what with them pioneers comin' in one after t'other. Getting so late in the season t'wern't expecting a fourth train. That man over thar, he been living a mite west since before this cabin got built, and he got the hankerin' to talk to a man who lives a mite closer than the fort. You think about chattin' to the fellow, find out what his problem might be. If'n you please, I got a couple letters for Missus Butler. 'T'ain't nobody else's bid'ness, so I'ds sooner place 'em in your'n hand." He walked to the man fingering the furs and pointed at George. The man turned and walked to the door. Grabbing him by the shirt sleeve, he led George onto the porch. He turned to look out at the settlers mingling around and back to George.

"You, monsieur, you live here permanent? American?" The man had a heavy half French-half English speech pattern that was hard for George to understand, but he didn't have time to consider it, for when he nodded, the man kept talking. "My name's Otto Thibodeau, came in yesterday with the wagons; left my partner back in the hills of Tennessee; he wanted to see his ma, but me, I don't like civilization much. I'm headed back to the high mountains spite of the fact the beaver trade's running out."

Thibodeau lowered his voice as though someone might hear what he had to say. George didn't see anyone nearby.

"They's a couple of pilgrims come on the train, but should'a stayed where they was. Man was a shepherd, had a flock of sheep, and the other men didn't like that much, for he had a Basque shepherd boy with him, what don't speak no English. The man died a few weeks back, and the people are all upset and don't want the woman to go with them, her being alone, 'cept for the boy. Be a burden on them to take care of her." The trapper looked toward the Indian encampments and the wagons standing some distance away before going on. "I thinks to myself, if there be a farmer hereabouts that would take the woman in and care for her, he could have her sheep as payment." He looked closely at George with his midnight black eyes.

George gazed back at him, puzzled. "I don't own the farm," he denied. "I just work for Mr. Butler; can't take care of no widow woman and her boy. Best to send the woman on her way with the others on the wagon."

"They don't want them. I'm thinking they'll wait 'til some dark night and rid themselves of the woman and boy, and keep the sheep for themselves."

George was horrified. Following behind the fur trapper, he moved out of the walls of the fort and to an area near the river where several wagons were parked. Thibodeau pointed to a small flock of sheep being guarded by a dark-skinned boy in a blanket wearing a battered felt hat on his head. He saw a shaggy, long-haired dog moving among the sheep. The wagon nearby was small, similar in shape and size to the wagon that he and William had found at the Cummings farm when they arrived.

Thibodeau halloed the wagon, and a female face peered out through the edge of the canvas top. He said something to her in rapid-fire French, and handed her down from the wagon. George's first impression of Mrs. Jemima Boudreau was of a tiny woman of about sixty years, with a pockmarked face and strong character. She came forward and shook hands with George after a few more words with Thibodeau. Then, in a clear bell-like tone in perfect English she said, "Mr. Thibodeau said you might provide a home for me."

George mumbled, thinking he'd said nothing of the sort, had just volunteered to talk to the woman. Before he quite knew what was happening, he was shown into the wagon and told about her possessions, taken to the flock and introduced to the boy, who shook hands with him in the same way that Joseph had that first time they met, showing half respect, half fear in his eyes. George looked around and found that Thibodeau had disappeared. Thoroughly befuddled, it seemed that he had acquired the responsibility for one middle-aged woman, one foreign boy who could speak no English, a shaggy sheep dog, and about a dozen sheep, both male and female

George tried to explain in his stammering way, "I don't own the farm, ma'am, I'm only a hired man, and I don't think Mr. Butler the owner would want any sheep." But, he got nowhere.

She looked at him out of soulful, dark eyes, "You look like an honest man of good character. Give me an hour to straighten the wagon and come back. I'll be ready for you."

It looked like the Mountain Man and the woman had settled it between themselves, and he was trapped. George walked to the fort and looked for Thibodeau. He couldn't be found, so he retrieved the horse and the canvas bags of supplies tied across the saddle, the two letters for Charlotte that Pedigrew had mentioned and rode back to the wagon.

The woman was waiting, with a large brimmed man's hat over which she had tied a dark blue checkered bandanna. It covered her hair completely. In spite of the heat of the day, she wore a wool sweater over her dress and brown high buttoned shoes, revealed at the hem of her skirt as she prepared to step up.

George, embarrassed and worried, handed the woman onto the passenger side of the wagon, tied the saddle horse onto the back, gestured for the boy to follow him, and climbed into the driver's place. He loosened the reins, and the four mules stepped out lively. As though in a trance, George saw himself back on the banks of the Mississippi River starting out with the Morgan wagon. The only difference he could see was these were mules instead of horses, and a widow woman instead of Joseph Morgan.

The woman spoke little on the way to the Green Meadow farm. George was grateful, for he spent most of the time thinking how he would explain to William how he'd gotten himself into this predicament, and the rest of the time thinking what he would do if his employer told him to leave the farm. About halfway there, he pulled on the reins to slow the mules.

Jemima looked around. "Why are we stopping?"

"Ma'am, can hardly see them sheep back there. Think we ought to slow for the boy?"

She leaned around the corner of the wagon. "Might better," she said in her dignified way. "Have you lived here long?"

"About a month, ma'am, came with a wagon train from St. Louis. Drove a wagon for Morgan. Work for Butler, now."

"Is the place much farther down the road?"

"Straight there and over the distant rise." He peered at her to see if he could get a measure of her intentions.

"No roads turning off?" She pinched her lips.

"No, ma'am, just Butler's place." They could hear the sound of a dog barking.

"Move on. The boy'll find us. He knows his way around a piece of land as well as any man." She nodded her head, and he released the mules to continue the journey.

The wagon topped the ridge and moved slowly down the slope that led to the house and barn.

*****

William looked up when he saw a wagon coming toward the house. His mouth dropped open when he recognized George with a woman seated beside him on the wagon, followed by a nice size flock of sheep, a boy of about Joseph's age and a dog, nipping at the heels of the sheep if they dared to stray.

He grabbed for his shirt where he'd hung it on one of the upturned logs. Wrapping it around his body and buttoning the front, he saw Joseph come out the front door, a look of wonder on his face. Charlotte followed him out, for she must have heard the wagon approaching the house. They stared as George brought the wagon to a halt a few yards from the porch.

He tied the reins of the mules to the side of the seat, then dropped down and went around the back of the wagon, reached up his hand, and half lifted his passenger from the wagon seat. The woman was barely five feet tall, and William and Joseph towered over her like giants in a fairy tale. She moved forward with grace and dignity, her hand outstretched in greeting.

"How do you do, Mr. Butler, for that must be who you are. I'm so pleased to meet you. I introduce myself as Mrs. Jemima Boudreau. I do thank you for offering your home to a wayward stray and her chattel. And, you, ma'am," she turned to Charlotte without calling her name, "it will be my pleasure to assist you in your endeavors to make a home in this wilderness."

Not only had William never heard such fancy talk from a woman, but he hardly understood it. He stared at George, who ran a finger around the collar of his shirt, and looked straight into the eyes of his employer, his back stiff, then lowered his hands to his sides. William had seen that defensive stance once before.

Charlotte invited Jemima Boudreau into her home and offered a cup of tea, asking her to call her Charlotte.

Joseph burst out, "Can I go see the sheep? That's a fine dog; can I go play with him, William?"

William responded, "Wait, Joseph. George, an explanation, please." He glanced at the boy, to see him standing, a look of amazement on his face. William drew himself up to his full height, which was considerable, indeed, and glanced at the mules and wagon, then to the sheep which the boy had allowed to scatter over the green grass of the meadow, the dog keeping them in a narrow circle. They dropped their heads in the grass and began to munch. It seemed it mattered not to the sheep from whence the grass grew; only its wonderful taste. The boy took a large cloth from a bag he had strapped to his back and spread it on the ground, prepared to stay a while.

"It's like this, Mr. Butler. I was standing around the office of Mr. Pedigrew when he come out onto the porch and gestured that he wanted to speak to me. So I went in the building and there was a man, a Frenchy, I think, from the way he talked, name of Thibodeau."

"Thibodeau, you say?" William felt his excitement rise. "But, he's the fellow with Elijah Perkins that persuaded James Morgan to come out west. You say that Otto Thibodeau is at Fort John? Was Perkins with him, too?"

"I don't know, didn't see him. This Mr. Thibodeau, he started to—"

Again, William interrupted him. "I sure would like to see the man. Was he alone then, you think?"

"No, he came in with a wagon train, arrived yesterday. A whole passel of people were milling about the fort, like it was the same day we came."

William was no longer listening. With giant steps he went through the open door of the house and found Charlotte sitting across the table from the strange woman. He glanced at the women for a moment and made up his mind.

"Charlotte, dear, make our visitors welcome to spend the night. She can take Joseph's room and he can sleep on the floor over yonder." He pointed to the living area. "I must go to the fort. George says that Otto Thibodeau came in yesterday with the wagon train. You remember he and Perkins were the ones who persuaded your father to travel to Oregon. George doesn't think that Perkins came with the group." He looked toward the woman for confirmation, but she was gawking at him with startled surprise. "It may be my only chance to talk with the fellow, and he can give me valuable information on trade routes. I'll try to be back tonight. If it gets too late, don't worry, but entertain our guests as you would if they were in the hotel."

William went into the bedroom, collected what he would need for the trip, came out and took his rifle from the shelf. Charlotte stood and began to gather some food and a glass jar with water for him to take. He kissed her on the cheek, acknowledged the presence of the other woman with a tip of his hat, and he was out the door, leaving two very confused women behind.

*****

Already anticipating the trip, George went to the barn to saddle William's horse. Joseph was asking questions which he didn't have time to answer. Leading the saddle horse to the front of the house, George waited for William to emerge from the door.

"Ah, Mr. Butler, what am I to do with the woman and the boy?" He needed time to get around this new situation.

"William, can I go with you to the fort?" Joseph spoke at the same time.

"No, Joseph, I'm in a hurry, maybe next time. George, unhitch the wagon and release the mules into the corral with the horses, if you think that's wise. Charlotte will see to the woman." Then, with a stern look, he finished. "I'll expect a full explanation of how this came about when I return. But, I must take this chance to speak with Thibodeau, if he expects to continue with the wagons on their journey to Oregon tomorrow." He loosed the reins, kicked his horse gently in the flanks, turned and was gone.

George watched his employer ride away, the lump still lodged in his throat. He started to unhitch the wagon as instructed when he suddenly remembered the two letters he had collected from Pedigrew. He climbed the steps of the cabin and knocked on the door. As he spoke to Charlotte, he could see the woman sitting at the kitchen table, her hat and sweater removed.

196

"Ah, Mrs. Butler, I'm sorry things have turned out like this. I didn't mean for this to happen, but if you would be so kind as to take care of Mrs. Boudreau, I'd thank you kindly. Here's two letters Pedigrew held for you; come in on yesterday's train." Feeling completely overwhelmed with the day's events, he stuttered, "I gotta unhitch the team of mules."

He handed her the letters, and Charlotte put them in her apron pocket. She prepared to close the door when he stopped her, and he shuffled his feet, again ill at ease.

"Pardon me, Mrs. Butler, but there's one more matter. Where you want me to put the lady's things?"

*****

"Things, what things?" Charlotte indicated for George to step back, and she closed the door as much as she could so Mrs. Boudreau couldn't hear them discussing her.

"Mr. Butler said I was to unhitch the mules, but he didn't say what I was to do with the things. And, he said you'd take care of the lady, but I feel something awful that I done put that burden on you. I can drive her back to the fort if you want me to take her off your place."

"I don't know what to do except to bring the lady's things in here. There's plenty of space in the front room until we decide what to do. Just bring them in and stack them here next to the wall between the root cellar and the bedroom. William said to let her have Joseph's room, so leave a place for him to sleep, or I suppose he could sleep on the sofa, but I never could get all the dust out, and he may be sneezing all night. I gotta get back, or she'll think we're talking about her." And, she shut the door in his face.

Turning to her unwelcome guest, Charlotte explained about the outside toilet, and that her husband said for her to use her brother's room for the present until he came back from Fort John. She walked with her natural grace to the bedroom door and pulled up the dark blue curtain for Mrs. Boudreau to pass, then led the way to the lean to shed. She apologized for her brother's clothes which were lying on the bed. She quickly grabbed them up and snatched his coat and sweater from the wall pegs. Holding her brother's possessions in her arms, including his rope and Jew's harp, she promised to bring her some fresh water for the pitcher and looked under the table to make

197

sure Joseph had emptied his chamber pot that morning.

Charlotte was abashed at the way George had brought a stranger into her home, and her husband was even worse because he'd ridden away without a thought to her predicament. Oh, that dratted man. Sometimes, she would love to let loose her temper on him. Leaving Mrs. Boudreau in the room, her last thought was surprisingly that the lady could stand up straight in the room, and no one else, including herself, could do that. She took Joseph's things and dumped them on the sofa to be put away somewhere later. Finding a clean cloth, she draped it over her shoulder, went to the fireplace and poured hot water from a kettle into a large baked clay bowl. Wrapping it in a soft cloth to protect her hands, she carefully carried it through the bedroom that she shared with William and knocked on the side wall beside the cloth door. Mrs. Boudreau pulled aside the gray blanket, and seeing Charlotte, exclaimed at the luxury of hot water.

"Thank you, Mrs. Butler, you are so kind." Jemima took the bowl still wrapped in the cloth, and looked for someplace to set it. She found a space on the table, and while holding the bowl securely in one hand, moved aside what looked to be fish hooks and set the bowl on the edge near the lamp. She turned to Charlotte, hovering at the door with the raised blanket in her hand.

Charlotte handed her the clean cloth she had draped across her shoulder and a fresh bar of lye soap. "If you want anything, ma'am, let me know." She turned to leave the room, letting the blanket fall.

Before Charlotte was out of the bedroom, Jemima pulled the blanket aside and called to her, giving her hostess an inquiring look. "Thank you. I see you're with child. When is the happy event to take place, if I'm not too bold to ask? I have acted as midwife many times, and have knowledge of herbs and roots used for medicinal purposes. I would be pleased to assist you if you feel I might be useful."

"November, ma'am, after harvest time." Charlotte's heart sank. "That would be a comfort, ma'am; thank you." Again, Charlotte started to leave, but the midwife wasn't finished.

"Mrs. Butler, would you ask Mr. Remmington if he would tell my boy, Pedro, to attend me here. I have some instructions to impart to him." Without waiting to see if Charlotte would obey, Jemima turned and placed the clean cloth and soap on the cot, in preparation for later use. The blanket door fell behind her.

Charlotte went to the door and called for George. He put down the box he was holding and walked up the steps. "George, Mrs. Boudreau has asked for her shepherd boy to come here. She wants to talk to him. Would you mind fetching him? Thank you." Charlotte shut the door.

She went to the kitchen, cleaned and put away the tea cups. She sat down on one of the ladder back chairs and dropped her head in her arms. She felt the baby kick inside her womb and rubbed her stomach. There was a crackle of paper, and she remembered the letters she'd been given. She took them out and tore them open. One was from her father at Fort Hall, the other from Jasper Smith.

She read the one from Jasper first. He asked his brother Abraham to write it for him because he wanted to get the right words down. He thanked Joseph for the letter and told him that dogs weren't always safe from wild creatures; he knew that because some of the horses that came to the stable had been bitten by snakes or wolves. His father was well, and the livery was doing good. Abraham was going far away to a school in the East in the fall, and he would miss him. Miss Bertha came to see him when she got Miss Charlotte's letter about the death of the dog. She gave him some hot doughnuts, and they tasted good. Would Joseph write him again? Your friend: Jasper Smith.

The letter from her father was shorter, just a note to tell her that he had arrived at Fort Hall with the train, and the new driver Lt. Jack Taylor was working out well with the mules. Your loving father: James Morgan.

It wasn't much comfort, but he'd kept his promise to write, so she would settle for that. She went to the door to see where Joseph had disappeared and found him helping unload the wagon. She decided her news could wait and put the letters back in her pocket. She paused in the entrance to the house and looked out over the length of green meadow from which the farm had derived its name. Some of the grass was beginning to turn brown in patches with the lack of rain and the changing seasons. Scattered across the grass were about a dozen sheep, grazing peacefully. It somehow was comforting to have them there, like the bucolic scene in a painting she had seen as a small child in her grandfather Prescott's home in Illinois. She wondered fleetingly what had happened to the picture.

The shepherd boy was walking into the yard with George, trying to keep pace with the man's long stride. George had a frown on his face, but he didn't say anything. He motioned for the boy to see Charlotte, and went back to the box he'd dropped on the porch.

Charlotte smiled at the boy and held the door for him to come inside. She shut the door to keep out the annoying insects. She turned, and Jemima was just coming from the bedrooms.

Jemima said something to the boy in his native language, and they moved to the sofa and sat down. Jemima glanced at Charlotte who hastily went into the root cellar for some potatoes and turnips, but she could clearly hear Jemima speaking in English. She remained a moment longer and emerged, and with downcast eyes, she placed her treasure on the table, and got out a pot and put a wooden bucket at her feet to catch the refuse.

"Pedro, hon, you must set up your tent, and I will see that someone brings you a meal." Jemima looked over at Charlotte scraping skin off her turnips, but Charlotte pretended that she couldn't hear her.

"You will sleep in your tent tonight, and let the dog keep guard over the sheep. If you feel frightened, you must run to the house and knock loudly on the door. I'll be here," and she pointed to the dark blue blanket. "I or Mr. Remmington will help you, but don't try to save the sheep. I would rather have you than a thousand sheep." She stood and hugged the boy, and walked with him to the door.

After the boy left, Jemima asked if there was anything she could do to help with supper. Charlotte rose and got another knife, took about half the potatoes from the bowl, and continued her scraping without a word.

28

William had ridden less than a mile before he realized what he'd done, leaving Charlotte in a predicament, but it was too late to turn back. He needed to talk with Thibodeau. He took his horse to the corral and paid one of the guards, a French-Canadian named Montreau, to care for the animal. He had met the man before and felt he could trust him. He was a large fellow with a swarthy face, bushy eyebrows and deep set eyes.

There were two men in the office, and they were peering over a stack of hides on the table. Both looked up when William walked in the door. Pedigrew he recognized, but the other man he didn't. He was dressed in a strange combination of furs, buckskin, cloth and leather as though he had all his possessions on his back. He had a faded red knitted cap on his head, and a couple of inches of snow white hair peeked out from under the cap, with soft Indian moccasins on his feet. He smiled because this was exactly how James had described Thibodeau in January when they first met.

William walked toward Pedigrew, the smile still on his face, and his hand outstretched. "Pedigrew, I'm pleased to see you. It seems that young partner of mine came home with a petite lady perched on a strange wagon, followed by a shepherd boy and a dozen sheep. There was another man with them, name of Thibodeau, perhaps. Now, you wouldn't be knowing about that, would you?" And he looked at the agent as he spoke, amused to think how he might answer.

Pedigrew burst out laughing. The man standing next to him watched them both as though trying to discern some foreign language.

"Butler, ya could'na mean this man you be lookin' for?" He clasped the man at his side on the shoulder. "Young George make it home with Mrs. Boudreau, no? What you be thinkin' of the little lady?"

"That he did, that he did, and a big surprise it was, too. I was chopping wood in the yard with my shirt off and hairy chest exposed to the world, when George drives up with a team of mules and that little lady perched beside him. She got off the wagon, and as bold as a peacock announced she had come to live with me." He gazed at Thibodeau, biding his time to find out more about the Mountain Man.

"This'n way. In the back room, we sit and discuss this like-a good gentlemen." Pedigrew led the way through a thick door to his real office, for the outer one was where he dealt with the Indians and fur trappers, but his other business of buying and selling land was done in the back room. The men spent the next half hour with Thibodeau talking about the predicament of Mrs. Boudreau and the other men in the wagon train, who he suspected of malice and thievery.

From that point, the men began to talk of wagons trains in general, and the one outside the walls, specifically, then to the possibility of war, which surprised William, because the nearest large defensive post was Fort Leavenworth, and if there was a war, most of the Dragoons and infantry men would be going south to Texas or Santa Fe.

From the ominous threat of war, the men progressed to what William had come to find out, a freighting business. He told them that not only did the settlers need necessities, but luxuries as well. Pedigrew pointed out that if there was a war, the trails south would become more dangerous or shut off altogether. Maps were brought out, and river crossings and shortcuts were discussed.

After midnight, the gathering broke up with Thibodeau saying that he probably wouldn't see the young freighter again, because he proposed to go into the high mountains where he found himself most comfortable. It wasn't until that was said that William remembered to ask after Elijah Perkins, to which the former partner gave a scornful answer that he'd left him in Tennessee with his mother. They wished each other a good night, and William found an empty room, where he

202

lay on his back and thought about what had been said, and finally drifted off just before dawn was breaking.

When he returned to his home, it was to discover that the front room was filled with trunks and crates, with a few pieces of furniture. He apologized profusely to the ladies for leaving them alone. But, he told them, he'd received the information he'd wanted, and he informed Charlotte that Perkins had remained in Tennessee with his family. Charlotte told her husband that she'd received a letter from Jasper Smith about Spotty, and one from her father telling her the wagon train had arrived at Fort Hall. Thus peace was restored in the household.

William was awakened before dawn by a ghostly sight walking through his bedroom. He realized it must be Jemima, going outside to the toilet. She stopped in the kitchen, and the sound of pots and pans banging proved that she was preparing breakfast. William didn't mind the lady cooking, but he didn't want her traipsing through the room he shared with Charlotte.

As soon as breakfast was over, William cornered George and told him that they must build Jemima her own cabin. "I will not have that woman wandering through my bedroom whenever she chooses to leave her own room!"

The younger man espoused feeling guilty that he was the one who had brought Jemima to the farm, and reminded William that there were some logs and cut timber in the barn.

William agreed that they could make good use of the timber, and it would be well worth the effort it would take. The men shook, and William returned to the house.

29

By the first of September, Mrs. Jemima Boudreau was firmly entrenched in the Butler household. A sturdy one room cabin with a fireplace stood beside the main house, a few yards to the west. The fireplace had been a challenge to the two men, for they had to gather hundreds of rocks, taking time away from other endeavors, but the men got in the habit of picking up rocks whenever they found them and tossing them into a pile beside the mountain of firewood.

The fireplace had been one of the hardest challenges William had ever met, for he had no skills at laying rocks and caulking with river mud. He insisted he would be the first to light the fire within, in case the flue didn't work as expected. The whole household gathered around the outside of the cabin to watch as a blue-gray plume of smoke arose out of the tall rock structure, and an assortment of trunks, crates and barrels were removed from the larger house. George made a primitive bed of wooden beams with a crisscross of heavy cord from one side to another to hold the mattress Jemima had brought with her. Joseph returned to his comfortable bed in the lean to shed.

The larger wooden piece of furniture proved to be a desk. William took one end, and George, walking backward, carried the other as they moved it from one cabin to the other. Joseph held the door open; his eyes wide open in awe. George stumbled as he took the one step up onto the narrow porch, and William had to brace himself to keep the desk from falling.

"Be careful, George Remmington. That is a valuable piece of furniture. My husband, Simon, brought it all the way from New York." Sidestepping, Jemima eased her way ahead of the men and through the door.

"Yes, ma'am." George sheepishly glanced at William, who felt rather gloomy himself.

"Now, put it over here against this wall." The men started to where she had indicated, only to have her change her mind. "Wait! I think it would be better placed here by the window, so I can get the morning light." At last the desk stood in its glory beside the front door of the cabin, and two relieved men almost ran from the house. Charlotte and Joseph joined them, after both agreeing that it was a fine piece of furniture.

William watched the two women. It seemed a sense of rapport he hoped for between his wife and the older woman took nearly as much time to grow as the fence. There seemed to be no spontaneous feeling of affection like that which had appeared with Bertha in the hotel at St. Louis, as Jemima proved to be a strong-willed and dominant character. He was proved right when Charlotte remarked one night as they lay in bed together how she resented the presence of another woman in her kitchen.

Everything came to a head one morning when Charlotte had a sharp pain in her belly and was told by Jemima to sit, and she'd bring her a cup of hot tea. William watched from his place at the table, and he was amused to see that after drinking the soothing tea, she discontinued complaining about minor issues to do with the planning or cooking of meals.

The early spring and summer flowers of pink, white, purple and red had stopped blooming, but the field in front of the house was aglow with bright yellow blossoms, and Charlotte regularly sat on the porch in one of the ladder backed chairs listening to the birds and humming bees. One day when William questioned her about her activities, she remarked that she liked to watch the sheep munch the grass. Occasionally Jemima would join her, but most days, she left Charlotte alone to her dreaming. Jemima had a small porch of her own, but she seldom sat on it.

George requested William's help one day. Following a bee, he told his boss, he had come upon a hive in the hollow of a log.

Together they went to the barn and built a small square box, put on gloves and one of Charlotte's woolen scarfs to protect their face and ears, and brought the comb to put in the box, hoping they had captured the queen. In no time, the worker bees were coming to the box instead of the log in the forest. Sweet honey was soon served to substitute Charlotte's dwindling supply of molasses.

William wondered about the lad in the meadow sleeping in the tent, and decided to confront Jemima about the matter.

"The boy much prefers this arrangement so he can be near the sheep. He is very responsible."

She explained that she and her husband were on a trip to the Bisquy area of Spain and had seen the sheepherders, the country's customs, type of government and been impressed. They had applied for a permit to bring some sheep to the United States and were told they could bring them over on a ship only if a Basque herder was with them. The man who came was the boy's father. He had married a sweet young American lass and the boy was the result.

She also explained she had no children of her own, but she knew a great deal about herbs and roots for medicinal purposes, and he might see her wandering along the riverbanks or the meadow. She hoped her behavior wouldn't alarm his wife, but she would find herbs, wild onions and mushrooms good for preparing meals.

William thanked her for warning him. He didn't mention it to Jemima, but Charlotte had told him of her mother, and he was afraid his wife would misread Jemima's wanderings as that of a crazy woman.

Jemima gave one final laugh, telling him something of the boy who accompanied her. He claimed to not understand the language, but he understood English and Spanish well enough, and Mr. Butler should watch what he said around the boy.

Armed with this new information, William went to the boy's tent and sat with him for a long time. "There's no need for you to be timid around me, Pedro. Miss Jemima has told me about your background, and I know that you were born in America, your mother was an American, and you can speak my language." Pedro gave him a look of half scorn and half awe, in the same manner that Joseph often did when being challenged on his school work. "I have a boy about your age, and he needs someone to play with. Come up anytime to the house and knock on the door." William walked back to the barn and stayed in sight so the boy could see him.

Jules Robertson kept his promise to bring his wife and children to visit the Butlers. William was pleased to see Charlotte interacting with a woman in her own situation. She appeared to warm to Ava Robertson, exchanging recipes, with Charlotte sharing Bertha's methods for the preservation of garden vegetables. Hanley, at age two and twenty, appeared tactless and cynical, interrupting the older men on several occasions. Jacob, the younger by two years, was caught by the strength and endurance of the oxen, but he was most fascinated with young Joseph's skill with the rope. He tried a turn at looping the length of rope over the head of Petey, the pony, and he and Joseph laughed when the lariat fell to the ground. He was allowed to try again, and this time was successful. Even quiet Pedro came up to enjoy the roping contest. At one point, William called for him to try the rope, hoping to pull him into the fun, but he remained aloof. After about three hours, Jules turned their wagon north and left for home, the boys riding their own horses ahead. Jemima declared the visit well managed, and Ava Robertson a pleasant woman.

William said since the weather was mild he would make a trip into Fort John for supplies. He returned several hours later with catastrophic information. The news came in several forms. The Eastern newspapers had made their way to Fort John, and beamed headlines and images from wood carvings of the tragic flood that had occurred in June. The flooding was so devastating that the course of the Mississippi was changed forever; hundreds of people were left homeless and many had died. The commercial area along the river was almost destroyed and would have to be rebuilt.

Three letters had arrived since he had last taken the trail to the fort. One came from Eileen Kincade, telling not only of the loss of their home and farm, but their precious weeks-old baby girl named Joella had been swept away in the rushing waters. Eileen had clung to her as best she could while holding one of the boys, Jesse, with the other arm, but one child had to be sacrificed, and she had chosen the girl. Jesse was fine now, but he'd caught the fever, and they hadn't known for days if he would survive. Peter had held the other boy, Neely, and they'd been rescued by a neighbor, who had later himself been drowned helping someone else. They were living in Springfield with Peter's parents. If everything went well over the winter, Charlotte was to expect them at Fort John by summer's heat.

The second letter came from Bertha, and told of another tragedy similar in nature. The flooding river had caught the hotel in its wake.

The building itself was still standing, but the lower floor was ruined, and it would take months to clean and repair it. All their personal possessions had been lost, including Clayborne's precious library and violin. Fortunately their money was in the bank, and they had the funds to rebuild, but several of their neighbors had lost everything. Trice's merchandise store was gone, but Benjamin and Rebekah were well and had taken shelter in a hotel for now. Good, kind Conk had carried Clayborne on his back to the upper floor and saved his life. At the risk of his own life, he'd returned downstairs to bring up the wheeled chair. The dog Nero must have been washed away for he was never found.

Margaret and the other permanent residents were saved, but Rachet Jones, a frequent guest, had been drowned while attempting to cross the street in front of the Red Rooster Saloon. Moses Brown's livery had been ruined but could be rebuilt. He'd lost all his horses and equipment, but Moses and his son Jasper were safe and had moved to Springfield. He'd asked that Bertha tell Charlotte and Joseph to write to them there in care of the Majestic Hotel. Moses intended to return to St. Louis as soon as he could recover from his losses. And, she was ever her friend: Bertha Hightower.

The third letter was from Jonathan Kincade, father of Peter, telling of the tragedy that had befallen his son and his family. He requested that, if possible, William build or buy a comfortable home for his son near Fort John, for the boy was determined to head west on the first possible wagon train. Kincade would, of course, pay all expenses if William would personally see to the matter. It need not be a large house or farm, something to give him shelter until such time as he was able to provide for his family in the manner in which they had previously lived. Kincade would forward funds in the care of the United States Army to Fort Leavenworth to be sent on to Fort John by currier or freight wagon.

After reading the note, William decided he would build it himself, now that he was an experienced carpenter and fireplace builder. After all, family was family, and he was certain that Charlotte would want her aunt nearby, and Joseph was apparently quite fond of his uncle.

George announced that he was satisfied with his garden plot, for it had produced cabbage, peas and squash from the seed packets sent by Clayborne. The wheat was sprouted and growing. About four inches tall, the shoots were a light green color, and made a sharp contrast to the brown grass surrounding it. If the wheat lasted until spring,

George remarked, they would have plenty of flour for the family. The new challenge was to keep the sheep from straying into the field.

A hard frost was seen in the first week in the new month. George killed a deer one mid-October morning when the fog was heavy over the meadow. It was salted and dried for eating during the cold months. The garden vegetables had been plucked and dug and canned. They stood proudly on the shelves in the root cellar. The pigs and chickens had been brought into the shelter of one of the sheds, after removing the current contents, which happened to be farming equipment. By the end of October the chill of the snow topped mountains could be felt in earnest.

In mid-November, Charlotte woke William, telling him of a sharp pain in her belly. He encouraged her to go back to sleep. Later she woke William again, telling him the child was especially active. He dressed and knocked on the door of Jemima's cabin, almost in a panic. Although everything was in order, the baby waited until midmorning to show himself. William held the new babe in his arms, given to him by Charlotte Butler, barely past her seventeenth birthday, in the home that William had purchased off Lawrence Pedigrew in Wyoming Territory far from her home in Illinois. William felt like his world had come right again. He tried not to compare the black fuzz on this son's head to the blond fluff of his first son, Samuel, but tears sprang to his eyes, in spite of his strong will. He sat, holding the boy until Jemima took the tiny mite into the kitchen area to give him a first bath. Charlotte slept the day away, exhausted after her ordeal.

Joseph seemed delighted with his new nephew. He gazed down at him from his superior height and declared him a fine fellow. George stood in an awkward pose over the cradle that he had made, then thumped his employer on the back and congratulated him on his success. Jemima gave him a sharp look at that statement, but she relented and smiled and told him to sit and eat his supper.

William lay beside his young wife in the dark and wondered at the strength of women, for he'd been nervous and almost as tired as she by the time the travail was over. Jemima had ordered her confined to her bed for a week, and he was glad of it. There abided in him a wealth of respect and affection for his young wife. He draped his arm gently over her chest trying not to awaken her. She gave a soft moan but didn't stir. He wished he could light the lantern and watch her sleep, but he would awaken Joseph just on the other side of the blanket door. William slowly drifted off to sleep, his large calloused hand gently holding the breast that gave sustenance to his son.

They named the boy Theodore Morgan Butler, and he was called Teddy. William watched in awe as his little limbs flew through the air in an attempt to catch the sun. The winter was mild according to the old timers in the fort by the two rivers. At last a warm southerly wind blew. The ice melted, and the wheat stood tall and brown in the field beyond the barn. George planted the spring garden from his seed packets, and tiny green sprouts appeared. Joseph was now taller than his sister, and William had to buy new trousers again. Jemima loved her little cabin and planted flowers from the seed packets near the door, but Charlotte whispered to William that she loved the wild flowers best.

The sheep produced of their kind, and at William's urging, the boy came often to the house to visit with Joseph. Pedro learned to rope a horse, play the Jew's harp and fish in the river. His initials were added in crude letters to the stump beside the J M. The two boys became almost inseparable when they had time away from their chores. William laughed as Pedro rode Petey, his legs dangling almost to the ground. Joseph would spring into his own saddle, and they would loop around the farm as far as William permitted, because the area was still wild. Soon, a trail was made as the horses tramped down the wild grass.

In the late spring, William and George tried their hand at sheep shearing. It was awkward at best. George had noticed an old pair of shears among the farm implements and said they would have to do, he supposed. William agreed, not knowing much about sheep or how they were sheared. They had Charlotte sew two pair of moccasins out of an old deer skin, like those the boy wore, so their shoes wouldn't be damaged and they could grip the ground better with the soles of their feet. Jemima told them to take the flock to a shallow place in the river and wash them so the wool would be clean of burrs, twigs, and soil. The two men and Pedro drove the flock to a likely place and made a game of it, splashing and dunking each other like children, but the sheep returned to the barn a lighter color. Following Jemima's instructions, they made a belly cut, and removed the soft wool from the shoulders, back, and legs.

William put Joseph in charge of stacking the fleece inside one of the farm wagons, to be taken to Pedigrew, for Jemima said that would be the best way to get a good price. They saved some of the wool for themselves. Jemima showed Charlotte how to card the wool to remove the leftover burrs and grass and to make it into long thin ropes to be woven into a rug or blanket. Since they had no spinning wheel, it was a long slow process, and Charlotte remarked in wonder at the skill of her new friend as she worked with the wool.

Jemima told Charlotte, "We have plenty of time before winter to complete the yarn. You'll be able to make caps and scarves soon."

William took the fleece to Pedigrew, and the man was overjoyed to see it. He paid him what he believed to be a good price and told him that he would send it on to Santa Fe, where the Spanish dons would examine the quality and value of the crimping and determine the final price. If it was more than he had given William, Pedigrew would then pay him the difference.

William exclaimed that the wool wasn't from his sheep. They belonged to Jemima. Pedigrew told him he'd have to work that out with her. William drove home, the wagon empty and smelling like sheep. He solemnly handed the government script to Jemima and told her what Pedigrew had said. She took the money and put it in her leather money bag.

William appreciated the change in Charlotte. She was again slender and graceful. Her freckles stood out like beacons when she forgot to wear her sunbonnet. She loved to wander through the wild flowers or ride with him, taking Joseph's horse, with her son in a canvas bag strapped across her back. They would ride along the riverbank and stop to kiss or lie down in the soft sand and make love. She was shocked the first time William tried it, but to William there was something exciting about lying on the blanket, with the sun filtered through the swaying leaves overhead, knowing that your wife's young, innocent brother was not in the next room. Charlotte seemed to give in and enjoy it, also. William told Charlotte that she was beautiful, but she claimed she didn't believe him, and would blush and turn away in shyness. She did remark on enjoying a sense of true freedom for the first time since she learned to cook, for Jemima was willing to attend to the kitchen chores whenever William asked her.

William noticed a restlessness in George and suspected he was ready to move on, but he didn't raise the subject, thinking George would come to him when he was ready. William would miss the man, but in another month or so, Charlotte's uncle and aunt with their children would be here to help with the work. They were kin, and George was not. It would be well for them to be with Charlotte when

William went on his freighting routes. The major work was finished, with wheat in the field ready for harvest, the barn roof repaired, the fences mended and the corrals secure against intruders. There were more sheep in the meadow, more chickens in the coops, and the oxen were healthy and strong. He had taken good care to see to that.

It was, therefore, no surprise when George came to the barn where William was currying his horse in the last week in May of 1845. The animal was getting old, and needed to be let out into the fields in retirement.

"What do you think, George, is it time to let the old horse roam free in the fields, and buy a new saddle horse for myself?" William brushed the horse with short, vigorous strokes. He looked over the withers of the animal, thinking to ease the pressure by asking about Jimmy.

George stopped in midstride. "Ah, how old is Jimmy, Mr. Butler?"

"Old enough to be given a break from the hardship of daily work." William chuckled.

"I suppose it would be a good thing to have a young frisky stallion under a man's legs of a morning. Do you think there are any horses for sale at Fort John? Might even get yourself a mare, too, start your own herd. Pedigrew said there was some horses and cattle here when Cummings ran the place, but I haven't had time to go looking."

"That's right. I'd forgotten what Pedigrew said about the cattle and horses; but the wagon train will be coming in a few weeks, and I guess you'll be wanting to go to Oregon with it."

George breathed out an obvious sigh of relief, and William moved over and laid the brush on the top of the stall where Jimmy was happily eating hay. He walked out of the stall and past the two new stalls built with the lumber that had once stood in the shadows. He motioned for George to follow him.

George began to talk as they walked. "I'd like to be on that train, if you think it would be right for me to go. Your family's coming in, and with Miss Jemima here to help Mrs. Butler, I figure there'll be people to take care of your missus when you go off to Santa Fe or back to Independence for supplies. I been thinking, Mr. Butler, I done saved what you paid me for the work, and if you'd loan me the rest, I could buy the supplies necessary for Oregon." As if a new thought had occurred to him, he stopped and glanced at William with an odd expression. "Come to think on it, we're almost halfway there already.

212

We already crossed the plains, only got the mountains to cross."

William took off his hat and scratched his head. "You got a point there. I'll tell you what I'll do. You can get most of your supplies here, what with the food you've grown yourself, if the things in the garden are ripe enough to can when the wagons leave Fort John. Got milk and eggs and butter and cheese. Should last a single man several days, or you could trade it in the fort for ropes, molasses or coal oil for the lanterns. We can grind enough corn and flour for your needs. Got an extra wagon and four mules with Jemima's vehicle here, and I don't think she's planning to travel. You make out a list of what you need, and we'll work it out."

He kept walking until he was out of the barn and George had shut the door. There in front of them was a cabin almost identical to the one in which Jemima lived, except it was twice as big, for he and George had built an extra room for the Kincade boys. He was proud of the fireplace, because he was experienced now and hadn't made the mistakes of the first one. He had to admit the last year had taught him many skills.

"I'm right proud of you, George, but I learned a long time ago that a man has to make his own way in the world. You've been a good worker and a friend. I wish James had seen in you what I do now. You'll feel free when you have your own place in Oregon. It'll be hard on the boy, though, you leaving. I wish you well." William held out his hand in friendship and went into the house.

Charlotte was talking with Jemima, who was stirring something in a large bowl. Joseph was in the rocking chair playing his Jew's harp. Teddy, now six months old and trying to raise himself on his fat legs, had given up and was crawling on the floor. William picked him up. He put his face into the babe's neck and took a deep breath of essence of boy. A feeling of pure joy rolled through his body like a stone. This was love. He knew that now. But, to find a way to tell Charlotte, that would take courage. He kissed the boy on the cheek, and when he put him on the floor, he started crawling away.

"George is leaving." William waited for the looks of shock on the faces of the women.

"No, you can't be serious. That fine young man?" Jemima, as usual, got in the first word.

Charlotte stared at William. "Did you tell him to go? What about your friendship? I'll miss him so much; he's part of life here on the farm." She looked at her brother. "Oh, Joseph."

"He's decided to go on to Oregon, like his original plan. He wants to join the first wagon train if he can, the one your uncle and aunt will be on, I expect, my dear." William turned toward their friend. "I been thinking, Jemima, that if I can buy that wagon and the mules from you, he wouldn't have so much of his own to buy. It would give him a nice start on his future farm."

Jemima dropped the spoon in the pot and exclaimed, her face damp from the steam, "What are you saying, William Butler? Me, sell that wagon and team of mules? Why, I'll give them to the man, that's what I'll do. And, I'll help him with what else he needs. I'm not going to need all that farming equipment." Her cheeks were puffed out like she was having trouble breathing.

He had completely forgotten the boy at the other end of the room. Joseph stopped playing his music. William looked in that direction in time to see Joseph coming right at him. He was about a foot shorter, but he was strong and healthy. He flew at his brother-in-law and started pounding on his chest and his stomach with a ferocity that William wouldn't have believed. "You sent him away! You don't want George here, I know you don't. I hate you! I hate you! I don't want you for a brother."

William looked down, and the baby was in the way of Joseph's feet. Instinctively, he grasped Joseph under the arm pits and lifted him off his feet and away from the baby, then swung him up into his arms. Holding him tightly, he tried to explain the situation.

"It's not true what you say, son. George decided of his own will to go to Oregon. He's our friend, and I love him." There was that word. He had without thinking said what he felt for his young employee. He gently put Joseph on his feet away from the baby, and turning on his heels, left the house. He went to the barn, saddled Jimmy and rode away. He rode to Fort John and for the first time since that awful night of the poker game over sixteen months ago, William Butler got drunk. He tied his horse to the railing and passed out in the hay. His last thought before oblivion took over was that he wasn't so different from James Morgan after all.

*****

George set the boy down at the kitchen table and told him the absolute truth. "I'm sorry, lad, if you think that your brother doesn't want me. The truth is, I feel stifled here. I need to go to Oregon to

214

find my own place. The land is free there, and I can start over with my own farm, like this one, if the good Lord is willing. I have to leave, Joseph, can't you see what's in front of your eyes? Mr. Butler not only accepted my decision with grace, but has offered to loan me the money to pay for the journey." He pointed out Teddy, now safe in his mother's arms while tears rolled down her face. "Mr. Butler picked you up to save his son from harm. You should beg your brother's pardon for the harm you've caused. You don't hate him. And, someday when you're older, you'll understand the meaning of love."

Jemima remarked that she had never heard such inspirational words, and she had listened to many preachers in her day.

Joseph started crying, and George took him in his arms for a while and told him that he must go away, but he would always love the boy. He was like his own son, but William was his brother, and Joseph belonged to him.

George looked up from his charge to see Charlotte hugging the babe in her arms, and tears were in her eyes. She walked to him and whispered that she now saw the true worth of a man. It wasn't in his beauty or his charm, for her father had those qualities in abundance. The worth of a man was in his inner strength and his ability to cope with any situation that presented itself to him.

She thanked George for helping her see that quality in her William. She now recognized it, because she just saw it exhibited in George.

George couldn't help himself, as he felt the sting of unshed tears. He sensed he was leaving his family behind, and breaking away was going to be very hard.

30

George found William lying in the hay the next morning. He was in a pathetic haze; his clothes were disheveled and smelled of liquor and vomit. His gray eyes were glazed and bloodshot, his hair tangled and unkempt. It took George a while to rouse him, and when he did, William promptly vomited again. George jumped back just in time.

"So, you love me, do you?" George had a twinkle in his eyes. He'd heard the shouting and had come in the house in time to see the baby crawling and William lift Joseph in his powerful arms to keep him from harming the child. George had gawked at William as he'd made his declaration of love, and turned to walk out the door. He tried to stop him, but decided to let him alone to his pain and grief, for he could see clearly what had torn the older man apart.

He cleaned him up as best he could and got him something to eat, for he'd missed two meals. Afterwards, he located him a new shirt and pair of trousers. He told him that Joseph was all right. He'd talked to him, and Joseph knew that George wanted to go to Oregon. The men rode back to the farm, one satisfied with his work; the other chagrined that he'd actually done something that he'd promised he would never do again.

When the two men rode into the farmyard, George went to find some work, for he needed something to do with his hands.

*****

William walked into the house and apologized for his behavior and absence the night before. Joseph came to him and held out his hand, and they shook as though they were truly brothers, although the boy acted awkwardly in his presence for some time after that. Charlotte handed the baby to William to see if he could quiet the child. Jemima was busy cooking and pretended nothing unusual had happened in the room the day before. William took Teddy in his arms, went to the rocking chair, and held him until the child fell asleep. Later, once it seemed the events of the day before were settled, he took the soiled clothes in back of the barn and burned them in the trash heap. It was like a baptism or a religious ceremony, and he planned never to forget the moment he arose from the hay, mortified and subdued, and grateful for George's care of him.

Six and a half weeks later, William saw George off as he rode away from the farm in Jemima's wagon, pulled by her four mules. Most of the supplies in the wagon were provided by her, or grown on the farm, or made with his hands. He hugged both the women, shook hands with Joseph, and then without resistance, took him in his arms and hugged him, too. He and William had said their good-byes the night before out of the sight of the ladies. William told him if things didn't work out, he would always be welcome at Green Meadow Farm.

Two days after George's departure, William received word from his friend and former employee that made him think of old, tired Jimmy. George sent word by one of the Indian fur traders about a small herd of wild mustangs that had been seen about a day's ride east of Robertson's place, across the river. With halting English, the Indian drew a map in the dirt and gestured toward the rock formation that marked the turn off to the Butler place, then toward the east. William gave him a shiny silver piece, which he put in his buckskin pocket, his black eyes flashing his approval. With a guttural sound from his throat, the Indian mounted his horse and rode back toward Fort John.

The next day the first train of the year from Missouri arrived at Fort John. It contained over one hundred wagons, carts, buggies, and carriages. Among the pioneers were Peter and Eileen Kincade and their two boys, Jesse and Neely. It was a bright sunny day in early

217

July when the new family arrived at Green Meadow Farm. The vegetables in the garden patch were at different stages of ripeness. The grass was green in the meadow and abundant with wild flowers. The sheep grazed in the field in serenity, watched over by Pedro, who still slept in his tent. That was a great novelty for two boys who had spent months in a large city. The Kincades brought with them mail from St. Louis and Springfield, Illinois. The trip had been tedious but with no major calamities. Upon their arrival they were shown to their new home, and Eileen burst into tears. It had been a bad year for her, losing her home and her baby, but with rest and care she had survived. She had proven stronger than her older sister, Priscilla. Within a few days of her entry in the family group, she was her usual exuberant self. The boys were tall for their age, and slender like their mother. They quickly renewed their relationship with their cousins, and were welcomed by the quiet Pedro.

Eileen looked closely at Joseph with her wise blue eyes and found a maturity she hadn't expected. He was now about the same height as Peter, but still shy of the stature of his brother-in-law. His voice had begun to crack and squeak as he passed puberty. But if the boys teased, he would shrug and say it was his throat getting ready for his adulthood. A man named George was mentioned several times in his conversations, and Charlotte explained he was the hired hand who had cared for him since they left St. Louis.

William showed Peter around the farm: the animals, the barn, the fields and the river. Peter seemed very pleased, and William couldn't help but puff up with pride.

"I have to admit it was mostly the work of George, the hired man, for I'm not a farmer by trade. I spent my life in the iron ore mines of Virginia or driving a team of mules or oxen. A fine young man, but with your coming, he felt he could go on to Oregon, take advantage of the free land, and build a place of his own. We'll all miss him, especially Joseph, for he drove the Morgan wagon from the Mississippi River, and the two became fast friends."

Peter was presented to the Conestoga wagon in which they had crossed the plains. William told him of his plans to start a freighting line, but recently the idea had ceased to hold as much importance, for William was content with what he had, his wife, his son and his home.

Peter appeared to be a placid, virile man, comfortable in his own masculinity, who had lived through the tragedy of the last year and accepted it as fate, working its will in their lives. Having never seen him before, William had learned from Charlotte that Peter was well educated. His father was an attorney in Springfield, but Peter had chosen another life for himself, leaving his four younger brothers to sooth the ruffled feathers of their father. William imagined that must explain the arrogant tone of the elder Kincade's letter. It must have been humiliating for Peter to return home after losing his farm and livelihood and ask for assistance from his father.

There was a letter which had been waiting for some time at Fort John, and Pedigrew had sent it on when he learned the Kincades were related to the Butlers. It was from James Morgan and sent months before, only now arriving from Oregon. He'd arrived safely and had found land to his liking, and had built a makeshift cabin until he could do better. He sent his affections and well wishes, for the baby must have arrived by now. He was in good health. The Oregon country was exactly as presented by the fur trappers. Did Charlotte recall that Fannie Landers girl who hung around their wagon, who had caused George trouble? Their wagon had hit a rock in the high mountains, and Fannie had been thrown overboard and broke her neck. Good riddance in his opinion. Always flirting around the single men. Bound to end badly. Peace and joy for the coming Season: James Morgan.

A second letter came addressed to Charlotte but was for Joseph from Jasper Smith. They were still living in Springfield, and his father had decided to stay there. It was a thriving place and good business opportunity for a livery stable, so please to continue sending mail to the Majestic Hotel, and they would receive it. His brother Abraham was at school in Boston. Did Joseph have another dog? Affectionately: Jasper Smith.

Joseph put the letter in his pocket, and William saw him more than once take it out to read again whenever he was alone, finally taking one of the books, and slipping the letter inside.

The letter from Bertha was not so cheerful. They had undergone some repairs on the hotel, but it wasn't finished. Margaret Brown had died of an overdose of laudanum; poor, slow-witted Gladys had found Margaret in her bed when she had gone to change the linens. Bertha believed she'd never gotten over the loss of her sister's affections. Mr. Hammond was sending some more seed packets. Bertha didn't know when they would arrive; she hoped before planting season. Clayborne was growing weaker. She worried about him, but he remained optimistic and worked hard. The real estate business had suffered greatly from the flooding. She hoped the baby had been born without her sweet Charlotte coming to grief. She remained her friend: Bertha Hightower.

William saw the signs that Charlotte was despondent after the news that her friends Fannie Landers and Margaret Brown had died, and he expected her mood to be a blight on her face for several days. When he spoke to her about it, she recalled Fannie's lovely face and her blond curls and laughing eyes, and of Margaret, flirting with the guests at the hotel, and remembered her fragrant white handkerchief waving from the front porch as William drove the wagon out of sight. She cried and moped about the house, cooked the meals, and tended the baby, until Jemima set her down, with William at her side to offer her a cup of herbal tea, and told her there was no need to wring herself dry like an old rag. They had all known the hazards of the trip across the continent when they started out; did she imagine that she was safe from losing her friends?

"Look around you, woman, you got a husband, a fine home, a child and food to get on the table. Now, take these beans and start shelling, afore I have to do them myself." Jemima slammed the bowl on the table and marched to the other end of the room, sat down in the rocking chair and started it moving back and forth, like she hadn't a care in the world.

William was wide-eyed at the woman's nerve, wishing he hadn't asked for her to speak with his wife.

Charlotte stared at Jemima in amazement, and burst out laughing. She got up from her chair and hugged the old woman, then kissed William, and did as she said. She began to shell the beans. Her natural equilibrium improved, and after finishing the beans and putting them in a pan to soak, Charlotte found the ingredients to make a cake for supper, and promised to save William the largest slice.

After completing his outside chores, William returned to the cabin to find Charlotte fully restored, and talking with Jemima about whether the beets and radishes in the garden were ready to be dug. The sweet smell of freshly baked cake permeated the room. He sniffed and his stomach growled in anticipation. Charlotte smiled at him, and he was reassured.

*****

William and Peter decided to go on a mustang roundup. They rode over to the Robertson farm to ask if one of the boys wanted to go with them. William was on Jimmy, and Peter was riding Joseph's horse, for he hadn't brought a horse with him from Illinois, but had driven the wagon.

William went to the door and knocked, leaving Peter still astride the horse. Mrs. Robertson came to the door, wiping her hands on her apron. Behind her stood her son, Jacob. Average in height, with brown hair and brown eyes, and about twenty years old, Jacob came around and took a defensive stance as though to protect his mother. He looked at Peter suspiciously, and as the older man slowly dismounted and strolled to the house, the two men gazed at each other curiously.

"Ahloo, Mr. Butler." Ava's dimples showed when she smiled. "I was just telling Jacob here, hadn't seen you in a while. Whut can I do for ya?"

"Hello, Mrs. Robertson." William took off his hat. He looked at Jacob, and the boy relaxed his body. William turned back to the woman. "This is my wife's uncle, Peter Kincade, just came in on the train from Illinois. George rode out on the same train bound for Oregon, but sent word before he left that a herd of mustangs have been sighted across the river, maybe ten miles to the east." He pointed across to the other side of the river toward the early morning sun. "I was wondering if Jacob, or maybe Hanley, would like to ride along with us. Take maybe four days, maybe a week of hard riding. We could sure use some young horseflesh." William pointed over his shoulder to his old horse.

Jules came around the corner of the house, his dirty buckskins looking worse than the first time William had seen them, but this time he had a blue plaid shirt sticking out from under his top. "Heerd you say you was looking for horses. That a fact?" Robertson's deeply browned face was almost hidden by his broad brimmed hat. He came forward and shook hands with his visitors. Jules looked Peter over, muttering that he looked more like a city man than a farmer, if anyone asked his opinion. He then opined that if he was with William, he was surely alright.

Peter withstood the scrutiny of these neighbors with his usual placid manner.

William had time to wonder if these were the only clothes Jules owned, before he acknowledged that he was planning to look for the herd that had been sighted by some Indians a few miles on the other side of the Laramie River.

"Pa, I sure would like to make that trip. You know I done all my chores, and Hanley got to go to Fort John, and I stayed here last time." Jacob looked hopefully at his father.

Jules took off his hat, rubbed his gnarled hand over his bald spot as though he could stop the hair from receding with the gesture. He replaced his hat on his head and looked closely at Jimmy, William's horse, and made a decision. "Tell you what I'll do, Butler. That old hag of yours won't last a day out looking for those wild critters. What you'll need is speed and endurance. If you can bring me back one of them wild horses, I'll lend you one of my cow ponies. Jacob can ride his own horse, if'en you think he'll not be a burden to ya. I could use a fine mare, if one's to be found."

Ava gave her husband an assessing look and went into the house. She gathered some food and fruit jars of homemade brew for the men to take with them.

William looked at Jacob and decided it was a good exchange, for he'd been worried about his horse. He tried not to look offended at Jules' assessment of his faithful Jimmy who'd come all the way from Virginia to this place. He held out his hand. "Done. Of course, it may be that we won't find those horses, or can't catch them. Might be a waste of time, but we'll try for a week, maybe ten days, then come on home, for I don't want to leave the women and children alone for long."

"Don't you fret about your women folk, I'll send Hanley over to see about 'em." The men went toward the barn, where Jacob took out his own mount and saddled it, while the others examined the stallion Jules said would make a good sturdy horse for William. He mentioned that he hated to see young George go off like that, but young men get restless, and he looked sharply at his son.

Peter inspected the stallion carefully. He looked at his teeth and his legs, and he nodded that the animal would be acceptable. William rode him to the house, prancing and pawing the ground, trying to get a feel of his gait and performance, and was satisfied. Jacob ran into the house to collect what he thought he'd need for a week's ride, came out with a bag of clothes, the food and the jars of corn liquor, and mounted his horse, waiting for the elders to say their good-byes. William promised to have Charlotte send over a leg of lamb and maybe some dried apricots and peaches that the Kincade's had brought from Illinois. They all shook hands, and the party headed back for Green Meadow Farm, with William leading Jimmy.

Jacob spent the night in the Butler's barn, and the next morning before dawn the men set out to find the mustangs, leaving three women, and four young boys behind. Charlotte cooked some extra biscuits and slices of beef, with some sausage links and dried apples to change their diets a little. Eileen gave them a sack of hardtack and coffee, and contributed her coffee pot and a couple of tin cups and plates. Peter assured the women that they'd kill some game if they were gone longer than a week. They weren't to worry about them, for they were experienced marksmen, including Jacob Robertson.

*****

With no small amount of trepidation, the women waved the men off, and returned to their normal routine. Eileen mostly cooked and prepared the meals for her own family grouping in her kitchen, but occasionally she would share or come over for the Saturday ritual of telling stories or listening to Charlotte read aloud from one of Clayborne's books. The Kincades had lost their favorite treasures in the flood, but they'd brought a few articles from the family home in Springfield.

Pedro watched over the flock of sheep, now looking fat and content in the meadow. Without the men there, the women wouldn't let the boys wander to the river, and they had no horse left but the pony Petey and the horse Jimmy. Each of them was becoming proficient in roping the pony. They shared in the chores of milking the cow, Lola, and feeding the chickens and pigs.

31

The men were gone eleven days, and the women were concerned. They were encouraged, however, by Jemima, who ruled over the whole household without giving offense. It was her nature to be dominant, and Charlotte had learned to accept it. She spent most of her time growing her herbs and roots in her small plot beside her own cabin. Eileen tried to avoid Jemima when she could, and spent most of her time with cooking, sewing or weaving with the wool yarn from the fleece garnered in the spring.

On a misty, cool afternoon, the men crossed the river from the east at the ford and rode into the farmyard with two fine mustang stallions and a yearling bay mare with a white face, with two colts trailing them. Jacob brought up the rear on his steed leading a second older mare. The boy sat high in the saddle. After greeting the ladies and children, he told everyone he'd caught the mare himself. He'd held the noose around her neck while Peter threw a second loop, while she kicked and bucked at the restraints on her freedom. Finished with his tale, he shook hands with the men and rode toward his home, leading the mare and the horse that William had borrowed.

The men had seen the leader of the herd, a fierce black stallion, which Peter declared he'd like to own. William had laughed and said he'd have to be sharp to catch that one. They'd missed the chance for another mare. She broke loose from the rope and ran away to join the black leader. Altogether, it was a successful trip, but the men were glad to be home. William decided, and Peter agreed, to put the mare in with Jimmy and see what happened. William, with the help of Joseph, added a large addition to the corral in which Jimmy and Penny, the mare, would have to themselves. The other horses were placed in the old corral where they would stay until broken to the saddle. Petey remained in the stalls next to the cow in the barn.

William was excited, for they'd seen cattle in the gullies and among the trees. Pedigrew had told him there might be some Cummings' cattle roaming the land. As soon as the men rested and settled the horses in the corral, they set off again to bring in the cattle. Five cows and a couple of calves soon resided in their own corral. It was a fine start to a herd of oxen for his freight wagons.

The next few days were spent working the horses, or catching up on chores neglected while they were away. William looked up from hoeing the garden plot, to see the same Indian who had brought the message from George ride up to the house. William had learned from Pedigrew that the man was a Shoshone named Bear Grease. Thinking he might be bringing news of trouble at the fort, William took his hoe to the barn and leaned it near the door.

The Indian dismounted, and with his guttural half-English explained that Pedigrew needed him at the fort. William's heart thumped loudly, for the last time he'd visited with the agent there had been a sighting of United States Army troopers in the area. In addition, news of a raid on a caravan of Mexican traders near the Arkansas River was in the newspapers from the East. William tried to get more information out of the Shoshone, but the man would only say Pedigrew needed him.

William tried not to alarm the ladies, but drew Peter aside to explain why he was going to the fort. It might be an entirely false alarm, but he warned Peter to keep one of the boys on the lookout for danger. He spent some time with Charlotte and his son, Teddy. He told her he might be gone a while, that she wasn't to worry; and with a casual kiss on her forehead, he whispered, "I love you," and he was gone on Jimmy, for the new horses were not yet comfortable with a rider and saddle on their backs. The Indian patiently waited, squatting on the ground and smoking a long-stemmed pipe. When William mounted his horse, the Indian put out the fire in his pipe, and rising slowly, accompanied him on the ride to Fort John.

The two riders arrived at the trading post in the early afternoon. There were several men in uniform squatting in the dirt of the stockade, and a few Indians milling around the grounds. They looked at William with curiosity, which he returned with an equal regard of his own. He rode directly toward the office of the manager, with the Indian following more slowly in his wake. Bear Grease dismounted and took the horses to a clump of trees near the building, and tied the reins to a knotty oak. William had no time to spare watching the Indian. He grabbed his rifle from the scabbard, took the steps at a leap and crossed the balcony to the office.

William opened the door to Pedigrew's office and saw the manager standing behind the counter, talking to a man in an Army uniform. A quick glance around the room revealed the presence of another two troopers, one apparently a sergeant, by the stripes on his shirt sleeve. There were two civilians, one dressed in the same manner as Otto Thibodeau.

"Ah, my boy, there'n you be. William, my friend, such a good time you make. Come to meet my new friend." Pedigrew remained where he was behind the counter but indicated the man with him. "This be Lieutenant Truman Aloysius Baker, of G Troop, United States Dragoons." He spoke with a note of affection and amusement in his voice, as though the name were a private joke between them. William relaxed, holding his rifle in his left hand, since there didn't seem to be an emergency after all. He walked closer and shook hands with both men. "Baker, he have some proposition for ya, and if'n I put on your'n boots I maybe make a good decision. Maybe say yes. The back room, it be all your'n."

The soldier crossed to the door indicated, and gestured that William should go before him. He stepped into the room and the lieutenant closed it behind them. "Please sit down, Mr. Butler." William sat, placing his weapon on the table, and Baker brought another chair close by so they could talk quietly without being heard in the other room. He was intrigued and leaned closer to the soldier, his hands relaxed in his lap. "As Pedigrew indicated, I have a task that may be dangerous, or may be only stressful. Hostilities have opened up recently with certain elements of the citizenry of Texas along the border with Arkansas. Also, there has been trouble with bandits in northern California. Pedigrew has sworn that you're an honest man that can be trusted with secrets, and have in addition the resources that we need at the moment."

William gave an indication with a nod of his head that he agreed with the lieutenant. Baker looked around the room, and began to speak again, looking William in the eyes as he did so.

"There's a shipment of gold bullion to be taken from Fort Leavenworth to Fort Gibson along the military road. This is already on its way, but must pass through the area of Arkansas that I've mentioned. My superiors have come up with a diversion plan to throw suspicion away from that area by directing a freight train from Fort John to Santa Fe surrounded by Dragoons, meaning my own troop, Company G. Most of the companies out of Leavenworth are stirring about in the area of Arkansas or Missouri. They're hopeful that with the increase in army traffic further west that the diversion will work."

William nodded his head and sat back in his seat.

Lieutenant Baker glanced casually around the room again and smiled. "Pedigrew tells me that you own a Conestoga purchased out of Pennsylvania. I haven't seen such a vehicle myself. I come from New York and attended the Academy at West Point. I should like to visit your farm and witness for myself the virtues of traveling in such a grand style. Would this be possible?"

"I'd be happy to show you my wagon." William realized that this was what the meeting was about. He wanted to employ him on this excursion to Santa Fe. "It's been forsaken since we arrived a year ago, I'm afraid, and is gathering dust in the shed. We've discovered that it's more practical on a farm to use the lighter more easily driven vehicle. I have five good oxen who have taken advantage of the abundant grass in the fields."

"It is, however, in good repair, you say?"

William looked thoughtfully at the lieutenant. "I would say so. Would today be a suitable time to show you the wagon? You'd be welcome to spend the night, of course. My wife is an excellent cook."

"Sounds like a fine plan. Let me tell my troopers of the change and to find a campsite for a few days." Lieutenant Baker opened the door and walked out, nodded to Pedigrew, and sauntered over to his sergeant and motioned that they leave the office.

William picked up his rifle from the table. He watched them go, and also the man dressed like Thibodeau. He walked toward Pedigrew, still standing behind the counter. He raised one eyebrow in a silent question, but the fur trader gave no indication that he understood the gesture.

"Ah, my friend," Pedigrew called jovially. "Ya have finished

227

your'n bid'ness with the lieutenant. A letter! A letter I have for your most excellent wife!" He withdrew a paper from the cubicles behind the desk, looked at the address to make sure he had the right one, and handed it to William, who had walked forward and held out his hand. He recognized the familiar handwriting of his father-in-law, and moaned. It was Pedigrew's turn to raise an eyebrow in question.

William shook his head and left the office, gazed at the soldiers more closely, and crossing to the trading post store, asked if there were any cones of sugar or baking soda available. He made his purchase and stepped out of the building. There was a cluster of civilians in store-bought clothes milling around, a few he recognized, but he only nodded at them.

The Shoshone sat against the trunk of a tree, guarding the horses. He had his long stemmed pipe in his hand and was obviously enjoying the taste of tobacco. William walked toward him, and Bear Grease rose to his feet and pointed toward the gate with the pipe. He placed his purchase in a sheepskin bag draped across his saddle horn. Walking his horse, he went through the gate and saw Lieutenant Baker and the man dressed like Thibodeau mounted, holding the reins of a pack mule. They seemed to be waiting for him. Bear Grease followed. The troopers, with the sergeant shouting orders at their heads, were erecting what looked to be canvas tents in a semi-circle near the Indian encampments. A cook wagon stopped. Another soldier dressed in a large white apron over his uniform was starting a fire, in preparation for the night's meal.

"Butler, this is Army Scout Orville Willowby, who works for the government. He's from Connecticut and has never seen a Conestoga wagon. I've invited him to join us if you don't mind. And, of course, you're familiar with Bear Grease." William acknowledged the presence of the Indian and shook hands across the saddle with the scout, and turned his horse in the direction of his home.

When they came to the rock formation cutoff, William pointed it out to the gentlemen, explained its importance as a landmark, and took the path to his place. When he'd first come to Fort John, this path had been narrow and covered in places with vines and underbrush. He and George had cut a wider roadway that could be traversed by wagons or horses. The men rode silently until the picture of serenity caused a shout of enjoyment from the scout. Plumes of smoke drifted up from the cabins.

Someone had seen them cross the ridge; and Charlotte, with

Teddy riding on her hip, and Joseph were waiting at the front door. William led the men to the front porch, saw ten-year-old Neely hovering nearby, and asked him to tie up the animals. The boy rushed forward, calling out to the horses and very nearly dancing with excitement.

"Charlotte, my dear, this is Lieutenant Truman Baker, and the army scout Orville Willowby, and you've seen Bear Grease before." Beside her, Joseph was open-eyed with amazement.

William took the child from her, then, with pride in his voice, introduced his wife Charlotte, his brother-in-law Joseph Morgan, and announced that this was his son, Theodore Butler.

"Pleased to meet you, gentlemen, won't you come in the house?" Charlotte's dark brown eyes shone with curiosity, and she indicated the wide open door, for it was extremely hot in the cabin in August. The Indian moved into the shade under a tree.

Bear Grease didn't have long to wait, for after a cool drink of water and a couple of biscuits to keep them from starving until supper time, the three men emerged from the house and sauntered to the shed where the Conestoga rested, covered with the sailcloth top that had protected the pioneers from the elements on the road to Fort John. William had removed the metal frames that kept the top high over the bed of the wagon, and laid them inside. The covering was draped over the bed as a sheet on a mattress.

Joseph followed behind the men, and tried not to get in their way, but William recognized what the boy was doing. He wanted to see the Dragoon lieutenant and army scout. He motioned the boy closer to the group of men, and satisfied the boy wouldn't interfere, began pulling the covering off his wagon. The army scout, without being asked, began to help.

It looked unimpressive standing in the shed without the high oval frame and white cover which gave it the majestic look people admired. The wheels were made of wood with iron rims, larger than most wagon wheels, made to withstand heavy burdens. The axles and tongue had been carved by superior craftsmen in far off Pennsylvania. The sides were deep and strong, the paint now weather-beaten and faded. The army scout pushed and pounded on the sides. Lieutenant Baker crawled underneath to bang on the underpinnings.

William heard a sound from Joseph and was uncertain what had caused it. He saw the boy run away. Lieutenant Baker rolled out from under the wagon; and the army scout ran his finger over the axles to see if there was grease leaking or caked dry around the surface. They both seemed to come to the same conclusion.

"Butler, you're to be congratulated. Many a man would give their fortune to have such a vehicle of splendor as this one. Now, may we see your oxen, please?" The men turned to follow William to the small pasture where the five oxen were grazing contentedly, along with the cattle he had recently found. William looked up in time to see the shock of amazement in the eyes of the scout. The five animals were not alike. They appeared in various shades of light brown, dark brown, one with a speckled rump, and touches of black and white markings on all five. The males each had a set of horns that reached the spread of a man's arms.

They didn't become upset when the strangers approached them and ran hands over their rumps and shoulders, raising the legs to see that they had been recently shod, for William took pride in his animals, especially Brownie and Jezebel, his favorite team.

"Yes, yes, I believe we can make a deal." The army scout wandered over to the Indian and began to converse with him in his native tongue, leaving William and the lieutenant alone. Lt. Baker looked around to see what happened to the boy, but the child was gone. He swatted at a fly that came too close to his nose, removed his hat, took out a kerchief and wiped the sweat from his brow, then replaced his hat on his head.

"Butler, the United States government is prepared to pay a large sum of money to young, enterprising gentlemen like you who are willing to take risks for their country. You have a distinct advantage over most since you have your own wagon and team of animals. I cannot with good conscience seek your services without mentioning the danger of the trip. I've met your good wife, child and brother-in-law. The government realizes that you have personal responsibilities, but I assure you, we need your help." Lieutenant Baker gazed into William's eyes for an instant. He dropped his glance and started to walk away toward the scout and Indian. Then he turned back as though he'd forgotten an important point.

"I've discussed with Pedigrew at the fort the possibility of leaving the Indian with your family to help with the work. This, too, you'll have to decide for yourself. I'm not familiar with the man or his tribal customs. The Shoshones have lived in this territory for many years, and I've heard they were one of the first tribes to use the horse as a domestic animal. Pedigrew vouches for the man's character." And, with this last bit of information, Lieutenant Baker went to stand with the Indian and the scout. They seemed to be having a heated discussion, but William wasn't watching.

He stood as if turned to stone. It was his dream, his opportunity to begin his freighting line, and with the authority of the government behind him, and a troop of soldiers as protection and support. He would be a fool to reject this chance of a lifetime. But, just as important to him now was his home here in the meadow and the people depending on him. He had to think this through. He started off toward the trail to the river, bypassing the rock fence. He could clearly see the rocks and the grass and the blue sky, but it was as if he was looking at them through the wrong end of a spy glass; they had become small in comparison.

His thoughts swirling around in his brain, William almost stepped on the young man lying under the canopy of green leaves on the slope of the river. He'd forgotten the lad. He knew that Joseph must have heard him coming, but he didn't turn or speak. It was their favorite spot, for there was a deep hole where the catfish liked to hide and wait for the minnows on a hook dropped down from above. Here beside the river it was peaceful and cool, even in the hottest months. William lay beside the boy. He put his arms behind his head and waited; his own problems would keep for later.

"William, do you think George is happy now? He said he felt stifled here. What does that mean, stifled?" Joseph continued to lie on his back and watch the leaves blow gently in the breeze, the hot August sun streaking through the limbs, yet not quite reaching their cool respite.

William was trying to think what might be in Joseph's thoughts. Was George happy? George always managed to be happy wherever he was. William had only lately come to realize that himself. "The word means that a person feels he no longer belongs somewhere, that he's being held down by responsibilities and burdens he can no longer bear. George decided to move on like a leaf in the breeze of a summer day."

"But, we loved him. He could have stayed longer. I would have helped him with his burdens."

"Son, George was unhappy when he joined the wagon train. His brother had cast him adrift, had turned him out of the only home he'd known. He didn't know where to go or what to do, but one night your father came into his life. I don't understand why James didn't want to drive his own wagon. I think it was because it would have stifled him, held him down to the responsibilities of caring for you, the animals and the food supplies. Do you understand that word, responsibilities? It means that no matter how sick you feel, or if you're tired of doing it day after day, you have to get up and feed the chickens or the pigs or they would die, because they can't feed themselves. You do that, Joseph, and I'm proud of you. Every morning without fail, you get up and go feed those pesky chickens and those lazy good-for-nothing pigs."

Joseph looked up with a gleam in his eyes.

William continued, "When George left he was glad to have had our friendship and a job to do, and to know that we'd be thinking of him always, like you are today. That made him happy. You're unhappy because the men pounding on the wagon brought you memories, didn't they, son?" He waited for an answer, unsure that he was making sense to the boy, but aware he was vocalizing his own problems and was beginning to understand what he must do.

"Yes, that's what George did the first day we met. He crawled under the wagon and banged on the floor, and he shook the sides and ran his finger over the grease. I watched him, but Papa didn't say anything 'cause he got drunk the night before and was feeling sick. I guess that's why Papa hired George, but why did he stay if he was stifled?"

William sighed under his breath. It was hard to explain to a young man of Joseph's age about why people left them.

"Joseph, George stayed because we needed him. He's a good farmer, and a good carpenter, and I'm neither. If left on my own here last year, we'd all have starved. When we needed him he stayed, but with your aunt and uncle coming he figured we didn't need him anymore. He left to find his own home and a wife like your sister, maybe a little boy like you." William decided it was time to go to the house. But, there was something he must say first. He sat up. Joseph looked up at him, a question in his eyes.

"Joseph, I'm going away for a while. It may be for a long time. I want you to understand that it isn't because I feel stifled, because I don't. I cherish every moment in my heart that I'm with you and your sister and Teddy and the others. Lieutenant Baker believes there's going to be a war soon with Mexico. And, that's shown in the newspapers we get from the East. That means there'll be killing and robbing and all sorts of evil things going on." He became still as he thought of the danger he would face on the trail to Santa Fe.

"The government needs men like me who know how to drive an oxen team and a wagon, so I feel it's my duty to help out in this way. Now, get up and clean yourself because the lieutenant and the army scout are staying the night. I want you to show them that you're ready to do your part, too. Can you do that for me, Joseph, while I'm gone?"

Joseph's gray eyes were as big as plates. He stood up and brushed the leaves and soil from his clothes. "Yes, sir, I can do it. I know I can, because you and George showed me how. He taught me how to fish and trap rabbits and follow a cougar's track, and you've shown me how to be responsible." And, he grinned again. On the way back to the house, Joseph talked about soldiers and guns, of horses and Indians. William didn't have the heart to lay any other burdens on him today. He answered his questions with simple words that a thirteen-year-old boy could understand.

As they turned the corner of the rock fence to go toward the house, William stopped the boy. "Remember, Joseph, for just a little while longer this is to be kept a secret between you and me. I'll tell your sister when the men have left." Joseph solemnly nodded his head in agreement, went to the horse trough, washed the muck off his face and hands, and slicked down his hair by running his fingers through it.

The visitors were sitting in the ladder back chairs brought from the kitchen, patiently awaiting their supper. They gazed at the scene before them of sheep chewing away on the grass and a shepherd boy watching over them, with the dog constantly on the move, nipping at their heels if he didn't approve of their behavior. William and Joseph joined the army men. There was a serious look on Joseph's face, one not of awe for the uniform, but with a new respect.

*****

While the meat stew was cooking, Jemima made her delicious leaf lettuce salad with tiny onions, carrots and pieces of the herbs and mushrooms she'd collected. Charlotte decided to take out the letters from her pocket that William had brought from Fort John. She knew one was from her father by the bold handwriting. She opened the other letter first.

"Charlotte, my friend, I have promised to write but didn't feel well for several months. We lost the baby. He started coughing in the night and it didn't stop for several days. Captain Foster was concerned for the rest of the party, so our wagon dropped out of line and we were at the back of the train for some days. After the short prayer service attended by one other couple who stayed behind with us to help dig the grave, we were able to catch up, but remained the last wagon until we reached the Willamette Valley. Bart went into Oregon City and filed our claim, and we have been working hard to build a shelter before winter sets in. All about us are tall trees, so high you can't see the sky through their leaves. Bart has started the plowing today and a kind neighbor is going into the city and will take this letter with him. I hope all is good with you and your family. James Morgan has filed a claim nearby, Bart was told. Your friend: Matilda Johnson."

Charlotte spent a few moments thinking of the sad-eyed woman, who had asked her to watch over her children so that she'd have time to tend her baby. Oh, it was so sad the baby didn't survive to see the tall trees and green fields of Oregon. She opened the seal on her father's letter.

"Charlotte, I have left the fields and land of Oregon, and joined a band of pioneers bound for Alta California. We'll arrive at the Mission San Francisco de Asis near the village of Yerba Buena tomorrow. I have seen the Pacific Ocean and it is a grand sight to witness. We had meant to spend several hours swimming but the water is too cold for comfort. The waves billow up like giants and we saw some sea lions sunning on the rocks off the shore. All about is talk of war with the United States. 'Tis strange to think that the Spaniards of California believe us to be their enemies. When questioned by one man, I answered in my broadest Scottish tones, and he let me be. I have lost my father's books and the family Bible. Blue Boy stumbled and fell over the side of a mountain. I have no horse, only a ride in the carriage of a beautiful Spanish lady from Oregon City on the Willamette River. I haven't received a letter from you. Your loving father: James Morgan."

Charlotte tried to hide her emotions from Jemima, so she rose and went to the bedroom she shared with William. She put the letters in her stocking box. She poured some water from the pitcher into the basin and washed her face and hands. She took out her comb and dampened it to pull the stray hairs off her neck and the sides of her face. She emerged from her bedroom with a brave smile on her face.

After the supper was over and the dishes put away, Peter and Eileen and the boys came and joined the group. Tales of the floods in

Illinois and Missouri were related without the addition of the loss of the baby girl, for it was still too painful to talk about. Willowby spoke of his time in that area and that his imagination couldn't grasp the significance of the change in land markers and devastation of farmlands and buildings. Lieutenant Baker spoke of the Military Academy, and his home in New York. The older women told of quilting parties and social events in their youth, and Jemima described the trip that she and her husband had made through Spain and France, where their ancestors lived.

Eileen told of a morning on the wagon train when one of the single men tied a red scarf on the tail of a mule. Everyone laughed hilariously as the mule took off across the prairie kicking and he-hawing in protest. A whole group of boys ran after the mule to get him back. The wagon master was most displeased, but it was funny, and people laughed for days over the incident.

The younger boys were getting sleepy, and Teddy was squirming in Charlotte's arms, fretful with teething. William took the boy from his wife's arms. Eileen wished the men a pleasant good night and took her boys to their cabin.

When the sun began to close down for the night, Charlotte excused herself, took Teddy from William's loving arms where he'd fallen asleep, and said that Joseph must retire to bed. They moved into her bedroom where Joseph sat on the bed, and she told him about Papa's letter, while placing her child, still asleep, in his cradle. Then with a quiet good night, Joseph went into his room and the gray blanket was pulled down between them.

*****

To give Charlotte privacy William moved the men's talk outside on the porch. For several hours they discussed river crossings and the trail, and swatted at the insects buzzing around their heads, attracted by the light from within. Finally the two army men went to their tents on the east side of the house near the rock fence. Peter returned to his cabin shared with Eileen and his two boys. The Indian slept in his bedroll under the stars. It was a pleasant night with the waning moon shining and the stars twinkling like fireflies in the Virginia hills, William thought, as he gave one final look over the barely visible sheep lying or standing in the meadow, and closed the door.

He checked the fireplace to see that no sparks might set fire to the surrounding area. He crossed the room silently in his stocking feet for he'd removed his shoes in the kitchen. The room seemed eerie in the gloom of the night. He pulled aside the blanket and moved into the room. He removed his clothes, raised the covers and slid into bed beside his wife. "Dear, are you asleep?" She turned toward him, and he took her in his arms. He felt guilty because he'd told Joseph of his plans and not her, but it wasn't the time for such a conversation. He whispered in her ear that she was beautiful and he loved her. He wasn't sure that she believed him, but she didn't resist as he began the dance of love that they shared in the night.

32

The next morning after a breakfast of flapjacks and fresh butter, and a choice of molasses or honey, and porridge and ham, the army men packed their tents and bedrolls onto the mule and rode to Fort John. The Indian followed them. Jemima made a flimsy excuse and went to her own cabin.

With an instinct equal to a mature man, Joseph went to the corral where Peter was working with the mustangs. There was a sense of urgency in the business for William would need the sturdy horse on the trip. The boys lined up on the rail with their long legs curled under them for balance as they watched the familiar routine of selecting the horse, separating him from the others, putting the harness and saddle on and climbing aboard without getting bucked off before a man was comfortably seated.

William had selected the taller of the two animals, since he had longer legs than Peter, and named him Mercury after the Roman winged-feet messenger god, symbol of trade, merchants and travel. Peter was more pragmatic; he named his horse Rudy after the man he had known in Springfield named Thomas Rhudy who had lost his life in the flood. When Neely asked his father why he didn't name him Tommy, the father answered that was too common a name for a horse. The mare was named Penelope and always known as Penny. She was a lovely shade of copper, and she was sometimes called Penny Copper.

William and Charlotte were alone except for Teddy, who was on the floor playing with some wooden stacking blocks carved by George. He asked her to sit with him on the horsehair sofa. She took, instead, the rocking chair, and he sat at an angle on the end of the sofa. She started talking while he rubbed his hand on the side of the sofa.

"It's time for the start of your business, isn't it? I know this because Neely said that the men were looking at the Conestoga and the oxen. Where are you going?"

William wasn't really surprised that Charlotte had guessed his reason for bringing the army men to his home. She was an intelligent person, and well-read for a farm woman. She hadn't had the advantages of Eileen, who had lived in a city environment, nor Jemima who traveled through Europe. But, she was quick-witted and retained what she heard or read to recall later in her stories of fact or fiction.

She rocked the chair slowly.

"Santa Fe." His words were a bold statement, and Charlotte blinked hard. William saw the surprise but also the fear in her dark brown eyes, and he understood. The town was in Mexican Territory, and there had been many articles in the Eastern newspapers about war with Mexico. The newspapers were several weeks or months late by the time they were passed on to them by Pedigrew or Jules, for they, too, had a keen interest in a war, especially Jules, with two boys of his own at the age to want to ride off and join the army.

William told her basically the same facts that he'd told Joseph the day before, eliminating the details of the diversionary tactics he determined weren't suitable for the ears of a tender woman of her years. He told her of Pedigrew's suggestion of leaving the Shoshone to help Peter with the work. This was plausible for two reasons, one that the Shoshone and the Bannock Indians who frequented the fort were for the most part honest and non-hostile, but there were elements prone to steal from their neighbors.

Further, with fall and winter coming on, Peter would need the help of an adult male, not three half-grown lads. The Indian had his own bedding and tent, but if it were extremely cold, he might use the empty room in the barn that George had slept in or come into the house in dire circumstances.

He went on to tell her that the troop of Dragoons would be with him, and there would be at least three wagons in a caravan across the prairie and hills. The length of the trip would depend on the weather and overnight stops along the way. They would shoot or trap wild game to supplement their diets. Lieutenant Baker figured three to four months. William stopped talking and waited for a reaction from Charlotte. There was none.

"Charlotte, what do you have to say?" He smiled, hoping for a good response. He'd have more trouble leaving, if she was angry or yelled at him.

"I accept that you must make the trip, and there's nothing I can say except to wish you God's speed and pray you come back to me."

She changed the subject by relating the details of her father's letter. He'd forgotten the letters he had brought back from Fort John in all the excitement and bustle of the visitors. She gave him her opinion of why her father had left the beloved Oregon country he had dreamed of and claimed in his first missive that was quite satisfactory.

"My lovely Charlotte, your father, once he gained his freedom from the farm in Illinois and the petty bickering of your mother, cannot now settle down in one place and be happy. He's enjoyed the sins of the flesh too long. I don't know enough of the situation to condemn him outright for the reason for his traveling in the carriage of the Spanish woman. It may be as he said, he needed transportation and she provided it. The woman may be married and her husband in the carriage with her or riding beside them on a horse. We mustn't judge what we don't know."

Teddy became fretful, and William picked him up from the floor. "I'll miss you and the lad and dream of the day I can return to your arms, for I do love you, my sweet Charlotte, even though you don't believe me." William came close and leaned over the warm body of his son to kiss her full on the mouth, and she accepted his embrace warmly.

To relieve the tension of the moment, William gave her the boy and went outside to chop wood for the fireplace, for it might be a hard winter. Besides, he needed some physical exercise to drive away the demons that beset him when he thought of leaving the farm.

He finished off the logs that he'd brought down from the high ridge above the farm, and yoked Atlas and Star for a trip into the forest for more logs. He hallowed to Joseph to come and help him. Peter was still working with the mustang stallion Mercury, but his two lads had taken to roping the pony, Petey. The pony had grown accustomed to young boys swinging ropes around his neck and stood still.

They brought back a dozen fallen logs from the forest above his farm. He and Joseph, with the assistance of Peter and the boys, laid them out to be cut into lumber or wood for the fireplace. Peter suggested he try out Mercury, and William mounted his new saddle horse and rode him around the farmyard and down to the meadow to speak with Pedro. He was very pleased because the horse had an easy gait and appeared strong. He kicked the horse in the flanks, and they flew back to the barn. Dismounting, he congratulated Peter on a job well done, unsaddled the horse and tackled some more logs, leaving a considerable addition to the wood pile. He asked Jesse to help him hone his ax at the sharpening stone. The boy smiled at the offer, as William expected he would, for William knew the boy loved the feel of the flint and sparks flying from the stone. William watched him at this task and thanked him afterward.

In the two weeks that followed, William took his oxen on the road to Fort John for practice in maneuvering in tight corners, backing and going forward at his command. He was convinced the animals had grown lazy and fat from pulling the lighter farm wagon. He used all five, because he planned to take the extra in case of need. The Conestoga was washed and axles greased, with one board on the back given some extra nails, for it seemed loose to William. The younger boys gazed in fascination at this activity, and he sometimes took them aboard for the ride. Joseph had ridden on the wagon and was more sanguine about the practice sessions.

One midafternoon in September, Bear Grease appeared with a pack mule of his belongings and settled into the routine of life on a farm. He set up his tent behind the house, and it was explored by the boys, but they didn't go inside, for the Indian made the guttural sound in his throat, and they left him alone. He was shown the small room in the barn in which George had spent the winter in comfort, and the Indian nodded but preferred his familiar army tent. The horse and mule were released into the corral with the mustangs.

Two days after Bear Grease arrived, William hitched the oxen to the Conestoga, tied the extra ox and Mercury behind, kissed Charlotte and Teddy, shook hands with Joseph and told him he was depending on him to take care of his family. He spoke for a while with Peter and the boys, gave Eileen and Jemima a hug, a salute of his hat to the Indian, and marched away beside his four oxen, his black whip flying

240

high above the backs of the animals once more. The crack of the whip echoed across the valley floor like a thunder clap. Pedro watched in awe until the wagon was over the ridge and lost to sight.

33

The Indian helped Peter in the wheat field and in harvesting the last of the corn from the spring garden. The fall and winter vegetables they left alone to mature. A small area was set aside for garlic and peas to be planted in November, weather permitting. Bear Grease was especially skillful at trapping and hunting wild game. He killed a deer in late October which provided meat for weeks. He showed the boys and Peter how to tan the hide and make soft shirts or vests out of the skin. Jesse wore his buckskin vest with the pride of achievement, although Eileen was not so pleased because it still had a wild smell about it.

Hammond had sent more varieties of vegetables because he didn't know what would grow best in the high plains. By sending different kinds, he wrote, they could enjoy vegetables almost year around except in the extremely cold months of January and February. It would become an experimental farm for the drummer, although he would never see the fruits of his largesse. He looked forward to their replies, as he was keeping careful notes in his book about what was sent and what grew or did not. He looked forward to the short missives sent by Charlotte to Bertha to be relayed to him when he stopped at the hotel in St. Louis. Bertha hadn't been heard from since the wagon trains had ceased to roll across the plains for the duration of the winter.

In late December, when the weather brought a harsh wind, some wolves were heard, apparently driven south out of the mountains by the cold air and snow. The next night they sounded closer, and the Indian went looking for tracks. They had come to the edge of the meadow, and Jemima fretted about Pedro and the sheep. But Pedro wouldn't abandon his responsibility, so stayed in the tent that night.

Shortly after midnight, the mournful sound of the wolves was even closer. Peter and Bear Grease went to the meadow, rifles in hand, and found the mangled body of the boy curled inside his tent, his clothes and blankets soaked with blood. The dog lay near the door. He had attempted to prevent the entrance of the wolves. Two sheep carcasses lay in the meadow grassland, slaughtered by the wolves. Peter blamed himself for he should have insisted the boy come into the house. The next morning, the faithful shepherd boy, only thirteen years old, was buried on the slope above the farm next to the grave of the Cummings woman, and the sheep were herded into the barn for their safety.

The winter was extremely bad. The cold north winds blew, and twice snow piled high over the fences so that Peter and Bear Grease, with the boys' help, were forced to bring into the barn all the animals it would hold. Jemima volunteered to keep the chickens safe in her one room cabin, but even she was driven into the Butler cabin, since she couldn't walk the distance from one place to another in the ice and snow. She again took Joseph's room, and he slept in the front room. Joseph begged to sleep in George's room in the barn, but that room had been offered to the Indian. One day shortly before Christmas, Bear Grease muttered, "Too cold, too cold," and rolled up his tent and adjourned to the assigned room. The women worried about him for there was no heat in the barn, but he seemed to bear the cold better than most as long as he was out of the wind.

Peter built a temporary cage in the barn and changed the newspapers under them so the chickens wouldn't foul the floor, but by January the newspapers and magazines had all been used. The Rhode Island Red rooster awakened them each morning with his happy good morning. The Kincade's mud roof began to leak, and Peter climbed up to see what he could do, but decided to cover the contents of the inside as best he could and moved the family over into Jemima's cabin, with her permission.

By the end of February everyone was tired of the snow and ice, even the boys who had played joyfully in the first snowfall of the season. As if in an answer to prayer, the north wind shifted to the south, and a warm, weak sun began to melt the snow and icicles from the trees and wooden sections of the cabins. As the month passed, so did the winter cold. The river rose and flooded its banks but not enough to reach the stone fence built to protect the cabins.

March was pleasant enough to move the animals out of the barn except for the pigs, milk cow and chickens, in case the snow returned. The wolves didn't return after the night of disaster in the meadow. The Indian had cleaned up the carcasses of the lost sheep, and green shoots of grass and wild flowers soon covered the area. Peter determined that it was safe to release the sheep so they could munch on the new lawn. A rider from Fort John came to say that a wagon caravan and troop of Dragoons from Santa Fe had been sighted about twenty miles to the south.

The message brought welcome comfort to the Butler household. Charlotte tried not to anticipate the arrival of William, for it might be a different wagon caravan or a different troop of soldiers. Teddy was now past his first birthday and walking with only a few tumbles. He had taken a liking to climbing onto whatever he could manage with his little butt twisted in the air. She had to watch him closely so he didn't get near the fireplace. Jemima had become a treasure in that regard. While Charlotte cooked, Jemima entertained the boy with his wooden blocks or a soft ball of yarn. Sometimes his clever hands would unwind the thread and pull on the strands; and with great glee, he would run away or twist the strands across the rocking chair or sofa. Jemima was found to exclaim, "That boy is going to go some-where, he is!"

Joseph was often seen reading a book with the younger boy sitting solemn-faced beside him. He played his Jew's harp, and Teddy would move from side to side to the music, or clap his hands. Joseph would laugh but couldn't play the harp and laugh at the same time, so the music stopped, and Teddy would give Joseph a mournful look in his beautiful brown eyes, and Joseph would laugh harder, bringing tears to his own gray eyes. Those were the good times, filling Charlotte's heart with love for her brother and her son.

Jacob came to check on the family as he'd promised William, and when told of the loss of the Basque sheepherder, he said they'd lost some animals, too. His mother had been sickly with lung congestion, but was feeling better. The heavy snow and ice had toppled a few large trees in the yard and nearly crashed into the house. His father and Hanley had chopped them up into firewood. Peter passed along the news of the wagon caravan and the soldiers in case the Robertson's hadn't heard, and Jacob gave out a shout of joy. Peter also suggested that he and the Indian might need help with the wheat harvest in the early summer. The youth went home with what was left of the venison and a few vegetables from the fall garden.

April came in warm and windy. New grass appeared. Peter was gratified to welcome a foal from the mating of Jimmy and Penny, a mare with Penny's bright copper coloring. There were lambs and piglets and a dozen chickens, in spite of Joseph's curses and threats to shoot them all. The repairs were done to the Kincade's roof by making shingles out of some of the cedar logs that William had hauled into the yard. Peter and Joseph climbed up and tore away the old sod roof much to the dismay of Eileen who lamented the dust it showered down on the contents. Peter yelled down that it was better a little dust than the snow dripping in. She yelled back that they wouldn't know whether it was an improvement until the next rainfall. When the roof was finished and the family removed to their home, Jemima moved back into her small cabin.

Peter was so successful with the cabin roof that he decided to repair Jemima's and William's too, but Jemima said to wait until they saw his own roof withstand the water. He accused her of siding with his wife, and everyone laughed, even Teddy who didn't understand what they were laughing about.

34

William spent three days at Fort John, impatient to see his wife and son. He regretted he'd missed Teddy's first birthday, but had brought him several presents from Santa Fe in consolation. He'd also brought a surprise for his wife.

He stayed while the supplies promised to the local settlers were unloaded and then pulled out. It was a warm day with the sun high in the sky and puffy white clouds floating by, with a hint of rain in the air. As he spied the rock formation and took the cutoff, his heart thumped in anticipation. He topped the ridge with his black whip cracking in the air. He walked beside the oxen team, and his spirits were lifted when he saw the green grass which gave the farm its name. He didn't see Pedro's tent, and he wondered whether Jemima was still at the farm.

Joseph was the first to spy the wagon and oxen crest the ridge and move down the slope toward the cabins and barn. William waved as the boy let out a whoop, jumping up and down. His shout must have alarmed Charlotte, for she appeared in a state of mild disarray and stood on the porch with Teddy, followed by a slower Jemima. William called with a wave, and Jemima went to her own cabin. The shout was heard by Neely, and he yelled that his father was digging in the garden for root vegetables for his supper, and he would let him know. Eileen came to the door to see what her son was fussing about, and she saw the Butler Conestoga wagon move down the slope. She clasped her hands to her bosom and thanked the good Lord.

The second thing that William noticed was the new brown roof on the Kincade cabin. He heard Joseph give a second whoop and saw him running toward the wagon. If a heart could break from sheer joy, William thought his would split wide open. He'd dreamed of this day for six months, and to hear that sound from Joseph was the most wonderful thing he could imagine. George had tried to tell him to be patient that day he had lain in the hay with the smell of his own vomit and spilled liquor on his clothes. The boy would come around in his own time. Could he also be so lucky that Charlotte had forgiven him for the way he'd married her and taken her innocence in the prostitute's bed in St. Louis?

William slowed the oxen, and Joseph caught up. He ran to William's side and reached out for him. "Wait a minute, son, you'll frighten the animals."

Joseph grinned and walked sedately beside his brother-in-law until the wagon came to a stop in front of the house, exactly the way it had those many months ago. William turned, and Joseph was in his arms.

"Hello, son, I love you." William wrapped the boy in his arms, thinking that the child seemed to have grown another two inches. He'd also seen his gray eyes shimmering with unshed tears. William's eyes were gritty with emotion of his own. When Joseph just hugged his brother harder, William squeezed him back.

"I love you, too, William." Joseph's words cracked, and he drew away, wiping his eyes with one sleeve.

"We wouldn't want anyone to see you crying, now would we?" William smiled. He set the boy down, and they turned as one and walked toward the porch where Charlotte waited with Teddy squirming in her arms. William swept the hat off his head. "Where's Bear Grease?" He picked up his son as he spoke. He was surprised not to see the Indian's tent in the yard.

"He's gone. We saw a string of Indians riding along the edge of the ridge. Bear Grease said they were his Shoshone brothers and ran to catch his horse and mule. He packed his belongings and was soon riding to meet his tribesman." Charlotte laughed. "Eileen is certain that's the last we'll see of him."

He looked into the dark brown glow of his wife's eyes and found the love and forgiveness that he had prayed were there. He would be patient until nightfall to reward her in private. For now, he tickled the baby in his arms. Teddy pulled back not recognizing William.

"You're a stranger to him. He'll get to know you again." Charlotte rubbed the boy's face. "Give him time."

William whispered in his ear, and the boy relaxed. William turned and put his arm around Charlotte's waist and kissed her on the mouth. They went into the house, but Joseph didn't follow. William heard the sound of whistling as the boy marched away.

It seemed awkward at first, both wanting to say something, but neither wanting to be the first to say it. William put Teddy on the floor, and he was off like a shot out of a gun, crossing the room at a gallop to his toys near the sofa. William watched him in shock. He looked into Charlotte eyes, and she was laughing at him. He began to laugh himself. The baby looked up and saw his parents laughing, and he decided he would join in, so he ran back and into his mother's arms.

"My God, I never dreamed he would be walking when I returned. Look, Charlotte, how big he's grown. He has your brown eyes." William took the boy from the mother's arms, and this time the child didn't resist but put his chubby little arms around William's neck.

"I've brought you home a surprise, my Charlotte. As soon as we can empty the wagon, you'll see how much you mean to me. There's so much to tell about the trip and Santa Fe. But I have to ask, did I see a shingled roof on Peter's cabin?" He grinned.

"Oh, we had a bad winter, William, really bad. The cabin leaked, and Peter had to fix it. The worst was when Pedro was attacked by wolves. The animals also got the boy's dog. Nothing could have been more horrific."

"By wolves, you say, little Pedro?" William remembered coming over the ridge and thinking that Pedro must be sleeping in the barn, but to discover he was dead was like a mule-kick to the gut. He bowed his head a moment. "Where did you lay him?"

"Beside the Cummings woman. And Honey, there's another grave there, one without a marker; just a board near the sunken ground. When you go to the fort again, you must ask Pedigrew who it might be so we can put a marker. I've wondered if Mrs. Cummings might have had a child after all."

As she spoke, she'd been moving toward the living area so they could sit. Teddy had four blocks lined up, then he reached a chubby hand and swatted them down.

"I'm afraid your son has a destructive bent. I asked Eileen, but she says it's natural for a boy of his age." She smiled as she watched the boy build his tower again.

"I was the same." William's words were little more than a murmur. After a moment of pondering, he asked, "Charlotte, how did the wolves get to the field? Did they come from the north or the west? Did the Indian look for tracks? I must know how the boy was hurt." He couldn't bring himself to say the word killed. He'd seen so much killing on his trip. He'd never been introduced to violence before, and to think the small boy was so cruelly hurt was devastating.

"I don't know the answers. Peter wouldn't let us go there. You'll have to ask him. The Indian saw tracks that day, but the boy wouldn't come to the house, insisting he must stay with his sheep."

Teddy tired of the blocks and came to her. She stopped rocking when he pulled on her skirt, calling out, "Mama, eat!" It was said so forcefully that William laughed, and the boy turned to him with a question in his eyes.

Charlotte excused herself and went to the kitchen area to find something to satisfy the boy until supper, and Teddy trotted after her, chattering in his little boy's treble voice. William couldn't believe the boy had grown so much. Charlotte was so beautiful; the hated freckles seemed to have faded a little. He wanted to take her in his arms and march to the bedroom; but it wasn't the right time. Tonight, he promised himself. Tonight.

He continued to ponder why the Indian would leave. He'd promised Pedigrew that he'd remain until William's return. He voiced his thought out loud.

"Maybe the Indians sensed the change in the wind, for it's almost certain that war will be declared soon by the Washington politicians. American troops will come to Fort John. I talked to Lieutenant Baker and Pedigrew about it. The manager of the fur company is already making plans to go east. He said the days of the fur business are limited, what with the increase in wagon trains on the move. He expects maybe ten caravans to come through this season, where there were four last year. Baker expects the Army to take over the fort in the next year or so. We had seven wagons on our train from Santa Fe. The trading post will be brimming with supplies for the emigrants this year."

"War? But, surely it won't come here to the fort. What would the

Mexicans have to do with this country? And, ten wagon trains, surely the man exaggerates." She left the boy at the table eating a biscuit smeared with butter and came to sit near him. "Will you have to leave again?"

"Not for a while." He took her arm and gently drew her into his lap, where she lay contentedly against his breast. "I'll have to wait and see what the Army wants. The lieutenant's left for Fort Leavenworth, where I suspect he'll be needed in the battles in the south. He promised to write." He kissed her deeply, "I've missed you so much, my lovely wife."

William stayed with Charlotte and the boy for a moment longer, and restless, he helped her to her feet and stood himself. He gave her a kiss on the freckles. "Dear, I must see Peter about unloading the wagon, for the oxen shouldn't be left standing at the door for long." Before Charlotte could blink, he walked out the door.

He stood on the porch for a moment, gazing down at the meadow. It seemed in many ways the same as when he left, but the boy's tent was gone, and there was no dog tormenting the feckless sheep. They were milling about without purpose. He'd speak to Jules and ask if he knew of someone with a reliable dog, or a shepherd. He walked around the wagon and headed toward Peter's cabin, for there were so many questions to be asked, not the first of which was how he'd made the shingled roof. Neither he nor George had thought of it. He stood admiring the newly shingled roof and glanced at Joseph standing beside his pony, brushing his coat.

Neely raced past him and flew in the door, only to hear his mother call loudly, "Neely Kincade, haven't I told you to walk, not run?" William mounted the steps behind Neely and paused at the door. He could see Jesse sitting at the table reading. It reminded him of George with his Bible. But, he sent that thought away, for he sorely missed George. Since the boy had nothing to say, he turned to his brother.

"Hello, Neely. Have you come to tell your parents that the hogs have gotten out of their pen again?" William winked broadly at the boy to make his jest clear, and glanced at Peter to find him smiling at the joke.

Neely laughed. "No, sir, nothin's got out, but we got a dozen new baby chickens, and Penny had a foal."

"Did she now? That is good news, a filly or a colt?"

Peter came over and laid his arm across the lad's shoulder, giving it a squeeze. "A filly, by God. She looks like her mother. The old boy

250

came through for us, William. We've been calling her Lucy. I expect you came to get someone to help you unload the wagon. Come on, boys. Let's help William with his chores." He started to the door, and William had to move first, being the closest. The others followed behind him, leaving Eileen to her cooking. They walked across the grass toward the wagon.

"I see you got rid of the sod on top of your house, Peter. How did you do that?" William looked up at the new wooden roof with awe in his voice.

While the men and boys were taking boxes and barrels out of the wagon, Peter went on to say how the snow had piled over the fences and the roof began to leak. Jemima moved in with Charlotte, and his family had moved into Jemima's house. "If you remember, you left an old cedar tree in the pile of timber over there. I looked at that cedar log one day and decided to use it for shingles. I saw a man do it once in Illinois and tried to imitate him. It took a while to get the size right, but I just threw the broken pieces into the fireplace. They put off a pleasing aroma."

"I imagine it might, if it smells anything like the cut wood." William chuckled, satisfied with Peter's resourcefulness in a difficult situation, one that was surely beyond his area of comfort.

"We put all the animals in the barn, and the chickens in your house, but Joseph got mad and said he'd shoot 'em all 'cause they kept him awake at night, cackling and pecking at the floor." For Jesse, this was a long speech. Joseph had come to the house and quietly started helping with the unloading. He looked at the box he was holding and turned red with embarrassment.

Neely took up the tale. "Wolves got the sheep and killed Pedro and his dog."

"But Bear Grease, he chased 'em away and put Pedro up there." Jesse pointed toward a brown spot on the western side of the wheat field.

William hadn't known where the Cummings woman was buried. He hadn't wanted to know. The story of her death and Cummings running reminded him too much of his own tragedy, and he wanted to forget about Virginia and its troubles. "Really, the Indian chased the wolves away?" He looked at Peter with a question in his eyes. Peter returned a look of, "I'll tell you later."

"Charlotte said the Indian left. When was that?" William hoped to distract the boys from the tragedy, but anything about the Shoshone

251

seemed to be a matter of importance to the boys, and they continued to rattle on about how he'd shot a deer. Jesse stuck out his chest and told how he'd made his deerskin vest. William had wondered about that vest, but had assumed Peter bought it. They removed all the boxes and barrels from the wagon and put them temporarily on the porch or the ground beside it. In the front of the wagon was a large object covered with heavy sailcloth.

"What's that, Mr. William?" Neely pointed.

"It's a surprise for my wife." William told Joseph to fetch Charlotte.

Joseph ran into the house, calling, "Sister, William says come; he has something in the wagon for you." He turned and walked back to the wagon, not waiting to see if she followed.

Charlotte came out the front door and stopped, Teddy in her arms. Jemima followed close behind and almost bumped into Charlotte. They moved forward, surprised to see everyone there but Eileen.

"Jesse, go get your mother." William stood as proud as Jesse over his deerskin vest, but he wouldn't let anyone touch the sheet to reveal what it covered. Joseph and Neely climbed into the wagon and whispered to each other. Peter looked at William, but he grinned and wouldn't talk. Eileen lumbered up the slight incline between the two cabins and stopped, wondering what was happening. Jesse was beside his mother, and when he saw the other two boys in the wagon, he moved forward, but William grasped his shoulder to keep him back, and jumped into the wagon bed himself.

"Charlotte, my dear—" William's pulse rate soared as he saw his wife and child standing at the back of the Conestoga. "On the way to Santa Fe, I asked myself what I could do to convince you that I truly do love you. Then I walked into a store like Trice's Mercantile in St. Louis, and saw something that might convince you. Darling, before all your family, I again make my vow to love you and remain faithful until the day I die." He turned and asked the boys to step aside, then with a mighty sweep of the cloth, there stood a wood burning iron cooking range almost exactly like the one Charlotte had cooked on in Bertha Hightower's hotel.

She gave a gasp of shock, and Jemima reached for the boy before Charlotte might drop him. She stood still, her brown eyes filled with tears. She looked at William and hadn't a single word to say. William understood. He motioned for Peter to help her onto the wagon bed. Charlotte ran her hand lovingly over the shiny surface of the front of the oven, down the black sides of the hot water well, and touched the four burners with care as though they were hot. She turned to William and fell into his arms. He held her tightly and whispered in her ear, and she blushed.

He helped her down from the wagon, then with the help of Peter and Joseph carefully moved the stove to where they could lower it and take it into the house. It took all their strength to move the heavy object. Eileen, always the practical one, hustled her boys into the cabin and started moving chairs and the large table to the empty center of the room so the men could place the range against the front wall. Peter used a thin-bladed saw to cut an opening in the sod roof for the vent pipe and slipped it through, attaching it securely to the back of the stove. It stood in perfect splendor, and the space in the center of the room was finally filled.

Neely was heard to comment that they couldn't put the chickens there next time it snowed, and everyone laughed to relieve the tension. William opened the oven door; for he'd worried that it might be damaged, what with all the boxes and barrels jostling against it on the long road to Fort John.

"Woman, I'll have me a taste of hot lamb stew tonight." William rolled his words off his tongue in a perfect imitation of a Scottish brogue, bringing their attention to the arrogant way in which James would use his native speech when he was emotional or angry.

It was Eileen's turn to gasp, but Charlotte laughed and said it was perfect, as if old Solomon Morgan had stepped into the room unannounced.

Jemima stood near the door, the child Teddy in her arms, admiring the black behemoth, and remarked that she itched to get her hands on the stove. She put the boy down and he ran to the other end of the room for his toys. Joseph followed him and brought out the Jew's harp from his pocket and began to play a merry tune. Teddy, arrested by the sound, said, "Moosic, Josie. Pay moosic," and began to sway his hips to the sound.

William, with another small kiss on his wife's forehead, motioned for Peter, and they went to the door, standing for a time, listening to the bustle of activity going on inside. Peter smiled when they saw Eileen step over to admire the stove, and the three ladies, all talking at once, and with great awe, ran their hands over the iron surface. The two men watched as Eileen went to the woodpile and got some kindling, and soon a fire was going. Jemima went to the water barrel in the root cellar and filled a bucket with water for the well. Charlotte found some potatoes, carrots and sat down at the table to peel them. Her gaze kept going to the shiny oven door.

"The women are happy as field chicks with a parcel of good food to eat." Peter chuckled as they left the house. "What do you have in mind for us to do?"

"I'd like your help with the animals." William pointed to the animals still tied to the porch railing, waiting to be released into the corral.

The two Kincade boys ran past them to find something more exciting to do. William released his saddle horse, Mercury, and Peter led him to barn. Jimmy came to the fence. William scratched and fondled the old horse's head and hugged him around the neck. He led the extra ox, Star, to the gate and released him into the field, where he immediately began to nibble on the grass.

Guiding his oxen team with the familiar commands, he drove the wagon to the rear of the house and turned it around to back it into the shed from which it had come before his trip to Santa Fe. He released the oxen to join Star in the field. There seemed to be a new corral, for when he turned around, it was west of the one where Jimmy and Penny, the mustang mare, were kept. As soon as the wagon and oxen were settled, he went to see the foal, Lucy, in the barn.

Peter took him around the farm to show the improvements and the damage done by the winter storms. They climbed up the ladder and Peter described how he had shingled the roof. He explained how they could build onto William's house and add a back door, which had always been his concern. They walked around to the back of the cabin, with Peter waving his arms, pointing and pounding on the wall.

William began to see how it would work. Peter stooped in the dirt, and picking up a stick, traced the lines and form it would take.

"My idea is to haul dirt from the new spot for the root cellar and fill in the older root cellar after emptying it of food. After the hole is filled and packed solid, we can place wooden flooring and extend the wall to the east about twelve feet, then build a room above it. Can you see it?" Peter gave his nephew an inquiring glance, while squatting on the ground, the stick in his hand. "You'll have two more rooms, one downstairs and one upstairs. The downstairs room will have an outside door." He stepped to the side and shrugged his shoulders. "Of course, it means anyone in the kitchen will have to go through the new room to the back door, but it's workable, if you think we can get the digging done, and haul more logs before winter sets in." He looked at William with anxiety in his eyes.

"The plan looks good, with one exception." William crossed out a few lines and put in new ones in the dirt with Peter's stick. "If we're to extend the wall by the root cellar thus, then let's extend it another six feet, making it even wider, then coming out of the kitchen, we can add a hallway and water closet. I'd like to get some pipe and the equipment for an inside bath. Charlotte can tell you how the Hightower's hotel had a combination wash room for the laundry and water closet for the guests. With a hallway from the kitchen, through to the outside door, no one would disturb the people in the rooms." William shuddered with remembrance of Jemima walking through his and Charlotte's room in the early morning hours. From anxiety, Peter's eyes now glowed with possibilities. He suggested they go to his cabin where they'd find writing paper and make better lines than in the dirt. They were still talking when the women called them to supper.

There was no question but that the whole family would eat together in the Butler cabin that night. The table seemed to fit perfectly in the center of the room between the two doors. The fireplace glowed with hot coals, and the new kitchen range was admired once again, for it had performed well. It had been many months since the women had used a stove, and they delighted in their work. There were hot venison steaks, fresh vegetables from the garden, biscuits with butter and a honey loaf that Jemima had learned to make in France. It was a feast, and when Eileen said they should ask the Lord to bless the return of William Butler, no one objected.

On that same night, April 25, 1846, Mexican troops attacked American soldiers on the southern Texas border and attacked Palo Alto on May 8, 1846. President James Knox Polk received word in Washington, D.C., on May 9, and the United States Congress declared war with Mexico on May 13, 1846. Busily unaware of the dramatic events taking place in the south, the inhabitants of Green Meadow Farm near the Laramie River pressed on with the routine of running a farm.

35

William and Peter, with the help of Joseph, carefully stepped off the perimeters of the new building, placed stakes into the ground at the corners, and strung cords between the stakes so they would have a guideline when the actual building began to take shape. The men decided to wait on the sheep shearing until later, and Jemima agreed that it wouldn't hurt for a few weeks, but at last the necessary chore was accomplished. William took the fleece to Pedigrew, but he wasn't as excited as he'd been the year before. He said there was no market for the fleece now that the lines of communication with Santa Fe were restricted. If William thought it best, he might take the fleece himself to Fort Hall to the west, owned by the Canadian Hudson's Bay Company, but he might not be able to sell it there.

William Butler walked to his farm beside his oxen and wagon still loaded with fleece. He had bought several burlap bags and a few yards of heavy cloth, hoping that if Jemima was willing, she could sew the cloth into bags, and they could preserve the fleece until the wagon trains started coming through. He might make a deal with the wagon master to have the fleece taken to Fort Hall or sell it outright to someone on the train, but he didn't have much hope of success. They would use what they could and wait for the matter to be resolved. When Jemima heard the plan, she agreed to sew the bags, and for an afternoon the other work stopped while the fleece was bagged and tagged and placed in the corner of the barn where it would stay dry, but not safe from the mice or varmints. It was the best they could do under the circumstances.

The summer garden vegetables began to ripen: pole beans, beets, potatoes, cabbage, carrots, mustard greens, onions, peas and corn. Each in its own time was picked, gathered and taken to the kitchen. Using the cloth that William had bought, Jemima and Eileen sewed small bags and larger bags and filled them with vegetables. They were stacked in the front room until the new root cellar was finished. The smell was both pleasant and unpleasant for the pungent odor of onions and garlic warred with the sweet smell of baking bread or pies.

In the last week in June, a day after Joseph's fourteenth birthday, a messenger was sent from Fort John that a wagon train was about ten miles to the east and would arrive in a few days.

Everyone was excited, and William decided they would make a holiday of it. He hitched two of Peter's mules to the smaller farm wagon, and everyone piled into the back. Jemima was given the honor of sitting on the seat with Charlotte and the child, Teddy. Peter rode his horse. Eileen agreed to ride in the back with her family. They had a baked chicken, ham sliced into thin slivers, mustard greens seasoned with bacon grease, new potatoes no larger than William's thumb and iced cake for everyone. The women brought blankets and pillows in case they had to spend the night. And an extra change of clothes for all.

William used his whip to guide the mules. The Kincade boys were so thrilled they kept glancing over the side, until Peter rode up to the side of the wagon, and in his deep, placid voice told them not to disturb their mother with their rowdy ways. The boys settled down in the wagon bed, but they laughed and pointed each time they heard the crack of William's whip in the air.

The wagon rolled toward the gates of Fort John, and everything seemed quiet and normal. William wondered if they'd made the trip on the wrong day. He'd carefully calculated how long a train of a large size would take to travel the ten miles since their last sighting. He found an out-of-the-way place near the gates. He parked the vehicle and told Peter he would inquire of Pedigrew at the office if anything was out of order. Everyone crawled down from their positions to stretch their legs. The boys looked around with awe. They'd been here a few times, but there were more settlers, fur traders and Indians strolling around today in anticipation of the new immigrants' arrival.

William mounted the steps and entered the now familiar office of the American Fur Company. Only Pedigrew was in the room. He looked up from what appeared to be a ledger book and smiled at his visitor. "William, ah, the rumors be not true."

"Rumors?" William laughed, unsure what he meant.

"That ya be leavin' us with your'n pretty lass of a wife. Come in, come in, t'ain't seen ya in weeks. It be paperwork keepin' me busy. Must make my bid'ness 'fore the settlers come raidin'. Everthin' goin' well up your'n direction?"

"Everything's going well. Pedigrew, I'm a farmer. I never thought I'd see the day when I spent my time chopping wood, growing vegetables and nursing sick horses. I enjoy every minute of it. There's something soothing to a man's soul to look out over your own property and see sheep and cattle munching on the grass. Did you say the wagons are supposed to roll in today? I brought my whole family for that very reason. What's the latest news?"

"Ya, sighted 'bout five miles back. Gotta Bannock Indian has been keeping an eye on 'em for me. Scouts shou'rn be coming 'bout the time we finish speakin'. Nay, tis not good news, William. There'n be a bad word. The Congress of the United States have declared war with Mexico. Tis a bad think, indeed." Pedigrew closed his ledger book and looked up at the ceiling as though for words to express his frustration and anger. "I been knowin' it be in the works for months. Since young Lieutenant Baker wern here. Before ya went off to Santa Fe. I may get caught up in it meself. I got me a notice from me superior thar's a new man comin' in on the train, or maybe the next one. Name of Watson, to take mine place. There's gonna be dozens of wagon trains rollin' through if them Yankees bust up the hostilities down south. It'll make them California rumors true, and Oregon, too. T'ain't nobody gonna stop them wagons."

"You say it's already started? A real shooting war? Where did you hear that?" William was thinking of the trip to Santa Fe when he saw things he never wanted to see again. They had turned his stomach and soured his outlook on the government, but he'd have to keep the information to himself, for he'd taken an oath of allegiance to the country.

"Place down in Texas, I hear, be where most of the bid'ness happenin'. Hear tell the Mexican army fired on the Americans, and a few days later, they lookin' for a wrangle and 'tacked another town, but we'll be waitin' 'til the wagons come in so's we'll have some newspapers, maybe. Probably not this train, 'cause they must'a left Missouri in February, mebbe early March, to be getting' here so soon. Real news be coming when them trains go through Leavenworth and see all them soldiers moving out for points south." Pedigrew opened his book. He sighed, a resigned look in his eyes. "Cain't say when I'll be pushin' on. That question lay with the owners of the company; them might send transportation for me, maybe not. May have to go on to California with the train and catch a boat back East. Been a pleasure knowing ya, son. 'Twer a fine day when ya chose to settle in these parts." He held out his hand, and William shook it, knowing once the emigrants started coming in, the man wouldn't have time to talk. This was possibly the last time he would see him.

All thoughts of celebration left William, and he returned to his family with a heavy heart. A sorrow for Pedigrew leaving Fort John, who had proved a good friend; and a rush of memories from his trip to Santa Fe threatened to overwhelm him. He put them out of his mind, for his family waited for him. They were eager for news. The boys, including Joseph, all gathered around.

"Might be any minute now the scouts from the train come in the gate. Main wagons are about five, six miles out. Suppose they'll pick up speed when they see the fort in their sights. Charlotte, why don't you and Eileen settle the children somewhere they'll be out of the way when the wagons roll in. Go shopping in the store if you've a mind to." He gave his wife some silver coins and government script from his pocket.

"I'm going to take Peter over to meet a fellow Pedigrew told me about might be willing to take those fleece off our hands." He looked at Jemima. "Might not be a price you want to live with, but it'd be better than them rotting away in the barn, 'specially since we'll have to deal with another load next year." He meant to tease her, but somehow the joke seemed weak even to his own ears.

*****

Charlotte gathered the brood together and looked around for some shade or shelter and found some trees near the fort wall. It wasn't much as far as trees go, but there was a dappled area where they could spread out the blankets for the children to sit and catch any breeze that might blow through the fort. She knew something had changed in William's enjoyment of the day, but it wasn't the time to question him. She took the hand of her son, led him toward the tree, and the others followed.

Jemima agreed to wait with Teddy, if the two women wanted to shop in the small trading post store. "There's not much I need, just a few hairpins, or a new comb for my hair if anything like that can be had." She took out some coins from her leather bag for Charlotte to use for her needs. "And buy some candy or a toy for the boys, if you please, Charlotte."

The women walked through the gates to the store, looked around at the variety of merchandise, and came back with their purchases: a new pair of shoes for Teddy, two dozen canning jars, and several bolts of material for making dresses or shirts, for they all needed new summer wear. Also, they carried a small tin of hairpins and two pretty tortoise shell combs for Jemima. Some stick candy and cherry balls for the boys were bought, but there didn't seem to be any toys. There were a few books left by some pioneer who had tired of them or traded for something more useful. They bought those, too, for they were all readers, and wouldn't mind if the pages were torn or water stained.

Eileen was more practical and bought heavier cloth for trousers and shirts for her boys. They seemed to grow so fast. When the women returned, they were accompanied by the assistant clerk who agreed to carry the heavier packages for them. They thanked him and the packages were put in the wagon. They sat on the blankets enjoying the sights and sounds around the fort, awaiting the return of the men.

*****

As soon as Charlotte and Eileen were out of hearing range, and Jemima sitting comfortably on the quilt entertaining Teddy and the boys, Peter asked William what had happened.

"It's bad news, Peter. The Congress has declared war with Mexico. Pedigrew didn't say how he knew when I asked him. He might be afraid of spies or maybe doesn't want to say until he knows more information. He said we'll have to wait for the Eastern newspapers or one of the later trains that went through Leavenworth. Pedigrew himself is leaving. His replacement, man named Watson, is supposed to be on this train. Sure hate to see that man go; he's been fair and just with his dealings with the Indians and the settlers."

"War? You said Baker was trying to prevent war by making that trip to Santa Fe. I sure wish I had a newspaper in my hands. That's one thing wrong with this western country, ain't no way of getting news. Back in Springfield it'd be on the newspaper next day. Petigrew's leaving? That is bad news. You really got some news about that sheep fleece? Or, are you wanting to get me away from the ladies?" Peter gave William a suspicious look.

"There really is a man I want to talk with, but I don't have any hopes of him buying that fleece. If Pedigrew can't find a market, don't suppose this man can either. Name's Damian Pembroke, Pedigrew said."

Leaving the boys with Jemima, they walked around the board-walk of the fort until they came to a low roofed building similar to the office of the fur company. William looked back at a noise like horses running, and there were three mounted men riding at full gallop toward Pedigrew's office. Fool men, William thought. They'll run someone down. He looked around for his family, but saw only some fur traders and Indians sitting or standing against the wall.

William turned and went up the steps to the building. Peter followed, still looking back at the riders, and almost stumbled into William when he stopped. William knocked on the door, and it was answered by a small, gray-haired lady, who gave him a look of inquiry.

"Good day, ma'am. Is this the Pembroke home?" She nodded in the affirmative. "I'm William Butler, and this is my wife's uncle, Peter Kincade. Won't keep you long; was wondering if your man's home."

"Sure is; wait and I'll fetch him," and the woman was gone from the door.

Peter was still watching the men who had ridden into the fort. They didn't stop at the office as expected but stopped at the sign that said, "Grayson's Saloon." William nudged Peter, remarking that he'd been in the place a few times, and it was crude and dark inside. Just a long flat board lain across three barrels to make a temporary bar. There were no tables or chairs. A person was supposed to get his liquor and leave or stand around talking to his friends. The two men turned when they heard someone come to the door.

"Butler, you the one with that big wagon from the East, with the oxen pulling it?" Pembroke wasn't much taller than his wife, William thought. He answered his question as though he was of equal size.

"Yes, sir, that's me, if you mean the Conestoga and the team of four oxen. I was through here with the team a few weeks back. I live north, northwesterly on the Laramie. This is my wife's uncle Peter Kincade, from Illinois." William stood perfectly still as the man examined him, then turned to Peter.

"I saw you when you were here. Sure do admire that wagon of yours. Saw your animals, too. What can I do for you today?" For such a short, stumpy man, he had a deep basal voice and gray hair that might have once been red, for there seemed to be a few streaks of orange or red in the white. He also had a snow white beard, and William had time to wonder if his might be that color someday. He'd already noticed some white strands in his beard and hair.

"I have a flock of sheep on my farm, and when I was here before, Pedigrew said there was no market for the fleece since the hostilities with Mexico seem to be heating up." William didn't want to give much away if Pedigrew's source was private. "He said you might be interested in good clean fleece." William held his breath, for he did want to help Jemima sell her only source of income.

"Sheep, you say? On your farm? How many and how much of this fleece you wanting to sell?" The man's eyes took on a greedy look, at least that's what William thought it was.

"About fourteen sheep; got some ewes, some rams, and three little ones. Can't say how much the fleece weighs, for I don't have a scale, but there's two large burlap bags and a couple of smaller ones. It's all clean because we wash the sheep in the river and get out as much of the twigs, leaves and grass as we can, finding it to be easier when the animals are still walking around. If we waited until they're sheared, the fleece would take weeks, maybe, to dry out." William groaned to himself. Good God, he sounded like an expert, and all he knew about sheep was what Jemima had taught him.

"Well, I tell you what, Butler, if you take as good care of those sheep as you do the oxen, you might have yourself a deal. I'll have to come out to your place and see for myself. I don't deal in beaver pelts and such like Pedigrew. I prefer wild animals like wolves, buffalo and bears. Big market in the East for such animal skins and the horns or hoofs."

William felt himself recoil. He sensed some danger in the man's eyes, as though he killed for the sake of killing. He didn't like that in a man. He'd talk to Jemima about whether it was worth the money to engage in commerce with such a person. They set a date for him to come to the farm and left to go back to their families.

William turned to Peter as they retraced their steps down the boardwalk. "Do you sense what I do, Peter? There's something about the way he said wild animals that puts my guard up. Man's greedy, too, if I read him right." William didn't want to influence Peter, but he was already wishing he hadn't made a date for Pembroke to come to his farm.

"I felt the same thing. I worked with my father in his law firm for a year before I got disgusted with the likes of men like that. Men come in accused of some shady practice and lie right to your face claiming their innocence. I know you're mighty anxious to get rid of that fleece, but I think you should be careful when the man comes out. And that talk of wolves; it was wolves that killed Pedro. Animals are the same to him, tame or wild." He spat on the ground, his disdain seen in his action. "Those riders that came in the gate? They went right to the saloon, not to Pedigrew's office. I'm thinking they're not the scouts from the train but single men like James Morgan wanting to get first chance at the liquor."

36

William found the women and children under the shade of the trees. All eyes were on Charlotte who was laughing and making expressive gestures with her hands. He heard the sound of horses and watched as four riders went through the open gates, two abreast, and rode toward the building marked, "Office." William looked at Peter. He looked back and smiled.

"I think we've found the real scouts, Peter."

"Aye. The wagons are on the way. How long, do you think?"

"Within the hour," William proclaimed. He stood in the wagon bed and saw a great cloud of dust toward the eastern horizon. He pointed his finger. "Here they come. Can you see them, boys?" The boys ran a few yards until they were called back. Neely lost his hat and had to scramble to retrieve it, with his mother scolding him all the while for his carelessness.

The caravan could be seen advancing from the hills. The first wagon arrived, not as large as the Conestoga, but imposing none the less. It was followed by perhaps fifty assorted wagons, pushcarts, and buggies. They began to line up along the opposite river bank from where William was parked.

William gathered his group together, and they sat in the wagon bed, the boys' legs dangling off the rear, while they had their midday meal, watching the new pilgrims moving about like ants at a picnic. It was still early, so he said they might as well go home since the excitement was over. He wanted to make one last trip to the office in case any mail or newspapers were brought to Pedigrew. Peter was left in charge of readying the wagon for departure from the fort, and William walked up the steps again. There were several men standing on the balcony. They gave the large man with the black beard a thorough scrutiny. William nodded and went inside.

Pedigrew was standing in the middle of the room talking to a couple of men; one had a rifle in his hand, barrel down. Of average height, he was a nondescript sort of fellow, one who would blend into the background in a crowd. Pedigrew called to William, "There'n ya be, friend. Glad ya come back. Haven't sorted mail yet. If'n you don't mind another hour, mine assistant is thar in the back room now. Gentlemen, this be William Butler come out from St. Louis 'bout two years ago, has a nice farm up a piece on the Laramie River. William, Bradford Watson, come to take my place, so guess your'n see plenty of each other. Planning to be 'board the train when her leaves, and be about ta Fort Hall and then ta Sacramento City, in Alta California."

"Taking a ship, then?" William grinned.

"Better'n Indian raidin' parties. Hopefully round the Horn to the East. This here'n other gentleman be Ezekiel Talbot, lookin' for a place of work. Carpenter by trade, he say."

William saw the gleam of mischief in Pedigrew's eyes. He didn't respond to the comment, but offered his hand to Watson and asked how the trip was coming out. "Pleased to meet you, Watson, I expect I'll be seeing you soon, but I have my family with me today."

Watson grasped William's hand firmly and shook, saying rather formally, "Understood. This is an unplanned meeting, and you have other duties."

"Thank you." William turned to the carpenter. "Talbot, I wonder if you can spare me a minute while I wait for the mail to be sorted. My wife will shore scold me if there's mail from the East and I fail to pick it up while I'm here. Pedigrew, I wish you good sailing. I'll have my boy, Joseph, come for the mail in about an hour, if that's what you think it'll take for it to be sorted." William had noticed a troubled look on the men's faces, indicating something must have happened on the trail. He shrugged it off, shook hands with Pedigrew and called to Talbot.

"Mr. Talbot, if you'll walk with me, please. I need to tell my family of the change in plans, for I only came to tell Pedigrew good-bye. He told me he'd be leaving soon. I hate to see him go, for he's a good man." William set a fast course and noticed the man was having a hard time keeping up. He slowed down. He figured Talbot to be a city-bred man, like Peter. That might not be a bad thing. He was a city man himself, although he hadn't been a merchant or banker.

"Pedigrew said you're a carpenter, wanting to settle around here. I don't usually nose into a person's private affairs, but I got a reason for asking." William gave Talbot a sharp look, and the man didn't flinch from his scrutiny. He had brown hair, cut short, and a mustache, with brown eyes that looked intelligent and knowing. He spoke with an accent that William couldn't recognize, with clipped words and a faster cadence, not unlike Lieutenant Baker and Government Scout Willowby. Must be from New England area, William decided.

"I can tell from your apparent rapport with the fur company's manager that he has a depth of respect for you, Butler. I find that amount of respect is shown in a person's actions and character, therefore, I'll answer you truthfully." Talbot was about to continue, but they had reached the gates to the fort, and William interrupted him with a motion of his hand.

"My apologies. Wait, if you please." They saw a group of people waiting beside a wagon, and William went to his wife.

"Charlotte, my dear, I'm afraid our plans have been changed. We're waiting for the mail to be sorted by Pedigrew's assistant. He said about an hour, so if you'll take the children back to your favorite tree. I'm sure you're anxious to know if you've received a letter from Bertha. This is Ezekiel Talbot, whom I've just met. He's a carpenter. Mr. Talbot, my family. My wife, Charlotte, my son Theodore, whom we call Teddy, my brother-in-law Joseph Morgan, my wife's uncle and aunt and their two sons. Peter and Eileen Kincade, Jesse and Neely, and my friend Mrs. Jemima Boudreau." Everyone shook hands or curtsied, and the group moved to where they had been sitting under the trees.

William walked over to the mules, patted one and gestured for the men to stand at the back of the wagon, so the ladies couldn't hear. "Peter, Talbot's a carpenter, and he's looking for work." He waited for a reaction from Peter, and he got it. Peter grinned from ear to ear, and looked very pleased.

"Talbot, I'm sorry for the delay in our little talk. You were saying that you were willing to be truthful in your background, perhaps?"

266

"Aye, I'm originally from Vermont. Plainfield, but my work has carried me to many places. I was recently in Independence City, helping to make repairs from the flood. With all the excitement of going to Oregon, and talk of war with Mexico, I awoke one morning and told myself I must see this new country. Alas, my wagon broke down about twenty five miles from Fort John, and I had no transportation except the four mules. One of the men on the train offered to sell me one of his horses, a mare, in exchange for the mules. It was a bad bargain, for the mules were much more valuable than the horse. Oh, she's a darling, and she's gotten me to Fort John, but I don't think she'll last through the high mountains. I agreed to trade two mules for the horse, but kept two of the mules, for how was I to carry my tools and food? Another neighbor on the train kindly let me keep a few clothes and trinkets in his wagon. But, I fear I am poor indeed. I have my skill as a carpenter and my tools. Watson, whom you met, said it would be difficult to find work since there are only a few civilized people living in the area. A most disagreeable fellow."

It was a strange mixture of pathos and acceptance. William looked at Peter. Peter smiled. They were in agreement.

"Talbot, we have need of a man such as you. We're attempting to build an addition to my log cabin. It's a poor effort, for I was trained a miner and oxen driver in Virginia. Peter was schooled to be a lawyer in Illinois. He has some skill with hammer and nails, where I have none. If you think you might like to share your talent with us, we can pay you a small stipend, and room and board. We might even build a log cabin for you, if you choose to stay. If you still wish to see the Oregon country or travel to California after the cabin is finished, I'll furnish you with the supplies and wagon and team to catch a caravan out of Fort John. I'm afraid it would require that you stay at least a year, for the trains don't come through in the winter."

William stopped talking when he saw a lad of about eight years running their way through the gates of the fort. The women stood on their feet, and the boys came to see what was happening. The boy had a parcel and a stack of papers in his hand.

"Mr. Butler, the man back there." He pointed to the office of Pedigrew, soon to be the office of Bradford Watson, just visible through the open gates. "He done told me you'd give me a dime 'iffen I'd bring you these things." He held out the parcel and letters.

William reached in his pocket, pulled out a dime and gave it to the boy, who handed him the mail in its place. "Thank you, boy, that was very kind of you." The boy scampered off toward the fort. The ladies and boys gathered around. William handed the mail to Charlotte to be distributed to the right person once they returned home. He then turned to Ezekiel Talbot with a question in his eyes.

Talbot took a step forward to bring himself in line with William, and he held out his hand. "Sir, I accept your offer and will do my best to please you. If you can wait a while longer for me to get my horse and mules, I'll meet you outside the gates. My friends call me Zeke." He waited for his answer, and getting a hand shake from both William and Peter, he turned and strode toward the wagons setting up camp near the river.

William watched as Talbot walked away. He helped Jemima and Charlotte to the wagon seat, and handed Teddy to her. He went to the mule team to get ready for the ride home. Peter helped his wife and boys into the back and mounted his horse. Joseph scrambled up on his own power. William explained to Charlotte and Jemima that he'd hired a carpenter to build the addition to the house, and although it hadn't been mentioned, to make shingles for the roofs of the cabins.

They waited for a few minutes for Talbot to gather his belongings from the friend who'd loaned him the use of his vehicle to store his possessions. The family moved over in the wagon bed so Talbot could place several boxes and barrels in with them. Talbot saddled his mare, whom he called Peg, said farewell to his friend, mounted his horse, and leading the two mules behind him, waited beside Peter for the wagon to pull out.

When everyone was comfortable, William climbed into the wagon, uncurled his black whip, tugged on the reins and Whack! went the whip over the backs of the animals. They stepped lively on the way to Green Meadow Farm.

It wasn't until after supper that Charlotte distributed the mail. There were several old newspapers rolled and tied with thin cords. The men pounced on them and began to read the Eastern news. There were two letters for Peter, one from his father, and the other from his elder brother telling of their father's failing health, something his father hadn't mentioned.

The packet was from the drummer Hammond with more flower and vegetable seeds. It said that on his last trip through St. Louis, thinking to stay as usual at the Hightower Hotel, there had been a for sale sign on the door. Hammond had gone to Trice's newly rebuilt Mercantile Store and been told that Bertha and Clayborne had sold the hotel. Hammond wished the Butlers well and hoped they would try the new tomato seeds. He advised they plant them in small pots or bowls until they sprouted and then replant in the garden in early spring. A few of his customers had raved about the uses for the vegetable, and he hoped that Mrs. Butler would find them tasty. He signed the missive: Hammond.

There was a wrinkled note from Bertha. After the necessary repairs to the lower floor had been made, they had sold the hotel and moved to Chicago, in Illinois, where Clayborne would be taking some special medical procedures for the benefit of paraplegics. Her husband seemed to be responding well to the treatments and was rebuilding his library. She'd gotten a job as cook at a local boarding house for the doctors who worked at the hospital. Trice had hired the dark-skinned man, Hezekiah Conklin, himself, for he was a good worker, and Bertha didn't want to see him displaced. She was to address her mail to the Doctor's Hospital, Chicago. Your loving friend: Bertha Hightower.

A longer letter was addressed to Master Joseph Morgan, Fort John, Wyoming Territory. It was from St. Gregory's Prep School for Boys in Pennsylvania, and Joseph's eyes lit up like candles in the darkness. Jasper said he was studying Mathematics, Science, Fencing, and Languages. He was very pleased except that he didn't like the stiff collar on his uniform. His father was well, and the livery business in Springfield was thriving. His brother Abraham had a job as clerk in a warehouse and had plans to marry soon. Please to write me soon: Jasper Smith.

That night, before Jemima retired to her own cabin, William told her that he might have a buyer for her fleece, but that he couldn't quite trust the man. He seemed to have about him the manner of stealth and greed. "He admitted that he preferred the skins of wild animals like mountain lions or bears. He's agreed to come to the farm to look over the sheep and the fleece. I may have made a mistake in asking him to the farm, but I was eager to get rid of the wool. I'm sorry for my impulsive move. I hope it'll turn out well, but I fear you won't receive a fair deal."

"Oh, William, don't fret yourself. Any amount of money will be better than the wool rotting away in the barn and being buried eventually. Do you think that my husband didn't make mistakes in judgment and lose money? I fear it's not the fleece that the man wants but the animals from whence it comes. You should take care to keep your weapon nearby when the man arrives." With that wise advice, Jemima went to her own cabin.

William showed Talbot his sleeping arrangements, laughing and saying he'd soon see his predicament. He led him to the small room in the barn in which George had kept residence. It had a bunk and table with a pitcher and bowl, with a new bar of soap beside them. Underneath stood a chamber pot. There was a peg holding a clean flannel cloth. There were no windows to let in the night air, and William reassured him that while he might feel stifled in the heat, and the smell of animals might penetrate the walls, it was better than a blanket under the stars and the chance of being drenched by rain.

The next morning after a breakfast of fresh eggs and ham, with biscuits and porridge, William discussed with Peter the matter of the fleece and Jemima's warning about the sheep. They decided to keep a lookout posted to watch the road and the river ford. There was one place that might be adequate, so William asked Joseph to sit there and watch, not to do anything, but give a warning by loudly playing his Jew's harp, if more than one rider came from either direction. It was a heavy responsibility to place on a young boy, but Joseph said he could do it. William explained he would have done the job himself, but he needed to hear what Talbot said about the addition to the house.

Talbot met with William and Peter to discuss the plans for two additional rooms to be built onto the house. Talbot carefully went over the diagrams and plans that William and Peter had made to fill in the present root cellar, then dig a new one. Talbot ran his finger over a line, hummed under his breath; sought out another line, and finally stood up. They walked to the rear and eastern side of the larger house that had been built at least seven years ago, according to the reckoning of Jules Robertson.

Talbot looked over the freshly dug hole, then at the walls of the house. He remarked on the yardage and scope, then walked to the nearly filled in previous root cellar. He nodded his head, commented on the cords carefully strung between the stakes in the ground, then folded his hands behind his back and paced the steps from one stake to another. He moved toward the west and looked at Joseph's lean to room, then circled the whole house. He took a small notebook and a pencil from a pocket and began to write down figures, looked up at the top of the house, then wrote more figures.

He paced back to the current root cellar. "What you planning to use for lumber, Butler?" He looked toward the barn as if expecting it to be filled with stacks of lumber and nails. William pointed to the pile of logs that he and Joseph had brought from the forest to the north across the river, high in the foothills of the Rocky Mountains.

Suddenly, the sound of a Jew's harp rendered a lively tune.

William sprang into motion. "Talbot, grab your rifle and stand at the side of the barn. There!" He pointed toward a place near the corrals. "Peter, get your wife and children in the cabin and make sure they stay there, then get Mercury and your horse. Grab your rifle in case it's needed. Wait for me with the horses." William ran for Jemima's cabin only steps away and knocked, and hearing no answer, he hoped she was with Charlotte. He ran to his own home and took the steps in a jump and opened the door.

"Charlotte, get my rifle! Jemima, stay with the boy! Don't move from this house, no matter what happens. Either of you." Charlotte took the rifle down from the shelf, for they had practiced this in case of an Indian raid or bandits, while William grabbed an extra box of ammunition and put it in his shirt pocket. He was out the door, jumped on his unsaddled horse, and he and Peter sped toward the sheep in the meadow.

Four men were galloping their horses, trying to circle the sheep, but the sheep were slow to move, raising their heads from their grazing, but not budging from their positions. The strangers started shooting above the heads of the sheep, then saw the two men coming at them with rifles in their hands and turned their horses. One fired a shot, and William felt a sting in his left arm. He kept going until he was behind the nearest man. He growled in his deep voice, "Keep moving, Mister, until you're out of my valley." The man raced his horse back toward the ford of the river, his partners taking a similar direction. They were almost to the crossing when William aimed his rifle and carefully shot over the head of the man who had offered to buy the fleece. Peter saw the man flinch and fired his weapon over the head of the next man in line. He kept firing just for the pleasure of seeing them run.

The horses kicked up water as they tried to run through the soft sand and gravel of the bottom. William slowed his horse and stopped. Peter was still firing.

"Stop, Peter, it's over."

They sat on their horses until the men had left the water and disappeared out of sight in the forest. They turned their horses back and headed west when William saw Joseph perched on a tall boulder

271

where he'd told him to keep watch. His heart flew into his throat, for what if the men had seen Joseph or tried to kidnap him instead of the sheep? He walked his horse close to Joseph and started to lift him up only to realize his shirt was bloody, and the arm was painful.

"William, you're hurt! Uncle Peter, William's been shot."

Peter looked over at the boy in astonishment, and saw the blood on William's shirt. "Oh, my God. Joseph, come here and climb on my horse. We've got to get William to the house."

They rode slowly to the cabin. Joseph leaped off Peter's horse and ran into the house, calling out, "Sister, William's been shot."

*****

Charlotte gasped. She ran out the door and saw the blood on her husband's sleeve. Jemima, with Teddy on her hip, followed her out the door. She saw William now swaying in the saddle, his face contorted with pain and shock, and she handed Teddy to Charlotte, and ran to his side.

"Peter, help me get him off the saddle."

Peter had already dismounted. Slowly, with Peter taking most of the weight on himself, he and Jemima half lifted, half dragged the much larger man out of the saddle and into the house. Charlotte, her heart thumping loudly, followed. She put the boy down and went to the hot water well and began to dip water into a bowl. She grabbed a clean cloth from a shelf and stood ready to assist Jemima, the closest they had to a doctor.

Jemima told Joseph to go into the bedroom and take the top cover off the bed, and light the lantern. The boy had been standing, staring at the red spot on William's shirt. With Jemima's voice ringing in his ear, he did as she said, hurling the top cover off and spreading the blankets to expose the sheet. He lit the lantern and left the room. He heard a clamor at the front door and saw his cousins and Aunt Eileen coming in. They were followed by the new carpenter. Eileen stooped, picked up Teddy and went to the living area, sat and rocked him, thinking to calm his cries. The two boys stood near her not knowing what to do.

"Mr. Talbot, help Peter get William undressed and in bed. Charlotte, put that pan down on the bedroom table and find William a nightshirt, or if he doesn't have one find something soft he can wear after I get the bullet out." The eyes of the two boys, Jesse and Neely, spread wide. "Joseph, go to the rock fence now and watch closely like your brother said. If you see anyone you don't know, start playing that instrument. I have to go to my cabin for my kit."

"See to the horses. Someone take care of the horses." William's voice was weak and strained, but clearly he was aware of what was happening.

The place turned into a beehive of activity when Jemima left the house. Zeke and Peter helped William walk to the bedroom and removed his clothes, except for the bloody shirt. Charlotte put the pan down, spread the cloth under his bloody arm to protect the sheet if she could, or for a swab if that was what was needed. She didn't take the shirt off the peg like Jemima said because she figured she could do that when he was ready for it. William lay naked except for the bloody shirt, and Charlotte covered his lower body.

37

Charlotte sighed with relief when Jemima returned to the house. She asked about Joseph, and was told he was with Zeke, who was talking fishing. Jemima shook her head, and in spite of the circumstances, Charlotte smiled. The older woman was of such a practical bent, she made even the worst occasions seem manageable.

Inside the living area, Eileen sat calmly rocking Teddy, and the area surrounding her was cluttered with his toys. She had a frightened look on her face, and she whispered to Jemima as she passed that she knew Charlotte needed to be with her husband.

Jemima placed a hand on her arm and nodded. She went directly to the bedroom with a small leather bag in her hand. Charlotte held the blanket to the side. She watched as the woman began to work. She had a brown-colored bottle in her hand, and she moved some items from the table and lay them on the floor out of her way. She placed her bag on the table and opened it. Charlotte watched, heart in her throat, as Jemima gently cut away the bloody sleeve and helped William to remove his shirt. Working swiftly, she probed the area and found what she'd expected. The bullet was still inside the flesh of his arm, but she murmured that she was sure it hadn't struck the bone or an artery.

Charlotte pressed her hand to her breast as relief flooded over her.

Peter returned to the cabin after taking care of the horses, leaning his head in to see the progress on his nephew.

"Peter, come this way." Jemima motioned with her hand.

"Excuse me, Charlotte." He stepped past her, carefully avoiding bumping the bed. "Eileen's in the living area watching Teddy play with his building blocks," he whispered to Charlotte. "He's a good lad to play so quietly at this terrible time."

"Aunt Eileen's a good woman for watching him." Charlotte smiled. William lay still and wan, but alert. Charlotte shuddered at the sight of his bare arm, but didn't draw back when Jemima gently washed the arm and dabbed some sweet-smelling milky power on the wound. She gave it a few minutes, wiped it off and applied a bitter-smelling liquid from the brown-colored bottle. William flinched but didn't squirm.

"Peter, I need you to hold his arm down tight; don't let it jerk. Charlotte, stand near me with the bowl. Now, don't panic if he screams out in pain. I'll be as fast as I can." She withdrew a small slim knife from her bag, and cleaned it in the hot water. She touched the surface of the skin and made a small incision, then dropped the knife to the floor and took a long probe she had placed on the table, pushed it in through the hole and swirled it around as if looking for something. William groaned and closed his eyes. Deeper the probe went, and William screamed in pain, and passed out.

"Just a moment longer, William. I think I feel it." With a slight twist of her wrist, she withdrew the probe and dropped a little pellet into the bowl of hot water that Charlotte was holding. It made a thunk sound. Jemima poured some more of the milky powder on the wound and reached for the bandages that Charlotte had brought. Taking care not to touch the wound itself, Jemima bound the arm, circling the damaged flesh again and again until the whole upper arm was covered in white cloth. She showed Charlotte where to split the end with the scissors, and taking the two ends, she encircled once around the arm with one end and tied the two ends together.

In the other room, Teddy began to cry. Eileen called out that she was taking him out on the porch.

"Charlotte, there's nothing more to do except wait. Your man will get better or he won't. If you've a mind, you might say a prayer for his recovery."

"You're good for us, Jemima." Charlotte so wanted to give her a hug, but she understood when the woman pushed her away, picked up her knife from the floor, gathered her tools and placed them in the bowl with the bullet fragment. She returned her powders and ointments to her bag and closed it. She looked at the silent, sleeping man on the bed. There was an eerie glow on his face from the lantern's light.

"Watch for signs of restlessness or fever, you hear? Come that sign, and you call me fast as you can." Jemima left and went into the kitchen area.

Charlotte pulled up a chair to sit at her husband's side. She gently reached to his beard to brush it with the back of her hand. She was brought to mind how much she'd been appalled at her sudden and unexpected marriage to this big man, and the saloon in which the ceremony had taken place. It had been more a circus event than a moment of joining hearts and souls. Now she saw her man as he really was. He was filled with courage, and he meant to protect those under his care no matter the cost.

She had once doubted him, and now she had no recourse but to trust in Jemima's handiwork to save his life.

*****

The people sitting around the Butler table that night were subdued and thoughtful. Talking in low voices, they discussed with Zeke how best to carry out the plans to add the two rooms to the house. Zeke and Peter did most of talking for they alone knew the details of the sketches and plans. The women chirped in on things they thought were necessary for comfort and durability.

Since William and Charlotte would be using the much larger room built over the former root cellar, Joseph said he would take the upstairs room. He took a plate to Charlotte who sat like a stone watching over William.

"I'm not hungry, Joseph, but thank you." She looked at him with soulful eyes, but there were no tears.

"But, Sister, you must eat, William will expect it of you."

She placed a hand on his face. "When did my little brother grow so mature? A few years ago you would've turned and run outside to play."

"Sister, Jemima has made her best honey cake for you." There was a twinkle in his eye as though he'd revealed a secret. When she made no move to leave, he shrugged his shoulders and went back to the table.

With a no nonsense huff, Jemima rose to her tallest height, took the plate that Charlotte had rejected and marched to the bedroom, everyone's eyes following her. The boys squirmed in their seats, for they'd seen that look before. She raised the blue blanket and stood at the entrance to the room. She glanced quickly at the silent figure on the bed, and placing the plate on a vacant spot on the table, took the hand of her best friend.

"Charlotte, when I first arrived in the valley, I was sad and angry over the treatment I'd received on the trail after my husband died. I wanted to stay with him in that lonely grave on the prairie. I thought my life was over without my friend by my side. I've told you of some of our travels, far off places and ocean voyages, strange sounds and smells, but none of those places were a home to us. We decided to move to Oregon where the land was free for the taking. We dreamed of building a special place where there were only smiling faces and laughing eyes. But, it was a dream, a fairy tale, not real. This place is real, Charlotte. I have watched in silence when your husband comes in the door at night. His eyes go instantly in search of you and the boy. Only when he sees you does he relax. Now, he's hurting. I've done all I can with my herbs and powders. The rest is up to you. In order for him to live, you must live. Eat, my love. William and the boy need your strength and love tonight."

She returned without the plate and looked at the rest of the family and friends as though wondering why they were so silent. Everyone began to talk at once about the garden, or the house addition, or the inconvenience of a sod roof and finished their supper. In a few minutes, Charlotte lifted the blanket door and brought the plate to the table. She took her usual place and began to eat. She asked questions of the carpenter, joined in the laughter of a joke against Neely and listened to their tale of the ant bed. She took her share of the honey cake and gave Joseph a grin. When she'd finished eating, she gathered her son in her arms and went to her place beside her husband.

The gathering broke up as soon as the dishes were finished and put in their proper place. Peter and Zeke went to the sofa and continued their talk of lumber and sawing and hammering, until Joseph took himself out on the front porch. They agreed to take turns through the night watching the entrance to the farmyard in case the thieves came back. In his usual placid manner, Peter told his family it was time to go, and they left, taking Zeke with them. Zeke, with his rifle in his left hand, continued to the tree stump near the barn where he and Joseph had stood guarding the passage from the ford of the river. Eileen went to the bedroom entrance and suggested it would be better if she took Teddy for the night. Charlotte knew she was right and surrendered her child to her aunt.

Jemima finished up and went to her cabin, leaving her bag behind. Joseph returned to the room but couldn't settle. When Charlotte sat beside him, asking him what was the matter, he began to talk to her.

"Sister, I keep hearing the riders coming through the shallow water of the ford, then I hear the gunshots and see the blood on William's arm. I was frightened while playing the Jew's harp, but I knew I had to warn William and the others." He put his head in his hands and wept, his thin body racked with guilt and pain. When Jemima returned to the cabin, she took Charlotte's place, and they talked quietly near the fireplace until he calmed himself. Jemima sat quietly with Joseph in the living area; she rocked back and forth; he stood and paced the floor.

On through the early night William slept, then around three of the clock he became restless, kicking at the covers, tossing and turning, and thrashing about. Charlotte was alarmed and tried to sooth him by whispering in his ear, holding his hand, but he thrust it away and muttered something under his breath. He burst into sobs, then lay still, then kicked at the covers again.

When William threw aside the covers and tried to rise, his face distorted and gray, Charlotte called out to Jemima. Together they lay him back on the bed, and he began to mutter, then shout, then reared up again. He was hot with a raging fever. Jemima sent Joseph after some cool water, the gourd dipper, a clean cloth and her bag. She motioned for Charlotte to bath his face with the cloth dipped in the cool water. She poured some water into the dipper Joseph had brought and put one of her powders in the water, and stirred with her finger. With Joseph to hold William's head, she poured the liquid down his throat, spilling some on his chin and shirt. He jerked back, almost causing Charlotte to fall on the floor. The room was small and crowded with so many in it. But, each was needed in his or her own way.

Then the words came.

"No, Papa, I won't go. Papa, it's dark in the mines. It's dark, Papa." William lay still for a while, and the watchers began to relax, then it started again. "Papa, I'll kill myself. I will, if you make me go

278

to the dark. No, Papa, don't hit me. I'll go, I promise. Don't hit me no more," William shouted again. For the next hour, the watchers heard horror tales they never dreamed a body could stand, a mine explosion, a tunnel collapse. William moved on from days of his youth to the death and agony of losing his wife and baby, then he stilled.

"Charlotte," he murmured.

"I'm here, William." She leaned closer at the mention of her name.

"Charlotte, why won't you believe me?" Again he tossed and turned. "Come back, don't leave me. Charlotte, please stay with me." He tried to rise in the bed, and screamed, "Come back. Please come back." Jemima and Joseph held him down. "Forgive me, Charlotte, please forgive me."

The words became blurred and they couldn't understand him.

With a nod from Jemima, Charlotte leaned close to his ear and repeated, "I'm here, Honey. I'm here beside you. I'll never leave you." She continued to sooth him with a calm, quiet tone, and applied the cool water to his face and chest. "I'm here, William. Don't be frightened, my love, I will never leave you."

William stilled. Jemima put her hand to his forehead. "The fever is passing. The herbal medicine is taking effect."

William slept, a peaceful, restful sleep. Jemima gestured for Joseph to take the bucket and dipper. She collected the soiled cloths and her bag, and they quietly left the couple alone. Charlotte removed her shoes, crawled onto the bed, and careful not to hurt him, she gathered her husband into her arms.

"So strong and generous with others; so hard on himself," she murmured, as she fell into an exhausted sleep.

*****

The day dawned dark and gloomy. The rain poured down and soaked the sod roofs of the Boudreau and the Butler cabins. Joseph and Jemima were kept busy finding enough bowls and pots to hold the flow. Down in the Kincade house, the inside was dry. All outside work, except that which was necessary, like feeding the pigs and chickens, and the milking of the cow, was suspended as the rain continued intermittently for two more days.

The boys grew restless. The men talked of many things, the war, the addition of California and Oregon to the country. Would they become states? How long would it take? Both city dwellers, the men felt they had much in common. The ladies cooked and baked, sewed and mended, their nimble fingers flying with knitting needles. It was a good time to card more of the fleece that no one wanted but them. The rolls of wool yarn grew, just as the rock fence continued to grow in the yard. Jemima mentioned casually that if she couldn't sell her fleece, maybe she could sell the yarn. Charlotte burst out laughing. Eileen chuckled and said they'd have to learn to dye the yarn into several colors. That started Jemima into a tale of colors and roots and berries.

And, in the bedroom behind the blue blanket, the man slept on. Jemima changed his bandages each day, and the swelling and redness gradually subsided. She was in despair for all the extra cotton cloths were used, because the rain wouldn't permit the hanging of clothes outside. Peter gave them a length of his precious cord, and they stretched a clothes line near the fireplace.

On the fourth day the sun rose hot and yellow as though it felt it should apologize for the misery it had caused by not shining. The ladies washed and ironed the clothes, and Peter retrieved his cord. Mud was tracked through the cabins, and the ladies rebuked men and boys alike. Zeke at last was free to roam over the area, familiarizing himself with landmarks and buildings. The rain had washed away any sign of the tracks of the would-be thieves. The animals, using their own native languages, neighed, and oinked, and clucked and mooed.

William Butler's voice was the loudest of them all.

Awakened from his long sleep, he was bored and hungry. He fretted about having to stay in bed when he felt fine except for a twinge and slight numbness in his left arm.

Finally, he rose from the bed and clothed himself. He went into breakfast, and, except for the arm held in a sling, no one would've known that he'd been ill. Peter and Zeke welcomed him back, and the three took to heart the schedule that had been arranged. It would be some days before William could crack his black whip or chop wood, but he did what he could to help. He took over some of Peter's tasks, and fetched and carried for Zeke and the ladies.

By the first of August, the household had returned to normal. William, Zeke and Joseph went into the forest and found dead trees, and the log pile began to grow. When a sufficient amount had been selected, Zeke turned his energies to making the logs into lumber and shingles for the cabins, using the carpentry equipment he had brought west with him, and leaving the felling of logs to the other men. When William wasn't in the forest, he was working with his oxen, hoeing, plowing or fishing with his son and the taller boys.

*****

Peter dug until the new root cellar was deeper than he was tall and he had to be helped out of the pit. He made a trench so an outside door could be constructed to keep the varmints out of the food. Zeke took some of his timber and shored up the side walls and roof. Shelves surrounded the room, and a table stood near the back for larger objects. A door was made and leather hinges put in place. The root cellar was pronounced finished. The jars, bottles, cans, barrels and boxes were removed from Joseph's lean to room and were once again in their proper place. It was farther for the ladies to have to go to pick up supplies, but once the new rooms and the back door were finished, it wouldn't be so far.

As the previous cellar filled with dirt, the younger boys found it a delight to jump and play in the fresh sod. Eileen told everyone who would listen that she'd become resigned that her boys would always be dirty and grimy as long as the work went on. She might as well let them have their fun, for soon there would be no dirt. Whenever the men found a rock they would set it aside, and the rock fence now stretched around a corner and across the back. It wasn't very tall, about two feet in height, but hopefully it would hold back the river in flood.

As Eileen had predicted, the dirt was packed solid by letting old Jezebel have her way with it. A wooden floor was lain over it. The excess dirt would be used in the garden. Every day the pile of lumber grew, and in the evenings, Peter and Zeke passed the time talking and making cedar shingles for the cabins. On a hot summer day, when the men were wishing they had some of that cooling snow, the first wall was erected. It was followed by the second, third, and fourth.

Like the Tower of Babel the rooms grew. William was busy with the boys, planting seeds for the fall garden. Jacob Robertson came to help him harvest the wheat, and William returned the favor by taking a team of oxen, Juno and Atlas, and helped Jules and his boys clear a field of tree stumps and burn them. Every day, without fail, William would spend time with his oxen, and with his horse, Mercury, to keep them from becoming fat and lazy. Two female cows were bought from a wagoner on the trail, and the herd soon grew to nine. William trained six of them to pull the wagon.

One night he shared with Charlotte that his dreams of a freighting route or trading post were fading, but he didn't know when he might have need of the animals. Every other Sunday, the Conestoga was taken out of its shed, four oxen were chained to the wagon and the crack of the whip echoed across the valley floor. The first time he saw it, Ezekiel Talbot sat on the porch in awe, his mouth open. He opined that he had seen mule skinners and oxen drivers a plenty while on his train from Missouri, but the sight of the tall man with his midnight black hair and beard walking beside the yoke of oxen gave him a thrill every time they came into view.

38

Near the end of August, Jules stopped to bring the mail. He'd visited Fort John to complain about something to the new manager, Watson, whom he didn't like, he informed William, and had been given mail from the west for the Butler family. An eastbound freight train had stopped at Fort Hall on its way to Santa Fe, and carried mail for the Fort John area, so the manager of the Hudson's Bay Company had passed it on to Fort John. There were magazines and newspapers, and they were a welcome sight to the settlers.

The local news out of Fort Hall was much bigger than the mail delivery, for that brigand, Damian Pembroke, who had tried to steal Miss Jemima's sheep, had been caught red-handed robbing the storage warehouse of the Hudson's Bay Fur Company.

"What's this you say, Pembroke tried to rob the warehouse at Fort Hall?" William had suspected the man was no good, even before he'd tried to steal Jemima's sheep. "Is this the same man that lived with his wife at Fort John, had a trapping business of his own?"

"That's him all right. Bold as brass the man was, broke open the door and had a wagon out back ready to pack up the furs and git away, but a dog started barking. The racket woke up the manager and the merchant next door. They run up to see what was happening and there he was, him and two others they said was Injuns, caught 'em with the furs in their hands. Didn't wait for no law neither, strung 'em up the next morning on the fort wall, and left 'em for a week as an example for the others. Ain't no messing with the Company."

Jules was excited beyond what a decent man should be, William thought, with a frown of distaste. He could tell he enjoyed telling the story. "What happened to the other three men that were here? Does anyone know?"

"Don't no one know for shore. Rumor says they took off north toward Dakota country. Won't last long there, I bet. The Dakota, they're fierce warriors, not like the Shoshone and Bannock that live around here."

William waited patiently while Jules seemed to talk on and on. William was troubled for he worried not so much for the ghastly death of anyone, but for the poor woman who was left to mourn his passing. He'd only had a glimpse of her, but she didn't seem to be the kind of person who would tolerate such behavior in her man. He wondered what would become of her; be ridden out of town, he guessed, but where would she go in a wilderness like this? He probed Jules for information, but he hadn't heard anyone speak of the man's wife; and at last Jules drove his wagon toward his home further north along the river.

William stood on the steps of his cabin and gazed into the horizon, wondering what he should tell the ladies, when Jesse came running up and stood near the porch column.

"Mister William, Mama wants to know if you got any mail for her; she seen Mister Jules, and she thought there might be something." He had run so fast up the slope, his breath was coming in gasps.

"No, I'm sorry, Jesse, no mail from the East. These came from Fort Hall by freighter. These are from California and Oregon for us."

The boy turned away, dejected, and walked back down the slope.

William saw Eileen standing in the doorway and shook his head. She went in and shut the door. He knew they were anxious to hear of Peter's father. They hadn't heard from Peter's brother since the missive that he was ill.

He paused to admire the rooms being built, for now the outside walls were finished, and the next step would be removing the sod roof and placing the shingles in its place. William opened the door and went in to find Charlotte with her hands deep in bread dough and flour, her freckles glowing in the sunbeam that fell across her face from the open door. William was so proud of his young wife's cooking. Jemima was a good cook, and Eileen was skilled, but his Charlotte was the expert in his opinion.

"We have three letters, my dear, one from Oregon, and two from Alta California; one has your father's handwriting. Jules stopped on his way home. He said they were delivered to Fort Hall by mistake, and they forwarded them to Fort John. Where's the boy?" William looked around, and neither Jemima nor Teddy was in the room.

Charlotte looked up, a pained expression crossing her brow. "I haven't heard from Papa since the note from him when he rode to the mission with the Spanish lady from Oregon City." She put the bread dough in the loaf pan, covered it with a cloth, washed her hands in the water basin and dried them. "Jemima has Teddy with her. She was going to card some of the fleece, and you know how he loves to play with the yarn."

"And Joseph?" William couldn't say why it was important to know where the boy was. He helped Peter and Zeke and sometimes wandered with the boys on his horse.

"I believe Zeke is showing Joseph how to make shingles. The boy is so quick to learn new skills." She stretched out her hand for her letters. "I'm worried about Bertha. We haven't heard from our friends in St. Louis for a year; only the seed packets from Hammond. His packet was sent from Springfield."

William moved to the living area, hoping his wife would join him, but she was intent on opening the second letter from the San Francisco mission. She shrugged, murmuring that maybe one of the people she'd met on the train coming out wanted to continue the relationship begun there. She let her gaze wander over the contents. Her eyes dilated, and she grew pale. William reached for her just as she collapsed at his feet in a faint. He picked her up, took her to the sofa and put her down gently. He brushed her face with his hand and ran to the door. "Jemima!" he yelled in his loudest voice.

The letters still lay on the floor. William pulled his hat from his head and fanned his wife. He impatiently scrunched his own letter still in his hand into a ball and forced it in his trousers' pocket.

Jemima appeared at the door with Teddy in her arms. She burst in, ignoring the letters strewn across the floor, and looked toward the sofa where Charlotte was lying prostrate, her large husband rubbing her hands and telling her to awaken. Jemima put the boy down and told him to stay nearby.

Eileen appeared, also, her breath coming in painful gasps by the time she entered the room. She picked the letters up, and a clipping from a newspaper fell from one. Teddy's crying caught her attention, and she took the boy in her arms and went to sit at the table. She laid the letters and the clipping away from prying hands and cuddled the child.

It was only moments before Joseph appeared, followed by Zeke, Peter, and Jesse. Peter looked to the left and saw his wife comforting the boy. There were some papers in front of her. To the right, Charlotte was attempting to stand, and was wobbling on her feet. Jemima was encouraging her to walk. Joseph was standing near the table.

William stood as if made of stone, uncaring of the people in the room. He could see them, but it was as if they weren't there. At last, he pulled himself out of his trance. "The letter. Where's the letter?" He walked to where Charlotte had been standing, but there was no letter. He knew she hadn't taken it with her when he carried her to the sofa.

"Over here, William." Eileen pointed to the papers on the table, her hand shaking.

In a flat voice, Charlotte said, "Papa is dead."

Everyone looked at Charlotte with various degrees of shock on their faces, except Zeke who moved to the other end of the sofa. William rushed to the table and grabbed the letter. In lightning speed he read the words aloud. James had been burned to death in a hotel in a small village in Alta California trying to rescue his son from the fire. A gasp was heard from Eileen. Joseph ran from the room. Peter exclaimed, "Damnation!" and he followed Joseph in an attempt to comfort him.

William read the newspaper clipping, and it told a different story from the account written by the woman who called herself Maria Concepcion Gomaz. The headlines read: FIRE IN BROTHEL KILLS MAN AND CHILD. It went on to relate that one of the guests of the proprietor must have overturned a lantern while having a dispute with one of the employees of the establishment. The owner and proprietor, one James Morgan of Illinois, had run down the hall to pull his young son, about three months old, from the blaze which had quickly spread from room to room in the old building. The deceased were buried in a single grave on the outskirts of the village. An inquiry had been conducted by the court and the deaths ruled accidental.

William tore open the letter addressed in James' handwriting. It was an announcement of the birth of his son. He laid the letters on the table and went to check on his wife. Charlotte seemed to be in a daze. Jemima suggested that she lie down on her bed. William thanked Jemima for coming so quickly, put his arm around his wife's waist, and led her through the blue blanket doorway and helped to remove her shoes and thigh high cotton stockings, then he unbuttoned her dress. He pulled it over her head, leaving on her undergarments. He pulled back the covers and helped her in, rolled her over to the far side, quickly removed his own shoes, and fully dressed, lay beside her.

*****

William was awakened by the sound of a closing door. Groggy, he looked around and wondered why he was in bed in his clothes in the middle of the day. He felt Charlotte's presence beside him. Everything came rushing back. James Morgan was dead as he had lived, through sins of the flesh. But, in the end he'd tried to save his infant son. That must have taken courage. William wondered if he could do that and knew he would. For the first time in months, he thought of his first wife Martha and his infant son Samuel. They had become a shadow, a dream of a life that had been lived in the past.

He turned in the bed and looked at Charlotte. She was so beautiful, both inside and out. He loved her freckles and her laughing brown eyes. She resembled her father in looks. William had never known her mother, but he imagined Joseph took after her, with his light brown hair and gray eyes. Suddenly, as with a jerk of recognition, William remembered that he had also gotten a letter and had stuffed it in his pocket. Easing himself out of the bed, he picked up his boots and crept from the room, letting the blanket door fall behind him.

The evening was waning, and on an ordinary day, the women would be in the kitchen cooking, baking and laughing. But, not on this day. William would have to cook something himself. The thought reminded him of Eileen. She'd lost her brother-in-law. He must go to her and see if she needed anything. And, Joseph, how could he have so selfishly forgotten Joseph? He must be suffering mightily. With a grieving sigh, he took the letter from his pocket. The information hit him like a thunderbolt.

"Mr. Butler, kind sir. I am well and happy. I met a wonderful girl on the train to Oregon. She is near to my age, two and twenty years. She is from Ohio, traveling with her parents and younger brothers and sisters. They have taken me to their hearts and eased my loneliness. Did I not tell you her name? It is Fredricka what used to be McGuire. We call her Freddie. She has long blond hair and the bluest eyes this side of heaven. We have a daughter now two months of age. We call her Isabella Clarice Remmington. Ah, my Bella, she is the dream I thought would never come true. I have a small farm, not unlike the one you have near Fort John. They gave me title to 640 acres if I can improve it. The soil is lush and deep. The trees are so large that a man cannot spread his arms around the trunk. The lumber business is large here with all the trees, but it is north miles from my place. It brings to my mind when Joseph was in the saw mill. I didn't know him then, but he told me of the days spent in the mill. Tell Joseph if you please that my love is true and I will not forget your kindness to me. Is Mrs. Boudreau with you still? Give her my regards. Is the outhouse standing tall? Best regards: George Remmington."

William's heart was singing for joy. The long time he had waited for this letter had seemed endless. He must take it to Joseph. He poked his head in the room, and Charlotte was still asleep. He hated to leave her so, but he wouldn't stay away long. He put on his boots and his hat and went out the door; and closing it softly behind him, bounded down the steps and almost ran to the Kincade house. He was so happy; he didn't want to mourn for James Morgan. He knocked on the door, and Peter came in answer. Although the smells of something cooking billowed forth, the place was like a tomb.

"Is Eileen well? I'm sorry, I didn't think of her loss, only Charlotte. Is Joseph here? I must see him." William caught a glimpse of the boys, who were reading.

Peter opened the door wide. "Eileen's asleep. She's exhausted. Joseph, your brother is here for you." He turned and went to the fireplace to stir something in a pot.

Joseph was solemn and pale. His gray eyes were enormous, but there was no sign of tears. "Will you come with me, son? There's something I want to tell you." William waited while watching the other boys, their eyes wide with something he couldn't recognize. They would barely remember Charlotte's father, but they'd remember her mother. Charlotte had spoken about her living with them while the rest of the family traveled westward.

"I'll keep him with me tonight, Peter. I'll see Eileen tomorrow. Give her my best. Thank you for caring for the boy."

William and Joseph left the cabin. They took the familiar path, around the rock fence and down the trail to the river. It would be dark before they returned, but he thought their favorite fishing hole would be the best place for their talk.

39

William and Joseph walked to the riverbank where the channel catfish came to the surface and nibbled at the minnows. On this night the sun was low in the sky, and it was too late for fishing. The weather was warm, and a soft breeze blew off the water. A bird flew away in fright. The frogs could be heard with their mating calls, and the insects were numerous. William hadn't considered the bothersome creatures that would share the riverbank with them, but he wouldn't stay long. Charlotte mustn't awaken and find them gone. In any case, she would understand why this was the only place that William could take Joseph to relate his news to him.

They sat down on the soft sand and looked around at the familiar place. Joseph was the first to speak. "It's because my father died, that's why you brought me here. He died in a fire in California, and he had another son. Was his boy better than me? Peter said he died trying to save his son. I saw a fire once in St. Louis. I was running an errand for Major Sanford, and the warehouse caught on fire. There were people jumping out of the windows. Could Papa be saved if he'd jumped out of the window?"

William groaned aloud. It was worse than he thought. He'd no idea that Joseph had seen such a sight when only eleven. It must have been a bad thing to see at such a young age.

"I'm sorry that you saw the warehouse fire. And I suppose that your papa could've been saved, and the boy, too, if he had jumped. It doesn't always happen that way. Sometimes people drown in the river, like the drummer, Rachet Jones. And, your Aunt Eileen's little girl. Pedro died when the wolves attacked. But, most people die of old age in their beds, and I pray that we'll live to be a great old age. But, son, that's not why I wanted you to come tonight to your special place."

Joseph looked at William with a question in his eyes, but he didn't speak. William reached to grasp his shoulder, and he smiled at the boy to let him know it wasn't a bad thing he had to say. The boy smiled back, and William knew it would be alright.

"Joseph, my brother, I have something nice to give you, and it will make you very happy. Would you like to have it?" Joseph nodded his head. William took the letter out of his pocket. "You see, I had a letter today, too, from a faraway place. The news of your father's death drove it out of our minds for a time. It's from George."

The boy jumped up and tore the letter out of William's hand. He tried to read it, but it was growing too dark to see well. "What does it say? Is he happy? Does he remember me?"

"Let's go back to the house so you can read your letter." William took the boy's hand to guide him over the rocks and brambles. "Put your letter in your pocket so you don't lose it on the trail."

Joseph carefully folded the paper and put it in his pocket. He broke contact and almost skipped with anticipation.

With a smile, William called to him, "Yes, he remembers you, and Miss Jemima and her sheep. And, he mentioned that you told him you worked at the saw mill, and he wants you to know that the trees are so big that a man can't reach around them with his arms."

Joseph stopped his antics and gave him a skeptical look. "No tree is that big. How can George say that? Does it really say that in his letter?"

"That's what he said. Promise." William made an "x" over his heart. "Sounds like one of your sister's tales, but I've heard that before, that they tower over the tops of houses."

They reached the rock fence, and the way was clear enough for Joseph to see, but William stopped him. "Joseph, I know this is good news and you're happy, but your sister is sad. You mustn't disturb her if she's asleep or with the baby. You must always respect the rights of other people in your life. We'll know whether it's a good idea to show the letter to your sister tonight. But, you may have to keep it a secret for a while. Do you understand?" He nodded his head, and a very sober Joseph entered the house.

But, all was well. Jemima had brought Teddy back and checked on Charlotte. She got up and started cooking supper. Her face was drawn and her eyes puffy from her tears, but she seemed to have accepted the fact of her father's passing and the manner in which he'd gone. She'd put the babe to bed earlier. In a short time they ate supper. Jemima stayed to eat. William knew she was concerned. He caught Joseph's eyes and winked.

"Jemima, I have received a very nice surprise today that I think you will like." William glanced at Charlotte to see her pause and turn her head his direction. He smiled at her and nodded to Joseph, and then he gave her a conspiratorial wink.

Jemima smiled. "And, my good man, what would this nice surprise be? Can it be that you have received a message from someone of my acquaintance?" She looked down her nose as though she were a queen; and he the joker in her court.

Joseph could wait no longer. He jumped up from the table in his excitement. He took the letter from his pocket and waved it above his head. "It's from George! And he remembers me, and he remembers your sheep. It's from George." He hugged it to his chest with a reverence that surprised William. Joseph placed it on an empty spot on the table. Running his finger along the page, he began to read. As he read, William watched the faces of his family. He wished he could share this moment with George.

40

Green Meadow Farm
Wyoming Territory
October, 1848

It was late afternoon, and the red-leafed bushes along the riverbank blazed with color. The powder blue sky was streaked with scarlet, orange and gold; the willows leaned low to the ground; and the war with Mexico was over. William looked up from the harness he was mending when he heard some honking sounds in the sky. It was a flock of geese in a vee formation, heading south for the winter. He watched them for a moment longer then continued his chore. All the signs of autumn were around him. There had been a heavy frost in the morning. He and Peter had done what they could to weatherize the sheds and the barn. Zeke had finished the new house for the chickens. William heard a crack from the black whip and looked to the road where Joseph was practicing driving a wagon pulled by a yoke of oxen. Just like everything else he tried, he was getting better.

He had wondered when Joseph had first come to him for permission to work with the oxen if he was serious, but he'd explained that it was what he wanted more than anything. They'd spent hours going forward, learning to use the power of his voice to back the animals, to turn left, and to turn right. Now Joseph worked alone. William watched quietly, proud of his brother-in-law's achievement. The boy was now sixteen, and growing taller. Only a few inches shorter than William, he towered over his sister. Not far behind him was his cousin, Jesse, at fourteen, who was the same height as his father, Peter.

The harness finished, he leaned the chair against the wall behind him and thought of the first time he had seen Joseph Morgan, shy and awkward, working in the saw mill in St. Louis. It was the night after his marriage to Charlotte, a Saturday. They'd been gathered in the dining room of the Hightower Hotel. The guests came and went in a whirl of distant, half-forgotten faces, but William remembered the permanent guests. Margaret Brown, her perfumed white handkerchief fluttering under her chin, was flirting with one of the drummers who frequented the hotel whenever he was in town, and her sister, Sarah Warren, who ran off to New Orleans on a steamer. At the head of the large dining table sat Clayborne Hightower in his wheeled chair. Joseph had come in late, his hair slicked down with water, and slid into his chair next to his father, sitting morose and silent. Bertha, bold and loud of voice, passed around the food, and Charlotte, barely sixteen and his wife, handed William the bowl of cabbage soup.

Ah, that brought back memories. Bertha's cabbage soup. Charlotte made it occasionally now, but it didn't compare with Bertha's. Of course, William would never tell his wife that, for she made up for the inadequacy with other dishes. Her lamb stew was delicious, and her yellow cake so sweet and tasty, a man could live on it alone.

The peace of the afternoon was shattered by the slamming of the door, and a toddler ran to his father's chair. William let the legs down gently and reached for the boy. Theodore Butler crawled up his father's long legs and plopped down in his lap. He sat there for a moment, content. Then he noticed Joseph up on the road with the team and wagon. He pointed his finger at the boy. "Papa, Josey. Look, Papa, Josey!"

"Yes, Teddy, Joseph. Doesn't he look proud, driving the oxen? Maybe, someday when you get as tall as Joseph, you can drive the big wagon, but it'll have to be different animals, I'm afraid, for these are getting past their prime and need to be let into the back pasture where they can munch on the grass and lie in the shade of a tree."

The door opened again, and a young woman stepped from the house, wiping her hands on her blue cotton apron. Behind her came Jemima Boudreau, a small lady of large character. She told William to see that he fixed the back left burner on the stove, for the flame wasn't burning as high as it should be. William said he'd get to it on the morrow. Satisfied, Jemima wished them a good night and walked slowly toward her own cabin a few yards away. She went in and shut the door behind her.

Charlotte laughed and went to sit on the top step of the porch. "All it needs is a good cleaning. Something must have boiled over onto the holes and stopped them up." She sat silently for several moments and then sighed. "Doesn't he look fine, Honey, in that new red shirt? I told him not to wear it around the fields, to save it for going to the fort, but he said he never goes to the fort, may as well get some use for it while he can. You should take him one day, just the two of you, and let him drive." She got no answer so turned her head to look up at her husband. The boy was fast asleep, his chubby hand clutched in his papa's long black beard.

William winked at her, wriggling his mouth. When she smiled, he knew Charlotte understood. If William spoke, he would break the spell and awaken the boy.

Yet another door opened, one further away, a two-room log cabin similar to Jemima's, and the latest addition to the farm. Zeke came out of his home, and giving the Butlers a wave, started to the Kincade house. He knocked on the door and entered when it was opened to him.

William sat, contented, his boy asleep in his lap, and his wife sitting at his side on the front stoop. His house was snug and tight, with a roof of cedar shingles and a primitive water closet. Ezekiel Talbot had proven himself to be a master carpenter, a plumber and genius, as well. He had sent a message by an eastbound fur trader to a company he knew about in Clinton, Missouri, to send metal pipes. They had arrived on a westbound freight train coming out of Fort Leavenworth in the spring. Jemima had agreed to pay the cost if he would build one in her cabin and in the Kincade's, too. She said it was the least she could do to repay William and his wife for giving her a home.

Joseph, finished with his practice sessions with Brownie and Jezebel, turned the team toward the home farm. The sitting couple watched silently while he brought the team to a halt near the barn. He yelled something they couldn't hear, but assumed it meant they were to stay where they were. Charlotte stood and laid her hand gently on William's shoulder. Joseph parked the wagon in its shed, unyoked the team and left them in the corral. Then with his long legs, he strode to the porch.

"I have something for your birthday, Sister. Zeke showed me how to carve animals out of wood." Reaching into his trousers pocket, he withdrew a crude replica of a sheep. "Happy birthday, Sister." And he ran into the house before she could thank him. Charlotte's eyes flooded with tears as she looked at the small object in her hand.

William eased himself out of his chair, shifted his son to a more comfortable place on his shoulder, and gently guided her through the door. They didn't move to the old bedroom with the dark blue blanket door, but to the larger room behind the kitchen that had once been a root cellar before the magic hands of Zeke and Peter started their work. Charlotte went in before him, and he laid the still sleeping boy in his cot beside the window. He went to the table by the back wall and removed a small package and brought it to her. She looked up at him, her dark brown eyes moist from her recent tears. She quickly tore away the brown wrapping paper, and inside was a cameo pin, the woman's profile carved in ivory. William took her in his arms. "I bought it in Santa Fe when I was there in the spring, for it reminded me of you. I love you, my sweet gentle Charlotte. Happy Birthday."

Epilogue

On Janurary 24, 1848, James W. Marshall of New Jersey, found several tracings of gold on the bank of the South Fork American River near Sacramento City, California, and reported his findings to John Suttler of Suttler's Fort. During the next seven years, approximately 150,000 people crossed the prairies and passed through Fort John on their way to Fort Hall, where the road was split. Some pioneers went on to Oregon, while others went to California in search of gold. A few courageous homesteaders and freighters took the southern route to Santa Fe.

Fort John was purchased from Bruce Husband, a member of the American Fur Company, for $4,000 in June 1849 by United States Army Lieutenant Woodberry on behalf of the United States Government. Company G, 6th Infantry, arrived on August 12, 1849 and took over as the post's permanent garrison for many years.

The fort eventually became known as Fort Laramie, named for the river, and was a principal site along the Oregon, California and Mormon Trails. The last soldiers left Fort Laramie on April 20, 1890 and all but one of the structures were sold at auction to private citizens. On October 5, 1891, the fort was opened up to homesteaders.

Zeke Talbot took a position as civilian contractor with the government and helped build the barracks and hospital at the newly commissioned Army fort. He died there in 1861.

Joseph Morgan joined the army, and after serving four years came home to Green Meadow Farm, but he remained restless and couldn't settle. With the blessings of his sister and brother-in-law, his nephews, Theodore and George Butler, and his niece, Malinda Carol Butler, and his uncle, Peter Kincade, Joseph packed food and supplies for a long journey.

One last time, the loud Crack! of the old black bull whip was heard in the valley, as Joseph walked beside the freshly painted Conestoga wagon, pulled by a team of six young oxen, and joined the first wagon train of the season headed west. The family gathered on the porch of the Butler cabin and watched until he was out of sight. He took the well-trodden route out of Fort Laramie to Fort Hall, and headed southwesterly for California.

On a cold, windy morning in November of 1856, now aged four and twenty, Joseph stood on the slope of a hill near the old Mission San Francisco de Asis, and gazed down at his father's stone at his feet.

JAMES AARON MORGAN
BORN 1792 DONEGAL, SCOTLAND
DIED 1846 YERBA BUENA, CALIFORNIA
R I P

SOLOMON JEREMIAH MORGAN
DIED FEBRUARY 9, 1846 AGED THREE MONTHS
BELOVED SON

He removed his hat from his head, in spite of the chill on his ears, and read the words on the stone. He replaced his hat, walked to the shipping docks and caught a freighter to the Hawaiian Islands in the Pacific Ocean. He perished in 1864, during a storm off the coast of Oregon.

William Butler made two additional freighting trips from Fort Laramie to Santa Fe and retired to his farm. His freighting business provided supplies for hundreds of emigrants along the Oregon Trail. He became famous for the apple orchard grown from cuttings he brought from the East. In the field where the winter wheat once grew, a two-story trading post was built, which was managed after his death by his second son, George Butler. Charlotte lived to see the turn of the century and the invention of the telephone, electricity, and motor cars. Her legacy outlived her, growing to seventeen great-grandchildren, including a state senator, and a courageous aviator who died in the skies over France. She was buried on the land she helped to tame, under a simple stone marker engraved with the words:

CHARLOTTE
BELOVED WIFE OF WILLIAM BUTLER
BORN 1828, ILLINOIS
DIED 1921, LARAMIE, WYOMING
AT AGE 92 YEARS, 3 MONTHS, 19 DAYS

Cast of Characters

KASKASKIA, ILLINOIS:

Morgan Family:
    James Aaron Morgan, farmer
    Priscilla Prescott Morgan, wife of James
    Charlotte Morgan Butler, daughter of James
    Joseph Morgan, son of James
Kincade Family:
    Peter Kincade, farmer
    Eileen Prescott Kincade, wife of Peter
    Jesse Kincade, son of Peter
    Neely Kincade, son of Peter
Trappers:
    Otto Thibodeau, French-Canadian
    Elijah Perkins, from Tennessee
Bar Patrons:
    Bartender, Golden Eagle saloon
    Burford Shaw, farmer
    Cavenaugh, merchant
    Sedgewick, merchant

Minor Characters:

    John Raymond, neighbor
    Solomon James Morgan, father of James
    Grandmother Prescott, mother of Priscilla
    Nehemiah Prescott, father of Priscilla

ST. LOUIS, MISSOURI:

Principal Characters:

    William Butler, miner, oxen driver
    Bertha Hightower, hotel proprietor
    Clayborne Hightower, real estate agent
    Jacobe Sinclair, ass't to Hightower
    Gladys Donne, servant
    Tom Giddings, Gladys' boyfriend
    Hezekiah Conklin (Conk), servant

Hotel Guests:

    Sarah Warren, widow
    Margaret Brown, widow
    Rachet Jones, salesman, housewares
    Hammond, salesman, seeds and saplings
    Josiah Filbert, lawyer
    Prudence Filbert, wife of Josiah
    Neva Devine, niece of Prudence
    Quarreling couple named Nassar
    Drummer from Clinton, Missouri

Local Businessmen/Officials:

    Judge Thomas Moore, marriage officiate
    Major Sanford, saw mill manager
    Wilhelmina Sanford, wife of manager
    Moses Smith, livery stable proprietor

Abraham Smith, son of Moses
Jasper Smith, son of Moses
Benjamin Trice, merchant
Rebekah Trice, wife of merchant
Webley, farmer, oxen trader
Shoppers in the Store:
Unknown woman
Townsend, banker
Man #2, stout, red face
Man #3, smokes cigar
Bar Patrons:
Hank Blessing, bartender at Red Rooster Saloon
Jenkins, waiter at Red Rooster Saloon
Duff, piano player
Flavia, saloon girl
Maizie, saloon girl
Priddy, card player
Slim, card player
Sylvester, card player
Arthur Bingham, saw mill worker

WAGON TRAIN:

Principal Characters:
George Remmington, employee
Captain Horatio Foster, wagon master
Landers Family:
Francine Landers (Fannie)
John Landers, father of Fannie
Mrs. Landers, mother of Fannie
Arthur Landers, twin brother of Amos
Amos Landers, twin brother of Arthur

Johnson Family:
    Bart Johnson, father
    Matilda Johnson, mother
    Nathaniel Johnson, son of Bart
    Molly Johnson, daughter of Bart
Soldier:
    Lt. Graham, Fort Leavenworth
Minor Characters:
    Harper, wagon driver

FORT JOHN, WYOMING TERRITORY:

Principal Characters:
    Lawrence Pedigrew, American Fur Co. manager
    Theodore Butler, son of William and Charlotte
    Bear Grease, Shoshone Indian
Robertson Family:
    Julius Caesar Robertson (Jules), neighbor
    Ava Robertson, wife of Jules
    Hanley Robertson, son of Jules
    Jacob Robertson, son of Jules
People on the Farm:
    Jemima Boudreau, midwife, French woman
    Pedro, Basque shepherd boy
    Ezekiel Talbot (Zeke), carpenter
Soldiers:
    Lt. Truman Baker, U.S. Army Dragoon
    Orville Willowby, U.S. Army Scout
    Sergeant at Fort John

Minor Characters:

Lt. Jackson Taylor (Jack), Morgan's employee
Damien Pembroke, fur trader, thief
Mrs. Pembroke, wife of Damien
Three sheep raiders
Boy messenger
Montreau, French-Canadian fur company employee
Bradford Watson, replacement for Pedigrew

MISCELLANEOUS CHARACTERS:

Jonathan Kincade, father of Peter, (by letter only)
Maria Concepcion Gomaz (by letter only)
Solomon Jeremiah Morgan, infant son in California